In order to [obscured by barcode] like
an e[obscured]

I asked my[obscured], where would my Uncle Walt hide a key—then bent down and lifted the mat below my feet.

Nothing.

Well, I really had no intention of breaking a window or door to get inside. My heart sank, thinking I'd gotten this far and wouldn't get to snoop around.

I stood up and leaned against the door. "Ack!"

My world spun in a flash.

When I felt pain shoot up my back, I realized I'd fallen onto the kitchen floor when the door, which had obviously been left open, gave way. I couldn't move for several seconds and shut my eyes, waiting for the pain to subside. I sure as hell wasn't going to call out for help. How could I explain me on the floor of a dead man's house?

Then I heard a muffled sound approaching. *Footsteps!*

I opened my eyes to see a shadow standing above me.

A scream flew through my lips.

Books by Lori Avocato

THE STIFF AND THE DEAD
A DOSE OF MURDER

Forthcoming
ONE DEAD UNDER THE CUCKOO'S NEST

The Stiff and the Dead

A PAULINE SOKOL MYSTERY

LORI AVOCATO

AVON BOOKS
An Imprint of HarperCollinsPublishers

AVON BOOKS
An Imprint of HarperCollins*Publishers*
10 East 53rd Street
New York, New York 10022-5299

Copyright © 2005 by Lori Avocato
Excerpt from *One Dead Under the Cuckoo's Nest* copyright © 2005 by Lori Avocato
ISBN 0-06-073166-4
www.avonmystery.com

First Avon Books paperback printing: July 2005

Avon Trademark Reg. U.S. Pat. Off. and in Other Countries, Marca Registrada, Hecho en U.S.A.
HarperCollins® is a registered trademark of HarperCollins Publishers Inc.

Printed in the U.S.A.

10 9 8 7 6 5 4 3 2 1

This book is dedicated to Sal, Mario, and Greg. Thanks.

Acknowledgments

To Erin Richnow, my wonderful editor, who actually "edits!"

To Jay Poynor and Erica Orloff, fabulous agents. Again, thanks.

To Leslie O'Grady, Sharon Schulze, Nancy Block, and Suzanne Baney—fellow writers who have taught me so much throughout the years.

And to all my readers—there would be no Pauline if it weren't for you.

The
Stiff
and
the
Dead

One

"Say *ah*." I leaned forward with my flashlight aimed into my friend Goldie's mouth. "Yikes."

He opened his heavily mascaraed eyes and shut his coral-colored lips. I wished I looked that good in coral. Frankly, I wished I looked that good in anything similar to what Goldie wore.

"What does 'yikes' mean, Suga?" he asked.

I touched his hand and had visions of all the times I'd done that with the many patients I'd taken care of in the past thirteen years. That is, used to take care of. I'd sworn off nursing months ago. I didn't miss my ex-career though. I'd burned out faster than a desert pine hit by lightning during a drought.

I rubbed his hand beneath the beautiful silver-and-turquoise bracelet that sparkled on his left wrist. As far as transvestites went, Goldie Perlman had class and damn good taste in clothes. I could learn from him where makeup was concerned, and actually had in the past. But, damn, I still couldn't wear coral with my pale skin and gray eyes. "Yikes means your tonsils look like giant zeppelins."

He raised his eyebrows. "What the hell—" A fit of coughing took his words.

"Remember the Hindenburg?"

"Before my time."

"I know, but your tonsils are about that big, Gold. I could yank them out with my fingers. You need to go to a doctor ASAP." I took my hand from his and set the flashlight down on his glass-and-chrome desk. Goldie had dynamite taste in furniture too, especially if you liked jungle themes. I flopped onto the zebra chair I'd grown so fond of since working for Scarpello and Tonelli insurance company.

I'd only been there a few months thanks to the connections of my roommate Miles, Goldie's boyfriend. Miles's uncle Fabio owned the place and after a "meltdown" of my previous career, I'd fallen into this new one. Working for Fabio. Ack.

"I hate doctors, Suga."

I smiled. "Don't we all." This after the doctor I used to date nearly killed me—and not from an error in treating me medically. Actually, it was more along the line of murder. "I'm guessing you need those tonsils yanked out as soon as the infection clears."

He gasped a high-pitched sound. Very flamboyant. Gotta love him. I looked around the office. Giant ficus trees draped in moss gave the feeling of being transported from Connecticut to the old South, specifically Louisiana, Goldie's home state. As I tried to think of some words of comfort for my ailing friend, our boss walked in.

Fabio Scarpello. Yuck. Now *I* felt sick.

He glared at Goldie. "You look like shit." Then Fabio handed him a file. "Here's your next case."

Goldie reached out with a perfectly manicured hand, then fell back against the chair.

"What the hell is wrong with you?" Fabio asked in his usual I-don't-give-a-shit tone. I think he reached down to adjust his crotch through his brown polyester pants, but I yanked my head to the side so I didn't have to watch.

Ouch.

I spun too fast, but the pain was worth not having to see Fabio. I hesitated, then without looking back said, "He's got tonsillitis, Fabio. He needs medial treatment." I felt about ready to pop the guy, but figured my fist would slide off the grease on his chin, so instead I rubbed my now sore neck.

Normally I loved Italians. Miles was one, even though he had been adopted into the Scarpello family, but this Fabio guy got under my skin. He was the consummate Hollywood version of Italian right down to the "wifebeater" tee shirts I'm certain he wore under his polyester suit jackets. Plus, he always wore brown. That more than likely wasn't an Italian thing, but it was a Fabio thing.

He looked from Goldie to me, then yanked back the file. He turned to go, but not before he shoved it at me. "Here, newbie, get your feet christened with your second case. Prescription fraud. Two jokers to tail. Pauline Sokol, medical insurance fraud investigator extraordinaire, gets to prove herself yet again. Even though this case is way past your abilities, I don't have a fucking choice." He shook his head. "Christ. This time, don't nearly get yourself killed."

Then he was gone and all was right with the world.

Except that now I was facing my next assignment—alone. I'd only worked for Fabio once, and that case was a piece of cake. Workers' Comp. Tail a suspect. Take pictures. Yadda. Yadda. Yadda. Okay, I won't go into detail about how the first set of pictures I took was of the suspect's butt. Suffice it to say, the camera was camouflaged as a beeper, and it hadn't occurred to me to take it off my belt.

I learned my lesson though, and was ready—to work alone.

Perfect, since that first case had been "hindered" by none other than the mysterious Jagger. Be still my heart. Jagger was an enigma in the investigation field, even if no one knew who the hell he was, what his last name was—or his first for that matter—or whom he actually worked for.

Me, I really didn't care.

There went my heart again—and something else. Okay, so the guy revved my engine, but, being the consummate professional, I never made a pass at him—nor he at me. Shit. Wait, there was that one kiss under the mistletoe at my mother's house, but she'd egged him on, so it didn't count.

Goldie started to cough. I looked at him. "You have a fever."

He rolled his eyes upward. "How can you tell?"

"Your eyes are all glassy, and a ruddy hue the likes of my mother's Christmas tablecloth is showing beneath your pancake makeup."

"I'm dying," he muttered.

I gave a soft laugh and a cluck of my tongue so as to convince him that he wasn't nearly deceased and opened the file. "Oh."

Goldie looked at me. "Oh? That's your most professional assessment of your second case?"

I looked up. "Well . . . shoot, Goldie."

He sat bolt upright. "What is it, Suga?"

I leaned closer to look at the file. I flipped several pages, leaned farther down to look at a photo and the name. "I think one of my suspects is already dead."

"That'll mean less work."

I looked up into his watery, feverish eyes. "True. But it's Mr. Wisnowski."

"Wis what?"

"Wisnowski. One of my Uncle Walt's cronies from the senior citizens center."

"So, old people die."

"Uncle Walt's been, well, for the last few days, he's been insisting that Mr. Wisnowski . . . he was . . . *killed*."

After consoling Goldie and his tonsils until he fell asleep on his zebra couch, I walked out of his office. Slowly I turned to shut the door without waking him. I'd promised to come back in a few hours and take him to the Hope Valley walk-in clinic. Mondays were usually busy, so he'd chosen to nap first and avoid the morning rush. Mondays were also senior citizens days. Well, truthfully, every day was senior day at the clinic.

Being a recently hired employee at Scarpello and Tonelli Insurance Company, I didn't have my own office. Fabio had said I had to work through my probationary period, which was probably a year, before he'd cough up the furniture and space. Goldie had been sweet enough to let me use his office and equipment when necessary, but it didn't make me feel as if I really belonged. As if I was truly a medical fraud insurance investigator.

I still felt like a burned-out ex-nurse working on a temporary job. Because, and this part wasn't in my plans, as much as I wanted to get out of nursing, my last case had dumped me right back into my old scrubs, working undercover at a clinic. That, of course, was because of the overpowering persuasion of none other than Jagger. With my help, he had cracked a multimillion-dollar medical insurance fraud case.

But two people had died in the process. Thankfully, I wasn't one of them.

I had made a sacred oath to myself that *no one* was going to get me back into nursing.

I headed down the hallway and into the receptionist's little cubicle. I imagined Fabio had promised her a bigger space years ago, but here she sat in a tiny eight-by-four room. "Hey, Adele."

She swung around, her earphone catching on the knob of the desk, yanking her back toward the wall. "Oops!"

I jumped up, but before I could untangle her, she'd reached up a gloved hand to do the job. Adele always wore white silken gloves. At first I'd thought it odd, but soon came to love the eccentricities of the displaced Canadian woman, who had become like a second mother to me.

Well, looking at her streetwalker-tight pink suit and bright pink lips that matched her nails, I knew my real mother would die at the comparison. You can't judge a book by its cover was a cliché proven every day around here. From flamboyant Goldie with a heart of gold to greasy Fabio with the Godfather complex, to darling Adele Girard, who often spoke of herself in the third person, to Nick Caruso, with his leading-man good looks, the cast of characters often made me feel as if I were working on some movie set.

"You all right, Adele?" I plopped down on the nearby gray desk chair.

She smiled and spun around until she twirled back with a coffee in hand. She held it out toward me. I still had a hard time believing this woman was an ex-con. But she'd had a good reason for doing what she did. I can still hear her explaining, although I hadn't asked. *"My old lady was sick. The big* C. *Ate her up to nothing. And, to boot, no medical insurance. I needed that money. The jury was right to convict me. Don't matter the need, you can't steal."* She'd held up her gloved hands for me to study. *"Burned in the joint."*

I looked over to see her watching me.

"Adele is always fine," she said.

I took the mug. She'd given me the one she'd bought that said INVESTIGATOR SOKOL in bold black letters. "Thanks. Goldie looks like crap today."

"Mmmm." She took several sips of her own drink. I assumed it was coffee, but often thought Adele added a bit of "flavor" to it. Rum flavor to be exact. Nevertheless she was a darling and a wiz of a secretary. She'd helped me out so much with addresses and private info, I often wondered if she wouldn't make a better investigator than I.

But there was the ex-con thing.

"Yeah, he's got tonsillitis, I'm sure. Needs them yanked, but I bet it will be a challenge to get him to go under the knife."

She laughed. "Have his boyfriend help."

"Miles?" Now *I* laughed. "He'd be more of a wreck than Goldie, facing that prospect."

"And he's a nurse?"

"A great one, but when it comes to those he loves, he's a basket case." I set down my mug and picked up my file. "Fabio gave me Goldie's case."

Adele's eyes grew dark. She gingerly set her mug down as if it would splinter into millions of pieces. "I see."

Suddenly my coffee floated up my throat. No, maybe

that was bile brought on by fear. Adele had me scared. Maybe it was her tone, maybe the look in her eyes, or maybe the way she pulled on the third finger of her glove. Up and down. Up and down until I reached out and shoved my hand over hers.

Startled, she pulled back.

I did the same, with an apology fresh on my lips. "Oh my God. I'm sorry. I have no idea why I—"

"Adele understands." With that she got up, scurried to the door, and before I could get her to explain, Fabio shouted for her.

Damn.

I leaned back in my chair. It wasn't often that I got bad premonitions about things. I left that sort of thing up to my mother, who still worried because I was single, had given up the career I'd been schooled in, worked in a field that almost got me killed and didn't eat right. Don't get me started on not having kids yet.

But, looking down at the folder in my hand, while I read the name "Sophie Banko" and "possible prescription fraud," a heat spread up my arms, and a rocklike thud sounded in the pit of my stomach.

And, for some reason, all I could think was, Mr. Wisnowski had been murdered.

Of course I had no proof that Mr. Wisnowski had been murdered, but as I got into my Venetian red Volvo and drove toward my parents' house, I just knew my Uncle Walt was onto something.

Call it female intuition—which, by the way, had served me well throughout my nursing career—or call it a hunch, but I had to find out, and talking to Uncle Walt was first on my list. He'd mentioned Mr. W several times in the past.

Canon

DIRECT
PRINT

I'd even met him at some social functions and had heard Uncle Walt talk about the real "catch" that Mr. W had dated.

Uncle Walt, my favorite uncle, had lived with us all my life. When my oldest sister, Mary, left the convent to wed—and yes, my mother spent the next few years doing penance in Mary's name—Uncle Walt had been the super glue that had kept our family together.

I actually applauded Mary, since her wedding took the pressure off of me for a few years, but my parents and my mother's other brother, Uncle Stash, had nearly come to blows. Stash was the rebel sibling who thought Mary was very "modern" by leaving the convent, and the fact that the Sisters had paid for Mary's college education was an added bonus. He lived in Florida but came to Connecticut in late winter for his annual ski trip. That was the extent of his skiing.

Come to think of it, he had to be due any day now. Imagine a seventy-nine-year-old skiing. I became a ski-school dropout after giving it a shot with Uncle Stash back in the late 1980s. Everything hurt. It wasn't fun. I often thought about heading south with him each time he went back. He was a trip, and staying with him could be fun.

I pulled into my parents' driveway and looked up. Stella Mary Maciejko Sokol, aka Mother, and Michael Joseph Sokol, aka Daddy, had lived in this house for forty-three years—and had never upgraded. When I watched reruns of Donna Reed and Lucy, I knew where my mother had gotten her "decorating" taste.

The white structure, aluminum sided with classic black shutters, stood there, welcoming me back. When I got out of my car and walked into the foyer, I sniffed. The aroma of kielbasa and sauerkraut hung in the air. But I knew that couldn't be possible. Today was Monday. Mother had to be fixing meatloaf.

You could plan your calendar on my mother's menus. She made the same meal for each day of the week. Kielbasa and kraut were Saturday's delicacy and the aroma hung around nearly a week. Not even my mother's Renuzit air freshener (fresh mountain pine) fetish could get the Polish scent out of the air.

Truthfully, the air freshener had grown to be a comforting scent, much like a fake Christmas tree. Several times a year it soothed me—much like Linus's blanket.

"That you, Pauline?" my mother called out from the kitchen. She spent hours in the kitchen each day. Didn't even have a dishwasher since she said she could do a better job. Each year we kids offered to buy her one for Christmas, but she always declined—and we got stuck washing and drying on Thanksgiving, Christmas, New Year's and any other holidays. With five kids—most with families—doing dishes was no short-term chore.

"Yes, Mom. It's me. Who else would just walk in?" I turned down the royal blue shag carpeted hallway and headed toward the kitchen. Who still had shag carpeting in their houses? Thing was, my mother kept it impeccably clean, and with the fibers standing at attention, it looked much like I remembered it over twenty years ago. Not even a spot on it.

I nodded toward my father, who was sitting in his favorite chair near the bay window. "Hi, Daddy."

He looked up from his newspaper, the sports section, and gave me his loving smile. "Hey, *Pączki.*"

I kissed him on the forehead where his brown hair sprinkled with gray had thinned to reveal too much skin. I couldn't picture Daddy bald and wondered if he'd keep thinning until it was all gone. Then I gave my usual internal groan at his pet name for me. *Pączki.* A big, fat, round, often prune-filled Polish donut pronounced more like "paunchki." That was my father's endearing name for me since I was born a whopping ten pounds five ounces. But in my defense, I had heard my mother once say the nurses claimed I looked much thinner.

As a bit of a chubby kid, I paid no attention when Daddy called me that. But lately—okay, since my sixteenth birthday—I wanted to run out of the room screaming when he used it. Thank goodness I hadn't fit the bill of a round, stuffed donut since then. Now—ta-da—I was a size four.

Still, he meant well, and I loved every balding cell in his body. He could call me whatever he wanted—but hopefully, not in front of my friends though.

Daddy was a hardworking silent type who'd retired after forty years in a factory making tiny parts for airplane engines, and now he spent his days golfing when it wasn't winter and reading the newspaper the rest of the year. The guy had no real hobbies, but the paper took hours to get through. Not that Daddy wasn't a good reader, it was just that he read everything—and sometimes out loud. When my mother gave him a project to do around the house, he took his time so you could count on not seeing him for days to months.

Like Houdini, my mother spun around and handed me a plate with a Dagwood-size ham sandwich on it. I never saw the woman even take the bread out of the breadbox. "Thanks, Mom." I sat across from Daddy, knowing she'd produce some beverage very shortly. Most likely milk, since Mother accused me of not having enough calcium for my age. Not even close to menopause, I always insisted that I took calcium pills, which she said is hogwash compared to getting it naturally.

I took a bite of my ham, mustard, lettuce and tomato sandwich. When she wasn't looking, I slipped out the hot-house tomato and stuffed it between the folds of my turquoise paper napkin. Matched the Formica counter-tops. January wasn't tomato month in Connecticut.

Yesterday's left-over ham tasted wonderful. Me, I'm no cook. Actually take-out food had become one of the basic food groups where I was concerned, and, as much as I hated to admit it, I loved hospital food. Thank goodness Miles cooked when he wasn't at work. Truthfully, I think the only reason I remained alive was that my mother still fed me. For now, I had to hurry and talk to Uncle Walt, since I needed to head back to the office to get Goldie.

"Where's Uncle Walt?" I asked after washing down a bite with the milk Mom had snuck in front of me.

Daddy never looked up from his paper. From where I sat I could see that he was mentally doing the crossword puzzle. "Should be back soon. Some lady called for him."

Mother shook her head. "Tell us something new, Michael."

I figured Uncle Walt was real hot with the ladies nowa-days, then I laughed to myself. "Mind if I wait?" I looked up to see both glaring at me with shock and confusion on their faces. Where'd that come from? My parents not only didn't mind if I waited, they usually—no, daily—suggested I move back in with them.

That's when I'd miraculously find myself back at the condo I shared with my roomie, Miles Scarpello. Often, I wouldn't remember the trip back but knew I made it at warp speed.

Mother sat down with a cup of coffee in her hand.

Ready to ask where hers and Daddy's sandwiches were, I caught a glimpse of the black wrought-iron clock with golden hands above the stove. Eleven forty-five. They never ate lunch until noon or dinner before six. Breakfast was at 6 A.M., before they went off to daily 8 A.M. mass at the Polish church, Saint Stanislaus.

Hope Valley was very ethnic and neighborhoods and Catholic churches divided up where the immigrants had settled.

"Actually, Stella," my father said, "didn't Walt mention some funeral?"

She took a sip of coffee and set down her salmon-colored Melmac cup on its saucer. Mother always used cups and saucers, not mugs. Melmac had been our family's dinnerware since before my birth. It was a tough, hard plastic created in the 1940s, used by the army in WWII, and which then became popular in the fifties and sixties, when my parents must have bought theirs. "Funeral? Oh, that's right. One of his buddies from the senior citizens center passed away."

Or was murdered.

I gulped. "A lady?" A long shot, I knew, but if she said yes, then I wouldn't have that murder issue to think of right now.

"Henry Wisnowski."

I dropped my sandwich onto the Melmac dish below.

"Watch out, Pauline!" Mother was up in a jiffy and wiping the crumbs off the table. Good thing I didn't spill my milk.

Of course, if murder were involved, I would have a lot to cry about over that milk. I shuddered, reliving my last brush with murder, despite the fact that Jagger had come to save me.

Jagger.

My heart pitter-pattered. Once Goldie and I made a bet that Jagger was FBI, but there was never a definitive answer from him. Not only wouldn't I don nursing scrubs again, but sadly, I'd never have to work or see Jagger again.

"Pauline? What is wrong with you?"

My eyes fluttered. I'd gotten stuck in a Jagger-induced moment. "Wrong? Nothing, Mom. Well, I have a new case—"

"Case, smase." Mother got up and reheated hers and Daddy's coffee. "When are you going to go back to nursing? The job you'd trained for all those years. Even a master's degree. You made such a nice nurse."

Nice? After thirteen years, I'd hoped for "excellent" or at least "well-qualified." "Mom, I *have* a job. It's investigating." I wiped the napkin across my lips.

Two slices of hothouse tomato fell onto the Melmac dish.

Mother looked at me. "If you didn't want tomatoes, you should have said so, Pauline Sokol."

And you still would have put them on. "I didn't think of it." *Since you materialized the sandwich before I saw the ham come out of the Saran wrap.* "I have to go take Goldie to the doctor. Tonsillitis."

"Can't his boyfriend take him?"

Mother loved Miles and had grown to love Goldie too. She even baked them apple pies for Christmas and gave them each condoms as stocking stuffers. I know she had the best intentions in mind, but . . .

I had to get out of there.

I hurried over and gave my mother a peck on the

cheek as I shoved the dish into the sink, thankful Melmac was indestructible, although it did stain and burn. But not my mother's set. Then I kissed Daddy on the forehead. "See ya."

Once in the driveway, I took a deep breath, hopped in my car, shoved it into reverse and hit the pedal. A loud clank hit the air. I swung around to see Uncle Walt getting out of a 1963 Ford Thunderbird roadster—a convertible, no less. The white exterior sparkled, and the red interior, which I could still see even with the top up, was immaculate, as was the driver.

I knew cars, since Uncle Walt was a car buff and I read all his magazines, mostly in my mother's john. I flew out of the car. "Anyone hurt?"

Uncle Walt came around from the passenger's side. "You can't hurt someone in a vintage car like this at that speed, Pauline. They don't make them like this nowadays. You should know that."

I stared at the Thunderbird's bumper. Not a scratch. Mine, however, had a dent, which needed a good plastic surgeon.

I looked at the purple-haired woman sitting behind the wheel. Wearing dark glasses the size of Where's Waldo's, she sat there fluffing her hair in the rearview mirror. I wondered if the crash had dislodged any of the strands. Didn't look it—she had to have had a can of hair spray all over that coiffure. Silver rhinestones sparkled from the frames of her black glasses, but they were nowhere near as bright as the gems hanging from her earlobes and around her neck. And wrists. And fingers. Well, four out of ten fingers.

Uncle Walt, you dog.

He looked in the window. "Helen Wanat, this is my niece, Pauline Sokol."

Helen. Helen something. So this was the woman Henry Wisnowski and now apparently Uncle Walt fancied. Hmm.

I reached my hand out to shake hers. Firm grip for a senior. "*Favorite* niece, that is," I said.

Uncle Walt and I laughed. Helen looked at both of us as if we were whacko. "Family joke," I added. I leaned near Uncle Walt while Helen went back to the mirror to wipe some fire-engine red lipstick from her tooth. Very white tooth. Original if I ever saw one.

Uncle Walt looked at his watch. "Oh boy, eleven fifty-five. You coming in for lunch, Helen?"

Never looking away from the mirror, she said in a rather deep voice, "We just ate at the restaurant, Walty."

I could only stare. Walty?

He shrugged. "How about you, Pauline?" He released my grip and started to turn as if he thought if he didn't make it in by noon, Mother wouldn't serve him. Of course, that idea wasn't far from reality.

"Mom fixed me a sandwich earlier."

He froze. "It's not noon."

"You got me on that one. No telling what she was thinking. Anyway, I came here to talk to you."

Before he could say anything else, Helen turned back, stuck her head out of the window and blew a kiss. I guessed it wasn't for me. She did nod in my direction, though, as I said, "Nice meeting you."

Once inside, Uncle Walt must have remembered that he did in fact eat after the funeral since he didn't touch Mom's coleslaw with vinegar. He told us that the Wisnowski family put on a pretty nice spread at the Polish Falcon Club. He apparently reconsidered and began to eat a ham sandwich. I smiled to myself when he slipped the hothouse tomatoes out and, more clever than myself, shoved them into the pocket of his black suit jacket.

I only hoped he remembered them soon after leaving the table. Not like me.

Uncle Walt and I excused ourselves and went into his room under the pretense that we were going to look up Helen's vintage Thunderbird in one of his magazines. Once I walked through the doorway into the "brown" room, I slunk into the overstuffed chair by the window. Mom kept the room clean, and Uncle Walt was almost a neat freak, although not as bad as Goldie or Miles. No one was as addicted to clean as Miles was.

Uncle Walt methodically took off his suit jacket and removed the tomatoes, which he wrapped in a tissue and then set on the end table. He reached over and switched on a lamp whose shade was a still life of Niagara Falls. Any second now, I expected the water to cascade onto his brown carpet. I looked at the dresser near his bed.

Uncle Walt had saved me financially during my last case when he miraculously produced a wad—and I'm talking a four-figure wad of cash—from a secret drawer. That's how I bought my first surveillance camera.

"So, Pauline, need more money?" He hung his jacket over the wooden butler near the closet door.

"Hmm? Oh, no. I don't need money." Well, I do, but this time I have to earn it. "No, Uncle Walt, I actually came to you on official investigator business."

"You mean how I know Henry was murdered?"

If my teeth weren't "original," I'd be wearing them on

my lap. I reached up to push my jaw shut. "Well, actually, yes."

Uncle Walt beamed. Suddenly, he looked as if he had a purpose in life—and that was to help me with my case.

Most times I didn't know what *I* was doing, but being a stubborn Pole, I persisted. I sure didn't need an eighty-year-old "helping" me out.

"He was cremated, you know."

How could I? "No, actually I didn't." I shifted in my seat at the thought. No body. Difficult investigation.

Uncle Walt settled on the bed and pulled at his suspenders a few times. "You need answers, Pauline, and I'm your man. But one thing I need to know is, why are *you* asking about Henry's murder?"

Two

Just as Uncle Walt was about to spill the beans as to why he thought Mr. Wisnowski was murdered, my cell phone went off. Thank goodness, too, since, honoring the confidentiality of my case, I had no idea what I would tell him as to why I was interested in Mr. Wisnowski's death. It also gave me time to try to think of a lie about that. Lying was not in my top-ten mastered skills.

Catholic school and all.

A scratchy, pathetic voice wheezed from the other end. Goldie's appointment. I told Uncle Walt we'd talk real soon, scurried out the door before having to stop for a cup of tea and some kind of homemade dessert, and headed back to Scarpello and Tonelli Insurance Company.

That's where I found Goldie curled up in the fetal position on his zebra couch, looking very much like a baby boy—no, girl. I leaned near. No, boy. His mascara—okay, girl—had smudged off onto the sleeve of his gold-and-white-striped blouse. Either way the guy looked pitiable.

I wrapped him in a faux fox jacket and hurried him out to the car, whispering to Adele on the way what I was doing. I didn't want Fabio to come bustling out of his office and insist Goldie stay to do some stupid work. That'd be like Fabio. As for me, my nursing instincts collided with my womanly intuition, which bombarded my motherly desires every time I ran across someone who was ill, and I had to help.

And darling Goldie was a mess.

I pulled up to the entrance of the Hope Valley Clinic and told him to get out and wait for me on the bench outside the door. Of course, with the number of elderly that frequented the place, he'd be lucky to get a seat. Still, it was a perfect clinic when you felt like crap. Not only could you get treated, but they also had a pharmacy and medical supply store on the same floor, owned by the same crafty conglomerate.

"Am I gonna die, Suga?"

I smiled at him before he stepped out. "Yes—"

"Oooooooh!"

I grabbed the faux fur sleeve. "Gold, joking. I was joking. We are all going to die, but not soon."

He stepped out slowly and shuffled his gold spike heels on the pavement until he slumped onto the bench between two senior citizen ladies. They each smiled at him.

I readied to park and saw Helen Wanat pulling into a space. Made me think of Henry Wisnowski and how I hoped to hell death wasn't going to be knocking on my door very soon. I made a mental note to call Uncle Walt from my cell phone while I waited for Goldie.

I hurried out of the car and took him by the arm. "Come on, Gold." As we ambled toward the revolving door, I noticed a giant red circle with a red line across a cell phone much like the no smoking signs. Damn. I'd have to wait a bit to call Uncle Walt.

The receptionist, a twenty-something bimbo with blonde hair and glasses halfway down her nose, was snapping bubble gum. She looked up without blinking an eye. I assumed she saw plenty of odd characters while working at this clinic and had learned to accept everyone, or she was so jaded that she didn't notice "not normal." She shoved a clipboard onto the countertop. "Sign in."

Goldie managed to fill in his information. I shoved the clipboard back at her. "How long does he have to wait?"

She looked over the glasses at me without a crack of a smile. "Until he's called."

I curled my lips so she could see, but figured I was wasting my time. "Duh," I whispered to Goldie. "Come sit over by the window in the nice sun."

He nodded and followed along. When he sat down, the nurse stuck her head out of the door and called, "Goldie Perlman."

"Wow. Good timing." I got up and gave him a hand. We walked to the door, where the nurse took a look at both of us.

"Who's Goldie?"

"The sick one," I said, patted his arm and turned to go. I swung back before the door closed. "I'll wait out here after I make my phone call, Gold."

He muttered something that sounded like "okay." The nurse interrupted with "No cell phones on inside the building."

Some days I just wanted to scream.

I went outside and sat on the bench, where I dug around in my purse. The cell phone was hidden on the bottom. I pulled it out and pushed the ON button.

Nothing.

"Cripes." I'd forgotten to charge it. This was a major thorn in my paw. I pulled myself up and headed to my car to find the charger that Jagger had given me.

Next to my car an old rattletrap of a Buick pulled in as I walked to the passenger side, where the charger was in the glove compartment. I was thinking about how Jagger had threatened to have a microchip put on my tooth so he could always find me, when the driver's side door of the rattletrap swung open—and slammed into my chest.

"*Whoosh!*" Air flew out of my mouth, which had to be a good thing or I might have been really hurt.

An older gentleman jumped out of the car. Very spry for a man who had to be in his seventies. "Oh, my, *Bellisima* young lady, are you-a all right?"

His heavy Italian accent fit perfectly with his black pin-striped suit, heavy mustache and head of gray hair. Looked as if he'd stepped out of Don Corleone's parlor after doing "business." He was rather tall for an elderly gentleman, but I figured he held himself upright with perfect posture and that's what made him look tall, and very handsome and—I'm sorry to say this, but I noticed—built.

Helen Wanat passed by and gave an award-winning smile to the guy who'd just winded me. "Hello, Joey."

I think she purred.

Suddenly I wondered if purring at a nice, elderly, handsome Italian man could be construed as cheating on my uncle. She looked at me. I looked down. The print of the door handle of the rattletrap was imbedded in my Steelers' parka. I was a diehard Steelers fan along with Uncle Walt and hated to see anything happen to my parka. "Accident. It was an accident," I managed while still a bit short of breath. "How are you, Helen?"

"Fine." She looked at me again as if to say that accidents like this probably always happened to me—and she wouldn't be far from the truth. I turned toward the man who was ogling Helen. "My uncle is a friend of Helen. I'm Pauline Sokol."

He held out a gray-gloved hand. I had visions of Adele, wearing her gloves. I shook Joey's hand. Firm grip. Geez. I hoped my muscles still held up like his and Helen's when I got to be their age. I figured Joey wore gloves as a statement of his past. He looked very traditional.

"Joseph Tino." He bowed.

Wow. No one ever bowed at me. How cute. I found myself liking this guy already and wondered if about forty years difference would be a no-no for dating him. I mentally shook my hormone-driven thoughts out of my head and said, "Nice to meet you."

He looked at my parka. "I can-a get that fixed for you?"

"Oh. No, I'll just hang it in the bathroom when I shower and the steam will iron it out."

Joey grinned!

Joey, you dog, you.

"And you are sura you are not hurt, *Bellisima*?"

I got stuck on the bellisima part and could only stare for a few seconds.

"He asked if you were hurt, Pauline."

Wow. That got my attention. Helen's voice packed quite the punch. Uncle Walt might be barking up the wrong tree with this one. I turned to her and said, "I'm fine." Then I turned back to Joey. "I am fine. Thank you for asking."

He excused himself and walked into the clinic. I hoped he didn't have a serious illness. Helen stared at him as if he were a prime roast of beef and then nodded and went off toward the pharmacy. What a waste of a vintage set of wheels, I thought, looking back at her car. Suddenly I really didn't like Helen.

Which reminded me of why I came out here in the first place.

Once the cell phone was connected to the charger, I called Uncle Walt. After a few minutes of chatting and telling him I'd seen Helen here, and Joey, Uncle Walt paused. "Joey the Wooer. Sheeeet."

I mentally pictured the dapper Italian man. Okay, he probably could woo a woman over sixty since there was something almost sexy about him. Eeyeuuw. That was a pathetic thought. I didn't even want to get into a mental argument with myself about how long it'd been since I . . . *That* I blamed on my ex-boyfriend, old Doc Taylor, and his shenanigans. Instead of allowing my mind to go down that road, I asked, "Wooer?"

"Yep. Old Widow Bivalaqua gave him the nickname after she met him in the clinic."

"Is he sickly?" He certainly didn't look it.

"Joey? Sheeeet. I would guess he's the Italian version of Jack LaLanne. You remember that old fitness guru who had the TV show Pauline?"

I pictured the man in the jumpsuit who ate healthy, exercised on TV and sold one of those juicer machines. Then I pictured Joey the Wooer. Hmm. Guess he could do his own over-seventy program. "I do remember, Uncle Walt. But back to why I called."

"Henry?"

I held the phone close to my mouth and whispered. "Yes, Henry. Tell me about why you think he was . . . murdered."

"Okay, but you're going to have to speak up."

I looked around the car. No one in sight. "Why do you think that Mr. Wisnowski was killed?"

Pause.

"Uncle Walt?"

"I had to shut my door, Pauline. You know how your mother is. And, besides, Stash is due in any minute. Your father went to get him at the airport."

I mentally groaned. Now we'd have a whole set of new problems to deal with. "Okay, so now you can talk."

"Yes. Henry first met Helen at the senior citizens center. Bingo night. No, wait—"

I heard a shuffling, then a cough. "Uncle Walt? Are you all right?"

"Your mother passed by my door. Maybe we should meet somewhere. Somewhere inconspicuous."

I mentally laughed. Imagine a thirty-four-year-old blonde in some clandestine meeting with an eighty-one-year-old bald man. Yeah, no one would notice. Maybe in LA or New York City, but in Hope Valley we'd stand out like the proverbial sore thumb. "I really have to get going on my case. Can't you just tell me now?"

"Okay. No, it wasn't Bingo night. It was Italian pasta night. Henry met Helen there and, well, everyone wanted to meet Helen; if you know what I mean."

I refused that mental image. "Yes, go on."

"She was new in town and well, this is a sensitive subject, Pauline. I sure hope no one is listening."

Stupidly I looked around. The parking lot was empty except for me. Helen's car was still in the space, but she wasn't in it. Maybe she forgot something in the building. "No one can hear us."

"Okay." He coughed a few times to clear his throat.

In the meantime, thoughts raced through my imaginative brain. Sensitive? As in, he knows who killed Henry if he really was killed. Or maybe sensitive in some million-dollar-money scheme sort of way. Or maybe . . .

"Sex, Pauline. It all boils down to sex. S—E—X."

Oh . . . my . . . God.

Sex and the senior citizens.

Three

What a thought. Actually, I respected and loved the elderly, and if they had sex, more power to them. They should live life to the hilt. Me, I guessed I was a wee bit jealous that they were having it—and I wasn't.

This time I looked around to make sure no one could hear me and whispered, "Okay, Uncle Walt, you are going to have to explain that one. What does sex have to do with Mr. Wisnowski dying?"

Uncle Walt paused again. I wondered if he was adjusting the suspenders on his pants. He did that when he was thinking.

"It has everything to do with it. She—Helen, that is—came breezing into town about six months ago. She's a widow. We're mostly single or widowers at the center. Moves in with Sophie Banko. You know her, Pauline. She lives over on the corner of Pine and Maple Avenue. That big white house with—"

Sophie? *My* Sophie?

"The black shutters," I managed to say so as not to sound too interested. "I remember her." Of course I knew her, since she was my new case! "Didn't she have a son who went to school with Mary?"

"The convent?"

"Uncle Walt. Behave. I think they went to Saint Stanislaus School together. They were grades ahead of me." Mary was knocking on the door of forty. No, wait. She passed through last November. My mind was acting as if I was approaching that door soon, but I had years to go. And don't get me started on that ticking-clock thing. In a few months, on March 24, I'd be passing through the door of thirty-five. I planned to sneak in the window so no one would notice.

Surely my mother would remember, though, and have some blind date over for dinner—and me.

"Forget the son. Loser, that one. Anyway, Helen sashays in, with that lilac hair of hers and that car—"

"Maybe you're just interested in her set of wheels?"

"Pauline, you should be ashamed of yourself."

My face flushed. I hoped Goldie was doing all right and not waiting for me. Then again, this was the clinic. Waiting was a way of life. "Sorry."

"So, soon as Henry takes a liking to her—he also takes her out to dinner. You know that fancy restaurant down by the water?"

"Madelyn's." I knew it very well since my old boyfriend used to take me there. Of course, after his incarceration, I stopped dating him.

"Right. Henry was always the swinger of our crowd. Well, he starts bragging about . . . you know."

Geez.

"I'm thinking he's got to be having problems in that department, like most of us. Old Man Richardson with a prostate the size of an eighteen-wheeler's inner tube. Benny, who works as an usher in the movie theater, says he hasn't had working parts since the eighties. Mr. Kisof-sky pees about every twenty seconds, and truthfully, I'm not exactly Valentino when it comes to that department either, Pauline."

That was more than I needed to know. More than I ever wanted to know. "I still don't get—wait a minute. You mean Henry started using medication to help—"

"Viagra. At first I guessed he got his doctor to prescribe it. I don't think that anyone should use that kind of stuff, Pauline. Let nature work or not. Then again, Henry smiled more than any of us, even when he was losing at poker. Even started to walk faster and not shuffle like so many of us do. Made us all wonder and feel a little pea green with envy."

I had to once again laugh to myself—then delete those thoughts.

"Do you think he took too much or there was something wrong with the medication—"

"No, it had to do with the way he *got* the medication. I realized he couldn't afford a prescription 'cause he told me his insurance wouldn't cover it—not many of us on fixed incomes, with the stinking insurance we can manage to pay for, could afford the stuff. Especially prescription coverage. The government should be ashamed of themselves for the way they treat us old folks. Oh, but Medicaid covers it. Covers Viagra for those folks. Imagine. Geez. The pills run into the hundreds. Thirty pills for about three hundred bucks. Criminal."

Criminal?

Was Uncle Walt insinuating that Henry got his Viagra illegally?

Suddenly I felt chilled even though I'd cranked up the heater. Although I had several questions to ask, he said my

Uncle Stash had just arrived with his usual fanfare so he had to hang up. Illegal Viagra? Murder? Sex and the seniors? I allowed myself another chill and watched a shadow darken my window. Gulp. I grabbed my purse to use as a weapon if need be and then turned to the right.

Damn!

Outside stood Joey the Wooer.

Thinking of sex was not a good thing right now, because I could swear the old geezer was ogling me.

After I'd given a nice, polite smile to Mr. Tino and said I had to hurry inside to see how my friend was doing, I sat there in the waiting room, waiting. I thought about Joey the Wooer. The clichéd Italian Stallion. There was something about him. He'd actually looked as if he was going to talk to me when I had scurried off. I kinda liked the old man, but felt loyal to my uncle. And if they were both after Helen, well, I had to root for Uncle Walt.

The nurse opened the door. "Ms. Sokol?" She looked around the room. "Ms.—"

I looked up. "Here. Right here." Then I jumped up. "How is he?"

She rolled her eyes.

"Good." I knew Goldie was being Goldie and as evidenced by her reaction, he had to be all right. After all, if he were near death, she wouldn't be wearing that frown of annoyance. I followed her to the examining room and stopped at the door. "Oh, my."

Goldie lay sprawled along the examining table, his long limbs hanging off three sides. His eyes were shut and the mascara had formed darkened circles beneath. What a sight. I stepped closer. "Gold. Gold, Hon, you all right?"

One eye fluttered open. He groaned.

"Let me take you home now." I noticed a prescription slip in his hand. "Here, I'll take that and get it filled. You can sit in the waiting room until I get it. Antibiotic?" I eased the paper free of his grip and looked at it. "Yep. This will fix you up in no time, Gold."

He opened both eyes and sighed.

I got him up and walked him to the waiting room. On the way, he stopped at the desk to take care of his copayment. Through the window in the reception desk, I saw Mr. Tino signing in. He'd come back in after scaring the stuffing out of me in the parking lot. Geez. The guy must have bunches of health problems to be here so much. Not so unusual, I thought, when I reminded myself how Uncle Walt went off to the doctor at the drop of a hat. I nodded to Mr. Tino on the way out, but I was too busy getting Goldie comfortable to be able to stop and chat.

But Mr. Tino had given me the warmest smile.

"Comfortable, Gold?" I tucked the zebra comforter around his neck once I'd settled him back at his apartment.

He gave a weak smile and nodded. Poor darling.

"I'll make you some Jell-O. That should be easy to swallow. You need nourishment." After he shut his eyes, I went into the kitchen and rifled around until I had the individual glass dishes filled with cherry Jell-O. When I went to put them in the fridge, I gasped. Goldie's refrigerator was nearly empty. In fact, the kitchen was nowhere near as organized as Miles's. Goldie wasn't the chef type. This led me to the conclusion that the two belonged together soon, or Goldie might starve to death.

But that left me in an awkward position.

I couldn't impose on my two best friends and stay in Miles's condo if Goldie moved in. But I also couldn't cough up the bucks for a down payment on a place of my own yet. Each month, like excruciatingly painful clockwork, I had to pay a car loan—for a hefty-priced Lexus—that I didn't own. A "friend" had me cosign her car loan—then hightailed it (in style) out of town. With my addiction to shopping, my savings account was quite sparse. Lately, I vowed to fatten it up, but Fabio only paid when the job was done.

I needed to nail Sophie Banko soon, and find out more about Mr. Wisnowski. Was there a connection? Not exactly my line of work. Besides, I had nothing to report to the cops yet and didn't want my previous dealing with them, when I'd almost bought the farm, to make them treat me like some whacko.

"Pauline? You still here?"

I hurried to Goldie's side. "Yep. Your Jell-O is now solidifying. I added ice cubes instead of cold water so it works faster."

He looked up, grinned and took my hand. "I'll never be able to repay you."

"Stop that. That's what friends are for. Besides, look at all you helped me with on my first investigation." He had been a doll.

He pulled himself up and tucked the comforter under his arms. I guessed he'd had enough of the "dying scene" and decided he was going to make it. "What'd Fabio give you this time?"

I was dying—no pun intended—to tell him. Tell him and ask what the heck I should do next. But should I really burden such an ill man? "Prescription fraud, Gold."

One eyebrow rose. "Interesting."

I sat on the edge of the bed and took his arm. Ever since

I was a kid, my mother used to tickle, oh so very gently, our arms when we were sick. Turned out it annoyed my siblings, but me, I loved it. Even stopped my bloody noses when Mother tickled my arm. I especially liked the bottoms of my feet tickled. Very soothing. Goldie needed soothing, but I drew the line at feet. Without a word, I rolled up his gold silk pajama sleeve and set his arm next to me on the bed. Gently I rubbed. Goldie sighed like a kid whose mom had just hugged him.

"Yes, it seems as if it will be an interesting, if not more complicated case."

"Um."

Shoot. Not getting me anywhere. "Actually, Gold, my uncle thinks Mr. W was murdered for interfering with some Viagra fraud ring."

His arm stiffened. He turned to look at me. Beneath the now smudged mascara and heavy pancake makeup—deep bronze tone—a smile cracked across his coral lips. "You shittin' me?"

"Actually, no." I proceeded to tell him the entire conversation I'd had with my uncle, not leaving out that all I had left was Sophie Banko to investigate. What I did leave out was that "my" car loan payment was due in a few weeks and I needed the money from this case, and a bit more, actually.

Goldie sat up straighter. "You don't want to hear this, but you need to hang more at the senior citizens center. Only way to find out the dirt. Can't rely on your uncle who isn't a skilled investigator."

I froze. "And neither am I."

Now he tickled *my* arm. "You're coming along. You're a fast study. You're going to do a bang-up job on this one like the last." He smiled. "Besides, Suga, you got balls."

I leaned back on the pillow while Goldie sat up with his silky golden legs over the side of the bed. "Last? I was nearly killed—"

A shriek of horror filled the room. Startled, I jumped up, then quickly fell back when I realized it had only been Goldie's cry of anguish at reliving the horror of my nearly being shot. He took my arm and started tickling more.

"Yep. You need to infiltrate the SS center and spend more time at the clinic. Maybe you could—Oh . . . my . . . God. Goldie Perlman, you are a genius. Suga, you are going to have to . . . Yeah, that's *it*!"

Famous last words.

Goldie had more wigs than the wonderful country singer, Dolly Parton.

I found this out after he'd sent me to Biniker's Drugstore, the local old-fashioned kind with a real soda fountain, to buy chemicals. Not just any chemicals, but hair products. Despite his throat ailment and maybe because of the whopping dose of Motrin he'd taken, he perked up enough to embroil me in a plan.

So here I stood in his bedroom, looking in the mirror—and seeing my mother in ten years.

Oh . . . my . . . God.

The wig he lent me was a short bob that he styled with a curling iron, but not until he'd bleached it and recolored it a lovely shade of white. I'm glad he didn't go with the purple tint that Helen wore. At least I didn't look like I was trying to emulate the elderly flirt.

However, I did look something like my late grandmother in a shirtwaist housedress that fell inches below my knees. Goldie had left his sickbed to raid the closet of his neighbor, Mrs. Honeysuckle. I hadn't met the woman before, but could see she too had a fondness for Goldie. Being in her late seventies—I guessed by the wrinkled complexion and natural (I assumed) gray hair—she had several outfits to borrow.

Although I looked like my mother in the future, I couldn't picture her in the polyester dress. The base color was yellow with tiny birds, darker yellow birds, flocking about the bodice and skirt. Tiny buttons went down to my waist and took nearly an hour to fasten. But the part that made me hesitate, okay, make that argue with Goldie, was the nylons. They were opaque tan, with built-in wrinkles. Goldie insisted they made me look more authentic. And who would have guessed that I'd fit in Mrs. Honeysuckle's black shoes with the one-inch, thick, square heels? Okay, they were very comfortable and a "senior" fashion statement.

Goldie was a cosmetics whiz, as evidenced by his looks. I'd tried to learn from him in the past how to brighten my ever-so-pale complexion and make my gray eyes stand out. I often thought I looked too Polish. But now, leaning near for a few seconds, I had to blink past the wire-rimmed glasses he'd stuck on my nose.

"I look ancient." My heart thudded at the thought that this was how I was going to look in fifty years. Not even a computer could have enhanced this kind of image. All I could think of was, I better get married before all this happens. In the meantime, though, I'd decided to become a career woman. Still, I'd tuck this image of myself in the back of my mind in case the marriage thing became a desire.

Goldie turned to give me a high five. "Perfect."

"I'm not sure I can go through with this." I stepped closer. "Don't you think someone will recognize me?"

"Do you?"

"Recognize myself or think someone else—"

"Yeah, recognize yourself." He leaned back, tugged at the belt of his gold and black paisley robe and tapped a finger to his lips. "I wouldn't."

After copious nudges from Goldie to leave and a half glass of chardonnay followed by a Budweiser, I found myself standing in the doorway of the Hope Valley Senior Citizens Center, looking very much, I hoped, not like myself.

I heard a shuffling sound and turned to see Mr. Richardson, whose prostate I hoped had shrunk, and Benny, the usher from the movie theater, coming up the sidewalk. The building was level with the sloped walkway, and so there weren't any front steps.

They both stopped—and stared.

I gulped loudly and tried to smile, although the makeup Goldie had pasted onto my face was nearly ready to crack. Suddenly I thought of Robin Williams in *Mrs. Doubtfire*.

"Hello, sweetie," Benny said.

I couldn't distinguish the tone. At first I thought he used it as if I were a thirty-something dressed for Halloween. Then he winked.

There is a God.

Mr. Richardson scuffled forward. "You're new around here."

As if I had dementia and didn't know that. I nodded.

"Come on, sweetie," Benny said, taking my hand from the door. He paused.

I looked down. Goldie had forgotten my hands! They didn't look over seventy. Then again, my eyesight had to be a thousand times better than the folks who came here. Benny was in motion again, opening the door for me.

"We'll introduce you and get you a nice, warm cup of

coffee." He stepped aside. "With those hands, you look used to having someone take care of you."

I sighed.

"Passed away, did he?"

He who? Oh, my husband. "Several years ago," I replied.

Once inside, it looked as if the world were running in slow motion. Men sat at tables playing cards, chatting and laughing. A group of women sat in rows of chairs ever so slowly doing arm exercises instructed by a young guy in a black leotard. Maybe I could have come here as that? But no, I stood between the two elderly gentlemen, disguised as an aged female, yet felt as if I stood out like a tick on a white dog.

I was introduced to everyone, fed melba toast sans butter, sugar-free cookies, and dried prunes. All was washed down with very weak coffee laden with Equal and nondairy creamer. My stomach flipped several times as I cruised the room by myself.

There in the back row of the exercise ladies sat Sophie Banko, rolling her arms as if she thought the slabs of fat hanging off would tumble to the ground. At least I thought it was her. I had to lift up my fake glasses to be sure. Looked just like the photo in my file.

Bingo.

I'd introduce myself as soon as her arms thinned. I swung around in time to see Uncles Walt and Stash walk in like an Oreo cookie with a Helen Wanat filling sandwiched between the two.

Suddenly I had to get out of there. I started to hurry, and then got a suspicious look from Benny. No one in this room except maybe Mr. Leotard traveled at that speed. I slowed, shuffled and tried to get to the door. Benny grabbed my arm and yanked me toward my uncles!

"Hello, fellas. Meet our new member." He turned toward me with a look of horror on his face. I readied for him to say, "Your niece," but all he said was, "I never got your name, sweetie."

"Pau . . . Peggy. Peggy—" I felt the fake sagging boobs Goldie had fashioned sag a bit more. "—Doubtme. Peggy Doubtme." I pronounced it "Doubtmay" as if I were French. "Real name is Margaret, but I go by Peggy," I rambled nervously. "My mother, God rest her soul, refused to call me Peggy and when someone would call on the phone asking for Peggy, Mamma would say, 'You mean *Margaret*.'" I chuckled. Alone.

Uncle Stash took my hand and shook it vigorously. He winked and said, "Nice to meet you, Peggy."

I tried to ease backward so Uncle Walt wouldn't get a direct look at me. He stood there staring.

Oh, boy.

Suddenly he took my hand from his brother's and said, "Very nice to meet you. I hope you enjoy yourself here, and don't hesitate to ask me anything. Anything at all." He dropped my hand.

I gulped.

He smiled.

Did he know?

Helen leaned in close. "Keep your distance, Doubtme." The words came out slowly, nearly silently and without her lips moving.

Benny interrupted with, "Get her another coffee, light and sweet, Walt. Peggy's a widow and used to being waited on."

Uncle Walt gave a slight bow and moved away, followed by Uncle Stash. I leaned against the wall and shut my eyes.

"Call 911! Call 911!" Benny shouted.

My eyes flew open in registered nurse mode. "What? What's wrong?"

He shook his hands as if to erase his words. "Holy mackerel, Peggy. I thought you was gonna pass out on us."

Oh, boy, again. I really had to have my wits about me in this place. Doing surveillance on Sophie to see how unhealthy she really was and did she need all the meds she got and trying to find the truth about Mr. W's death was a hell of a lot harder than tailing a workers' comp case.

After an hour, I had forced down the third cup of coffee Uncle Walt had brought me, played six games of gin rummy with a mixed group of seniors, and watched my Uncle Stash flirt with every woman in the room. All the while, I made up a fake family of three married children, six male grandchildren, and a dead husband who had been a math schoolteacher all his life.

Then, I set my sights on Sophie.

Thank goodness my uncles didn't seem to recognize me. I said a silent thanks to Goldie and my favorite saint, Saint Theresa, although I knew I should be mentioning something to Saint Jude, the patron saint of hopeless causes.

Sophie walked to the food table, but not before several men came up to her to chat. Geez. Maybe size doesn't matter. She sure seemed popular with the males.

I wove my way through the gang now dancing the polka. Before someone could commandeer me to dance, I sidled up to Sophie. "Nice place this here is."

She turned, looked at my waistline. Goldie had stuffed some old sweaters into my underwear to make a wonderful elderly potbelly, but I was still only a size nine. Sophie was in double digits.

"Yeah, good cookies."

I made small talk with her until the cookie tray was empty and my stomach ached. I swore I wouldn't eat desserts for weeks even if my mother made my favorite homemade chocolate cake with one-inch-thick frosting and eight ounces of cream cheese in it.

I leaned nearer to her. "So, any of these guys capable of any action?"

At first she hesitated, then she turned to me. "If they aren't, things can be fixed."

I readied to ask what she meant when I felt a hand on my arm. I turned to see Joey the Wooer. Great.

His smile nearly melted the last sugar cookie I held in my hand.

"So, Sophie, who's-a the new bellisima?"

Sophie introduced us and then split. I tried to get away, but found myself alone with Joey. Who would have thought a woman the size of Sophie could disappear so fast? Maybe she and Joey were in cahoots. Maybe they were working on the Viagra scam. Maybe he helped her commit prescription fraud.

But he looked so damned dapper compared to every other man in there.

Before I could think of a question to trip him up, he said, "*Bellisima*, will you do me the honors?"

Before I knew it, I was polkaing across the room in the arms of Joey the Wooer, all the while thinking I might be in the wrong profession.

Also, how I was insane to come here.

And, Joey smelled good.

Damn good.

What the hell?

Four

Polkaing in the senior citizens center in Joey the Wooer's arms was not like any nursing job I've ever worked on.

If it weren't for the fact that I had little knowledge of what to do to investigate Sophie Banko, this wasn't a bad gig. But in my Polish stubbornness, I intended to investigate till I *did* know what to do.

I inhaled Joey's cologne.

My insides tingled. What? I yanked myself free. Just because my body *looked* older, I shouldn't be finding myself attracted to him! "I . . . my . . . I have to go. Go. Yes. Go."

Damn, but my body was confused.

Joey gave me a polite smile and gestured toward the hallway. "Second door on the left."

"Hmm?"

"Ladies' room?"

As I nodded and scurried away from Joey, I wondered if my red-hot complexion showed through the layers of pancake makeup and fake wrinkles. I had to look ruddier than feverish Goldie.

I didn't know what was more humiliating, my reaction

to an old man or his thinking I was a candidate for adult diapers. That crossed my mind as I ran down the hallway and into the ladies' room. With my bladder only a third the age of most women at the center, I really didn't need to be in here as Joey assumed, but when I got a look at myself in the mirror, I was damn glad he'd gotten confused.

The "wrinkles" Goldie had fashioned with some tape and pancake makeup were sliding to the side of my face. Gave my eyes an Asian flavor. Oh, boy. I hoped no one noticed. Then again, most of these folks had vision that ran in the triple digits. I convinced myself I was safe. Then I hurried into a stall and grabbed a handful of toilet tissue. Back at the mirror, I wiped the sides ever so gently so as not to yank the wrinkles off.

The door opened.

My hand froze.

I turned around in time to see Helen lighting a cigarette. No wonder the deep voice. Her head flew up, our gazes locked, and I'm not sure who was more embarrassed, she or I.

When she looked at the tissue, I decided it was me.

Then I noticed the huge "NO SMOKING" sign on the wall to the left. Gotcha. I squinted at her—and then began to cough my brains out.

"Shit." She nonchalantly headed to the sink, took one long pull on the cigarette, then ran water over it and dumped it into the trash.

Suddenly I remembered the wrinkles and figured if I coughed too hard, they'd end up on my droopy chest. After a quick peek in the mirror showed me my wrinkles would pass for now, I started to turn.

"So, where the hell did you come from anyway?" she asked.

I'm guessing Helen was not known for being tactful. "Excuse me?" I tried to make my voice sound like my grandmother's, but truthfully, I sounded more like a thirty-four-year-old trying to sound over seventy. Helen didn't seem to notice or if she did, she didn't care. She was more concerned about where I had come from and how long I'd be here. *Cutting into your territory, Helen?* I wondered.

She pushed past me and headed into one of the stalls. I could make my getaway now, but that would be rude. I didn't want to be a rude elderly widow. Helen seemed to have that label down pat.

Two other women came in and nodded. One went into the other stall and the other went to wash out her dentures. Damn. I found my tongue running across my teeth, thankful they didn't come out.

"Where'd you come from and how long you gonna be in Hope Valley?" Helen asked.

Feeling foolish talking to her feet, I turned and looked at myself in the mirror. The woman without her dentures leaned closer. "Stay out of the sun, honey, and give Botox a try," she said with her tongue slapping at her gums.

Hmm, she had darn smooth skin. "Thanks." I sighed and turned enough so she couldn't see my slipping wrinkles anymore. "I'm here, visiting my nephew, Helen. Dear boy."

The toilet flushed. The door opened and she walked out still zipping up her slacks. "How long?"

"Well, maybe a month or two." *Or until your buddy Sophie is locked up.*

"Month or two." She came closer.

I backed up.

Didn't stop her as she nearly stepped on Mrs. Honeysuckle's shoe. "Keep away from Walt and Stash."

My elderly hackles rose. "Well, I never. If I want to dance with any of those gentlemen—"

"Then you'll have to deal with me, old lady." With that she turned and walked out.

"Your breath smells like smoke," I called out after her, then turned to see the toothless woman grin. What a stupid thing to say, yeah, I knew it. But at least the toothless woman found it humorous. Me, I needed to slink out of there and get back to being myself.

This case might prove much more complicated than I thought.

After my run-in with Helen, I tried to stay clear of her. For as much as I wanted to head back to my condo and change, I hadn't really accomplished anything here yet. Goldie had said I needed to "hang out" around this place more, and I knew he was right. He always gave me the best advice to learn how to do my job, and I had yet to give up even when reality hit me in the face. I'd always been that stubborn kid who persisted when everyone else quit.

Pretending I couldn't see a wave from my Uncle Stash, who, I'm guessing, wanted to dance, I turned to look around the room. Hey, the poor vision of old age had its benefits, and I drew the line at dancing with either uncle— and not because of Helen's threat. There at the snack table stood Sophie. Mental note to myself: When looking for Sophie, find food.

Before Uncle Stash came up to me, I scurried over there and wriggled between two elderly women to get next to Sophie. "This is such a lovely place. I'm so glad I came here."

She gave me an odd look while she chewed what I

guessed was her six dozenth cookie. Sugar-free, yeah, right. What about the fat content?

"It's a place to meet folks." She took a swig of coffee.

"Yes. Yes it surely is. Where else could we go—"

"Saint Bartholomew's has Bingo tonight."

Bingo. Maybe this disguise wasn't such a good idea. Now I had to sit through Bingo. I'd had years of that, keeping Uncle Walt company because I was the only single one in our family—don't get my mother started on that. I never could keep up with the numbers and letters being called and who the heck could remember if they were looking for a straight Bingo, corners only, postage stamps, diagonal or whatever. I never could. I'd have to think about this one.

One of the ladies I'd shoved over to get next to Sophie turned to me. "Yes, Sophie is a wiz at Bingo and all the men make a point to sit at her table."

I told myself a nice, hot shower would erase *that* image, but then realized something. If Sophie were ill and needed all the numerous medications that she filed claims for, Peggy would have to spend more time with her to form a diagnosis. One thing for sure, she didn't have any digestive problems, by the way she packed in the cookies.

"Bingo sounds like fun. May I join you tonight?"

Her mouth too full to talk, Sophie shrugged.

I said my goodbyes and walked as slowly as a woman of my "age" should until I got outside. Then I jogged to my car and leaped inside. Goldie had some work to do on this makeup stuff, and I had to borrow another dress. Couldn't go to Bingo in the same outfit.

Then a comforting thought struck.

After this glimpse into my future, I realized I would remain pretty much the same person, only wrinkled.

* * *

Miles opened Goldie's door after I'd rung the bell. As I pushed past him, he grabbed my arm. "Excuse me, ma'am. May I help you?"

I turned around. "Queen."

He screeched.

A pitiful laugh emanated from the bedroom. I looked to see Goldie, wrapped in a golden silk robe, hanging onto the doorframe.

Miles looked from Goldie to me. "I don't see what is so funny." Then he focused on me. "Why, I never!"

Compassion had been inbred in me so I leaned near him. "Relax, Miles, it's me. Pauline?"

"What the hell?"

Goldie continued laughing as he came into the living room and collapsed on the couch. After covering him with a spotless white afghan, Miles sat next to him.

I explained the situation to Miles, who finally chuckled. Then I turned to Goldie. "I know you feel like crap, but I have to go to Bingo tonight. Which means I need a new outfit and—" I pulled the wrinkles up on my face. "—a makeover. Something slide-proof."

They both stared at me.

Miles rolled his eyes. "Maybe you should come back to nursing, Pauline. I mean . . . look at you."

"I don't have to. I know how I look." I decided not to tell them about the "Asian incident" in the Ladies' room. "And, Miles, you know I can't go back to nursing. I still have scorch marks from being burned out."

"But with the shortage in the country, you could pick and choose your job." He rubbed Goldie's shoulders as if that would make his throat feel better.

Goldie purred.

I smiled. "I don't want to pick or choose a nursing job. In fact, I've sworn off donning a pair of scrubs or comfy shoes for the rest of my life. I like my new job."

"I know you do, but when the novelty wears off—"

"Novelty? Wears off? Look at me, Miles. I'm wearing Mrs. Honeysuckle's dress and shoes. The novelty of this job keeps changing. I like the change."

"What?" His hands slipped off of Goldie's shoulders. "Sorry, Gold. You like the change, Pauline? You who have lived in this small town all your life and never ventured farther than Long Island Sound for a vacation?"

"Okay. Okay. That was the old me. Besides, I don't think I could go back to a job where I had to get up at five in the morning and follow some boss's rules. Fabio doesn't care what I do or how and when I do it as long as I get the job done."

Goldie turned toward me. "And how is that going?"

I sucked in a breath and collected my thoughts. When I blew out the air, I said, "Well, I've become buddies with Sophie so that I can find out about her illnesses. I've already ruled out the gastrointestinal tract by the amount of food she consumes. She really doesn't appear sickly, so I'm guessing Fabio is correct. She's got prescriptions for illnesses from her head to her toes. Cardiac. Diabetes. Migraines. Arthritis. You name it. Sophie may be scamming the insurance company. Thing is, I'm not sure how."

"You have to stick closer to her, Suga."

I nodded toward Goldie. "I know. That's why I need a change of outfit. To go to . . . Bingo tonight. You up to it?"

Goldie smiled. "For you, Suga. For you."

* * *

I stood in the doorway of Saint Bartholomew's Church and looked across the room. Nearly every overweight woman looked like Sophie. Damn. I should have planned to meet her at the door, but she wasn't all too thrilled about me joining her. I shuffled down the steps and into the hall in Mrs. Honeysuckle's brown pumps. They did go well with the brown-and-white dress Goldie had picked out for me.

I ran my fingers across my cheeks and prayed that when this night was over, I'd get these wrinkles off my face. Goldie had sworn I would, but I had my doubts when he layered globs of Vaseline on my face, formed the wrinkles—and then set them with superglue! He swore the Vaseline would allow me to peel off the glue.

Please don't make me permanently wrinkled, I prayed to Saint Theresa. I thought it was appropriate since I was in a church hall. Then I found my mark. There, near the stage, sat Sophie and her friends. Uncle Walt, Uncle Stash, Helen and Joey. Damn. I didn't expect the usual crowd. But, oh well, I had a job to do and would have to ignore them.

"May I join you?" I asked as I approached.

All the men stood except Joey, who looked at the others and then followed suit. Next, he actually hurried over and held the chair for me. I thanked him, ignored him, and was glad the empty seat was near Sophie.

"My feet are killing me tonight after dancing. Arthritis, you know," I complained.

She nodded.

Shit. Did that mean she had it too? This wasn't going to be an easy case. I felt it in my pretend arthritic bones. "You suffer from it too?"

Uncle Walt leaned near. "Had it in my knees since the seventies."

I know. I know. But I smiled at him and looked toward Sophie. "How about you?"

She gave me an odd look.

Joey cut in with, "Why the interesta in Sophie's joints, *Bellisima*?"

For a second, I forgot my disguise. Geez, the guy had a way about him that confused me. "I . . . well . . . don't we all suffer from it?"

"My joints are like well-oiled machines," Uncle Stash added as he nudged Helen, who gave him a feisty grin.

I did not want to go there.

So, I smiled back, focused on my Bingo cards, all six of them, and decided I needed to get Sophie alone.

After three hours, forty-five minutes, and ten seconds of Bingo, I felt the hairs on my wig stand on end. If my face were pliable, I'd scream. Then I vowed I would never join a senior citizens center or play Bingo when I really became of age. I was even putting it in writing so, if dementia set in, my family wouldn't have a confused me playing Bingo.

Plus, I was pissed that I hadn't won. I'm sure Miles would tell me I was a sore loser since everyone at the table had won Bingo except me. Damn. Maybe he'd be right.

Sophie started packing up her Bingo equipment. I couldn't believe they all had their own markers and chips. I must have looked like the rank amateur that I was. I jumped up when she did. Guess that's the fault of "aging" so quickly. I needed to think things through and prepare better. Then again, I had no idea how to prepare for any part of this job.

"Can I give you a lift, Sophie?"

She shook her head. "I only live a block away."

"Oh, my. I guess my mind is going on me." I giggled as maturely as I could. "I also walked. Bad night vision, you know." Mental note to myself, pick up your car later.

She nodded. Sophie Banko, woman of few words. Damn it.

Once at the doorway, I latched onto her arm and said, "Let's walk together." With my death grip, she couldn't say no.

After we got out past the parking lot, I released my hold when she kept pulling away. "Sorry. I'm always afraid of falling."

"No problem." She walked on.

The night was moonlit, which made it easier to see, along with the good lighting around the church and nearby neighborhood. When we crossed Pleasant Street, Sophie turned into the yard of a white house.

"So this is where you live?"

She gave me an odd look. "That's why I turned here."

"Isn't that house next door where poor Mr. Wisnowski lived?"

She froze.

When she defrosted, she glared at me. "How would someone who just came to town know about him?"

Oh . . . my . . . aching arthritic feet.

I chuckled in as elderly a way as I could. "Know about him? I don't, dearie. But I heard someone at the . . . oh, no. Silly me. When I was driving with . . . someone told me he lived here."

She curled her lip and leaned in.

I backed up and prayed the moon would eclipse so we'd be in total darkness, and I could sneak away.

"You may be heading into Alzheimer's, Peggy. Get a checkup." With that she nodded as if to dismiss me and started to go walk up her porch stairs.

Good. She wasn't suspicious of me. Well, of my really being elderly, that is.

"Wait!" I yelled before she hurried up the steps.

She swung around and bobbled like a top. A woman her size should know better than to spin around at that speed. Thank goodness I caught her before we both fell down. Well, I really couldn't catch her; it was more like I shoved all my weight against her to keep her upright.

She steadied herself and turned back without so much as a thank-you.

I made a mental note not to startle her again. My mental-note list was growing at warp speed. Good thing I had a great memory. Came from my nursing background.

"I . . . wonder if I can come in for a . . . drink of water."

She shrugged. I followed her inside.

Once in Sophie's house, I stood like a jerk while she glared at me. "I . . . oh, the water?"

The place was creepy. That's what got my attention and made me forget that I'd asked for water. The old Victorian-style living room looked more like the parlor of a funeral home. And the smell. Old. Musty. I followed Sophie down a dark hallway and into the kitchen. The stove looked like an old coal job. Pale green. I felt as if I'd stepped back in time, and not the same way that I did every time I went into my mother's house.

This was downright eerie.

"Glasses are in the drainer." Sophie hobbled to the kitchen table and flopped down. The chair groaned.

I walked to the white porcelain sink and looked at the

glasses. Suddenly my thirst disappeared. Not that the glasses weren't clean, but I had an odd feeling that I shouldn't touch anything in Sophie's house.

What if she *was* a criminal?

My fingerprints would be all over—and maybe even covering up hers. Instead I turned and decided to snoop while I talked. "Tired?"

She looked at me and wheezed. "Aren't you?"

I readied to say at my age I jogged several miles before getting tired, then remembered my age was supposed to be in the seventies. I sat across from her and nodded. "Beat."

She probably forgot the reason I'd gotten myself invited in as she took a napkin from the lazy Susan in the middle of the table and wiped her forehead. It wasn't really warm in there, but maybe her size had thrown her internal thermometer off. Plus, she hadn't taken off her jacket yet. When she swung the lazy Susan around, I noticed two prescription bottles.

Damn, that's it? Sophie couldn't be too ill. But, according to her file, she was sending in claims for a hell of a lot more than two prescriptions.

I smelled a rat the size of a kangaroo.

I started to ease closer to read what they were for, but suddenly Sophie's face was in mine.

Geez.

Close up, she looked gigantic.

"What the hell are you doing here?" Her accusing tone had me pull back.

"I—" What the hell was I going to say?

"Is something wrong with your hearing?" Her weight when she leaned near pushed the table, which pinned me between the wall and the other end of the table. "I asked what the hell are you doing?"

I looked at her. For several seconds I couldn't respond, and figured this was good. Even though the reason was that I was so squashed I could barely squeak out a breath, it would make me look confused and even hard of hearing if I played dumb. I caught my reflection in her toaster. Shoot. I was turning the color of a boiled lobster.

I held up a hand and waved it about. "Breathe. I can't . . . breathe." I pointed to my chest.

"Oh!" Sophie pulled back and yanked the table. "Such a skinny thing. Why didn't you say something?"

I blew out such a strong breath, Sophie's hair danced about. While she straightened it, I decided I had to get out of here. She was too suspicious about me scrutinizing her medicine. I stood.

She stood.

I smiled.

She didn't.

"Well, thank you for the water."

"You never had any."

"Oh." I turned toward the kitchen door not wanting to go back in time through the parlor. "Silly me. Mind isn't what it used to be." But I couldn't leave. Not just yet. I hadn't found out anything. Not even what the prescriptions were for. And maybe she had more of them stashed in other places. I tried to stall for time. Shifted my legs. Pulled down on my dress and yanked my jacket tighter.

"Goodbye." She stood staring at me. No wonder. She probably thought I was crazy or some criminal.

"Mind if I use your little girls' room?"

She wrinkled her forehead. "I only have boys. Grown ones."

"Oh." I laughed. "That's nice, but not what I meant. I meant the powder room." I laughed again. Alone.

This time she shook her head and pointed toward the stairs. "Only one in this place is upstairs."

I followed her pointing finger thinking, *Good. One less place to have to snoop around in.* When I got to the top of the stairs, I saw only one open door. White tile covered the floor, so I knew it was the "little boys' room." I was tempted to sneak a peek in the other rooms, but I figured I wasn't adept at opening a door quietly while the suspect was home. So, I headed into the bathroom.

Sophie was neat and clean which made my job easier. At least there weren't any piles of clothes thrown on the floor that I could slip on or have to dig through. I opened the medicine cabinet above the sink.

No medicine.

Facial creams. Shaving cream. An old bottle of rubbing alcohol and two peroxides, but no prescription bottles. Hmm.

Someone with all the meds she had gotten reimbursed for had to keep them somewhere.

Unless she never got them.

"You all right up there?"

Uh-huh. "Fine. Fine. Support hose, you know." I quietly shut the cabinet door, did a quick look in the linen closet to find only linen, flushed the toilet and hurried out.

When I got downstairs, she was really giving me an odd look now. No doubt I deserved it, but so what if I got a reputation around the senior citizens center as a nut case.

"Thanks so much. Feel better now. Too much coffee."

"Goodbye."

I smiled and headed toward the kitchen door. When I opened it, I noticed how close Mr. Wisnowski's house was. Only a few feet away with a joint driveway in between. The house was dark. "You must be pretty close to your neighbors."

She looked at me like I had two heads. "Obviously. These houses were built after the war. Not much property, so they are close."

"You must miss having someone next to you."

She paused. "How do you know no one lives next to me now?"

Oh, boy.

"I . . . someone mentioned it. That he was . . . that he died. They mentioned Mr. Wisnowski died. For the life of me, though, I can't remember who. Who told me. Not who died. You know how we forget things at our age."

She looked at me suspiciously but said, "Won't be long before someone moves in."

Hmm. "Oh, are you getting new neighbors?"

She shrugged. "Soon. House just went up for sale today."

Then that meant someone looking to buy could get a tour of Mr. W's house. I reached out my hand to shake hers. She just looked at it.

Before the words could filter through my brain, I said, "*I'm* looking to move here." Where the hell did that come from?

She looked at me, again oddly. "I thought Helen said you were only here for a few months."

Damn. For gossip to spread so fast, there had to be a senior-citizen grapevine the size of which could produce oceans of wine. "I . . . you know, Sophie, my mind isn't what it used to be. I don't know what I said to Helen. She kind of makes me nervous, you know." I moved closer as if pulling Sophie into my confidence. Worked too.

She nodded.

"Anyway, I love it here and the people are so nice. So I said to myself, Pau . . . Peggy, why not stick around?"

Again she nodded, then looked at the door.

"Right. I should be going."

She nodded a third time. Sophie was a woman of few words.

I scurried away from her house and started back toward the church. But then I realized what a great opportunity was smacking me in the face. Admittedly, I had a long way to go before I could call myself a real medical insurance fraud investigator. But I was determined—and curious.

One would think I would have learned my lesson about curiosity getting me into trouble, but what the hell? I needed to find out if Uncle Walt was laboring under dementia—or if he was correct.

And even if I wasn't a good liar, my curiosity was advantageous for this profession.

So, I looked back to make sure that Sophie was not watching me through the window. And thank goodness, she'd left her side porch light on. I turned around and walked past her house to the sidewalk in front of Mr. Wisnowski's house. How convenient the two were, side by side.

Although dark inside, the moon, along with Sophie's light, allowed me to walk around to his backyard. Every once in a while, the inside of the house seemed to glow from the moon. There was an enclosed porch out back, which I assumed led to the kitchen, since that was the setup in Sophie's house.

The house on the other side of his, which was a mere ten feet away, was also black inside. Good. No snooping neighbors. I figured Sophie would be passed out on her sofa by now as I walked up the back steps. My hand shook when I reached toward the screen door. This was not good, I told myself. Any investigator worth her salt should not shake, even though my brain kept shouting that I wasn't a *murder* investigator. Then, I also told myself a person would be a fool not to be a little nervous while breaking and entering and shaking.

Damn.

Could I really do this?

I would have to in order to find out if Uncle Walt had been correct. Murderers shouldn't get away with it, and maybe there was some evidence in here that would help my case with Sophie.

With my hand poised near the door handle for a few seconds, I thought about it. Then, before I could stop it, my hand grabbed the screen door and yanked, and I was inside the porch.

Since the screen was unlocked, I rationalized that this wasn't actually "breaking." The entering part was arguable. Hey, I was looking to buy and wanted to beat the rush. Sophie, a suspected criminal herself, could vouch for me. Is that what my world was coming to? I looked through the window. Yep. The kitchen.

Okay, in order to get inside, I had to think like an eighty-year-old man. Dressed like this should help. I asked myself where Uncle Walt would hide a key—then bent down and lifted the mat below my feet.

Nothing.

But there was an impression of a key in the dust on the floor. Hmm. Maybe Mr. Wisnowski had used it, like my Uncle Walt might do, and had forgotten to return it before he died. Well, I really had no intention of breaking a window or door to get inside. My heart sank as I thought about how I'd gotten this far and wouldn't get to snoop around.

Something in my gut said my uncle was onto something, thinking murder instead of death by natural causes. And with Sophie so close . . . there just was something gnawing at me.

I stood up and leaned against the door. "Ack!"

My world spun in a flash.

When I felt pain shoot up my back, I realized I'd fallen onto the kitchen floor when the door gave way. Obviously it had been left open. Even my wig had sailed off in the fall.

"Damn." I couldn't move for several seconds and shut my eyes to wait for the pain to subside. My medical background said I shouldn't move in case a vertebra had cracked, but I sure as hell wasn't going to call out for help. How could I explain this getup and me on the floor of a dead man's house? I squeezed my eyes tighter—as if that would help my situation.

A dull light shone through my eyelids. Wow, the moon was really bright tonight to cause that phenomenon. I reached my hand up to cover my eyes and let out a satisfying moan. Then I pulled at my "wrinkles," which were suddenly annoying me. Had to be from the pain caused by my head smacking the floor. Thank goodness I didn't feel any warm liquid running down any part of me.

A muffled sound came near. Footsteps!

I opened my eyes to see a shadow standing above me. A scream flew through my lips.

The figure leaned near. A flashlight blinded my eyes. I shut them again as if that would beam me out of there.

"Jesus. Is that you, Pauline? What the hell are you doing here?"

I didn't need to see who it was. The voice made it embarrassingly clear. I moaned again and managed, "You?"

Then I remembered how bizarre I must look.

Five

My "you?" filled the silence of Mr. Wisnowski's kitchen and, despite the pain in my back, confusion filled my thoughts.

I finally opened my eyes. Yep. I hadn't been hallucinating. "Hi, Jagger."

"Again, what the hell are you doing here?"

I inhaled and remembered. Remembered his familiar scent and had to control my urges, despite his being a few inches away. You are a professional, I told myself and looked up.

Dressed all in black, which wasn't unlike him at all, he looked good. Yum. He even had a five-o'clock shadow. I figured it was to aid in his breaking and entering disguise, but it also made him look sexier than usual.

And that was hard to do.

Even in this dim light I could see his dark eyes, noticed his hair a tad shorter and windswept in a delicious sort of way. His jacket was suede, and beneath it he wore a knitted shirt that had to show off the definition of his arms.

One could only hope.

"Move that damn light out of my eyes." I swatted in the

air, but missed. "And, you could at least ask if I'm all right. I mean, I could have a concussion." I tried to sit up and felt strong arms aid me.

"You landed on the braided rug, and you didn't black out."

Hmm. He must have been watching me. Although a tantalizing thought, it also sent waves of embarrassment throughout me when I realized—I was still dressed like Peggy Doubtme—sans the wig and the Vaseline/super-glued wrinkles, which were now in my hand.

I must've looked wonderful.

I'm surprised he recognized me. I peeked at him staring at me. On second thought, no, I wasn't surprised at all.

His hand tugged on mine. "Get up."

He wore gloves, I realized. And I also thought he must have taken the key from under the mat. But why? Why would Jagger be snooping around here?

And why hadn't I thought of wearing gloves?

"Don't touch anything," he said, as he helped me toward the door.

So much for my golden opportunity to investigate.

But then again, I was known for my persistence, even if it got me into trouble sometimes. Okay, lots of times.

I shrugged free. "Ouch!" My head pounded.

He stopped. "You all right?"

I rolled my eyes. Even that hurt. "Yes, I'll live. But I'm not moving from this spot until you tell me why *you* are here." I even attempted to pull myself up straighter so that might make me look more formidable to Jagger. What the hell was I thinking? My five-foot-six body couldn't hold a candle to his six three. "Well? What are you doing here? Remember, I'm not moving until you spill."

He grinned.

I was surprised that he didn't say, "Wanna bet?" I knew damn well that's what his grin meant.

"Pauline—" He leaned near and his grin deepened. "The real question is, why did you come crashing through the door?" He touched my arm. "Spill."

"Uncle Walt thinks Mr. Wisnowski was killed. Murdered." Damn! Just 'cause he touched me didn't mean I had to spill my guts.

He leaned back against the wall and looked at me.

Well, Jagger, I had learned, didn't just look. He kinda pulled you into his stare and made you his slave. Not literally, although some nights that became the plot of my dreams.

So, I rambled on. "I don't know why, but I think Uncle Walt is right. And you . . . you insinuated as much . . . with that look. Just looking at me. And the grin. Why are you here? You don't investigate murders." I had no idea why I said this, because I'd never, in fact, learned whom Jagger worked for. He very well could be FBI investigating whatever the hell he felt like.

"I have my reasons, and you, of course, know that I'm not good at sharing."

"I'll bet you were a blast to play with as a kid."

"Loners don't play with other kids. But, I will tell you this much since I know why you are here, I will share what I know with you . . . if . . ."

I knew Jagger was talking. His firm lips, the top a bit thinner than the bottom, kept moving. Me, I couldn't hear a thing since a cloud of doom rolled over me.

Jagger was going to pull me into his web.

And, me being me, would let him.

Before I knew it, he did, in fact, manage to get me to the

door. With his firm hand at my back, we walked through it. He locked it, bent down and stuck the key under the mat. "Don't even think about it."

Once outside, he walked me toward the back of the yard and close to an old shed, where he sat me on a concrete bench, much like the ones in my church's cemetery. A chill sped up my spine. I told myself it was from the morbid cemetery thought, but also realized it could have come from being so near.

Jagger. Damn it all! Now he would know I was parading around like an elderly lady. But then again, knowing Jagger—he probably already knew.

I looked at him and ignored how the moonlight gave him an almost "Casablanca-type" haze. And, it looked damn good.

"What are you doing here, Sherlock?"

Sherlock. Oh, boy. Jagger had given me that pet name when we first met. Although he could have meant it sarcastically, I always chose to view it as more of an endearing term. "I . . . well. Hey, I could ask you the same thing. What the hell are you doing here?"

He shook his head twice and clucked his tongue. "You already did."

"Okay. Okay. I should know better than to question you. But, really, Jagger. Why would you be snooping—"

He stared a typical Jagger-stare.

"Mr. W really was *murdered*," I mumbled.

The closemouthed Jagger had not volunteered any info, but got me safely back to the church parking lot—without my even telling him that's where my car was. Didn't surprise me though. He also didn't ask about my outfit, but when he'd tucked me into the driver's seat, he had whispered, "We'll talk. *Soon.*"

Before I could open my mouth to ask about what, knowing damn well he was going to involve me in something I'd regret, he was gone. Again, no surprise. I knew he'd show up somewhere else, when I least expected it. All the unanswered questions of why Jagger was in Mr. Wisnowski's house, was he really murdered, what did Jagger have to do with it and—ta-da—the $64,000.00 question, who the hell did Jagger work for, would only be answered when and if he wanted me to have that info.

I was convinced he already knew why *I* had been there.

I made it back to my condo without running into anyone in the parking lot who knew me—and had already repressed my feelings after meeting up with Jagger. Good thing, since I looked like my grandma, Babci. When I got inside, I grabbed Spanky—our five-pound shih tzu-poodle mix—who growled at my outfit. I kissed his furry head and said, "Why the hell did I tell Sophie I was moving here? I mean—" I sat on the couch.

Spanky merely stared into thin air when I continued, "I just told Helen I'd be here a few months. Don't ever lie, Spanks. Lies always jump up and bite you in the ass."

He curled up on my lap and this time looked at me as if he cared what I said.

"I mean it is a good idea, the moving here thing, since it will give me access to the inside of Mr. Wisnowski's house to see if he was murdered and if Sophie is in danger too. Or Uncle Walt! So, you see, I really need to know if he's right, and while I'm a 'senior citizen,' I could probably find out. But how the hell am I going to snoop around with some realtor on my butt?"

Spanky looked at me with his dark eyes that were far too big for his little squirrel-size head. "You bring along a diversion."

I stared at him. Had he talked? Then I realized I needed a Budweiser. *I* had talked while staring at Spanky. Damn. A diversion. Not a bad idea even if I was going nuts.

The next afternoon, Goldie met me at Wisnowski's house bundled up in his white fox coat. It was real, too, since Goldie was a wiz at investigating, and we got paid in proportion to our cases solved. "Gold, I really appreciate your help."

He smiled while the realtor, Ms. Barbara Lawrence, went to unlock Mr. Wisnowski's door. It had taken me all morning to call around town to see which realtor had the listing and insist on a showing before the sign went up.

"I'm feeling much better now, Suga. Anything to help. Besides, with Miles back at work and having watched Maury, and reruns of Jenny and Oprah until my eyes blurred, I needed to get out. Not ready for my own case yet, but love to help you."

Barbara, whom I had gone to Saint Stanislaus Grammar School with but, thank God, didn't recognize me as Peggy Doubtme, turned to look at us. She held the door open while we stood by her black Chevy station wagon. "Do you and your aunt need any help, Ms. Goldie?"

Gold and I looked at each other. If only poor Barbara knew.

"No, darlin', Auntie Peg and I are fine." With that he slid his arm under mine, and we walked up the stairs—intent on distracting and snooping.

When we walked inside the living room, I gasped.

Goldie tightened his hold. "Everything all right, Auntie?"

"I . . . I'm fine. Fine."

Barbara stood staring at me. "Can I get you something?"

"Water," I moaned.

I leaned close to Goldie and whispered that the place looked exactly like Sophie's, right down to the faded white doilies on the end tables. Weird.

Then again, nothing should surprise me. Since leaving nursing, lots of weird stuff had happened in my life—Jagger being one of them. I was beginning to wonder if I was being punished for leaving a profession that had fallen into crisis.

Barbara came up with a glass of water in her hand. "Here."

I looked at it and then remembered I'd asked for it. Seems when I got nervous I asked for water. This time I took it and drank it all down. Then I nearly spit it back up when I realized it was Mr. Wisnowski's glass!

Damn!

"Since you seem all right, shall we continue with the tour?" She waved her hand as if we were to follow.

"Fine." I took Goldie's arm as we went upstairs, and forced myself to forget that I'd just drunk out of a dead man's glass.

Barbara proceeded to point out the obvious. "This is the master bedroom. See the large window?"

She must think Goldie and I were dumb bunnies. I was getting a bit anxious since we were wasting too much time and not finding any useful info. I gave Goldie a look and a wink—as best I could with superglued wrinkles near my eyes.

Goldie, darling Goldie, swung into action. "Barbara, honey, is that a closet over there?"

I took two steps back and was out in the hallway. As I heard Goldie "ooh" and "ah," I scurried down the stairs. At the bottom I paused, feeling as if I might run into Jagger again.

No such luck this time. As I told myself that was a good thing, I went into the living room. I ignored the creepy feeling and went to Mr. W's desk.

Then I opened the purse I'd borrowed from Mrs. Honeysuckle, and took out her white gloves.

So there, Jagger.

Once the gloves were on, I opened drawer after drawer to look for . . . something, but I had no idea what might help me with the truth. Bills, cancelled checks, and old letters from Helen, which I stopped reading when I came to the "last night was wonderful" part. I noted two prescription forms on the bottom of the pile. One was for a diuretic. Water pills. Real common with the elderly. Especially ones with congestive heart failure. Then I lifted up the other prescription, which had a tiny coffee stain on the left side.

Viagra.

I held it for a few seconds.

"Mrs. Doubtme? Are you all right?" Barbara called.

I froze.

Goldie's wonderful voice said, "She's in the little old lady's room, Babs. Don't wait for her. Could be several minutes or longer."

"Oh . . . fine. Here is the hallway that leads to the spare bedroom. It would be great for you when you come visit your aunt, Goldie."

"Sure, great."

I unfroze and smiled to myself, picturing Goldie upstairs grinning like the Cheshire Cat. At least he'd bought me some time.

I looked down and thought about what Uncle Walt had said. The old geezers were using Viagra. At least Mr. Wisnowski had a genuine prescription for it from the Hope Valley Clinic's pharmacy.

I wondered if Mr. W's doctor had gone over the side effects and safety precautions of the drug. I knew if he was on any nitrate drugs, often used to control chest pain or angina, he shouldn't have been taking Viagra. It also reduced the blood pressure, which could have suddenly dropped to an unsafe or life-threatening level. Or killed him. Maybe Mr. W wasn't really murdered, but had suffered some effects of taking the Viagra?

How the hell would I find *that* out?

"There you are, Auntie," Goldie called as, I'm sure, a warning before Barbara came down the stairs.

"Oh, dear. I seem to have lost my way," I said, pretty damn proud of my "elderly" voice.

Barbara was fast on Goldie's heels. "So, do you want to see the upstairs, Mrs. Doubtme?"

"I . . . my nephew has better taste than little old me." I brushed my fake forehead. "Stairs. Take the breath out of me sometimes. Did you like it, Goldie?"

"It has potential. We'll think about it." He turned to Barbara while taking my arm. "We'll probably need another look or two before making up our minds."

While we followed Barbara out the door, I marveled at Goldie's foresight in leaving the opportunity open for more snooping if need be.

Barbara let us off in the parking lot of the Century 21 real estate office. We said our goodbyes and promised to call when ready for another tour. She also said she'd be on the lookout for other houses that would meet my needs.

I smiled and thought it would be wonderful if I really was looking for a house—and could afford it. Goldie and Miles were getting closer in their relationship and about ready to move it to the next level. I really thought they belonged together, but I was in the way.

Goldie opened the door of his banana yellow Camaro. Sixties vintage. Looked as if he'd just driven it off the lot. "That was fun, but I'm bushed."

"I really appreciate your help, Gold."

"I know you do, Suga, but you really need to get back on your case. Fucking Fabio has little patience."

"And I need the money. Besides, Mr. Wisnowski was one of my original suspects for prescription insurance fraud. The opportunity was too great to miss to see if my Uncle Walt was correct, too."

"What did you find?"

I sighed. "Nothing really. Guess I should stick to investigating medical insurance fraud and leave the murders up to the professionals."

Goldie stared at me. A thin grin wanted to appear. Classy as he was, he held back.

"Okay. Okay. I don't know shit about investigating anything!"

"But you're a damn fast learner and persistent as all get out. Then there's that balls thing you got goin' on."

"Thanks. I need to get back to work." I turned and paused. Then I looked back at Goldie who stood there watching me. I had no idea what to do next.

"You gotta keep up your charade to get in good with Sophie and find out about her medication claims."

I knew he was right, so I nodded and absentmindedly unlocked my car door and slumped inside.

In my haze, I watched Goldie drive off.

"Seems as good a time as any to have that talk I'd mentioned," Jagger said from my backseat.

Six

It isn't every day that one is startled nearly to death. But when someone pops up in your backseat your time has come.

I don't think that I was able to catch my breath, or had taken a breath since hearing Jagger's voice, but a tiny sound of some kind did pop out of my mouth.

"Sherlock?"

I could feel him leaning over the back of the front seat near me, his heat on my neck. His hand rubbed against my shoulder. "Didn't think I had such a startling affect on you."

Being the levelheaded, organized person that I was, I summoned my faculties and turned slightly. His hand remained in place. Thank goodness my mouth still worked when I noticed he hadn't moved his hand yet. "What the hell? You nearly scared me to death, Jagger."

After a pause, he removed his hand. "Hold it."

With that he opened the back door, got out, and got into the front. "Drive out and head toward Pleasant Street."

For a second I looked at him, then my damn body did as he said. When we turned the corner onto Pleasant, he said, "Pull over. Not near any houses though."

Hmm. I found the most deserted section of the street I shut off the engine. "Okay, why all the secrecy?"

At first he stared at me, and then he said, "I need your help."

My heart wanted to flutter, but I wouldn't let the stupid thing act so, well, stupid. "My help? Again?"

He didn't even nod, but merely stared as if I'd spoken in Greek.

I knew I should shut my mouth. I knew I should ignore him staring at me, and I knew I should start the car and take off—after I'd thrown him out the door.

But, I said, "What kind of . . . help?" It only took a few more seconds of his staring at me to know. *Scrubs. White clogs.* It would definitely involve donning my never-wear-again scrubs! He was going to get me back into my old career. I still had those before-mentioned scorch marks on my butt from burning out of nursing, and he was going to throw me right back in without any fire retardant protection.

Now I knew how a cow felt standing in line at the slaughterhouse.

Jagger wasn't going to hurt me—not physically. But my mental state around him was always in question.

I looked him straight in his eyes. Eyes that had a way of capturing my soul. Well, okay, that was a cliché, but sometimes clichés seemed a way of life with Jagger around. Gorgeous, sexy guy and all. After several blinks, I figured I might have escaped his influence unscathed and said, "No. No. No!"

He did that head thing again. "You *need* me."

True. But I couldn't let him think I was so needy in my new job. Okay, his help had gotten me my last paycheck—

and maybe I'd still be working on that case if Jagger hadn't "bargained" with me. You know, one of those "I'll help you if you help me" kinds of things.

But stubborn Pole that I am, I said, "I'm doing fine on my own."

He looked me up and down. I felt Mrs. Honeysuckle's support nylons constrict around my ankles where earlier they had bagged. Then I felt the blood shoot up my veins back to my heart where it caused my chest to burn. Damn. This man was a public nuisance. A health nuisance. No one should be allowed to follow someone around and pop up in her car to scare her—and then ask a favor.

Or, more truthfully, point out the obvious.

"Stop staring at me like that, Jagger. I have started this new case . . . and . . . and I'm almost done." I had to fight the urge to stick out my tongue, because I knew it wouldn't convince him anymore than the lie I'd just told.

"So, you have Sophie Banko caught red-handed in prescription fraud? Good. Fabio will no doubt give you a bonus for such fast work. And here you only had to dress up in Mrs. Honeysuckle's clothing a few times. Great. Perfect, Sherlock. Atta girl."

My mouth dropped open, despite the flecks of superglue, which should have at least held it semi-closed.

Sophie Banko?

Prescription fraud?

And Mrs. Honeysuckle!

With the tip of my finger, I pushed my jaw up and said in a voice that reminded me either of my childhood or a Chatty Cathy doll, "Okay."

* * *

I stood in the boiling-hot shower to peel off the remainder of superglue only minutes after driving Jagger back to his car and rushing home. I made a mental note to tell Goldie that we needed more Vaseline or this stuff was going to take the outer layer of my skin off.

I shoved my face toward the showerhead and shut my eyes.

Jagger!

My eyes opened, water forced soap in, and I yelped.

But not at the soap. How could Jagger know all that he did? How could he keep up with my life and do any work of his own? And *why* did he keep up with my life?

We didn't keep in touch, since, well, it wasn't as if we were best of friends—more like temporary coworkers.

But now, how could I get out of working with him, when I knew damn well—as he knew I knew—that I needed him *more* than he needed me?

With the soap washed out of my eyes, I shut the water off, grabbed my towel, yanked off my shower cap and stepped out. Miles was at work, and Spanky fast asleep on the floor next to the counter. I dried as fast as I could, wiggled into my powder blue panties and pulled my jeans on over them. After I had my bra and navy sweater on, I pulled my hair into a ponytail and looked in the mirror. Felt good to be dressed in clothes more appropriate for my age.

My skin glistened. I needed blush and lipstick, but was too frustrated and in a hurry to care.

I grabbed my purse, keys and jacket, and after a quick goodbye to sleeping Spanky, I hurried out to my Volvo.

When I opened the door and got inside, I froze.

His scent clung to my leather seats.

I'd have to get one of those horrible peppermint air freshener cardboard tree thingies that you hang on your rearview mirror to get the scent out.

But did I really want to?

Sure I was angry with Jagger over butting into my case, but that scent could work wonders—just like my mother's Renuzit did. As I pulled into the parking lot of the Scarpello and Tonelli Insurance Company, I told myself maybe this job wasn't such a good idea.

But I loved it, so far, and made great money for not having to get up at five and work an eight-hour shift.

With my insides still knotted, I stormed in the front door.

"Hey, *chéri*," Adele called out.

I waved to her and barreled down the hallway. Before I got to the end, I turned toward Fabio's door and pounded my fist against it. "How could you, Fabio? How could you tell Jagger about my case? How do you even *know* Jagger?" I didn't even let him say anything before I pushed open the door in a huff.

Fabio leaned across his desk.

Jagger turned around.

I felt faint.

Then I realized I didn't have on any makeup.

The pain in my feet reminded me that I was still standing in my huff state in the doorway of Fabio's office in a weird position. Fabio, on the other hand, sat staring.

The biggest shit-eating grin I've ever seen formed across Jagger's face.

This was not good.

The first thought that came to mind was to say, "Oops. Wrong office," and then slink away.

But I had every right to be here, I told myself, and I had every right to be annoyed. So, I sucked in the stale cigar air of Fabio's office and stepped forward, leaving the door open.

I wasn't a fool.

This way they'd have to be civil to me, or I'd have witnesses. I stepped closer. "Fancy meeting you here," I said with a passing glance to the still-grinning Jagger.

He nodded.

Fabio stood. "What the hell is going on, Sokol? What's got your panties in a—"

Jagger flew up.

I leaned back.

But his furor was aimed at Fabio. "Is that any way to talk to a lady, Scarpello?"

Wow. Had me blushing.

I'd give him credit for manners.

Fabio's greasy complexion, the darker side of a cheap virgin olive oil, reddened. "What the hell are you storming in here about, newbie?" He gave a sideward glance to Jagger as if asking if that was better.

Jagger ignored him. "Look, Pauline, leave Fabio out of this. There's no use involving him anyway."

That I agreed with. Working with Fabio was like setting up a tent near a nuclear power plant. Any second and there could be a disaster.

For a minute, I paused and thought. Jagger was right. He might have legitimate business here for one of his assignments—in which case I was betting that he worked for an insurance company, not the FBI. Then again, Jagger could have no good reason to be here other than to spy on me.

I shook my brain. Why would Jagger waste his time on that?

"Okay," I said to him, "then *you* tell me what the hell is going on. Why are you here?"

He turned toward Fabio. "Catch you later." With that he took my arm and "guided" me out the door and down the hallway.

When we passed Adele's office, I heard her sigh. Loud.

I felt the same way with his hand on my arm, but forced myself to ignore it and remain pissed. Once outside he aimed us toward his black Suburban. I'd had a few trips in that SUV. A family of four could live in the darn thing, and sometimes I thought Jagger actually did. Anything I needed, he had somewhere in the Suburban, and since no one knew where he actually lived, my mobile-home theory was entirely plausible.

"Get in."

I looked at him and wondered if it was worth wasting my words to ask where we were going. So, I just got in with my mouth shut.

Again, I always felt safe with Jagger—although every logical cell in my body said I probably shouldn't. He could have killed me or done any number of things to my body—some of which I'd welcome—but he never did.

We drove out of the parking lot and headed west.

Dunkin Donuts.

Our "hangout."

At the entrance he pulled up to the drive-thru window, ordered without asking me what I wanted and handed me my hazelnut decaf, light and sweet, followed by a French cruller.

Exactly what I would have ordered.

The January air was unusually mild today. The sun cast rays of gold across the dashboard to land on his now shaven face. Yum.

And that wasn't for the aroma of hazelnut decaf.

He stuck his black coffee into the cup holder and pulled over to the side. This time there wasn't any fear that someone was following us as there had been in the past, but I still felt a shiver of suspense run up my back.

Again, being approximately thirty-three inches away from a hunk of a guy could have caused it.

He shut off the engine and turned to me. "You need to take a job at the Hope Valley Clinic. Miles should be able to get you one."

Soon I'd need a huge elastic band to wear around my head if Jagger kept "surprising" me like this. This time the recovery of my jaw was much quicker. "What? What? What?"

He shook his head. Twice.

Since our first encounter a few months ago, Jagger could have easily suffered several cases of whiplash when we were together. I'd learned that one shake meant perturbed, two more like exasperated. "Look, Sherlock, I'm working a case . . . that is . . . in the same location—"

I waved my hand in the air. "Hold it right there, buddy. I've heard this song before and it led me to . . . You're going to tell me everything will be fine. Ha!"

He sat silent. With Jagger, silence spoke volumes.

"See? You're speechless." A bold-faced lie to be sure, but I gave it a shot. Anything to get him off this subject.

"You'll get done with your case much faster—and get paid faster—if you cooperate," he said quietly, almost hypnotically.

"Cooperate with you?" I took a sip of my now lukewarm coffee. We hadn't been here that long, but I liked so much cream in it, it cooled fast. I figured Jagger didn't have a microwave in his SUV. "Cooperate. Yeah, right."

There went that grin again.

Nonchalantly I crossed my legs, as if that would take the emphasis off his effect on me. Pheromones gone wild. Might make a good reality TV show.

His grin deepened.

I let out a deep sigh. Inside I felt as if something was slipping. Slipping from my grasp. Then the words, "What, as if I don't know, do I have to do?" came out. Damn! I summoned every ounce of assertiveness I could and only came out with, "And how do you know Miles can help me?" As soon as I said that second part, I realized how foolish that was. This was Jagger I was talking to. "Forget the second question."

He smiled. Best teeth I've ever seen and white enough to do commercials.

"Take a temporary job in the clinic. The pharmacy is next door. Staff floats back and forth getting medication for the patients. Easy to check on prescriptions that way."

"Did Fabio tell you about my case?"

His look told me that Fabio, or anyone else for that matter, didn't need to tell him anything.

"I said I have a case of my own there. Leo Pasinski, one of the pharmacists."

Hmm. "I'm guessing you're not going to tell me what it is about, who hired you or how my helping you will get my case solved faster."

He stared at me.

I swallowed and wiped my now sweaty brow.

"Trust me, Sherlock."

* * *

As soon as I'd left Jagger, I called Miles to ask his friend at the Hope Valley Clinic to get me a job there. Miles had friends and connections all over town. That's how I'd gotten hooked up with Fabio. Miles had come through again, I thought the next morning as I yanked my mauve scrub pants up over my white bikini panties. Damn, but it felt good to be dressing appropriately for my age—even if I was in scrubs.

Once dressed, I headed to the kitchen for a quick breakfast, hating getting back into a routine. I loved the freedom of my investigative job and although I was technically still working it, I was also technically back in nursing.

Jagger was going to owe me big time . . . again.

With that X-rated thought on my mind, I managed to make a cup of tea in the microwave and throw a slice of wheat bread into the toaster. If I was going to get to work on time, I had to put Jagger out of my thoughts.

Then again, once I got there, I had no idea what I was going to do to help him—yet. I knew he'd tell me when he was ready.

"And over there is where you hang your coat," Randy Johnson said. She was the nurse who'd been assigned to "orientate" me to this job. I'd been hired to fill in for Maggie Pepperwhite, who was out on maternity leave. Thank goodness I didn't have to deal with the bubble-gum-snapping, blonde bombshell of a receptionist—the one who must have owned stock in Dubble Bubble.

I said a silent prayer that my case would be solved before the Pepperwhite kid was delivered. My feet already hurt and the clinic hadn't even opened yet.

The old cliché of riding a bicycle after not riding for years is true of nursing too. It didn't take long before I was schlepping patients in and out of examining rooms, taking blood pressures and temps along with taking histories and reasons for the patients' visits. I had to keep reminding myself that I was working a case and not become complacent as I fell back on my nursing skills.

Several times I'd tried to snatch the patient charts of ones whom I thought would need prescriptions. Since the clinic was attached to the pharmacy, often the nurses would help out the patients and get their meds for them just as Jagger had said. I'd at least get to meet some pharmacy personnel and maybe even snoop a bit.

But no such luck.

Soon there were only a few minutes left before the clinic closed. Thank goodness the pharmacy stayed open two hours longer. Not sure how I'd manage, I was determined to get over there today and see what I could find out. So far, with no Jagger in sight, I was *not* getting my case solved.

I grabbed the last chart on the rack. A young man with some kind of rash. It would be a welcome relief after all the elderly patients I'd met today. Oh, I did love the elderly, but since becoming Peggy Doubtme, I was having a personality crisis.

Last night I actually tried to take my teeth out to soak in a glass.

An examining room door closing behind me pulled my attention back to my job. I looked at the chart in my hand and walked toward the waiting room. Only two patients remained. One, a heavily pregnant woman, and the other a throwback from the sixties. Although not much older than myself, the guy had hair longer than mine, dark glasses on and a mustache that hung down past each side of his lips. Didn't look bad even if not my type.

Then again, I reminded myself, anyone with my "dance card" shouldn't have a type other than *breathing male*.

I looked at the guy and called, "Mr. Lance Feathermoon."

He didn't look American Indian but could be, with a name like that. Actually, he looked more like Johnny Depp, and that alone was reason to pick him instead of the pregnant lady.

He set down his magazine and came toward me.

My heart skipped—twice.

I mentally pulled out my list of no-nos and added, *No caffeine at lunchtime.* Had to be the cause of my cardiac arrhythmia.

I waved for him to enter Exam Room #3. "Have a seat on the table. So, what brings you here, Mr. Feathermoon?"

He remained seated on the edge of the green enamel table, looked around the room several times, paused, then finally said, "Rash."

Oh, boy. Last patient of the day and I'd picked a doozie. Not only was I certain he wasn't going to be too cooperative, but I had to keep my wits about me since every time he looked at me, I felt his gaze undress me through his Foster Grants.

I had to get a date soon.

Deciding it'd be a waste to add that to my mental list, I smiled at him. "Where?"

"Foot."

"Please remove your shoes then."

"Foot," he repeated and slipped off one well-worn Nike running shoe from his left foot. "Not feet, doll."

Doll? Suddenly the weird attraction to Lance drained out of me. I actually looked down to see if I was standing in some sort of puddle of hormonal insanity. My feet were dry, and when I looked up, so was Lance's left foot. As a matter of fact, I couldn't see a rash at all.

I stared at him a few minutes. Really studied him. I'd been working on honing my investigational tools, and this guy seemed a good study. There was something familiar about him, but I was fairly certain that I'd never met Mr. Feathermoon. It'd been a long day so I ignored the familiarity and proceeded with my job.

Now my head started to pound as it did so often when I was frustrated, overworked or horny. The last obviously not the cause at this moment. I shook myself and wondered how I'd let myself be talked back into this profession. Even if it would help my case, I figured it wasn't worth it to have patients like this. I was losing precious time heading over to the pharmacy.

"I don't see any rash, sir." Maybe I should just chart what he said and leave it up to poor Dr. Handy, who was working my section today. No. I couldn't do that. First of all, he was the oldest physician here, and second, the most experienced. I figured if I wrote "rash" down on the chart when I didn't see one, Doc Handy would have me fired immediately before the end of my shift for wasting his time.

Mr. Feathermoon gave a loud sigh. "You have to look closer."

I looked at the foot again, rolled my eyes, and turned back. "I actually have very good vision, sir. Twenty-fifteen. But even if I wore magnifying glasses, I couldn't see a rash that wasn't there. Perhaps it went away before you came here?" *Please, let him go now.*

He grinned.

My eyebrows rolled up to my forehead. Wait a minute. I

studied him. I looked at his face—closely. I inhaled. The familiarity hit me. Jagger—in his "arrival upon a new case" disguise.

But I bit back my urge to yell his name.

Seven

My observational investigating skills *were* sharpening.

At the moment, my gut instinct was not to let on that I knew he was Jagger. As a nurse, I was always quick to notice signs and symptoms and now the knack had paid off. I looked at him and gathered my thoughts.

What made it most difficult was, "Lance" looked damn tasty.

Hey, if aged Joey the Wooer could float my boat, then why not some spring chicken who appeared years younger and sexy as hell?

Then again, this was Jagger.

"Well, *Lance*. It seems the rash is very faint. Almost can't see it. I'll have to . . . do a check before the doctor comes in."

He looked at me a bit skeptically. I wondered if he was ready to fess up.

Apparently not. So I decided to pull one over on Jagger. At least give it the old college try, since it'd surely be an accomplishment. I turned to the counter and took a wad of cotton from the jar.

"What the hell is that for?" he asked.

Good question, I thought, but said, "Oh. I need to . . . just hold your leg out a minute, sir." I proceeded to run the cotton up and down the bottom of his foot, saying, "I have to check for feeling in the foot. Make sure nothing is affecting the nerves." This was all bull and I hoped Jagger wouldn't pick up on that yet. He knew his investigating, but I was finally able to do something I knew more about than he did. Nursing.

I whisked the cotton around in circles.

He looked as if he'd explode.

Now I come from a family who loves the bottoms of their feet tickled. My siblings and I always used to argue about who would tickle whom, but that was unusual. I knew most people were very sensitive when it came to that area of their feet.

And Jagger proved no exception.

I ran the cotton back and forth. Back and forth.

Slowly.

Then quickly.

He grabbed my hand. "What the hell does that prove?"

I looked at him. "It proves, Mr. Feathermoon, that your feelings are intact. That the *rash* hasn't affected your nerves."

He merely lowered the sunglasses and glared at me.

The door opened behind me and in walked the old doctor.

"Hi, Dr. Handy, this patient is complaining of an itch on his foot." I handed him the chart and stepped back, ready to bolt out the door.

After a few seconds and my escape into the hallway, I heard the doctor's voice. "Why did you write 'rash' then, Nurse? I don't see a rash. Nurse?"

Okay, I thought, I could keep going and pretend that I didn't hear him, or be honest and turn back and lie. I shut my eyes, and then opened them to see one of the other doctors standing right in front of me. "Excuse me," I said and headed back into the room.

"Did you say something, Dr. Handy?"

He was already peering over Jagger's naked (be still, my heart) foot.

"Yes, I asked why you wrote down 'rash,' Nurse—" He leaned over to read my temporary name tag. "—Sokol."

"The patient said he had a rash. But I agree with you, Doctor. I don't see one."

"I . . . had one when I called this morning, Doc. Damn thing is, when I took my sock off for the pretty lady, it wasn't there no more. Does itch though."

I smiled in a "gotcha" sort of way.

Felt damn good too.

The doctor looked at me and then at the chart. Then he examined Jagger's foot and asked more questions. I held my breath, wondering if Jagger would mention the cotton thing. He didn't.

The doctor said, "Not much to look at, but if it itches, I'll give you a prescription for a stronger steroid than one you could get over the counter. Nurse, come to my office, and I'll give it to you." With that he turned and walked out the door.

"You may put your shoes and socks back on," I said and headed to the door. "I'll get your prescription." A prescription! I was going to be able to go to the pharmacy after all.

Then it hit me, Jagger had this all planned out, and it could help both of our cases.

Before I turned to go, I said, "Nice job, *Jagger*."

He actually looked surprised.

Warmed me inside before I ran out.

I wasn't too proud to admit that I needed help in this business. After all, Fabio had assigned me to work with Nick Caruso on my first case. Still, it did make my day that I had "fingered" Jagger. Despite my heart's protest, I decided I'd see if Nick could help again, since Jagger came and went like this on a whim.

Nick had freelanced for Fabio. Been doing it for years. And, as knockout handsome as Nick was, my feelings never reached the boiling point with him. That let me concentrate on work. But the best part was, Jagger thought they had. I smiled to myself and felt a bit wicked. That just might work. Besides, Nick and Jagger had a past.

And not a very amicable one.

"Hi. I'm the temporary nurse over in the clinic, and I need a prescription filled." I looked to see a bench full of people waiting on the other side of the counter. The clinic staff had access to a back door to speed things up for the sick patients. Very helpful, I thought. For my case, that is.

A young woman, most likely in her late teens and dressed very punk in more black than an Italian mourner, looked up from a stack of white prescription bags. "Leo's gonna shit a brick. Hang it!"

I was going to ask "hang what" but figured that was some kind of personal-curse word and with her temper, I kept my mouth shut.

"Leave it over there." She motioned with her head to another stack. "This one's full of prescription orders."

Damn. I couldn't just leave. "I . . . the clinic is closing and the doctor wants this medication filled now."

She rolled her eyes at me and grabbed the paper from my hand. "Yeah, right. I'm sure a steroid cream is a life-saving medication." She blew a pink bubble from between her—were they really black—lips and popped it with her nail. Black polish too.

"Look," I leaned in to read her name, "Hildy, I'm not a doctor, so I don't presume to think what they do is right or—"

Her eyebrows rose in what I'd clearly term "annoyance." I didn't want to piss off Hildy. She could be helpful. Then again, someone with so much black on and red painted hair teased out as if frightened by the proverbial bogeyman might not be much help. Still, with friends like Goldie, Miles and Adele, I wasn't choosy. You really couldn't judge a book by a cover where any of them were concerned. They were all the best, despite appearances. So, I changed my tune and said, "You must be so overworked. Can I get you a drink?"

She looked at the crowd waiting. "Yeah, tequila. Worm in."

After a moment of shock, I chuckled. "How about a soda? Cola?"

"Don't do caffeine. Anything clear."

"Fine." I turned to go and stopped. "My name is Pauline. Pauline Sokol."

From behind she mumbled, "Hildy Jones. I'll try to have your prescription filled as soon as Leo gets the chance. But, I can't promise 'The Shit' will cooperate."

I smiled to myself.

When I got over to the clinic side and went into the waiting room where the soda machine sat, I looked around. No Jagger. Where the heck had he gone? Then I reminded myself it really didn't matter. He'd pop up when least expected. Thank goodness it was usually when my life was being threatened. I hurriedly grabbed a dollar bill from my pocket, got a ginger ale and went back. If I had to wait at the pharmacy, I could maybe do some snooping. Good thing no more patients were around.

Of course the pharmacy was packed, so I'd have to be careful—and crafty, I thought, on the way back to Hildy.

After I'd handed the can of soda to Hildy, I sat opposite her desk and decided how to do "crafty," wishing my buddy Goldie were there. Amazingly enough, Goldie, even dressed like the Fourth of July fireworks, could do sneaky and inconspicuous very well.

Hildy got up. "I'll go check on Leo. He's freaking out with so much work to do. Bastard. Hang it!"

Hmm. No love lost between Hildy and Leo. This was good. I smelled a possible mole. Dear Hildy who might just serve unwittingly in that role, looked as if she might need a friend—and Pauline Sokol was nothing if not friendly.

I watched her go, wondering how and why she'd chosen to wear such gigantic platform shoes with her long skirt. I mean, someone could fall off those things and get hurt. As I was pondering Hildy's clothing, I couldn't believe my luck. Something caught my eye at the pharmacy counter.

Well, not something, but *someone*.

Someone you'd have to be legally blind to miss. One Sophie Banko, standing there, big as, well, to be charitable, I'd go with the cliché big as *day*, knowing *house* would be more appropriate. But, I'd decided, in my new line of work I needed all the help from above that I could get, and insulting someone, even just in my thoughts, surely couldn't do me any good.

I leaned forward to try and hear what Sophie was saying to the pharmacist. It wasn't Leo, I assumed, but someone else. An older gentleman with graying hair, stocky build and wire-rimmed glasses perched on his nose. Then I saw

Sophie give a wave to another man who I guessed was Leo. Back in my floor-nursing days, I'd been known as "psychic Sokol" because I could almost predict when a patient's condition was going to go into the toilet. Not literally. But more like when they were going to have some complications.

Gut feeling.

And I had that right now as Sophie waved again.

Hmm.

When Hildy got back and sat down, I looked at her and was about to ask a question about Sophie. A nonchalant question so as not to arouse any suspicion. Then she yawned and I got a load of her tongue. Biggest tongue ring I've ever seen. Had to be the size of a sourball. A big silver sourball, which jiggled a bit when she yawned. I couldn't stop myself from staring, and noticed Hildy had more artificial holes in her body than a piece of Swiss cheese. Ears—about ten earrings between the two—nose—both sides—and two on each eyebrow. When I looked down toward her chin, she said, "Yep, bellybutton and nipple rings."

I gasped. "Ouch."

"You have to suffer to be beautiful."

I sensed little Hildy was trying to cover up a lack of self-esteem by trying to show the world she didn't care. But I doubted that when I looked into her green eyes. There was a sadness there, and, my old nursing skills had me wanting to help the poor kid. Besides, I could be helping Jagger and myself too.

"Suffer to be beautiful. Who's the moron who came up with that one?" I laughed.

She hesitated and then joined me. From behind, a ghost of a man appeared. Again I gasped.

Hildy turned. "Shit. What?"

"This isn't a social, Jones. Get these passed out." He threw a handful of white-bagged prescriptions onto her desk.

I didn't know what to say as I watched his beady eyes give me the once-over, then he turned to reveal a "monk-style" balding head. He'd spoken with a lisp, and I believe I'd noted a pocket protector in his white shirt. A nerd with attitude.

"Who was that?"

Hildy curled her lip. I thought the silver sourball had to hurt in that position. When she uncurled, she said, "Leo 'The Shit' Pasinski." She grabbed the bags. "Gotta go."

"Let me help you." I stood.

She looked at me oddly. "No one's ever offered to help me."

A bit saddened, I touched her arm. "I'm off duty now and free. Let me help."

"What about the patient that needs the prescription?"

Caught up on observing Hildy and Leo, I'd forgotten about "Lance." "Well, I guess he'll come get it himself. You're right. It isn't a life-saving medication. Maybe he skipped out without it."

Fat chance, I told myself. But I also told myself that Jagger would come get it on his own terms.

I called patients' names while Hildy worked the cash register and insurance info. *That* I was interested in. I gazed down at one clipboard Medicaid patients had to sign when they got their medicine. Another was for all other insurances. The second list was minute compared with the Medicaid one, although I'd noted a lot of seniors had supplemental insurance since they didn't qualify for Medicaid. So, Leo dealt with the elderly more. No great surprise though, since this entire conglomerate catered to the elderly. Who else used doctors and medicine more?

A line had formed with everyone waiting for his or her name to be called. I'd found out from Hildy that the pharmacy stayed open a few hours after the clinic closed. When that tidbit had come out, I excused myself and ran back to get my purse and jacket before the doors to the clinic section were locked.

Now, with no date to hurry home to, I planted myself in the pharmacy to "help" Hildy. Another pharmacist came for her shift, which made more work for Hildy. I hadn't seen that pharmacist before. She had dark hair and seemed to keep to herself.

Jagger never showed, so his medication was put in the bins. I actually noticed there were a lot of bags left in there. Nothing unusual about that. Lots of times doctors called in medications or patients left the prescription and came back later. I knew that much without asking.

Hildy reached into the bin after a patient came to the counter. She rifled through the bags and then cursed.

"Something wrong?" I came closer.

She stuck her finger into her mouth. "Thupid shit. He always screws up with the thapler."

At first I could only stare. Then the words sunk in as my mind translated Hildy's finger-in-the-mouth-talk. "Oh, here. What are you looking for?"

With her finger still in place and sucking, she said, "Fwed Fwanklin."

Fred Franklin. "Let me." I gingerly reached into the bin marked E–F. I lifted a few bags. Hm. Several felt too light. I scowled and turned to look at Hildy. Caught up in her injury, she wasn't looking. So, I looked down to read the bag I held in my hand. Erythromycin. A prescription should feel a bit heavier. I examined the bag and did feel the round plastic bottle. Then, taking one more look at Hildy, I shook it. Nothing. Sounded empty. The pharmacist who had "filled" it was Leo.

Hmm, again.

"I don't have all day, ladies." This from a tiny wrinkled man waiting at the counter.

I wondered where he'd be going in such a hurry, but kept my mouth shut and found Fred Franklin on a white bag. I turned and handed it to him. "Any questions for the pharmacist?" I'd heard Hildy say that several times.

"Yeah. Why the hell am I so constipated?"

"It could be the medication, but you should ask your doctor about taking a daily stool softener."

With that he nodded and took out his supplemental insurance card. Hildy finally took her finger out of her mouth and rang up the charge.

A few hours later, complete exhaustion had set in, and I'd noticed Hildy had another body part pierced, I sank down into a chair. "I'm beat."

She finished writing something on the clipboard and looked at me rather strangely. "I'm not sure why you stayed here, Pauline, but . . . thanks. Lots of nights I'm here way past closing. Leo leaves me in the lurch, the shit. But thanks to you, I can take off now."

Take off now?

I'd helped, but hadn't learned anything to help my case. Leo was gone, too. Damn. If I could get Hildy to stick around a bit longer, maybe I could find something out. "I know what you mean. I'm starving."

She looked at me. Maybe someone with all that metal piercing her body had a lack of appetite. The sourball thing alone would knock the hell out of mine.

"Yeah. I could eat too."

Bingo. "Hey, let me take you to . . ." Where? Where could I take Hildy that no one would notice us? Me in my scrubs, Hildy in her pseudo-vampire attire.

At first I thought my mother's eyes were going to jump out of their sockets so she could stare at poor Hildy a bit longer. But, true to the core, mother kept her eyeballs in place and said, "How many of those . . . jewelry things do you have, dearie?" She pointed to Hildy's ears.

Obviously Hildy didn't embarrass easily, although I was still convinced her self-esteem was low. Too obvious in trying to be different for her own good.

She smiled, more politely than humorously, and answered my mother. "Lost count after the second nipple ring."

My mother grew pale. I gasped again, and my father came into the room, looking at all of us strangely. No wonder. We must have appeared an odd threesome. After introductions, my mother insisted on feeding us. It was way past six, so naturally, the kitchen had been cleaned for the night. But she pulled out Monday's left-over meatloaf and made two dishes of food.

Hildy ate as if she were truly starving and had no silver sourball in the way. She even took seconds, while I passed on the offer. The poor kid probably didn't earn much at the pharmacy. I'd gotten her talking during dinner to find out that she was an only child, had run away a while ago at seventeen, and rarely talked to her mother, whom she seemed to hold a grudge against. She briefly mentioned a grandfather, but I think I noticed a tear forming in her eye right when she stopped. Leo had hired her last year. No relatives in Hope Valley, and she had run here from Natick, Massachusetts, because the name sounded as if she might have a better life here.

I had to help out this kid.

Yeah, Pauline, I thought, *along with doing your job and helping Jagger*. Hmm, suddenly I wondered where he'd gone off to.

Trying to shift the focus back to Hildy and my case, I offered to get her a ginger ale. When she agreed and I got up, I started with small talk about whether she liked working at the pharmacy.

"Pays some of my bills." She cleaned the rest of the meatloaf off the plate.

In the background, I could see my mother fixing a "doggy bag," the likes of which could feed a litter of wolfhounds, for Hildy, and I smiled to myself.

"That sure is a busy pharmacy. How many work there?"

At first she looked at me like why the hell did I care, then she shrugged. "Me, three pharmacists, one pharmacy tech, and six assistants. I don't help fill stuff, I only do the front counter and paperwork."

No great surprise there, I thought, looking at her. Then I hoped Hildy wasn't involved in any "wrongdoings." But, if her pay only covered some of her bills, damn.

I handed her the drink and sat back in my chair. "Oh, Hild, I forgot to tell you. When I was helping out with that Mr. Franklin, I picked up a bag that felt, well, empty."

I paused and observed.

At first she looked—maybe—suspicious. It was hard to tell, since strands of ruby and black hair fell over her eyes. I never could understand how anyone could stand their hair in their face.

I leaned a bit closer. Hildy pushed the hair back a second. Her eyes looked more pissed than suspicious now.

"The Shit again." She polished off the ginger ale.

Maybe Mom had used a bit too much salt this Monday in the meatloaf. "Excuse me?"

"Why? What did you do?"

"Er. Nothing. I meant, I don't understand what you said about The Shit."

"Leo." She got up and took her dishes to the sink and set them down gently.

Good for you, I thought. There had to be good in a teenager who cleaned up after herself. "Leo?"

She stood by the counter. "I wish I had a buck for every time The Shit filled a prescription but forgot to put the freaking medicine in the bottle."

Why would a pharmacist keep making mistakes like that?

"Wow. How on earth does he manage that? I'd think it would be second nature to stick the pills in the little orange bottles."

She shrugged again. "No telling what he has on his mind."

"Do the other pharmacists make that same mistake?"

Now she glared at me. "You sure are curious about the pharmacy and stuff. Answer is no. Sometimes the female tech misspells a person's name, but no one but The Shit forgets to put pills in the bottles."

I wanted to ask what happened when she returned them to Leo but gut instinct told me I had to stop. Hildy was fed and looking very tired. Plus she was looking suspicious—at me.

Or at least thinking I was some nutcase.

I dropped the questioning and decided to build on our "friendship" before interrogating her again.

After Mom gave the doggy bag to a grateful Hildy, we headed out and left with pleasant goodbyes. I'd told her I would see her at work when I had to get a prescription filled, and she told me she'd put mine on the top of the pile unless Leo noticed.

What I saw was a certain fear in Hildy's camouflaged eyes when I mentioned his name. Somehow she'd manage to give me a look that was nonreadable. But why?

Interesting. Had to follow up on that one.

With my stomach full and realizing I had not only worked a nursing shift but part of one at the pharmacy too, I was beat. I headed home, hurried into my condo and after a quick hug to Spanky, ran up to the shower.

Miles had left me a note on my bedroom door saying he was spending the night taking care of Goldie. I felt horrible that I hadn't checked up on Goldie all day, so while I yanked off my scrubs, I gave him a quick call.

"So, Suga, how'd it go?"

I filled him in on Hildy, leaving out Lance/Jagger. Goldie thought it was a good idea to pursue the empty prescription bottles and my friendship with Hildy. He said maybe I could then find out more about Sophie. Geez, I thought, as I hung up the phone and stepped out of my white silky panties, I'd forgotten about Sophie. Besides her waving to Leo, I had nothing.

I shoved the shower door open and stepped into the steamy water. Felt wonderful. I shut my eyes and let all my problems wash down the drain. But, when home alone, relaxation had never been the same since I was once nearly killed. I opened my eyes, half expecting to see good old Norman Bates from *Psycho* standing outside the glass shower door with a knife. Instead there was only Spanky, sleeping on the mauve carpet next to the sunken tub.

Yes, Miles had a professional decorator's taste.

I decided I needed a bit more hot water to relax, but this time I'd keep my eyes open.

Ring. Ring.

Damn it.

I shoved the door to the side and reached the portable phone I'd earlier set on the brass-and-leather makeup chair, which Miles got more use out of than myself, and pressed the ANSWER button. "Hello."

"So, what did you find out from Hildy Jones?"

Eight

There was something very mindblowing about standing naked and hearing Jagger's voice on the phone.

Of course *mindblowing* wouldn't be the term I'd use if I'd heard his voice in person while standing here naked.

Suddenly, I grabbed a towel. Foolish, yes, but it felt better to be wrapped in terrycloth while Jagger was on the other end of the line. Thank goodness technology didn't have television-screened phones in every condo yet.

"You there, Sherlock?"

Oops. Wrapped in terrycloth and my fantasies, I'd almost forgotten he was on the line. Well, okay, truthfully I'd almost forgotten the question. Then it dawned. "How the hell do you know about Hildy?"

Long pause.

"Okay." Forget that. I sat on the leather makeup chair. Yikes. Cool to the touch after a nice, hot shower. "She needs a friend and might be a good helper." Then I told him about the empty prescription bottle.

"I'll pick you up in five."

With that he hung up. I looked at my mauve terry-cloth-covered body and wondered how I'd manage to get dressed in "five" let alone put on makeup, look sexy, appealing and damn good. I also wondered where he was that he could get here in "five."

Once dressed, I opened the door on the third ring. Surely opening after the first ring was a no-no. Made one seem too anxious to see the person.

Jagger stood under the golden lighting on the front stoop with the moon's glow behind, streams of his warm breath floating in the cold night air, and wearing his black jacket and jeans.

Thank goodness I hadn't washed my hair, since it'd still be damp. Not that it needed it. But washing was one way of getting out the "wrinkles" of wearing my hair up in my "nurse's" French twist. Instead I'd used the hairdryer to tug out the crinkles. I'd put on jeans and my Steelers jacket too. Underneath I'd picked a black sweater since it made my hair look a brighter shade of blonde, and my skin, which needed all the help it could get where color was concerned, never looked quite as pale in black. Odd but true. Don't get me started on beige.

As usual Jagger had very little—no, nothing—to say until we got in the car, headed to Dunkin Donuts, ordered, got my hazelnut decaf, his black coffee and my one donut, and pulled into "our" spot, the farthest one away from the streetlights.

"Our" spot. Sigh.

Then he took a long sip of his coffee and turned to me. "She's been busted for drugs. Nothing big time, though. Weed. Using. Not selling. She comes from Massachusetts—"

"Natick. Yes, I know. But I didn't know about the drugs. Oh, my God." Suddenly I felt even sadder for Hildy.

Jagger shook his head once. "In this day and age, the cops don't much mess with small-time users, Sherlock. If you poll any local high school, statistically speaking, about sixty-five percent of the kids would admit to occasional weed use. At least sixty-five percent. No big deal."

"*I* think it is—"

He waved away my words. "No kidding. Everyone's entitled to their own morality. Back to Hildy Jones. She could be of help. I don't want you lecturing her and turning her off."

"I wouldn't!" I would have if I'd known about the drugs. As a nurse, I couldn't see why anyone would need a chemical to make them feel good unless they were in pain. I took a chunk of the donut, which I really didn't need at this time of the night, and swallowed. Hildy should eat donuts instead of doing drugs. After washing the donut down with my tepid hazelnut, I said, "Do you smoke? Weed?"

Where'd that come from!

And, did it really matter?

"Pauline, I grew up in the early seventies."

I did too, but decided not to admit it. Foolishly thinking I didn't want Jagger to know my age—when he more than likely knew my bra size. He had to be closer than me to forty. "Okay, weed is a moot point. What about the empty bottles?"

Jagger took another long sip of coffee. I wondered if he thought better when he did that. "Find out how often it happens and what they do with them."

"Oh, yeah, okay." What the hell?

Before I knew it, I was standing on the curb of the parking lot in front of my condo. Jagger said good night through the open car window and started to pull away. Then he stopped, backed up. "Sophie Banko was Mr. Wisnowski's sister-in-law. She had been married to his late brother. Then she married some guy named Banko."

He drove off before the entire neighborhood could hear my "What?"

Damn him.

How could he drop a bomb like that one and just drive off? I could still see the taillights of his Suburban as he waited to pull out of the driveway, so I shouted, "I'm going to have to have help with my case. From Nick. Nick Caruso!"

Now the entire neighborhood could hear the squealing of the Suburban's tires as it sped out.

I smiled.

Some women would say Nick Caruso was every bit as handsome as Goldie was gorgeous. Except that Goldie's hair, for the past month, had been blonde, while Nick's was gray. Prematurely gray. A bit streaked with brown. Not unlike Richard Gere's, and looking just as good. Couldn't have been past forty. Damn sexy too. I heard his deep, mellow voice when he entered Fabio's office the next morning.

"Hey, Pauline." He came near, bent and kissed me on the cheek. "Hear you been asking for me."

Okay, I wasn't dead. My insides shimmered. But he was not Jagger.

I stood and turned toward him. "Thanks for agreeing to help."

Fabio cleared his throat. I'd noticed that since Jagger had "straightened him out" about my being a lady he'd been a bit nicer. Of course, where Fabio was concerned, if he didn't openly curse at you, that was considered "a bit nicer."

Nick took me by the arm and led me to the door. "I've got a few free days until my case winds down. Let's go talk."

"Not at Dunkin Donuts." Geez. We'd gone there before, but since Jagger and I had been there lately, it seemed like "our spot." How dumb that must have sounded to Nick. Obviously by the way his eyebrows rose when he glared at me, pretty dumb.

"Okay, fine. Whatever."

"Goldie said I could use his office until he's back to work or until I get my own." I gave a weak smile. "Okay, I know that's stretching it."

Nick smiled. "Someday."

Once in Goldie's office I filled Nick in on my case, leaving out Lance/Jagger but telling him that Jagger was working a case in the pharmacy. I wondered if Nick knew as much as Jagger, but doubted it. No one could.

Nick ran his nicely manicured finger across his chin. "How the hell is he?"

"Jagger? No change."

Nick chuckled.

That said a lot. Jagger was indeed an enigma. All I'd been able to learn about the two is that they'd served in the Gulf War together and things didn't turn out right. Whatever had happened, they weren't best friends any longer.

They had flown sorties in February of 1991. An air bombardment. Four hundred killed in an air-raid shelter in Baghdad. Nick took a desk job in intelligence after that.

Jagger separated from the military and became a PI out in California. They both had left what they must have loved because of the accidental loss of civilian lives. War casualties, but no less harder to take.

I could only stare. Wow. But I still never knew why the rivalry existed.

My shallow side said thank goodness it wasn't over a woman.

Nick was gorgeous, I told myself, as he sat there telling me what new equipment I needed to buy. I should be nervous as a virgin on a first date, sitting in this room with him, but there was no spark.

With Jagger, there was detonation.

"Get a digital camera," Nick said. "You can take hundreds of pictures and edit out what you don't need. Saves a bundle."

"Do they come small enough to hide?"

Nick smiled. Damn.

"Yes, they come small. Let's check online."

As he booted up Goldie's computer, I sat and waited.

"How's Goldie feeling?"

"Oh, better. Miles is taking good care of him. He's still not ready for work. That's why I'd asked Fabio if I could get some assistance from you. I'm not sure what to do next." It was hard getting that last bit out. I hated not knowing what to do in my job. Yet, it was a trial-and-error sort of position. In nursing, I'd been trained and so well experienced that this "not knowing" business didn't sit well. Yet, I was determined to learn and do a good job.

No—a great job.

Nick had found several digital cameras I could afford that would be perfect for the job. I ordered one that was camouflaged as a pair of reading glasses. Of course I was too young to need them, so they had no prescription lenses. The cost wasn't as steep as I'd expected. It was amazing what one could buy online to spy on others.

Nick turned off Goldie's computer and swung around toward me. "Okay, now you need to go find your suspect."

I looked at my watch. "Yikes. Now I need to go to work."

"That's what I said."

I waved my hands. "No. I mean at the clinic. The temporary job."

"Good. You can sneak in some time to go through the files. See if Sophie Banko does in fact have several illnesses that would warrant so much medication." He stood and headed toward the door.

Right behind, I said, "Good thinking."

When I got into my Volvo and Nick climbed in the other side, I had to fiddle around to find my keys. Apparently around good-looking men, my fingers turned to Jell-O.

Before I cranked the engine I looked at him. "If you ride with me, you'll be stuck at the clinic all day. I really don't have a long-enough lunch break to drive you back here. Sorry."

He grinned. "You're stuck with me for the day, Pauline."

"Well. Alrighty then." I turned the key, backed out and headed to the clinic. Nick and I made small talk until I pulled into the parking lot. The clinic didn't open for ten more minutes, yet several elderly people sat on benches outside.

Thank goodness it wasn't snowing today. The winter's nip did hang in the air, and I hoped none of them caught pneumonia sitting there. When we got out, Nick followed me to the door. Before I could sneak inside, Joey the Wooer popped up from the bench.

"Bellisima. I hope you are not-a ill."

With my snuggly Steelers parka covering my scrubs, he must have thought I was a patient here.

He bowed.

Man. I was born in the wrong generation. "Hi, Joey. And no, I'm working here temporarily." I looked around. "Have you seen Sophie today?"

He gave me an odd look. Why not? What the hell was I thinking, asking about my suspect?

"Not yet. Is she-a due here?"

I shrugged. "Have no idea. Well, hope you feel better." I started to go inside.

Nick was right on my heels.

Joey stepped closer. He nearly put an arm out to stop Nick. "The clinic is-a not open yet." He looked at me. "Is-a he following you?"

"I . . . no, Joey. He's fine." I couldn't think of a lie. That was one thing I was not good at, having been raised with a Catholic-school-induced conscience. Even in my new line of work, I had a hard time coming up with lies. So, I practiced avoiding explanations.

Nick hesitated. He looked about ready to clock poor Joey. Then he stuck his hands into the pockets of his jacket. "Excuse me, sir."

Nice one. At least Nick had the courtesy not to beat up an old man. Despite Joey looking pretty good, I'd figured he was only a few years younger than Uncle Walt, putting him in his late seventies.

Once inside, I realized that I had no explanation for why Nick had come to work with me. We walked down the hallway where I hesitated in front of the door. "Nick, what the heck am I going to say about you?"

He grinned his Nick grin. When a guy who looked like Nick even noticed you were alive, it made you feel good.

He leaned toward me. "Say I'm your boyfriend."

"O . . . kay." I stuck my hand on the doorknob then yanked it off. "Boyfriend? Boyfriend!" Now I stuck my hands into my jacket pockets before I clocked Nick, by accident. Flailing arms were not an attractive sight, I decided. "I'm not going . . . How can I say you are my . . . Why would I bring you to work?"

He stared at me. "Catholic, right?"

I curled my lip. "Even Catholic nursing school. All girls."

"You need to work on telling a few 'fibs' that are necessary to the job, Pauline." He leaned over, and opened the door. "I came all the way from California to surprise you."

"You did? Oh, I get it. That's the fib. Good one." With that we went inside, and I lied my pants off to all the staff, waiting for lightning to strike at any second. I was pleased with myself when I'd said Nick had nowhere to go to wait for me and had to hang around.

Halfway through the morning I realized that my little white lies were getting better.

With the day half over, I was exhausted and kept telling myself I had done the right thing in leaving nursing. I did manage to get over to the pharmacy three times, but couldn't find out anything. It was nice to say hi to Hildy, who was wearing a new nose ring. I was actually quite proud of myself for noticing.

Liar I wasn't. But observant I was.

Except, of course, when it came to recognizing Jagger in

disguise. I won't even go into the story about the poor patient who I thought was Jagger—and yanked at his beard, which turned out to be real. I was more on the lookout now and, as I said, learning. A feeling of pride surged through me, managing to knock the tiredness out of me. At the end of the morning, I said goodbye to the other staff and went to find Nick, who'd spent most of the time in the waiting room.

I hoped he hadn't caught something from all the sick patients.

"Sorry you had to wait here all morning."

Nick stood and smiled.

Hmm.

Nice.

"It's my job, Pauline. I've been doing work out here, just as I'd be doing in my office."

"Oh. I feel better now."

He smiled again.

"Well, let's go," I managed after that smile.

"Find anything out?"

I looked around. Mary, one of the nurses, was standing by the door ready to lock it. I leaned toward Nick. "Didn't get the chance to look at the files."

He looked at Mary and said to me, "Silly, you have to have your car keys to drive." Then he leaned over and kissed my cheek!

"I . . . My keys are—"

When his kiss moved to my lips, a shimmering inside me sped up like a tiny tsunami. Yikes!

He didn't prolong it, but pulled back and said, "We'll have to go back and look for your keys, hon."

Hon? I had to mentally shake my head and tell myself that I was a professional—even if not very experienced.

"Yeah, Mary. Wait. I need to go find my purse."

"Keys," Nick said, taking me by the arm and pushing me through the door. He gave Mary one of his "Nick" smiles.

I figured Mary's insides were still shimmering when Nick and I got inside the door and shut it so she wouldn't notice my odd behavior. "Phew."

"No problem, Pauline. You need to try and remember you're working a case. I'm thinking you get so hung up on your nursing, which is totally understandable, that you forget you're in a new profession."

I sighed. "That's absolutely true. How can I help that?"

"You probably can't. Even though you're working as a nurse under cover, you still have real lives to deal with." He brushed a kiss across my cheek. "You're doing it right."

The kiss? I touched my cheek and stood like a jerk for a few seconds. Then I managed to snap my mind back into working gear. "Thanks. Come on. The file cabinet is behind the reception desk."

He followed me slowly, making sure no one was left in the office. I knew there was an outside answering service that took calls during the lunch break, so no one needed to hang around. Sure enough, not a soul was in sight.

At the file cabinets, we pulled out the "B" section and thumbed through.

"There. Banko," Nick said, pointing to a huge file.

Before I pulled it out, I felt my heart plummet. "Shit. She looks as if she really might be sickly. That's a damn big file."

"You never know." He took it out before I could and motioned toward the desk. "Don't move anything."

I readied to ask if he thought I was stupid, but figured if

he hadn't said that, I would have cleared a section of the desk to put down Sophie's chart. We sat at the same time and opened the file.

Nick looked at me. "Good thing medicine is your expertise. I'd have no clue about any of this."

Pleased, I smiled and leaned in farther to look at Sophie's chart. After several minutes, a "hmm" snuck out followed by a "damn."

"What's 'hm' and 'damn' mean?"

"Well, interestingly enough, Sophie *has* had some medical problems through the years. The most recent visit was only for her hypertension. Which, by the way, seems to be very much under control. But she has had plenty of problems. Diabetes. Congestive heart disease. Two warts frozen off her fingers last year . . ."

I looked at Nick.

"Bingo," he said.

"Well, not exactly. I mean she does take medication for those health problems, but mostly maintenance doses. Even with a chart this thick, she doesn't warrant all the prescriptions she files."

He took my hand and said, "Good job."

The warmth spreading up my arm had to come from being congratulated on a job well done as an investigator. On the other hand, when a guy looked like Nick, the warmth was a no-brainer.

"We need to get the hell out of here," he said.

"Oh. Yeah." I took the chart, tried to set it back so no one would notice that it was ever moved and we hurried out, locking the door behind us. I looked at my watch. "Shit. Only thirty minutes left to get something to eat."

"That's why they call it fast food."

I laughed as we headed out the door to my car. The parking lot was nearly empty now with the clinic closed, and the pharmacy was probably madly filling all the prescriptions ordered this morning. We went to the closest fast-food restaurant I could find. When we pulled into the lot and got out, Nick looked around.

"Do you think someone followed us?" I wondered.

"Not sure. Guess I'm always on the lookout."

Which is something I should be, too. I turned to give the lot a once-over. "Hey, wasn't that black Toyota at the clinic?"

Nick turned to where I was pointing. "Could be, but there are hundreds of cars like that. You have to start noticing license plates. Make it a habit."

I thanked him for the advice as we went inside to the counter. Nick had two Big Macs and chuckled when I ordered a Happy Meal—Chicken McNuggets—for myself.

"Hey," I protested, "I'm not too hungry." Actually, I was watching my diet, hence the children's portion, but didn't want to share that info with him.

When we sat down, we talked a bit more about the case, deciding we needed more information on Sophie. The chart wasn't really good enough to help convict her of prescription insurance fraud. I'd shared with him my "Peggy Doubtme" persona. He loved it and thought I needed to go to Bingo tonight and get chummier with Sophie. Already feeling exhausted, I groaned.

Nick chuckled and pulled me close. His breath brushed across my cheek. Wow.

I didn't have to look in any mirror to know my face was redder than Ronald McDonald's hair.

I should pull away, but suddenly I had a vision of my mother, staring at me. I know, on the tip of her tongue, were the words, "You are not getting any younger, Pauline. He is a nice man. And handsome. What are you waiting for?"

"Pauline?"

"Hmm?" My motherly vision disappeared. "Sorry. Did you say something?"

He smiled. "I asked if you wanted to go out for coffee after Bingo tonight."

My eyes widened. Nick was asking me out. All I could think as I turned to look at him was that my "imaginary" mother must have done something to make him ask me out. I stared straight ahead to see if she'd appear again.

And, in my peripheral vision, I saw *Jagger*.

Nine

I slowly pulled away from Nick, with Jagger a haze in the background.

Nick stared at me. "Pauline, you all right? You look as if you've seen a—"

"Ghost?" Jagger said.

Nick spun around. "Christ. A ghost would be a welcome sight."

I sat motionless. Silent. Scared.

What the hell should I do? Where was my figment of a mother when I needed her? Or at least needed her advice.

Jagger sat himself down, right next to me. I felt like the water boy between two fullbacks.

Jagger started to say something, but Nick waved his hand. "Hold on. Pauline was just about to answer my question."

My mouth was as dry as the Sahara.

Nick continued, with a rather unflattering shit-eating grin: "My question of going out tonight for coffee. With me."

Unfortunately he looked directly at Jagger and not me.

If I had a magnifying glass, I might have been better able

to tell if Jagger had even flinched—a minuscule amount. I squinted to see better. Naw. I'd need more than reading glasses to see a reaction from him. More like a magnifying glass or one of those telescopes used to see outer space.

I'd give him this; the guy had disguises, brains and *control* down pat.

He sat there like some gorgeous manly mannequin. Damn, but I wished he'd have shown a bit of jealousy.

What the hell was I thinking? It wasn't as if Jagger and I were an item. Ha! Jealous indeed. With his reaction of steel, he obviously didn't have one iota of interest in me.

I wished I didn't care.

I had to snap out of this infatuation and concentrate on work, and the fact that I should have a life outside of investigating. So, I turned to Nick and said, "I'd love to go for coffee."

My head spun around toward Jagger like the little girl's in *The Exorcist*. Damn. Still nothing.

Nick smiled. "Great. I'll pick you up at your place around ten."

Ten? I was usually in bed by ten. Thinking how pathetic that was, I decided to graciously agree and not mention my bedtime in front of these two.

Interesting two.

I wondered if, over coffee tonight, I might get more info from Nick about their past. Then I told myself to be honest and admit the only reason I wanted that info was because of my Jagger infatuation.

I'd keep my mouth shut.

Nick scooted closer to me.

I fought the urge to move closer to Jagger. He looked at us, but again, nothing.

"So, what brings you here, Jagger?" Nick asked.

My intuition told me Nick was going to drape his arm around my shoulder at any minute.

Bingo.

Not bad. It felt damn good to have a man's arms around me. Especially some gorgeous guy like Nick Caruso. I stayed put and looked at Jagger. "Aren't you going to eat something?"

He looked at my food. "What's the toy this week?"

For a second he'd lost me. Then I felt my face flush and said, "Some little horse from a Disney movie. I er . . . get the Happy Meal so I can give the toys to my nieces and nephews."

He wasn't buying that but remained silent for a few seconds. "Find out anything today?"

Work. Investigating. I'd nearly forgotten all about it, just as most of the women who entered the restaurant and noticed Jagger and Nick must have forgotten why they were there. I've never seen so many females staring at once.

Wow. Pauline Sokol, the envy of Hope Valley.

Amid bites of my nuggets, I filled Jagger in on Sophie Banko's chart and her ailments.

"Not enough to go on," he said as if Nick and I hadn't already come to that conclusion.

Miffed, I felt Nick's muscles tighten and figured he felt the same as I did.

"You need to get closer to her. Go to Bingo tonight."

Like a boa constrictor, Nick's arm tightened around me, causing a little sound to come out of my mouth. Sounded like some squeaky kid's toy. Nick released, apologized to me and then looked at Jagger. "We already have it taken care of."

Jagger looked at a loss for words, but I knew, just knew, that couldn't be possible. Not Jagger.

"I already have that little horse," he said.

Before I knew it, he was up and out the door faster than the breeze that blew in from the cold.

On the way back to the office, Nick and I were silent despite the gnawing feeling in my brain to question him about Jagger.

Back to work, I thought. Back to reality. Back to hooking up with Sophie.

It dawned on me that since I'd be wearing my Peggy Doubtme clothes tonight, I'd have to give Goldie a call. When we entered the office, Nick stopped at the door.

"I have something to take care of. I'll be around, though. Try to get over to the pharmacy if you can. At least make contact with Hildy. I'll be on the lookout for Sophie."

I'd almost forgotten about Hildy, but I had told Nick about her this morning so as not to leave any part of the case out. "Will do. See you later."

"If not, see you tonight at your place." He leaned near.

He's going to kiss me!

And he did. Soft, gentle on my lips. Wow. I touched my upper lip after he turned and walked out. One lady patient asked, "Did you bump your lip, honey?" Three others came through the door and looked at me oddly.

"Hmm? Oh. No. I . . . no bump." Bumbling idiot. I smiled and hurried into the nurses' station, where I looked to see I had four minutes left before I had to call in the first patient. So, I dialed Goldie's number. "Hey, Gold."

"Yeah."

"Oh, shit. Did I wake you?"

After a few mumblings, he said, "Yeah, but for you, Suga, I'd wake up at midnight. What's happening?"

I gave him a two-minute update, leaving time to discuss Peggy's wardrobe. He said he'd take care of me. Before I hung up, the words flew out of my mouth. "I'm going on a date with Nick tonight!"

"Sheeeet! And don't you hang up, girl."

I held the receiver. "Have to get to work in a minute."

"Tell me a minute's worth."

I gave a synopsis of the luncheon events.

Goldie howled. "Damn. That hurt my throat, but it was worth it. Only thing better would have been to see it all in person." He paused to cough.

"You all right, Gold?"

"Fine. Look, Suga,'member what I done told you about Jagger. He's like cocaine. He'll make you feel wonderful, then like shit. Stick with Nick. Nick's got class."

"Jagger has—"

"Jagger has your hormones all in a tizzy. Try to think with your mind on this one, Suga. You're a smart cookie. As mysterious and fabulous as Jagger appears, go with Nick. Nick's a done deal."

"You know something about Jagger you're not telling me."

He shrieked. "Ouch!"

I reminded myself this was Goldie that I was talking to. My second best friend. "I'm sorry, Gold. Didn't mean to imply that you were holding back on me. I don't know what's gotten into me." I looked at my watch. "Hey, I really have to run."

As I went to set the receiver down, I could hear him

mumbling, "I know what's gotten into you. Jagger's mesmerized you. That's what's gotten into you . . ."

The receiver clicked into place—and so did my heart.

I took the prescription from Dr. Handy and hurried over to the pharmacy. Mrs. Wentworth needed some Zoloft to deal with her teenage daughter and being as upset as the dear lady was, she wasn't in any condition to get the meds herself. I came up behind Hildy, who was waiting on a man at the counter.

"Hey, Hildy. How are you?"

She didn't look up from the cash register. I wondered if all the piercing metal had been weighing down her head. "Fine. Great. Usual shit. Hang it!"

"Hildy, it's me. Pauline."

She swung around and a faint smile crossed her purple lips. "Oh, hey. It's you."

I looked around. "Busy?"

She shrugged. "What's new?"

As she said that, Sophie Banko came into the pharmacy. Yikes! I wished I'd had my camera glasses. "I need this filled. I'll add it to the pile on your desk and wait over there."

Perfect. I could legitimately sit there and study Sophie. With my decent 20/15 vision I could even see what she was here to get.

I aimed my beeper camera at her and pressed the button.

Hildy handed the man at the counter his white bag of medicine, spun around and nearly ran toward me. She snatched the prescription off the top of the pile. "I'll get Leo right on this!"

Then she was gone, and I was pissed. Oh, not at her, but

at life. Here I was, making a friend to help my case and her in the process, and now I got preferential treatment, which would get me out of the pharmacy too fast to see the comings and goings of one Sophie Banko.

Pauline Sokol was not born under the brightest lucky star.

I was, however, born determined. So, I got up from Hildy's desk and headed up to the counter. Sophie had a paper in her hand. I looked at her and smiled. "Can I help you?"

Hopefully Leo or the other pharmacist wouldn't come out of the back and ask me what the hell I thought I was doing. I could say I was helping Hildy, but she hadn't returned yet. I pictured her standing over mousy Leo with a whip and a chair until he filled my prescription. Then they'd ask me why I was hanging around here so long. Most of the nurses dropped off the prescriptions, ran back and came to get them later or let the more able-bodied patients come get theirs themselves.

I'd use the excuse that poor Mrs. Wentworth was so stressed that she needed the Zoloft *now*.

Sophie gave me the once-over and said, "No. I'm waiting for the pharmacist."

I worried that she recognized me.

"We ever met?" she said.

"Er. Nope. Okay, then. I'll let you wait." I stood there, moving a box of carob bars back and forth to look busy. All I could see on her paper was that it looked like a list. What kind it was, I couldn't see. But I kept trying to stand on tiptoe to film her with my beeper.

Didn't think I got much though.

An elderly lady came over and started to chat with Sophie. Perfect. I moved the carob box closer to Sophie's list. Her meaty hand covered most of it, and she held it with a death grip.

The carob bars moved closer.

I heard a noise from behind. Leo was coming! My hand went to grab for the box, but instead, I pushed it.

Carob bars flew off the counter, pelting Sophie's side. The other lady screamed as if the bars would kill a woman of Sophie's size.

"Oh! I'm sorry!" I shouted, still trying to look at the paper, but also reaching for the rest of the bars at the same time.

Leo started to yell.

Hildy hurried over and yanked me away from the chaotic counter. "Get out of here," she said into my face while shoving Mrs. Wentworth's meds into my hands.

I could only grab the medicine and take one last look at the list. Upside down, I could read the letters.

M,A,C,I,E.

My uncle Walt's name?

I sat in the restroom of the clinic on the toilet seat cover, my cell phone in hand. Problem was, I didn't know whom to call.

Jagger?

Nick?

My logical mind said to call Nick. After all, he was supposed to be helping me on my case. But then again, to be fair, I was helping Jagger. I knew my film from the beeper was lousy. A real waste.

I punched in #1. Jagger's cell phone number.

Now, Jagger's phone number was not only unlisted, but I'm sure even the FBI couldn't find it. He was that elusive. But, on my last case—my first case that is—Jagger had trusted me with his number—once people had been murdered.

I know he wouldn't be upset to have me call now.

"Yeah."

I jolted back on the commode when I heard his voice. My voice, on the other hand, wouldn't work worth a damn.

"Look, Sherlock, I'm in the middle of something here. You all right?"

My first thought was to listen to the background noise to see if I heard some woman sighing, moaning, or . . . never mind. My second thought was to snap out of it, and I said, "I saw Sophie bringing a list to the pharmacy."

"What kind of list?"

No female chatter. No giggling.

"Pauline?"

Damn! When Jagger used my real name, he wasn't fooling. Then again, I don't think I've ever seen Jagger fooling around.

But . . . oh, those smiles.

Thinking quickly, I made some fake static sounds. "You're breaking up. Wha . . . what did you say?" Proud of myself, I smiled as I walked out of the stall with the phone at my ear.

Dead silence. Good. He bought it.

A slight breath. Or make that an annoyed breath from him.

Then, secluded alone in the bathroom, I felt my face burning. He never bought my static.

"Okay. I saw Sophie hand a list to . . . Well, she was about to hand the list to Leo. I think."

Through mental telepathy, I knew Jagger was shaking his head, but not how many times.

"You know, Jagger. One of these days you're going to shake your brains so much, you'll forget who you are."

No comment.

"Anyway, I saw her get ready to hand the list to him . . . when . . . well, something happened."

"Throwing carob bars at your suspect is not a bright move."

My hands flew up to my cheeks again. And here I'd just cooled off. Damn. The cell phone spun in the air and landed smack in the sink. Thank goodness it was dry. On the other end I knew Jagger was again shaking his head—and grinning.

He'd been watching me all along.

Tap. Tap.

"Pauline, you all right?" Josie, one of the nurses, asked through the door.

Shoot. I'd almost forgotten I was at work. "I'll be out in a few seconds. I'm fine. Thanks for asking." I grabbed the phone and whispered, "Jagger?"

"I don't even want to know what just happened."

I leaned against the cold porcelain. "I'm surprised you can't see me to know what happened." What? All I needed was to worry he could see me in the bathroom. I quickly said, "Okay. The only thing I could see on the list was the name Macie."

"Uncle Walt's name?"

Jagger had befriended my uncle, the car buff, and had even let him take a drive in his SUV. "Yes. Uncle Walt's last name is Macie. Why on earth would she have his name on a list that she's giving to a pharmacist?"

"She must be stealing insurance numbers."

Ten

"Stealing insurance numbers? From my uncle?"

"Maybe from everyone at the senior citizens center," Jagger said. "Leo and maybe the other pharmacists could be filing claims on them, then not filling the prescription."

"That'd be silly. What would they do with all that medicine?"

"He doesn't actually *fill* them, but gets the insurance claim money and sells the medication to someone else."

"Wow. How could anyone think of doing that?"

An audible sigh came across the phone. "Maybe you are in the wrong business, Sherlock."

My heart sank. If I never could have my "fantasy fling" with Jagger, I at least wanted him to respect me as an investigator. He'd given me a few positive comments about my work in the past and, of course, I'd blown them out of proportion in my mind.

"Sherlock?"

He must have noticed my hurt feelings even through the cell phone.

"Look. What I meant was, you are too trusting and honest. You have to think like a criminal to catch them in the act. We need to work on that."

We. '

That simple little word was all I needed to mend my stupid hurt feelings. Jagger had said "we," and I agreed and said goodbye.

Once I finally left the bathroom, I noticed a few of the nurses staring at me. I guess I'd be pissed off too if I had to do all the work while someone sat on the "throne" and talked on the phone. "But I *was* working!" I wanted to shout to them.

So, I grabbed my next chart and headed to the waiting room, not allowing them to make me feel guilty. After all, I had, of course, gone into the bathroom only when there were no patients scheduled for the next fifteen minutes. Even as an ex-nurse, patients always came first with me.

I finished my shift without any prescriptions to fill. Damn. I got my purse and jacket and thinking I'd at least found out something about Sophie today, I could go to Goldie's and get dressed for tonight. With the dread of Superglue and Vaseline to look forward to, I opened the door to the waiting room—and ran directly into Nick.

Funny how talking to Jagger made me forget Nick and our date tonight. "Oh. Hey." I fumbled around in my purse for my car keys.

"Anything today?"

Ready to spill that my talk with Jagger was strictly business, I came to my senses and told myself that I didn't need to go into that with Nick. After all, he knew I was working with Jagger anyway. I did tell Nick about the list and little bit of wasted film.

"Hmm. Interesting. I'm thinking you've stumbled upon

more than Sophie Banko bilking the insurance company out of just a few thousand." He gently placed a hand on my shoulder and led me to the door.

I found myself smiling.

Having a real man next to me was way better than a fantasy.

"Suga!" Goldie wrapped his white-silk-draped arms around me and held for a few seconds. He gave me the biggest hug I'd had all day.

When he eased free, I inhaled Estêe Lauder's Beautiful cologne and said, "I think you've been out of work too long, Gold."

"I'm going nuts here, Suga. How much *Jerry Springer* or *Oprah* can one watch?"

We laughed, and he led me to the living room, which was decorated the same jungle theme as his office. He sat me on a leopard lounge chair and scurried to the kitchen to fix me some hot tea. Through the open door I told him all about my day. The list. The lunch. The lousy luck of shooting carob bars at Sophie Banko.

Goldie screeched, howled, coughed and complained I hurt his throat. When I told him what Jagger had said about my having to think like a criminal, Goldie hurried out of the kitchen, set down the hot tea and gave me another big hug.

"I have to agree with him on that one. You can't be nice in this business, Suga. The crims will walk all over you."

I took a sip of tea, thanked him for it and nodded. "I know. I know. You two are right, but how do I change a lifetime of honest living to try and catch a criminal?"

He gave me a few suggestions, some too X-rated for my

conscience. I finished my tea and decided that if I wanted any dinner tonight, I'd have to hurry up and get dressed like Peggy. Goldie helped me, did the makeup thingy and off I went, forty or so years older.

When I got to my place, Spanky growled at me, and I knew I could fool anyone if he didn't recognize me.

I had to keep reassuring him it was I so he wouldn't take a chunk out of my ankle. He didn't. After a fast chicken-salad sandwich, I was off to Bingo.

Saying little novenas all the way.

Uncle Walt, Helen and Uncle Stash were all sitting at a table together. I looked around and didn't see Sophie but figured she'd be with them, so I headed their way.

Before I reached my seat, I stopped to pull up one knee-high. It had bagged at my right ankle, very senior-citizen-like, but I couldn't stand the feeling. Goldie had gotten me bright pink polyester pants this time with a matching pink-and-white cardigan over a white frilly blouse. The collar buttoned all the way to my throat, and, although tempted, I knew I couldn't leave it open. No woman my "age" would.

I bent down and pulled at my left pant leg to see if that ankle looked like a Chinese shar-pei dog, and a shadow caught my eye. Without standing back up, I noticed the highly polished shoes and heard, "Bellisima—"

I swung up so fast I'm certain my blood pressure crashed, which made me appear right in character of a swooning senior citizen.

I swayed into the arms of Joey the Wooer.

Yikes! For an old man, he had a damn good body. His arms were firmer than mine, for crying out loud. "Oh, Joey. You frightened me."

"I'm-a so sorry. Here. Come sit." He pulled out a chair.

With knees still knocking, I slumped into the seat and gave a nod to my uncles and Helen. She kinda sniveled back at me.

A warning, no doubt.

Ignoring her, I turned to Joey. Hey, on principle, she had Uncle Walt and Uncle Stash and should learn to share. Not that I wanted to lead Joey on, but I decided to ignore her threats and be nice to him. "Thank you, dear. I guess I got up a bit too fast. Blood pressure, you know."

He nodded and sat next to me.

I looked up as Sophie lumbered toward the table. Good. Back to work. "Sit here, Sophie, I saved you a seat," I said, as she got closer.

Giving me an odd look, she sat down without a thank-you.

No problem. At least I could get to talk to her. She opened her satchel and pulled out all her Bingo gear. I looked around the table and realized I didn't even have a card in front of me, and everyone else had at least six. Oops.

Joey must have noticed too, since he waved to the girl who was selling the cards. She hurried over, and he bought me two.

Damn. He must have known I could only handle two. "Thanks. Here . . ." I opened my purse and took out my wallet.

His hand flew over it so fast I thought he was going to rob me. "Put that away, Bellisima. It is on-a me."

He then shoved my wallet, with my hand still attached, back into my purse.

"No. I can't let you pay for me." I started to grab for my wallet again.

"B—eleven," the announcer called.

Shoot. I couldn't be fiddling for money and watch these stupid cards, even if I did have only two. So I politely thanked Joey and stuck the wallet back. As I did, my license slipped to the side.

PAULINE MALVINA SOKOL.

Oh . . . my . . . God. If it had fallen out earlier, Joey and the entire bunch would have seen my picture and real name. Thank goodness for chivalry.

The game progressed, and again, I was the only one at the table who didn't ever get a Bingo. Now I was mad. A pissed-off seventy-four-year-old is someone to be reckoned with. Good.

All these old folks seemed so nice, even darn Sophie. I had to remind myself that she was more than likely a criminal, even though she was kind enough to help me find B-7 on my card when I'd missed it.

During the break, refreshments were served. I figured this would be a good time to corner Sophie, by the cookies, and see what I could find out.

I found her eating chocolate-covered strawberries and a chocolate-chip cookie that was the size of a saucer. So, I grabbed one for myself, telling myself it was all right since I'd eaten such a small dinner. "You sure have the luck, Sophie."

With a mouthful, she nodded.

We stood for several minutes eating before I realized I had to go to the ladies' room. Too much tea, and not a good time to leave. But my luck changed when Sophie said she'd go with me. Joey had come up from behind, and I could see his questioning look as to why women had to go to the ladies' room in tandem.

I for one thought it was great, since I'd get Sophie alone. We excused ourselves and headed up the ramp to the hallway. I let Sophie go first and gave her enough room in case she started to slide backward. Even with all my padding, a woman her size could squish the daylights out of me.

Once in the bathroom, I opened the door to one of the stalls.

"Want me to hold your purse, Peggy?" Sophie asked way too sweetly. "We do that for each other ever since poor Betty Wheelman, who suffers from Parkinson's, dropped hers into the commode. What a mess. All her Bingo winnings soaked." She held out her hand toward me.

Hmm. So that's how she gets the numbers from unsuspecting women. Wow! I was thinking like a criminal. I mentally patted myself on the back. Even so, at first I was ready to say no because I didn't want her to find out about me. If she snooped, she might find my license. But then again, this could be my big break.

But no camera glasses yet!

And no beeper on Peggy, since I'd never be able to explain that one.

Still, I'd at least get a good lead and know what to catch her on the next time. "Aren't you sweet." I handed her my bag and hurried inside. I couldn't pee right now though. I had to peek over the door to watch her. So, I silently put the toilet seat down, stood up and looked over the door. If she looked as if she was going for the license, I'd zoom out.

Another woman was washing her hands. Sophie stood by watching, waiting. That a girl, Soph. Hang yourself. When the woman left, Sophie looked around. I could jump down or nearly fall to my death. Okay, I wouldn't die from falling from this height, but from embarrassment, yeah. Especially if Joey and Uncle Walt had to come in to pry me out from between the commode and the wall.

She set my borrowed purse on the counter. Then, with her chubby fingers, she started to pull at the zipper. Thank goodness Mrs. Honeysuckle had purses the likes of which Brinks couldn't get into very quickly.

Sophie pulled and tugged.

The zipper opened.

I stumbled off my lookout perch, shoved the toilet handle down and flung open the door.

She stood smiling at me, my purse all tidy and appearing untouched.

Very clever girl, Soph.

Next time you'll be on film.

I looked at the satchel Sophie carried and wondered why on earth she would need to lug around such a huge bag. Had to do with crime and insurance fraud. I felt it in my thirty-four-year-old gut. She headed toward the stall. I held out my hand. "You wouldn't want your purse to take a dip. Would you?"

Her face grew as red as the strawberry drippings on her blouse. For a second she hugged the purse to her chest. Sophie didn't trust me—she was protecting whatever was in the bag. Then she gave me a smile and held it out.

"I only have to pee. Very quickly," she said, as if I couldn't be trusted not to look in her bag!

She shut the door behind her. I heard the toilet seat lift up.

I opened the top of her bag with such silence, I became teary-eyed at my skills. Nursing had come in handy once again. Efficient. Clean. Organized. That was me.

As disgusting as it sounded, I just about timed her peeing, and looked inside her bag for a second. Good thing I had a strong stomach from my nursing days.

About ten prescription bottles were inside her purse.

I pulled one out. Colchicine. Used for gout when needed for pain. The name on the bottle was "Mr. Richardson." The man with the gigantic prostate. What the heck would Sophie be doing with this?

The toilet flushed.

It'd take a few seconds for her to shimmy up her undies.

I dug deeper.

Next bottle was Bennie's. For Clarinex. Used for allergy symptoms when needed.

Damn.

Now I was confused.

I could just about hear her pulling down her blouse and straightening out her outfit. What the hell? I looked at one more.

Blue pills.

Viagra.

Name on the prescription: "Mr. Henry Wisnowski."

On the way home to change for my "date," I said several thank-you novenas to Saint Theresa. After all, it had to be some divine intervention that had the bathroom stall door stick on Sophie so I had time to shut her bag and stand there innocently smiling like some demure seventy-four-year-old.

When I pulled into my driveway, I knew I had to do something with the information I had found. Obviously it was a good thing that Nick was coming for me in fifteen minutes. Damn. I might need to say another novena that I could be back to myself in that short a time—and looking, please, God, at least a little sexy?

I shut off the car, hurried inside, gave a quick pat to

Spanky, who growled at Peggy, and shouted, "Miles!" No
answer. Great. I was thankful that he must have been at
Goldie's, so we didn't waste time talking. I looked at my
watch. Twelve minutes to show time.

Not that I was nervous, but it had been eons since I'd
had a real date. The years I'd spent using Doc Taylor for
sex, and vice versa, didn't count. Despite his being a
loser in the end, I always felt comfortable with him. As I
hurried toward the stairs, I slipped off Mrs. Honeysuckle's black pumps, pulled the slacks off and left item
after item on the stairs as I ran up in my own—thank
goodness—undies.

I figured Spanky would have the clothes in a nice pile in
my room by the time I got out of the shower. "Get the nylons, too, Spanks," I called as I adjusted the hot water noz-
zle and stepped in.

With only minutes to go, I took the fastest shower on
record. Didn't even have time to listen to Miles's shower
radio. It was a bright plastic pink-and-white fish that had
great reception in the shower. He called it his "tune-
a-fish."

I jumped out and ran into my room with only a towel on.
Then it dawned on me that I had no idea what I was going
to wear. Did I really want to impress Nick? Encourage
Nick? Or make him want to *peel off* what I chose to wear?

Whoa! I had to take a deep breath at the thought and
grabbed my black bra and black panties. I drew the line at
thongs. A thin line that felt as if I had a constant wedgy. I'd
stick with the lacy panties, bikini style.

Once in the sexiest underwear that I owned, I looked
into my closet.

Ring. Ring.

Shit! I didn't have time to talk to anyone. Must be

Goldie. I opened my bedroom door to hear whoever it was when they started to leave a message.

"Pick up, Sherlock. I know you're home."

I froze.

Froze in the doorway of my room, nearly naked.

And wondered if Jagger could see me now.

I unfroze at the sound of the doorbell. Damn! As exhausted as I was from such a long day, I sprinted into action and shoved on my silky black, long-sleeve top—I think Goldie had actually left it over here one day 'cause it had shrunk too much for him—and shimmied into my jeans. Nick wasn't a jeans sort of guy, but I wasn't the sort of gal to answer the doorbell in my undies either.

Spanky did his barking-at-the-doorbell routine. What a watchdog.

"Be right there!" I shouted.

I gave a quick glance in the mirror and told myself that my messy blonde hair was the new rage.

I looked damn sexy.

As I ran down the stairs, nearly tripping on Mrs. Honeysuckle's clothing, I decided I had to talk to Jagger about Sophie.

From the kitchen came, "Okay, play it your way. Catch you later." *Click.*

Phew.

I opened the door and audibly gasped, then promptly turned red.

"Hey." Nick leaned over, gave me a peck on the cheek and walked inside.

Nick. Nick was dressed in black pants—no, they'd be called slacks—and what had to be a very expensive black leather jacket, suit style, and a cream-colored cashmere turtleneck (I guessed without touching) sweater under-neath.

He took one look at the clothes tossed on the stairs. "Am I interrupting something?"

"Ha." I tried to make my face look as if what he said was funny. "No, silly. I was in a hurry and the dog—" Did he really think those were my clothes? Suddenly I felt frumpy instead of sexy.

Because no matter what I wore now, Nick thought I dressed in polyester.

Eleven

"Another wine?" Nick asked.

Another? I'd barely finished my first when my mind began to spin around like a dog chasing its tail. Not having eaten much tonight, my alcohol tolerance was low.

But boy did Nick look tasty.

Probably because of my unexplained protest of going to Dunkin Donuts earlier, he'd taken me to a wonderful and secluded little Italian restaurant instead of just a coffee place. Sammy's Place. Classic red-checkered tablecloths, black enameled table legs and matching chairs with red seats added to the décor. Thing was, at any second now, I half expected some mobsters to come through the door shooting tommy guns.

But as far as I knew, there was no mob in Hope Valley.

Crime we had, but apparently not organized. I looked over my wineglass to see Nick staring. "What?" Did I have drips of chardonnay on my nose or something?

He smiled. Nice. "Nothing. Okay, truthfully, I can't stop looking at you."

"What did I do?"

He chuckled. "Nothing, Pauline. It's just . . . you look so different tonight."

My hand flew to my face. Did I still have a glob of Superglue stuck to my cheek? Felt smooth.

Nick reached over and took my hand away from my face, then held it. Whoa, boy. His grip wasn't tight, but gentle. Much like Nick himself. I imagined Jagger grabbing my hand in a much tighter hold. A hotter hold, if that was possible.

Stop that! I shouted inside my head. Stop thinking of Jagger. You're with Nick, who *asked* you out.

"More wine?" He still held my hand.

I smiled. "I'm afraid if I have any more, I won't be responsible for my actions." As soon as the wine-induced words came out, I froze. That sounded like a come-on!

Nick smiled at me—and then poured.

I thanked him and kept telling myself this was chardonnay and not grape juice. Sip slowly. Sip slowly. Swip swolly. When I took the time to look at Nick, there was a fuzzy haze around him. Very romantic. He had a kinda Casablanca-meets-Bond thing going on.

Suddenly our gazes locked. I felt myself sway. Thankfully I was still in my seat. Nick leaned over and moved the wineglass to the side. I noticed his flawless complexion, with only a hint of beard.

When his finger touched my chin, lifting it ever so slightly, a very ladylike gasp slipped out of my mouth.

He came closer. His lips touched mine with his finger guiding my chin to meet him.

Wow. Wow. Wow.

Tipsy interest zoomed throughout my body, reminding me that I was a woman. Apparently a very desirable woman, if this guy was kissing me. Who would have thought I'd be Nick's type. Probably not even Jagger.

Jagger!

I pulled back.

"You all right?"

He looked adorable when confused. "I . . . Nick, I have to ask. Are you doing this—" I waved my hands about the restaurant and table to make sure he knew I meant this date tonight "—to get back at Jagger?"

Nick looked as if I'd wounded him with a pizza cutter.

"I'm sorry. I shouldn't have asked such a stupid thing." I felt like a fool. No, a jerk who just insulted a really nice guy. And, besides I told myself, that implied that Nick thought Jagger cared.

Nick leaned back.

I assumed he was composing himself. Maybe controlling some urge to throw the wine at me.

"Pauline, you're a great person. Considerate. Smart. A sexy woman with brains. I asked you out because I'm *attracted* to you."

Again I tried to shrink. This time I wanted to end up under the table where I couldn't see Nick's hurt expression.

"I really was out of line, Nick. It's just—"

He touched my lips with his finger. "I, above all people, know what kind of effect *he* has on women. But this isn't about him, Pauline. It's about us."

My heart fluttered like a damn butterfly. Nick was really interested in me. My mother would have a conniption if she'd heard me insulting such a great catch. I decided then to ignore any "Jagger thoughts" and give Nick a chance.

After all, it was about *us*.

Us. Us. Us!

I'd finally been labeled an "us" with a dynamite guy.

Even though Jagger had called he and I a "we" earlier, he'd only meant it as partners.

I took that second glass of wine and sipped until my lips were sore. Then I excused myself and headed to "powder my nose." As if men didn't know what women really did in the bathroom.

When I opened the door, a woman the size of Sophie nearly plowed me down. Sophie! Despite nearly being squashed, at least the woman reminded me about my job. I waited until a stall was empty, hurried inside and took out my cell phone.

I pressed #1 and waited.

"About time."

I nearly fell into the commode at the sound of his voice. Who was I kidding? Even over a cell phone with lousy bathroom reception, his voice made me hot.

Damn it.

"I was busy."

"Right. How's the date going?"

I tried to decipher a tone of jealousy, but, then again, this was Jagger I was talking to. He didn't let you "decipher" anything about him that he didn't already want you to know.

"Fine. Great. Nick's a babe." My words came out a bit slurred. Good. Maybe Jagger would think Nick could now take advantage of me.

Wishful thinking.

"But that's not why I called."

"You all right? You sound a bit—"

"I'm not drunk!"

A pause. "I was going to say overtired, Sherlock. Overtired."

"Oh. No. I'm not tired. Anyway . . ." I had to get him on

track here, and it took me a moment to remember why I had called him. "Anyway. I found some information out tonight."

"Nick's not a gentleman?"

Hmm. Maybe it did bother Jagger that I'd gone out with Nick. "No. I mean yes. Nick is a gentleman. Stop doing that. I found several prescription bottles in Sophie's purse at Bingo."

I knew he was shaking his head.

"She didn't see me! They weren't her medications, but bottles from some of the men at the senior citizens center. Medications that are PRN."

"PRN?"

"Oh. Sorry. Only taken when needed. In other words they weren't medications that are life sustaining, like heart meds or blood-pressure meds one would take daily. And the last bottle I saw was—"

"You're breaking up. I'll meet you at your place in an hour."

Silence.

I'll never know if Jagger cut me off so we could meet up tonight—or because the reception was really rotten.

Back at my condo parking lot, Nick held my car door for me.

I can't remember a guy doing that, ever. He was a babe and a gentleman any girl would go nuts over. Don't get me started on how my mother would vote for him. Vote? More like start a shotgun wedding—aiming the gun at *me*.

"Thanks, Nick. It was a wonderful evening." We walked to my door.

"It was. Look, Fabio gave me a new case that I need to get started on."

My heart sunk.

I was left in limbo again—with only Jagger to help me. Even with the second glass of wine, I could clearly think about how confused I was becoming.

But before I had time to react, he leaned near and kissed me again. This time my left foot lifted up toward the back of my knee like some movie star. His lips warmed me to the tips of the toes on both feet. He ran his hands up my cheeks and pushed back my hair, all the while keeping his lips on mine.

His tongue touched my top lip.

I pulled back. "I . . . it was a great night, Nick." Thank goodness Miles had not left the porch light on because then Nick could see the stupid expression on my face.

He gave me a quick peck on the cheek. "I'll call you."

I touched my cheek—gently—and watched him walk away and drive off—knowing he really *would* call me.

Damn. What a great feeling.

Suddenly someone stepped from the shadow of the giant pine tree that stood near our porch. I gasped, and then let out my best B-movie scream.

A hand covered my mouth! My breath held, then . . . darkness.

"Whaaat . . . what the hell?" Something cool touched my forehead. It rubbed across it. I opened my eyes. Spanky lay nestled next to me on the couch. I looked to see if there was any blood on me or if my attacker had injured me. Nothing hurt.

Then I realized someone had just woken me up from my faint. "Miles?" I turned my head.

"You really have to work on strengthening your instincts," Jagger said.

I pushed his hand away. Damn, he'd carried me inside while I was conked out. "You scared the shit out of me! Why do you have to lurk in the shadows like some demonic stalker?"

He laughed.

And here I thought Jagger didn't have a sense of humor.

"What if I really were a stalker, Pauline? Or a crazed ex-suspect come to get even with you? You'd faint?"

Damn. I needed to strengthen my instincts and maybe even take Karate. Groaning, I leaned back.

"You scare too easily. I got to the door just as you two drove up and didn't want to interfere."

My insides weren't sure how to feel about that one. Should my heart sink in disappointment? Should my stomach knot in anger? Or should the common sense part of my brain ignore his comment because Nick Caruso liked me?

I pushed to sit up and swatted away his hand when he tried to help. Poor Spanky was momentarily squashed. I moved over, lifted him and kissed his little head. "I'll take a self-defense course."

"Not a bad idea." He leaned back and lifted his legs onto the couch. "Just don't get a gun and go shooting yourself."

"Aw, Jagger. Thanks for the concern." I shook my head and curled my lip so he'd notice.

"What else did you find in Sophie's bag?"

For a second I almost asked Sophie who? Then I remembered Jagger was here as part of the case. Plain and simple. "Viagra."

No change in expression.

"The prescription was in Mr. Wisnowski's name."

"He was her brother-in-law."

"I have two brothers-in-law, but I don't carry around their Viagra."

This time his look took the place of shaking his head. "She must be trading the Viagra for the other prescription meds."

"What would she do with all that medicine?" I petted Spanky, who leaped off my lap onto Jagger's. Little canine traitor.

"Back to Investigation 101, Sherlock. Why would she do that? Think."

Ready to tell Jagger to take a flying leap out of here, I realized he was trying to help me. His "bedside manner" stank though, but that was him. I decided to take advantage of his knowledge and learn something. "Let me see." I tapped a nail to my tooth. "*If* she was related to Mr. W, she might have had access to his house. Then if she stole his Viagra when he died and—" And what? What would she do with it? I know women used Viagra too, but Sophie Banko?

He nodded.

A nod from Jagger was like a gold star from your kindergarten teacher. "Okay. I'm on the right track here. She gets the Viagra and . . . sells it. No wait. Trades it!"

"Why the men's prescriptions in her purse?"

"Maybe she sells them too?" I could mentally hear some buzzer going off as if I'd said the wrong answer on a game show. "No, wait. If she's committing prescription fraud for the money, then she must be doing something with those medications—for money."

"But what?"

I curled my lip at him again. "You're not going to help me out even a little, are you?"

He got up. "You've caught on so far. We need to follow her every move when she comes into the pharmacy."

Excited, I jumped up. "Aha! So *you* don't know why either?"

Yes!

I felt like doing a little "happy dance" but held myself under control. The urge died quickly, and the last thing I remember before falling asleep that night was the grin on Jagger's face before he'd left.

The next morning I hurried to get ready for work. Miles had already left, waking me up, thank goodness, on his way out. I'd overslept after my big day yesterday and my big date last night. Well worth staying up past ten.

Facing a birthday next month on March 24 though, I decided I was getting too old to do that much in one day.

I made it to the clinic just in time to call my first patient. The morning went by uneventfully and quickly. The only good part was that tucked inside the pocket of my navy scrubs top were my new camera/glasses.

I was dying to use them.

I ate lunch by myself in the staff lounge and kept thinking about my investigation. What did Sophie do with those PRN medications? Why steal Mr. W's Viagra only to trade it for medication she more than likely didn't use? Was there some way she was getting money from the insurance company from those PRN medications?

I took a bite of my Caesar salad and decided that didn't make sense. I couldn't see how she could file claims on their medications when they were already filled. Damn it. Jagger probably had this all figured out. He was still using me to help prove his case. Interesting, though, how our cases once again overlapped.

I ate the last bite of lettuce. I'll show him. Determined as a toddler reaching for a piece of candy, I got up, cleaned up, headed outside so I could use the pharmacy's front door. I had twenty minutes left of my lunch break.

And I was going to figure all this out before Jagger.

The waiting room was full of people. Hildy was at the desk so I sauntered over. "Hi. Just passing through to the clinic. I have a few minutes. Man, you look busy. Need some help?"

She looked at me with her sad, dark eyes. I think there was a new loop earring in her right eyebrow.

"Hey, Pauline. I'm swamped. Leo's out to lunch and the other pharmacist is out sick today. Bummer. If you could help me file the prescriptions Leo filled before he left, that'd be great."

I stood by the door to the back of the pharmacy and waited for her to buzz me in. Once inside, I looked around. Just Hildy and one pharmacy tech on duty. Good. She showed me what to do, and I started to stick the little white bags into the bins in alphabetical order.

And I kept looking around for Leo.

With only a few minutes to spare, I cursed to myself. Waste of time. As I stuck Mrs. Zucowski's cardiac medication into the last bin, I noticed a young guy come into the waiting room.

Not just any young guy, but a punk. His hair was redder than my face got when I was embarrassed. He could match Hildy one for one on piercing. And he also sported a dog collar around his neck. Not a fake jewelry one either. A real dog collar.

Damn. I hoped he wasn't here to see Hildy.

But he came up to the desk and waited like any customer. Hildy didn't seem to recognize him. She kept waiting on the elderly gentleman who was asking a million questions about what stool softener worked best. I could see Hildy's frustration reaching the boiling point, so I leaned over. "Go with the generic brand, sir. I'm a nurse. I know it works the best for the price."

Hildy gave me a look of thanks and rang up the sale.

I turned to the punk. "Can I help you?"

He sneered. "What'd ya have in mind, gorgeous?"

Geez. First Nick, now Billy Idol here was putting the moves on me. How popular was I? I stared him down and said, "Do you have a prescription to drop off?"

He looked around. "Relax, gorgeous. Where's Leo?"

"At lunch, but there is a pharmacy tech here—"

"Forget the tech. I want Leo."

"Then you'll have to . . . There he is now." I watched Leo slither in the doorway and get a load of the punk. Leo looked around the room like a frightened spindly legged bird. One with a long beak. Maybe an egret or something like that. Either way he looked . . . damn!

I reached into my pocket and took out my new glasses. When I put them on and pressed the tiny button on top, I had to follow Leo with my head as he walked. He sure as hell looked nervous. I also got a shot of the punk at the same time, and switched on my beeper camera.

Could be my lucky day.

"Hey, Pauline."

I spun around to see Hildy. "Oh, I was just—"

"Helping. I know. When did you start wearing glasses?"

"Oh. These." Shit. I took them off. "Old astigmatism. Don't use them as much as I should. I have to get back now."

"No problem. I have to give these to Leo." She held a handful of prescription forms.

I nearly knocked her over, grabbing them out of her hand. "I have to go past him. Let me." I knew she was ready to argue, as well she should, since I really had to go out of my way to pass by Leo.

But Hildy, overworked as usual, just thanked me and started to help another customer. I headed toward the back door, but stuck my glasses on before I got to Leo and snuck to the side of the prescription drop-off desk.

There he stood, talking to the punk.

"I said forty a pop now, kid." Leo looked as pissed as a "mild nerd" could look. But then again, he appeared almost sinister if it wasn't for his cowlick of a hairdo and the pocket protectors. What was that about? Who wore two pocket protectors?

"Jerk. I could get them for thirty-five—"

Leo turned.

I ducked behind the contraceptive display. With a bit of effort, I shoved two boxes of condoms—Trojan Naturalamb—to the side so I could still keep filming.

The kid grabbed Leo by the collar. "Bastard. Give me three of them."

Leo brushed his hands away. "If you ever touch me again, Billy, I'll . . ."

Hildy had picked that precious moment to turn up the volume on the intercom. "Mr. Alan Rococo. Your prescription is ready."

Yikes!

I had the two on film discussing some sale and the kid's name was Billy. *That* I could remember. I couldn't wait to get home and see what I'd filmed.

Or find out what Leo was selling for forty bucks a pop. And, damn, natural skin condoms were expensive.

"Miss Sokol, we are going to have to let you go if you repeatedly can't get back to work on time," old Dr. Handy said.

I felt as if my father were reprimanding me.

I wanted to tell him he couldn't fire me because I needed to use this job to fight crime, but instead said, "I am so sorry, Doctor. It won't happen again. I have over thirteen years of impeccable attendance in my nursing jobs. It's just . . . my life isn't what it used to be."

He nodded and said, "One last chance."

I reached out my hand and shook his. "I appreciate that, sir. Thanks."

I behaved and finished my last shift without incident. When I had to go to the pharmacy, I made it in record time, figuring I'd have to find another way to do my investigating. One that wouldn't get me fired.

At the close of the shift, I apologized to the other nurses who'd taken up the slack earlier when I got back late and ignored their "yeah, right" looks. I really had been sincere.

On the way out, I noticed Sophie walking into the clinic with Joey the Wooer. They chatted on. I followed several steps behind. Geez, I hoped when I got old I could spend my time somewhere else besides a clinic or pharmacy.

Of course, good old Sophie was probably making a profit as she walked.

She headed to the counter and waved to Leo, who motioned for her to sit down. I noticed Hildy didn't even ask if she could help her. Odd. Joey started looking around at the over-the-counter medication section.

The poor guy. Must have a little pharmacy of his own at

home. If he was anything like my Uncle Walt, Joey probably went to the doctor at the drop of a hat. My dad, however, had to be bound and gagged just to get him in for his yearly flu shot.

I reached into my pocket and put on my glasses. Then I headed over to the side of the counter, still sneaking lots of filmed peeks at Sophie.

Hildy was bent over her work at the counter. "Can I help you?"

"It's me, Hildy." She hadn't even looked up, the poor thing.

"Oh, hey. I'm sorry. Busy day today."

"I have a few minutes. Want me to help file or something?" *Please say yes.*

"I hate to keep asking you to do my work."

"I'm the one who offered, as long as Leo doesn't mind. Does he?" I held my breath.

She shrugged. "He said since you work for the clinic it's about the same thing and as long as he doesn't have to pay you . . . cheap bastard."

That as twice in one day someone called Leo that name. Interesting.

"Buzz me in." I opened the door and went in while Sophie waited at the far end of the counter. Hildy nodded toward the bins full of·white bags. "No problem," I said.

She looked at me oddly. "Your astigmatism acting up?"

I nodded.

"Don't worry about the prescriptions," I said, trying to get her mind off my glasses. "I'll get them done in a jiffy."

Hildy looked at me as if she had no idea what a "jiffy" was. My age was showing. I ignored the fact of my imminent birthday and started to file the bags into the bins. I kept looking for letters in the last part of the alphabet so that I could get closer to Sophie and Leo. Every so often I lucked out. While I filed Mr. and Mrs. Hollander's diuretics, I got close enough for a great shot.

Leo leaned near Sophie. "Freaking Billy only bought three today."

Sophie growled.

I pulled back slightly.

Sophie reached into her bag and took out a medicine bottle. There was a small coffee stain on the left side. Mr. Wisnowski's prescription! She handed it to Leo. He took it, opened it and after looking around (and me nearly ducking into the bin), he poured out a few Viagra into his pocket.

What the hell?

Click. Click.

I was on a roll here.

Then Sophie took out the list she'd had the other day. "Here's one more. There's a new broad that hangs with us now, but I couldn't get hers."

I nearly jumped at her. She *was* trying to steal Peggy's insurance number! I made sure to get this all on film.

The female pharmacist with the black hair came near.

Sophie and Leo shut up, and he went back to work.

Sophie bounded out as gracefully as she could.

I noticed Joey heading out after her. Geez. I hoped he wasn't using the Viagra with . . .

Eeyeuuw.

Hildy dropped into her chair, looking totally wiped out.

"All finished, Hild." I came up and sat on the edge of her desk.

Leo came up next to me.

Yikes. I gave a nice smile and became a statue.

"Lock up the desk area. I did the back already."

He never even acknowledged me. So much for working for him for free. Bastard.

Three strikes and you're out, buddy.

Hildy sighed and watched him leave. "Go kiss your mama's big butt, you shit."

Mama?

I looked around to see the waiting area empty. What would Leo's mother look like anyway? A pencil of a woman, long and skinny like a beaker?

"Does Leo live with his mother?" Please give me something to go on, I prayed.

"Nope. But he might as well. She's in here nearly every damn day."

"Ha. I noticed that about some customers. Like that Sophie woman."

Hildy looked at me with eyes as tired as my feet felt. "That's the big butt he should be kissing."

Twelve

I sat in my car—in shock.

Leo was Sophie's *son*. No, Sophie was Leo's mother. Well, after my teeth nearly fell out, I'd gotten it straight from Hildy: Sophie was Leo's *stepmother*, making Mr. W his step uncle.

Sophie'd raised him since he was thirteen, so that was just as good. I couldn't wait to tell Jagger. If he didn't already know, that is. Nick had called me earlier, and we were "on" for dinner. On. I smiled despite my earlier shock.

I wouldn't mind Jagger finding out about my plans for tonight.

Damn. How lame to keep thinking about him. I was pissed that my mind had a mind of its own.

A siren yanked my attention back to the present. As I watched the blue lights of two cop cars drive by the parking lot, I dug inside my purse and pulled out my cell phone. Once again I punched in #1. Had to. I needed to share this info with Jagger. The phone went into voice mail. Darn it all.

"It's me. You won't believe what I found out today. Leo Pasinski is actually—"

The passenger door flew open. Jagger jumped in.

"Drive."

As if he had some kind of control over me (which, in fact, he did), I cranked the engine and drove toward the end of the driveway, where I had to slow to wait for traffic—and take a life-saving breath.

"What the hell are you doing?" I looked at him instead of the cars zooming by. "You scared me. Again!"

He was wearing his usual black jacket, jeans, and shirt, the wind had mussed his hair just the right amount. Where Nick was clean shaven, Jagger always had a shadow of a beard, as if his razor was set too high, like an adjustable lawnmower. But that five-o'clock shadow gave him a damn mysterious and sexy appearance.

One that took my breath away each and every time.

Damn it all.

"The question is what the hell were you doing?"

"I was trying to leave you a message to tell you—"

"Insurance Fraud 101, Sherlock. Don't discuss the case over the phone. Especially in public in the very parking lot of the building where suspects are under surveillance. Or leave voice mails. What if you called the wrong number?"

I felt like a neophyte. And well I should. Why didn't I think of these things? Mental note to myself, call Goldie. He has to be better now, and I needed him—so I could stop looking like a teenage Nancy Drew in front of Jagger.

All I could say was, "I'm sorry."

Jagger nodded. "What's the news?"

A horn honked in back of me. "Should I go or let you out here?"

"Go."

I pulled out of the parking lot. "Where to?"

"Anywhere until you've told me."

Okay. So I got to ride around, inhaling rugged man until I told him my news. I felt tempted to drive like a New York cabbie and take him the longest route. But then I noticed the time on my car's radio. I had an hour to get ready before Nick picked me up.

"I can't take too long."

"'Nother date?"

I figured he already knew, but his tone didn't sound like it. "Yes."

"Then talk fast."

No interest in my dating Nick. Damn. "Okay. I learned today that Leo Pasinski is Sophie Banko's stepson."

"Goddammit."

"Why? That's not a good thing to find out?"

"It would have been. Turn back and drop me off."

Feeling as if he'd popped my balloon, I pulled into a Staples parking lot, turned in the other direction and headed back to the office parking lot. Since it had nearly emptied out, I could see Jagger's SUV sitting all by itself on the west side. I pulled up to it and shoved my heater on full blast. Once the sun went down in the early evening, the days grew much colder.

Jagger opened the door and stepped out, shutting it behind. I pushed the electric window opener with my finger. "Hey. Wait!"

He turned slightly.

I actually turned off the heater's fan to hear him better as the wind blew through the open window. "Hey, Jagger. No fair. What did you mean by 'it would have been?' I mean, I think that's pretty helpful to know they are in cahoots. And related! What more could we ask for to help our cases?" Really getting pissed, I shut off the engine and shoved open my door.

As I stepped out, I asked, "Why are you so negative about everything?" I came around the fender.

He started walking to his car. "Go home and get ready for your date." He looked in the direction of some cops who drove out from around the building.

Date? Damn, again I forgot poor Nick. "I have plenty of time." I hoped he believed me, because that would mean he thought I didn't *need* much time to look sexy and beautiful. He didn't argue. Good. "Hey!"

He opened the driver's door of his SUV.

I hurried toward him. "I tell you a wonderful morsel like that and you say it's not a good thing. I've stumbled onto something here—" I looked around to see if anyone was in the parking lot. Empty. I still whispered, "—and Leo's connection to Sophie is enormous. What could be better?"

"If he were still *alive*."

"Take a deep breath," Jagger said, rather hushed. Or maybe rather annoyed.

I inhaled and let him fan me with a magazine he'd had in his SUV. I hadn't passed out again, but got a bit woozy at his tidbit of info.

Leo Pasinski was dead.

Damn. Murder was not covered in Insurance Fraud 101. This was two for two, and I didn't much like those scores.

"How? What happened? When?"

"A few minutes ago a janitor found him in the men's room."

"Shot?"

Jagger just looked at me. "Why would you think someone shot him?"

"I . . . I don't. I don't know. Maybe déjà vu about me almost getting shot. How else would someone kill a sleazy pharmacist . . . Poison?"

"Well, the place is full of medication. Maybe someone gave him an overdose of something. Lieutenant Shatley's investigating it."

"And he'll let you know? I saw the cop cars earlier, but had no idea that a possible murder had been committed."

"Leo's death will be treated as a murder—until proven otherwise. Could be natural causes, but until the autopsy, any accidental, unattended or unexpected deaths are suspect."

"Unattended. That means no one was around to see what happened."

Jagger had a way of locking your glance to his. "When was the last time you saw Leo alive?"

I was still mesmerized and mumbled something even I didn't understand. Then it dawned on me. Jagger was questioning me!

My mouth dried instantly as if I'd been given a bottle full of antihistamines.

"You think *I* killed Leo?"

"Did you?"

"Whaaaaaaaat?"

"Sherlock, I hope the hell you have the sense not to kill off one of our suspects—even accidentally, but the police are going to question everyone—and I want to make sure you can stand up to it."

Shit. There was that time I had blacked out when Jagger had stopped the elevator between floors to question me.

Hey, I never sought therapy for that phobia because I never expected anyone to trap me in an elevator!

I pulled back. I should be honored that he cared, but his implication was that I'd fall to pieces when the bright lights hit me. Then again, I'd certainly been affected last night when he'd scared me, and when he told me about Leo, whoa, boy.

I pulled myself up straight and repeated in my head over and over that Polacks were strong as bulls. "I saw Leo a few minutes ago—"

"That'd be right about when he died. So you saw him being murdered? Possibly murdered?"

"Oh my God! Jagger, stop that. You are making me nuts, and confused. I can't think straight."

"Well, you said a few minutes. Was it really that amount of time that you sat in the car? The cops aren't going to be as nice as I'm being."

A traitorous tear formed in my eye. I hated almost crying in front of Jagger, but murder did that to me. I sucked it up and blinked a few times. Here I thought this case would be so different from the last one. But again, a person had lost his life.

I sniffled.

Jagger reached in back and pulled out a tissue. He took it and touched my cheek.

Oh . . . my . . . God.

I'd never be able to think clearly *now*.

"Call Nick and cancel."

Nick! Even Jagger remembered my date when I'd clean forgotten it. Well, when you were out of circulation for so long, dating doesn't come back like riding a bicycle.

"Why? I can get ready in—" I looked at my watch. "A half hour."

He looked at me. "Obviously you've been sitting in your car longer than a few minutes. And—" He looked me up and down. "I'm sure you could get ready in a few minutes, but this is important."

As if my date wasn't.

I dug around again in my purse and called Nick. He understood about work—but I hadn't mentioned that I was with Jagger. "Tomorrow?" I asked, trying to see Jagger's reaction through my peripheral vision.

Nothing.

So what was new? "That'd be great. And, sorry, Nick." I made sure Jagger could hear and added, "I really was looking forward to tonight." I tried to sound sexy, but came out sounding more like a middle-ager who'd just exercised. I pressed the red button and tried to shove the phone back in my purse.

"What the hell do you carry in that thing?"

I looked around the car. "At least it doesn't look as if I live out of my purse. I pulled out my calculator, tissues and . . . I shoved the Tampax tampon further inside.

My glasses case fell out.

Jagger bent to get it at the same time I did.

Whoa, boy.

My hand touched his. His fingers burned mine. My breath held. His breath burned my cheek. And together we picked up the glasses case.

"I didn't know you wore glasses, Sherlock." He took back his hand.

"Oh. I . . . don't . . . They are . . ." *Pull yourself together, Pauline!* I blinked a few times, as if that would clear my mind. "They are . . . oh, my, Jagger!"

He pulled back.

"They're a camera. A camera! Nick helped me buy them, just like my beeper."

I think Jagger growled.

Maybe I imagined it, but he did make some sound that said, "Not Nick again." I waved the glasses at him. "I have pictures of Leo and a Billy Idol lookalike! Arguing. I think they were arguing."

Jagger shook his head once, turned on the engine and drove out.

Before I could ask a clear, nonsensical question, we had pulled into the parking lot of his "friend's" place where my film was developed, and then we drove to my condo to view the photos.

When the engine turned off, Jagger looked at me. "I hope this isn't like the beeper film."

As I walked across the parking lot, inside the condo, and through the kitchen door to let Spanky out and back in, I mumbled on and on about the beeper film not being my fault. Jagger had stopped listening around the first step up my porch. I could tell by that glassy look in his eyes, but I kept rambling on as if that would convince him of something I knew was my fault.

This time, on my coffee break, I'd studied the directions of the camera/glasses.

But that didn't make me any more confident as I clutched the envelope in my hands, sat next to Jagger on the couch—and held my breath.

"Let's see the video first," he said.

Gulp.

I took the remote, turned on the TV and the VCR and held my breath even longer.

The screen turned royal blue. I figured my lips would soon be that same shade if I didn't take a deep breath. I did and then the screen flickered, fuzzed and then brightly colored packages of condoms filled the picture. I thought I'd been looking at Leo and Billy—but apparently not.

Jagger turned to me.

I refused to blush. "Hey, I was in a pharmacy, for crying out loud."

Then Leo and Billy appeared, arguing. Every once in a while a package of Ortho Tri-Cyclen, Nordette or the Ortho Evra patch would show up in the picture.

That's when I'd swallow so loudly even Spanky looked up.

The camera kept panning in to them, then to the birth control stuff, then back until I thought I'd get seasick. I had to learn not to keep looking away when I had on those glasses.

The screen turned blue after several minutes.

"That's all you took?"

"I . . . I didn't want them to see me. Besides, that was good stuff. Maybe Billy killed Leo because he was gouging the price of Viagra. What the hell would a kid his age want with Viagra anyway?" I really didn't want an answer to that, I realized, when Jagger turned to me. "Something illegal?"

"Kids use it to enhance the effects of Ecstasy. Mostly at Rave parties. Sustains an erection . . ."

I know Jagger was talking. His lips were still moving. But my Catholic-induced conscience had shut down my hearing.

Erections!

I was sitting in my living room with a guy fantasies are made about (at least mine were), and he's talking erections.

Maybe I *should* go back to nursing.

* * *

Jagger had left last night soon after the viewing of my surveillance tape, but not before a snide comment about sea-
sickness, and the photos weren't any better. Good thing
he'd left, 'cause I couldn't have sat there staring at him
much longer. There was something that tested my self-
control each time I was alone with him. Something I
wasn't getting any better at ignoring.

So, I got up early this morning to meet him at Dunkin
Donuts. We'd have a few hours before I had to be at the
clinic. I couldn't imagine what work would be like with
Leo's possible murder hanging over everyone.

I had tossed and turned all night worrying about Hildy.
I hoped to hell that she didn't have anything to do with it.
After all, she'd never had a good thing to say about Leo.
Then again, I'd heard him being short or snappy to several
of the pharmacy staff. Leo didn't seem to have any friends
there. It had dawned on me around midnight: my case
with Sophie might come to an end—without my help.

If her stepson was killed, would she continue her illegal
claim filing? And how would I "get her" on that?

But the real clinker that stole my beauty sleep was, now
that Leo was dead, was Jagger's case over?

I'd called Goldie around one thirty in the morning not a
bit worried that I'd wake him. Goldie was an owl. He re-
quired very little sleep and had said I could call him any-
time. He'd agreed to meet me at lunchtime to go over
some things. It was then I'd decided not to ask Nick for
help with work.

After all, we were an "us" now, and pleasure came before business when you were still single at my age.

I did my morning routine, kissed Spanky on his little
squirrel head and ran out the door. Today was a beautiful

sunny winter day. The old snow from weeks ago had melted, leaving golden yellow grass and twigs of trees to hint at spring. I only wished it would come soon—except for the fact that it would then mean my birthday would have come and gone.

Nick was looking better and better.

On the drive to meet Jagger, I allowed myself to wonder if Nick liked kids.

Why? I had no idea, I told myself when I pulled up next to the black SUV and felt a bit Jagger-induced jittery before my first cup of caffeine.

Jagger already had our order in the car and motioned for me to come sit in the passenger's seat.

I opened the door, inhaled hazelnut mixed with his scent of male. "Smells good," I said, taking the coffee into my cold hands. I held the cup a few minutes before taking a sip. I noticed my French cruller sat on the dashboard. "What if I wanted jelly today?"

He looked at me.

Damn. I hated him knowing me so well when he was such an enigma.

"I talked to Shatley. He wants your tape and photos."

"My tape!" Suddenly I felt scared. "My photos!" It made sense that a homicide investigator would want my surveillance stuff, since I might have been witnessing a pre-murder argument.

And the killer was still at large.

If it got out that I had the stuff and had seen them . . .

"Do I have to give them to him?" I took a large bite of donut that I really didn't want anymore.

"Why wouldn't you?" He looked at me. With one finger, he wiped a dollop of sugar from my lip.

Suddenly I forgot what we were talking about.

"Look Sherlock, whoever killed Leo, if, in fact he was killed, more than likely murdered Wisnowski, too."

That's right. Murder. We were talking murder. "Right. But if that's the case, the kid Billy might not be the one."

"Let Shatley deal with the deaths. Your job is nailing Sophie—before someone bumps her off."

"Whaaaaaaaat?" I started coughing on a piece of donut. "Do you really think someone will kill *her* too?" I nearly coughed up my coffee and the cruller bites I didn't want.

"Sherlock, in this business, anything is possible. You have to start thinking that way."

"Be suspicious until proven not guilty."

He took his coffee, looked at me over the rim, and swallowed. "We have to go talk to Shatley now."

I couldn't eat another bite.

"Good to see you again, Pauline," Lieutenant Shatley said, taking my hand in a firm grip.

I smiled, not being able to shake the nervous feeling from being in the police station.

And being questioned about a possible murder.

Why did I feel guilty?

Had to be that old conscience thing again. Someone who had little, if any, conscience wouldn't be nervous. I sucked it up and answered all of the lieutenant's questions and gave him my tape and pictures.

They really didn't help my case anyway.

Truthfully, they really didn't help Shatley's case either.

I had to get back to Sophie. Fabio would be calling me any day now, asking for an update. And what could I give him? Sophie is doing something illegal—but I can't prove it. Sure. That would go over big with my boss.

We said our goodbyes, and Jagger walked me to the parking lot. I'd taken my own car from Dunkin Donuts.

"You all right to drive?"

I looked at him, kneading my fingers inside my mittens. "Of course I am. Why wouldn't I be?"

The look.

"Stop insinuating that I can't handle myself. I'm fine." I looked down to see my watch, but had a hard time reading it since my hand shook so.

Jagger reached over and steadied my hand.

"Eight thirty. I have to leave."

He didn't let go yet. "Be careful around the clinic today."

Like I needed *that* warning! Before he'd said that, I really wasn't worried. It was a good thing I'd seen the time earlier, because now my watch might go flying off my shaking arm if I tried to look at it.

"I'll be fine." I tried to sound convincing, but even I wasn't buying it. "Jagger, does this mean your case is over?"

"Nope."

That was it? Nope? He wasn't going into any detail of why he still had a case. "Do I really need to stay working at the clinic?"

He just grinned.

"Shit. Then I'll see you around."

He nodded.

Now I felt better, knowing he would be there in some disguise—to protect me.

The clinic's grapevine was swelling with gossip today. Talk of Leo's death had the place in an uproar. Thank goodness the word "murder" hadn't surfaced—yet. It took all of my control not to get into any "discussions" about it with any of the staff. I thought that was the professional thing to do. I did hurry over to the pharmacy on my coffee break to see Hildy though.

She was out sick today.

Damn it. That didn't look good, and I didn't even know her home phone number to call and see if she was all right.

I only hoped that she really was sick and not out—to cover up something.

Not much investigating would get done today.

Once the clock hit noon, I was outta there, to meet Goldie at the diner across from the clinic building. I went inside and looked around.

"Suga!" Goldie sat in the last red booth by the window. He'd worn a silver-blonde wig today with a ski jacket, a paisley pink-and-gold ski jacket and matching neon pink leggings. His size elevens were covered in furry pink boots that hit him mid calf. Despite the heat in the diner, he kept on a gold knitted headband over his ears. Beneath dangled lovely gold and diamond earrings matching the bracelet on his right wrist and the rings on every finger of that hand.

That's my Goldie.

I gave him a big hug. "You feeling better?"

"Heavenly. I'm going back to work next week."

"That's great, Gold. I can't wait. I'll clean my stuff out of your office."

"And go where?"

"Good question." I laughed.

He leaned near. "You'll stay put."

I had more on my mind than to argue with such logic.

The waitress came over with two glasses of water. "Coffee?"

Goldie said, "High octane for me."

"Decaf," I said.

She scurried away, a stream of cheap rose-scented perfume hanging in her wake.

"So, tell me everything," he said.

I looked at my watch—and momentarily cringed. Then I filled Goldie in on the case, on Nick and on Jagger.

The waitress came and left with our order. Goldie, the club sandwich without mayo. Me, the tuna with extra mayo, although one might assume by the smell in there that fried food was all they served.

He looked around and leaned close before the waitress came back. "Don't forget my Jagger warning."

"I know, Gold. It's not easy though."

He shook his head. "Tell me about it, Suga. If it weren't for Miles, I'd be hunting and pecking around too."

Hunting and pecking? I barely remembered that I had a date with Nick tonight. "Gold, what do you think of Nick?"

"Not my type, but a doll for you. He's not macho or rugged, like Jagger. He's more suave, movie-star handsome. Yeah, suave handsome. That's Nick. But, Suga, Nick'll treat you right. I've already told you that."

"I know. How do I get my emotions to know?"

Goldie laughed as the waitress brought our food, set it down and pulled the check off her order book. She put it on the table, turned and left.

We made some small talk over our sandwiches. Goldie really sounded as if he felt much better, and that made me happy. Maybe today was going to be better than yesterday.

Of course, if there were no homicides the rest of the day, it would be even better.

"So, Suga," Goldie said, dabbing a paper napkin to his bright pink lips. "We need to get you going on your case. Fabio will shit a brick if you don't give him something to placate him soon. He call you yet?"

"I've been avoiding him." I took a bite of my sandwich and sip of my decaf. "I really have to get on Sophie's good side. If she was giving Leo insurance numbers, I need to find the proof before the case is over and done with."

"Back to Peggy Doubtme."

I groaned, knowing he was right.

Goldie laughed, very ladylike. "What you planning next, Suga?"

"I figure if Sophie was making money with Leo on the Viagra, she may just keep up that end of the business. Maybe she even was selling on the side, too. I hear one pill sells for twenty-five to thirty bucks on the black market. Imagine?"

"Suga, I *can* imagine. That stuff's like gold to some of us."

I blushed, knowing my color made me look like a Raggedy Ann doll. "Gold, you don't mean—"

He waved his hand. "Not anymore. Not needed with my Miles. Speaking of Miles, Suga . . ." He touched my hand.

"Oh . . . my . . . God, Goldie. What is the matter?"

He squeezed my hand. "Nothing is wrong, Suga. It's just, well, I promised Miles I'd wait to tell you together, but . . . I just can't wait!"

My hand turned numb from the pressure. "What is it? You've got me all excited!"

"Miles and I are moving in together. He asked me to live at your place."

Which meant I was now homeless—with no solved case to get paid for—and two dead bodies.

Thirteen

"Suga," Goldie said with concern in his eyes. "Now don't you go fretting. You don't have to move—"

"Gold, I do. You and Miles deserve your privacy. To be together. Alone." I leaned over and kissed his cheek. "I'm thrilled for both of you. And don't you worry about me."

I'll worry enough for the both of us.

And worry I would. I really couldn't afford a place of my own, didn't have any other friends I'd care to share a condo with, and knew in my logical mind that the only place I really could go to live was . . .

"I'm so thrilled!" my mother yelled when I went over there after work—and asked for my old room back.

This was the worst day of my life.

Daddy leaned over, setting the morning newspaper to the side, even though it was nearly five. "*Pączki*, that is nice. It is nice that you'll be back here with us."

Uncle Walt looked over from his seat near the television. He winked.

I knew he thought we'd be working on the case of Mr. W's death together.

This truly was the worst day of my life.

"I have to go."

"Dinner is almost ready. It's nearly six." Mother jumped up, ready to blockade the door.

I decided I wouldn't put myself through eating any meals here—until the fateful day when I moved back in. "Can't stay, Mom."

"Why not?"

I edged past her, bumping into the coffee table, sending a statue of the Blessed Mother careening to the floor. Thank goodness deep shag provided such a nice cushion.

"Look out, Pauline!" Mom tried to catch the statue but without avail. "You could have broken it."

"Not intentionally. I really have to go."

"Why the hurry?"

My father had gone back to reading his paper. Uncle Walt's eyes had shut. And Mom stepped closer.

Shoot. She had some kind of mental telepathy with us kids. She knew when we were lying or at least trying not to tell her something. It was no use. I blurted out, "I have a date to get ready for." I spun around, hurried to the other side of the table, and tried to make a dash for the door.

She grabbed me as if her arm was rubber, like Stretch Armstrong's. "A date? A date? And you didn't tell us? Walt, Michael, did you hear that? She has a date!"

Uncle Walt let out a long snore.

Daddy looked up from his paper and nodded. "That's nice."

I sighed. "It's not like it's some earth-shattering news, Ma." She hated when I called her "Ma."

"That's *Mother*, Pauline. And yes it is, when *you* have a date."

"Thanks."

She eased up on her grip. "I didn't mean it that way. Just that, well, it's nice to know you are dating some nice man." She had some of the same skills as Jagger with her eyes. They locked onto yours and wouldn't let go. You really couldn't even turn your head. And, you *had* to tell the truth. "It is a nice young *man*. Isn't it?"

I know my mother had her moments of thinking I might be gay, and, believe me, I was tempted to lead her on a few times for the hell of it, but decided, how pathetic was that?

With my dating history, it really wasn't my mother's fault that she thought that. "Yes, Mom. He's a nice *man*. A good-looking man. Even a dynamite investigator."

"Jagger?"

Speechless, I shook my head, waved to everyone in the room whether they were looking or not, and yanked myself away from my mother's staring.

Okay, she'd never met Nick, and she had met Jagger. That's why she assumed I was dating him. They'd met a few months ago and consequently he came for Christmas Eve, and she egged him on to kiss me under the mistletoe.

Don't get me started on that night.

But damn if it wasn't hard to hear her talk about Jagger.

All the way home, I could hear my mother asking if I was dating Jagger. And, all the way home I kept telling myself how great Nick was. How handsome. How debonair. How smart. How . . . he wasn't Jagger.

When I pulled into my parking lot, I sat in my car a few minutes, looking at the front door of our condo. I wouldn't be living here much longer, I thought. My heart sank.

Once I'd pulled myself out of the car and gone inside, I grabbed Spanky and sat with him for a good ten minutes, knowing that I wouldn't have as much time to get ready. But depression had set in.

Who would Spanky live with?

Damn. This was like getting a divorce. Both Miles and I loved him equally. I looked into his gigantic dark eyes, "Shit. What are we going to do?"

"Don't leave."

Again I thought the dog had talked to me. Then I sat back and told myself that maybe I really wouldn't have to move to 171 David Drive, home of the Sokol family. Maybe I could stay here and keep out of Miles and Goldie's way.

I kissed Spanky on the head and hurried to go shower. At least a night out with Nick might take my mind off my problems. Possible murder. Possible moving. Possible never finishing my damn case.

Finally ready in record time, I ran to answer the bell on the third ring.

Not only was Nick impeccably dressed in a camel-hair jacket, black trousers and camel-colored suede overcoat, but he also was punctual. Thank goodness I'd showered, done my makeup with old tips from Goldie and let my hair fly around again after taking it down from work. I'd picked out a slinky outfit Goldie had made me buy on a shopping trip to Lord and Taylor.

I wore a hunter green miniskirt and matching blouse, which I felt great in. I went with sexy on my feet instead of "comfortable" as was my usual choice and wore my black heels with the sling backs that complemented my Maciejko legs. If I fell, I'd die of embarrassment, but the way Nick looked at me right now would make it all worth it.

Shimmer. Shimmer. Wow.

He took my hand and kissed it. "You look great. Hope you're hungry."

Hungry? I couldn't remember eating in the past century. My mind clouded with a male's attention on me, I merely smiled and said, "Thanks. I could eat a little."

"Good. We've got reservations at Madelyn's."

The infamous restaurant near the river that everyone went to. I'd gone there with Doc Taylor and even once with Jagger. After that, I'd actually never wanted to go there again, but it was the best place in town, so I'd had to change my standards. This could be an interesting night.

"That's my favorite place." Okay, the little white lie was for Nick's benefit so as not to disappoint him, since it was his choice. This day had to have a better ending than the way things had been going up to now.

On the way there, I filled him in on my case, and he told me he was working on a suspected fraudulent neurosurgeon over in the West Hartford area. When the valet took Nick's black Porsche, he held his hand on my lower back and guided me into the restaurant.

The hostess gave Nick a huge smile. "Hi, Nicky, the usual table?"

Me, she ignored.

"Thanks, Kristi."

Nick gave her a nice smile, but never let go of me. So there, Kristi! We wove through crowded tables toward the back of the restaurant, which faced the water. Tiny white lights sparkled year round outside the window, giving the place a festive atmosphere. With a dusting of snow on the back patio, it really looked magical.

Tonight would make up for today.

"Ah, Bellisima."

I swung around to come face to face with Joey the Wooer. He sat at a table near the window with Helen, Uncle Stash and a woman from the senior citizens center. I think the one who had taken her teeth out that day. The usual crowd except for my Uncle Walt. Obviously only one at a time could date Helen, and poor Sophie was not there either.

"Oh, hi. Joey. Uncle Stash." I nodded toward Helen, who kind of growled at me and drooled over Nick.

I'd never liked that woman, from the first time I'd rammed into her Thunderbird.

And I only hoped she wasn't getting her claws into my Uncle Stash. Poor Uncle Walt.

After brief introductions, Nick said, "Well, we'll let you folks enjoy your dinner." He took me by the shoulders, but Joey jumped up before we could leave.

"Why-a not join us?"

I think Nick growled now, but he was very polite to the elderly man. After several minutes of well-mannered arguing on both sides, I found myself sitting between Nick—and Joey.

I had to smile inside. Felt kind of nice to have two guys vying for my attention.

Then I reminded myself that one was as old as my uncles. That kind of took the wind out of my sails until I looked at Nick—and shimmered.

Damn. He was looking better and better each time. Maybe the fact that he seemed to like me, and had said as much, made him more appealing.

I decided I wouldn't even think of Jagger the rest of the night.

"Oh my God! Oh my God!"

I swung around to see Miles and Goldie exclaiming together. Gotta love those two. After making sure everyone knew each other they, too, joined us.

So much for my date with Nick.

Wrapping a diamond-studded-bracelet-covered arm around me, Goldie bent toward me before he sat. The diamonds went perfectly with the winter white fitted suit with white mink collar that he wore. Only Goldie could pull off the fabulous outfit without looking pretentious or overdressed.

Every guy in the place turned to stare.

Of course, being over six feet, Goldie kinda commanded everyone's attention. And he definitely had mine when he whispered in my ear, "You go, girl. Forget Jagger."

So much for not thinking about Jagger the rest of the night.

Goldie's reminder had me look at Nick, smile and pray that he hadn't heard the comment. I quickly turned to Joey, hoping his hearing wasn't that great. He merely stared at me. Oh, boy. Maybe he had heard.

Back to Nick. I put my hand over his and said, "I'm famished," knowing I probably wouldn't be able to eat a bite.

Joey shoved the breadbasket toward me. "Bellisima, you shouldn't have to starve when out on a date."

The muscles of Nick's hand tightened under my hold. Yikes. I felt certain he'd love to pop old Joey over the gray head. But Nick was a true gentleman.

"You're right, Joe. Such a beautiful date as mine shouldn't have to wait to eat." With that he waved the waiter over and looked at me. "Allow me?"

I nodded, knowing I'd eat just about anything right now with my stomach shrinking by the minute. Before I was near anorexic; now I could eat an entire tuna.

"Let's start with two shrimp cocktails, a bottle of your

best chardonnay, and—" He now took my hand into his and kissed it.

Joey nearly spit his wine out.

I smiled inside at the darling older man.

Nick finished with, "Chateaubriand for two. How's that sound, Pauline?"

"Wonderful," came out of my mouth on a very soft, ladylike breath.

Who knew I could do soft and ladylike?

When the waiter brought our shrimp and Goldie and Miles had ordered, we all settled in chatting and eating. The first crew was served their dinners, but being the seniors, they all ate in slow motion.

Joey kept leaning toward me and talking—make that interrupting—each time Nick started a conversation. It struck me as funny, but obviously Nick's patience was being challenged. The woman who had taken out her teeth and most likely came here with Joey, merely kept on eating.

Occasionally I'd look up to see Helen nibbling my uncle's ear and would have to take a gigantic sip of wine. When she'd catch me, she'd give me a dagger of a look.

Nick leaned near. "Maybe we should go elsewhere for coffee?"

The pleading tone in his voice had me agreeing.

Before the check came, Goldie took Miles's hand in his and made their "announcement."

I forced a smile on my face and caught Miles looking at me. I winked.

He excused himself to go to the men's room and nodded to me on the way.

I followed and met up with him in the hallway. "I'm really so happy for you, Miles." I gave him a peck on the cheek and a huge hug.

"Look, Pauline. I didn't want you to find out like that—"

I touched his lips. "Shh. Nothing makes me happier. And don't worry about me."

"I won't if you agree to stay. You won't get in our way, and we both love you."

How tempting. "I know, Miles, but—"

"No buts. If you don't, I won't have Goldie move in."

"You're not being fair!" To not have to move back to 171 David Drive. Was this a dream or what?

"Let's see how it goes before you make any major changes in your life. I know how you hate change, Pauline. Besides, Goldie can help you with your case."

And that way I wouldn't need Jagger as much.

I kissed his cheek. "Agreed. For a test run only."

Feeling as if I were walking on air now that I didn't have to move—yet—I headed back to the table.

Joey had Nick in some kind of death grip!

"Oh my!" I shouted and hurried to the table. I yanked on Joey's arm. "Let him go!"

"Pauline," Uncle Stash shouted, "let them alone. He's showing Nick some maneuver he learned in the war."

I'd apologized to both of them, but I know I saw competition in both of their eyes when I'd tried to pull them apart.

I couldn't bear to go for coffee with Nick in this state, so I feigned a headache and settled for calling it a night. What a night.

At the door I turned to him. "Thanks for a wonderful time."

He looked at me and laughed. "Not exactly what I had in mind."

I chuckled. "Me either. Guess that's the problem with living in such a small town."

"Yeah." He took my cheeks with both his hands.

When he kissed me, I felt my leg start to turn up again, but kept both feet planted on the ground. His lips warmed my already hot face as he gently kissed me.

Wow.

The shimmers were intensifying.

Thank goodness I could still react this way. I even toyed with the idea of asking Nick in—but decided my life was complicated enough at the moment.

Sure I missed sex, but Nick wasn't the kind of guy I wanted a one-night stand with. Or a few nights a week with. Actually, I really didn't want only sex from him.

When he said good night and turned to walk down the steps, I touched my lips and let out a long sigh.

This was way better than fantasizing.

I'd sat and held Spanky for about an hour last night, thinking and thinking. What a dinner that had turned out to be, and what the hell was I going to do about my case? I decided it wouldn't be bad having Goldie living here, and I would do my best to stay out of their way.

Since I loved them both, it wouldn't be hard.

As far as the case went, I figured I wouldn't get to see Sophie at all so I'd have to turn into Peggy tonight. With that thought, I hurried to the clinic.

The morning progressed as usual. I had three prescriptions to fill and ran over with the first one to see Hildy. Out sick again. Damn. One of the pharmacy techs had taken Hildy's job for the day so I decided at the end of the day maybe I should schmooze with her a little to see what I could find out.

"Hope Hildy's not seriously ill." I sat on the edge of the

desk and held out a prescription to her. Her name tag said MS. WATERMAN. "No big hurry on this, Ms. Waterman. I know you all must still be in shock about Leo."

"It's Kathy, and no one on God's green earth is upset about Leo."

Geez! Did she realize there was a possible murder investigation going on?

"I see. But, I mean, the possibility that he might have been . . . killed."

Stone faced, she grabbed the prescription out of my hand. "You ever met Leo?"

"Why, only briefly."

She clucked her tongue at me. "Murder or not, no one will miss him." With that she turned and walked toward the back of the pharmacy.

I leaned to the side to see her stick the prescription in front of the female pharmacist. I'd never gotten her name since she had only been here a few times, but she looked middle-aged with dark hair, heavy, dark black glasses and stood about as tall as Kathy. I decided I'd leave and tell the patient to come pick up her medication after she took care of her copay at the clinic.

Kathy headed back to her desk. I started to go, and the pharmacist walked toward the counter. I turned and there, in all her large glory, stood Sophie Banko—talking to the female pharmacist.

Fourteen

Oh, my gosh! Sophie was here at the pharmacy, when her stepson had died only yesterday. She really must need her medication badly, was my first thought. A very kind thought indeed, because my second thought was that she didn't care two hoots about Leo and was scamming some more.

Could be a golden investigating opportunity here.

I dug into the pocket of my scrubs and pulled out my glasses. Before I could stick them on and start clicking, I pressed the "record" button on my beeper camera. With having to aim my waist at the two and my glasses at the same time, I figured I could have been a damned good contortionist on the old *Ed Sullivan Show*.

A few customers on the other side of the counter got in my way, but I bent and shimmied to the side in order to get a better view. From behind, I heard a shuffling.

Oh . . . my . . . God.

Had someone caught me? What would I use for an excuse?

I swung around and clicked.

"Don't waste your film on me, Sherlock."

Standing there in a doctor's white lab coat, with short and sassy-looking blond hair, stood Jagger. Make that sexy-looking. Damn it. He wore wire-rimmed glasses and sure as hell looked taller—until I realized I was crouching. Crouching tiger, hidden Pauline. I figured if investigating didn't work out for him, he could make a bundle as a makeup artist or costume designer for films.

"What the hell? Stop sneaking up on me and scaring me, Jagger." I straightened to see Sophie walking out of the pharmacy. "Damn it. Now she's gone. Soph—"

He put his hand over my lips.

Darn! Broke another rule. I mumbled, "Fraud investigating 101."

He looked at me. "Common sense. Parking lot in ten."

I turned to see Kathy staring at us, but when I looked back to warn Jagger, he was gone.

In his wake was the scent of *male*.

I leaned against the wall—and sighed.

Then I reminded myself that Nick liked me. Nick actually asked me out. With those thoughts in mind, I hurried to collect my purse and jacket and headed out to my car.

When I looked around the parking lot, I didn't see Jagger's SUV. Well, I decided to just stay there a few minutes—and surely he'd show up. Snowflakes danced about the parking lot as the temperature took a nosedive. I opened my door after one more look around for Jagger and sat inside. Cranking the engine for a few minutes, I waited for the heat to kick in. Winters were my least favorite time of the year, since I was a "ski-school dropout," twice.

Okay, I jogged, but I'm not exactly athletic. As I pondered the idea of how painful learning to ski had been, my passenger door swung open.

The *real* Jagger jumped in. "Don't you lock your doors?"

"If I did, how would you get in?"

He grinned.

Damn it again. I knew he'd find a way. I shoved the car into drive and took off, assuming we were going to get coffee and talk. When I stopped at the light across from Dunkin Donuts and put on my signal light, Jagger looked at me.

"Go straight."

"What?"

"Straight. Then take a left onto Pleasant Street."

I knew better than to argue or tell him that I had actually been looking forward to a hot cup of coffee to warm my insides. But this was Jagger—and this was work. Coffee would have to wait. I guessed he was taking us somewhere that would have something to do with our cases.

"Who lives here?" I asked as we stopped in front of an old, white three-family house. Siding, half falling off, thumped against the house in the evening wind. An old red Chevy sat in the driveway, with one tire looking very much in need of air.

Jagger walked toward the front door.

Not mentioning that he had ignored my question, I hurried behind. When he hit the doorbell to #3, I looked at the name on the mail slot.

Jones. H. Jones.

"Hildy?" I asked as the door swung open to reveal a pathetic-looking Hildy dressed in ripped gray jogging pants, wrapped in an old green plaid blanket and sans jewelry. My God, she looked naked. "Hildy, hi."

She was barely able to take her eyes off of Jagger. Poor

girl. Even with illness fixing her eyes in a glassy stare, she still noticed him. "Pauline?"

"Hi. Yeah." I coughed a few times, not sure what the hell to say.

Jagger held out his hand. "I'm Pauline's friend, Jake. Nice to meet you. She asked me to bring her here to see if you were feeling all right. I believe she said you'd missed work a few days."

Hildy took his hand and shook it, all the while staring at him—which I did too.

Jake?

Okay, I decided I better go along with the ruse or else we'd never find out any info about Leo—and Hildy's involvement.

Now I wondered if she really looked sick. Hard to tell, even for me.

"Why, yes, Hildy. Jag . . . Jake brought me here to see how you are. Need anything? Chicken soup?"

Jagger nudged me in the side.

"What?" I whispered as Hildy started to blow her nose. "Chicken soup is a surefire cure for the common cold."

Hildy stuffed her used tissue in the pocket of her pants. "How'd you know where I lived, Pauline?"

Good question. "Oh . . . I . . . well . . . you know—"

Jagger glared at me. "One of the pharmacy techs told her."

That was so damn easy for him, and Hildy bought it.

"I'd ask you up, but, well, my place isn't very nice."

"At least it is warmer than out here," Jagger said, smiling.

Before I knew it, and I'm sure before Hildy could protest, we found ourselves sitting in her pathetic living room. Being on the third floor, the heat congealed in the tiny rooms, making me feel as if I'd suffocate. Old pipes clanked, the wind howled through window cracks, and Hildy kept sniffling and sneezing.

I knew I'd end up with a cold, if she really had one. Hard to tell if it was real or not, since sometimes the sneezing sounded fake.

"So, how do you feel?" Sure the question was stupid, since she looked as if the cat had not even wanted to drag her in, but I'd asked anyway.

Again Jagger's head-shaking thing. Once. I was ready for two though.

I wanted to smack him, but instead turned to Hildy. "Do you need anything?"

"Naw. My stomach couldn't handle it."

Stomach. I thought she had a cold. "So, nothing you need?"

She chuckled, a pathetic, cold-camouflaged chuckle. Poor thing.

"Sick pay would be nice."

"You don't get paid when you are out sick?"

"Not yet. I haven't worked at the pharmacy long enough, and Leo is such a shit he wouldn't bend the rules for me."

"Was," I said nonchalantly.

Hildy gave me an odd look. "What?"

Jagger looked about ready to interrupt, but I said, "Was. You meant Leo *was* such a shit."

"No, he still is a shit," she said amid sneezes.

Jagger poked me in the side.

"Ouch!" I turned to him, but he silenced me with a look. He and my mother were pips with those eyes of theirs.

He looked around the room, then at Hildy. "You don't get a daily paper, do you?"

"Excuse me? I can just about afford electricity."

"I didn't mean anything by it." He shifted in his seat, causing his leg to brush my thigh.

Whoa, boy.

Nick asked me out. Nick asked me out. Nick *asked* me out.

"What the hell are you talking about?" I said, getting annoyed, partly 'cause of my body's damned reaction to a little leg brushing.

"What I meant was, you haven't seen the newspaper today or read the obituaries." He didn't even look at me.

Fine.

Hildy said, "Never read them. Too many of my customers end up there eventually."

"Hildy," Jagger said. "Leo ended up there."

I thought she looked pale when she'd first opened the door, but what little color was there now drained out. Hildy really looked shocked. Good. Not only didn't she know about Leo's death, she hadn't had anything to do with it.

As I leaned back to relax, Hildy excused herself to go find a new tissue.

Jagger watched her go, took his handkerchief, and then opened the drawer to the coffee table in front of us.

I grabbed his hand. "What the hell are you doing?"

He looked at me.

I let go, but waited for an answer.

"Investigating, Sherlock. The reason we came here? Investigating?"

"For what? She said she didn't even know Leo was dead."

Head shaking, again. "And you think a *killer* wouldn't *lie*?"

"No, but—" Flustered, I shook my hand in the air. "But, Hildy said."

Jagger reached over, took a tissue from Hildy's end table and lifted a prescription bottle out of the drawer. "Digitalis. What's it for?"

"Heart medication."

"Think Hildy might be a little too young for heart problems?"

"Of course. She's only in her late teens, although it isn't impossible. Here," I said, grabbing the bottle with Jagger's tissue (hey, he taught me well). "Let me see what that really is."

The top of the prescription label, where the name of the patient would be, had been torn off. I opened the bottle. Inside sat little white pills. Digoxin, I knew from my prior nursing. This medication was used to strengthen the pumping of the heart, and Hildy didn't appear to have any cardiac problems. I never heard her sound short of breath or have poor coloring, lips that looked bluish instead of pink or any of the symptoms of congestive heart failure. And this dose seemed a bit much for someone of Hildy's size too.

I closed the bottle before spilling any when the horrific thought hit me that these pills could be crushed, dissolved and hidden in Leo's coffee while he'd been at work.

Otherwise, what the heck would they be doing here?

She could have easily stolen them and torn off the real patient's name.

"Ah choo!"

Jagger grabbed the handkerchief and bottle faster than Hildy could sneeze again. Before she stepped through the door, he had everything back in order.

Me, I sat there staring at my hand that he'd torn the bottle from, marveling at his skills.

Would I ever be such a good investigator?

I looked up and smiled at Hildy. "You sound awful. Sure you don't need anything?"

She sat down and looked at Jagger. "What happened to Leo? Car accident?"

He told her as much as anyone who read the newspaper obits would find out. Good thinking, Jagger.

She looked directly at me. "No one has ever cared enough about me to come check on me."

I smiled at her. "Call the clinic if you need me." I felt horrible not wanting to give her my home phone number.

We then excused ourselves and left. Once outside, I took a deep breath of welcome cold air and looked at Jagger.

"You think she did it."

"My job isn't to think, Sherlock. It's to investigate."

"Investigate insurance fraud or *murder*?"

Silence.

"Fine. Then tell me who the hell you work for." I demanded as he walked to the passenger side and got in. *Nick always opens my door*, I thought, as I got in my side, but decided not to share that info with a silent Jagger.

I turned the key, shoved the transmission into reverse and pulled out. On the way back to the office, I asked, "Do you think she did it though?"

"Not my job or yours to think about that, Sherlock."

"I know. Investigating 101. But give me your gut impression, Jagger."

"I don't speculate."

By now I'd turned into the parking lot, but still didn't see his SUV.

He pointed to the western side of the building, where only physicians parked. I turned there and sure enough, there sat his Suburban complete with a doc's parking sticker. The guy never ceased to amaze me. He opened the door as soon as I stopped.

"Wait, Jagger. Please. Do you think she did it?"

He held the door for a few seconds. "Don't get personally involved, Sherlock. Go home. Get dressed and have a good time with Nick."

My heart sank.

Partly because his not answering could be interpreted as a yes. Partly because he nailed me on getting involved and caring about Hildy. And partly because I was going out with Nick.

When I opened the door of my condo, I gasped and started to turn around. Surely I had the wrong place. Miles's stark white living room had been invaded by jungle mania. Palm trees danced in the breeze of the opened door. The couch had a zebra throw the size of my mother's house on it. And the chairs had all been replaced with leopard and tiger covered recliners.

Spanky barked.

I looked at the number on the door, nodded and went inside.

"Hello, Suga!" Goldie pranced out from the kitchen, holding Spanky in his arms. The little dog nuzzled against Goldie's arm, and why not? Certainly gold, sparkly, silk Kimono robes were pretty damn comfortable to rub against.

Better than my scratchy wool one.

He also had on gold flip-flops made of leather. I wondered where Goldie shopped. Had to be either the Internet or a West Hartford boutique.

At first I felt like a visitor, but as soon as Goldie put Spanky down and hugged me I knew I was home.

He'd fixed me a cup of hot tea, knowing, as Miles always did, that I needed it when stressed. It was either the tea or my favorite Budweiser, but with the cold weather, I went with the tea.

Over his teacup, he said, "So, tell me, Suga. What's wrong?"

I filled him in on our trip to Hildy's. "I really don't want her to be involved, Gold. I like her, and my gut instinct says she's innocent."

But was Jagger's gut more experienced and *correct*?

It looked bad having the name label torn off the digoxin. And, her switching illnesses midstream from respiratory to stomach didn't look good either. Of course, to be fair, she could have had the flu and both kinds of symptoms. But she did seem to hate Leo. Maybe she found out about the Viagra and threatened to call the cops. Wait. Then he'd have killed *her*. No, maybe she was in on the fraud and wanted more. Got greedy. And Leo cut her . . . I had to stop this mental rambling when I didn't believe any of it.

Goldie and I figured the cops would investigate Hildy soon enough. Me, I had to get back to my case. Fabio had called today and left a message on my recorder.

"Look, newbie, I need something. Something soon if you want to get paid."

Short and to the point.

"I have a date with Nick tonight, but first I have to dress up as Peggy, Gold. Bingo's at eight. I . . . as Pauline am meeting him at nine thirty. Not much time to clean up. Go easy on the glue."

He touched my arm. "You're going to be exhausted."

I already was.

But I persisted because Pauline Sokol was not a quitter. Sure I didn't like change—or make that didn't used to like change, but I'd been learning to adjust lately.

I reminded myself of this as Goldie did the final touch of makeup to "Peggy." I was looking so very real with this getup, I even had myself convinced. Before Goldie had moved here, Mrs. Honeysuckle had cleaned out her closet as a "going away" present for him. I now had a complete over-seventy wardrobe and two pairs of shoes. One black. One brown. Both so damn comfortable I wished they were in style for the real me. Also she had thrown in an old purse. Not the one Brinks couldn't get into, but a huge one much like Sophie's. Thank you, Mrs. Honeysuckle.

After a kiss to Goldie, Spanky and Miles, who'd returned home with three lobsters so we could celebrate our first day together, they graciously accepted my decline. Then I headed out to my car, careful to slow my pace when dressed like this.

On the way to Bingo, I kept reminding myself that I needed something, some picture, some film that I could turn over to Fabio to placate him a bit longer. I had no idea this case would take so long—or get so complicated—although I should have.

Nothing in my life had ever gone easily.

Don't get my mother started on her twenty-nine hours of labor to produce only one baby, me. She always had said for all that pain, she should have at least earned triplets.

I parked in the lot and took my "purse" in hand. The

other night I'd stopped at the local Wal-Mart and gotten some Bingo equipment. Hey, at least I'd fit in.

I checked my bag to make sure I had my beeper and glasses. In this getup, I certainly couldn't wear the beeper on my belt. What on earth reason would I give some snooping senior? And they did snoop, so I fit right in.

The card lady was walking around selling like crazy. Across the room, at their usual table, sat my usual group. Sophie was there as big as day. Okay, a bit bigger, but I was still in my "being kind" mood.

Imagine her showing up when Leo's body wasn't even cold.

Good for me. Not good for Sophie's reputation.

I bought my two cards on the way to the table before Joey could. I didn't want to owe him anything, and I didn't mean monetary-wise here. The guy looked as if *he* didn't need the Viagra that so many of the others coveted—and possibly died for.

"Hi, everyone," I said as I pulled out my chair. I purposely sat across from Joey, who had jumped up and was headed my way. "I'm fine. Thanks anyway." I plopped down and wondered if I should offer my condolences to Sophie. I think dementia came along with this outfit, because for the life of me, I couldn't think if Peggy was supposed to know that Sophie was Leo's stepmother.

I figured it'd be better to keep my mouth shut and look callous than be found out.

I set my purse down next to Sophie's.

Dementia!

Thank you, Saint Theresa. The idea had popped into my head like some divine intervention. Had to, since I still wasn't that good at thinking of ways to investigate on my own. Without Jagger or Goldie's input, I thought I had come up with a doozie. Before I set my plan into motion though, I reached down and took my glasses and beeper out of my purse and tucked them into my pockets. Good thing Mrs. Honeysuckle liked pockets.

The game had started. Eight minutes later (since I had little time to waste), I yelled, "Bingo!"

Everyone at the table cheered. After all, this was my first win.

When I had to call out my numbers, Sophie leaned over. "You don't have B-3 or B-4, Peggy. You have 34. N-34. Your mind must be going."

Bingo, I thought. *Bingo, my dear Sophie.*

I hoped that I blushed appropriately when I waved my hand in the air. "Sorry. So sorry. You are right, Sophie. My mind isn't what it used to be."

Sophie harrumphed.

Helen ignored me.

My uncles Walt and Stash looked concerned and genuinely sorry for me. Thanks, Uncles.

Joey the Wooer gave me an odd look. Not being an expert on reading people, I wasn't sure what it meant. But for my money, I would have guessed suspicion. Did Joey think that I had cheated?

That hurt although it shouldn't have. I merely kept my face down and continued on with the game, calling only one more "false" Bingo.

"Oh dear, oh dear," I said at the coffee break. "I don't know where my mind went tonight. I seem to have been having a few days like this lately." I hated lying to such a nice group of seniors—well, nice except for Sophie and Helen, whom I didn't like out of principle.

Uncle Walt said, "Now don't worry, Peggy. A visit to your family doctor should help. I don't hesitate to go for whatever ails me."

I smiled at him since it seemed appropriate and also since I knew how true that was. Then I bent to get my purse—and took Sophie's instead.

I shuffled to the ladies' room at the fastest speed a woman my age should move, and went inside. Two ladies were at the sink. Damn it. But, then again, how would they know the purse wasn't mine? Other than my strap being beige and Sophie's a honey color, the bags looked similar enough for a "confused" Peggy to take by mistake.

I opened the door to a stall and slipped inside. Once I had my glasses on, I pulled out item after item. Bingo! I got pictures of two prescriptions with men's names on them. The bottle of Viagra wasn't there, but I did find a list of numbers. I took a picture and a little bit of film. You go, Pauline!

In my haste, I dropped my beeper. It slid out from under the door!

"Shit," I mumbled and shoved everything back inside. When I opened the door, there stood Sophie—holding out my purse as if it was a snake.

Fifteen

Oh, boy. Sophie didn't look too forgiving, even to a confused old lady like myself as she picked my beeper up from the floor. She wiggled the beeper at me a few times. "What the hell is this?"

Before I could think of a lie, she grabbed her purse from my hands and shoved mine and the beeper at me.

"Oh!" I pretended to stumble.

One of the other ladies reached out. "Take it easy, Sophie. Peggy's fragile." She patted my hand, which didn't look as old as it should. "You all right, honey?"

I wiped at my dry brow. "I'm . . . oh, my, I'm getting so confused." I tried to force a tear out but apparently all the makeup and Superglue had clogged my tear ducts. Oh, well, a few moans and shake of my head still made me look "fragile."

"Why did you take my purse?" Sophie said, but kept her hands to herself.

Hmm. Covering up something, Soph?

I held my purse to my chest. "Oh, my gosh. I . . . I don't know. I didn't even open it, Sophie. They look alike." I turned to the woman by the sink. "Don't they?"

She nodded very sympathetically.

Maybe I should be a movie star. I sighed very loudly and as pathetically as I could. "See. They look alike." I waved mine toward her. "I didn't do it on purpose."

Sophie clucked her tongue at me. "All right. All right. Calm down before you stroke out." With that she hung her purse over her shoulder and went out the door.

As I watched her go, I touched the cameras in my pocket—and hoped to hell that I had *something* to give Fabio.

"Who the hell is this broad in the picture?" Fabio asked not all too politely the next morning.

He pointed at the female pharmacist, who almost looked familiar, but I guessed that was because I had, in fact, seen her a few times. "She's a pharmacist there. A part-time one. Guess she's working more since Leo's death."

I shuddered.

After coming from a profession where I tried to prevent death, it was still hard to deal with murders. Possible murders. Or actual murders.

I looked at Fabio, who was lighting up a used cigar that he'd fetched out of the over-full ashtray on his desk.

I coughed.

He ignored it. "What the fuck are these numbers on this list?"

I explained my theory (okay, Jagger's theory) that they were stolen insurance numbers. This lying thing was getting easier.

Fabio puffed and glared at me. "There are no names showing on these lists."

I was hoping he wouldn't notice. When I'd taken the

film to get developed last night after my wonderful but short date with Nick, I was aware of that fact. But, I still came here today and gave the lists and the pictures to him—since I had nothing else. At least he should realize that I *was* working.

My video was of Billy and Leo chatting, but not within earshot, so it was more a silent film. Damn it.

Fabio took a long drag on his cigar.

I stifled my cough, not wanting to upset him anymore.

"Look, newbie, this doesn't prove shit. We need proof that Banko is committing fraud. Fraud that costs me—and you, doll. Costs you too." With that he waved me away. "I want something by next week," he said as I scurried out the door but still heard him say, "Unless you don't need the money."

I leaned against the wall. Today was Friday. I needed to find out something this last shift of the workweek. I had the weekend, but what could I do? The clinic was closed on the weekend. The pharmacy too. Shit. Now what? I decided I needed to talk to someone so I peeked into the reception desk window.

Adele sat with her earphones on. I'd learned my lesson about sneaking up on an ex-con when she'd tipped over that one time. So, I stood here, waving my hands and hoping she would see me from the corner of her eye.

After several minutes, my arms about to drop from exhaustion, Adele looked up. She waved to me and kept typing.

Great.

Guess it wasn't meant to be. I went out the door and looked at my watch. I had a half hour to get to the clinic. After I stopped for coffee, I headed toward the clinic, thinking I could get there a few minutes early to see if there was any work I could do, since I'd been late . . . a few times.

When I parked and went inside the building, the hallway was empty. The patients weren't allowed in yet, so there were a few sitting on benches outside. The door to the pharmacy was open. Maybe I could pass through there.

Kathy was at the counter. "We're not open yet. What do you want?" She didn't even look up.

"I was just passing through, Kathy."

She looked up. "This isn't a walkway. Go through the clinic door."

Behind her I noticed a shadow on the wall. It moved and before I could turn to go, the female pharmacist poked her head out from behind the shelf. "Something wrong, Kathy?"

Damn. She sounded like a movie star instead of a pharmacist. Even had kind of a French accent. Wow. I envied women with those deep, sultry, scratchy kinds of voices. The ones that made men take notice. I soothed myself by thinking her voice came from smoking and my higher pitch was healthier.

"Nothing's wrong," Kathy said.

I'd be back, I thought as I went into the clinic the correct way.

The morning went along without incident, although I half expected each male patient to be Jagger in disguise. He seemed due to show up. Besides, neither of us was getting anything done about our cases since Leo's death threw a wrench into our work.

I wondered if Leo's funeral was today, but then thought the body might not be released to the family yet if the investigation was ongoing. Guess no one jumped the gun on the police and cremated Leo, the way they had with Mr. W.

When Dr. Handy gave Mrs. Tennenbaum a prescription for her psoriasis, I thought maybe I could go meet the female pharmacist and get it filled.

"I'll take this over to the clinic for you, ma'am," I said. The poor woman was a mass of cracks, wrinkles and rashes anyway.

She sat there scratching. "Thanks. I'll be in the waiting room if you don't mind. I don't like folks to see me like this." She put on her woolen coat although the clinic was kept quite warm since patients often had to disrobe.

"No problem. It may take a few minutes." I looked at my watch. Lunchtime. I had to hurry.

Kathy turned toward me when I opened the back door and came into the pharmacy. "Lost again?"

I bit my tongue. I might need her help someday, so I chuckled. "Actually, I have a prescription that needs to be filled before lunchtime."

She held her hand out.

I gave it to her and sat down.

Kathy looked at me. "Tell your patient we're swamped and to come get it later."

Damn! "I could do that, but, Kath, the poor woman is in such discomfort. She is also hiding her condition under a very heavy, very hot coat. Poor, poor thing." I leaned over and gave her my "empathetic" look.

"Well, with one pharmacist short, it will take a while."

"I thought that woman was working more hours. The female pharmacist." I pointed.

Kathy looked around. "Lois Meyers is a pharmacy tech."

Damn.

"But she can help. I'll give this to her. With Leo gone, I guess Lois will be around a lot more." She groaned.

I leaned in closer, taking Kathy into my confidence, and hoping like hell that she'd do the same. "Doesn't sound as if Lois is too popular."

Kathy stiffened. "No. I didn't mean that. I didn't mean anything." She pushed me away. "Everyone is so upset since Leo died." With that she scurried off.

I stood there wondering why she hadn't said, "Everyone is so upset *that* Leo died." Seemed more appropriate—unless no one really was upset that he died. When I first met Kathy, *she* wasn't.

I knew Hildy wasn't. I couldn't get over her cold, un-emotional reaction when Jagger had told her the news. And I really hated that, since it didn't look too good for Hildy. I hoped to hell my gut was more accurate on this account than Jagger's.

I couldn't let myself think about him now. So, while I waited for the psoriasis prescription to be filled, I thought about Nick. It really didn't take too much effort. Our late date last night had turned out pretty darn good. Since I was so exhausted, we had had a bottle of wine and shared a pizza at an Italian place over in Hartford. Nick liked egg-plant on his, just like I did.

Cute.

I thought we did make a cute couple. When the night was over, he took me home and . . . the kiss. It kept getting better as the novelty wore off. Nick's kisses were starting to cause shimmers to turn to waves. Not tsunami-quality yet, but at least decent surfing ones.

Nick liked me.

I smiled.

"What's so funny?"

That voice. Jagger's voice. I turned around to see the "doctor" from yesterday.

My hormones stood at attention.

Then, with the speed of light I ordered them "at ease," and said, "I was just thinking of my date with Nick."

A pause.

Good.

Within seconds, Jagger said, "That good? Wonderful. So, what about your case?"

That was it? Well, truthfully I wasn't that surprised. I mean, what did I really expect? Jagger to fly into a jealous rage?

"Nothing too new. The part-time pharmacy tech, Lois Meyers, is working more. Haven't met her yet, but Kathy didn't seem too thrilled with her. She tried to cover up that fact."

"I'm not even going to ask how you know all that, Sherlock. I'll trust your observational skills this time."

I felt my chest poof up like a prize-winning peacock's. "Thanks. You find out anything more?"

"The fraud hasn't stopped with Leo's death."

"You mean because Sophie was back here so soon after his death?"

"Atta girl." He turned to walk away as Kathy came toward us.

"Here you go, Pauline. Er . . . Lois said next time, you don't get preferential treatment. They're too busy."

Bitch. "Oh, no problem." I looked behind her to see Lois staring at me. What did I do? Then again, this place was in a mess with Leo gone, so I decided to continue my "kind" streak and give Lois the benefit of the doubt. She probably didn't want to be here so much lately.

I waved to her.

She ignored me.

I hurried the medication over to Mrs. Tennenbaum, who kept thanking me over and over until I walked her to the front door. The poor woman was sweating and surely that wasn't good for her condition.

When I got back, I looked around for Jagger. No one was left except the bubble-gum-snapping receptionist. After a quick "have a nice weekend," I was out the door.

The ride home gave me time to think. First I thought of a nice, long, hot shower. Nick had business in New York City, so no date tonight. I was actually glad. Being two people forty years apart was getting to me, and I really needed to relax.

The second thing I thought of was Hildy. It worried me that she might be involved. I wondered about going to her house, but figured Jagger would have my head.

Beep. Beep.

I reached into my purse and yanked out my cell phone. "Hello."

"Be ready at eleven. Wear dark clothes and bring gloves."

The caller ID had been blocked, but I recognized the voice.

"How do you know I'm not busy tonight?"

"Nick's out of town. If it makes you feel any better, consider this a date."

My hands were still shaking when I pulled into the condo parking lot.

A date?

Jagger at eleven.

Stay tuned.

* * *

I dug deeper into my closet to find the sexiest black outfit that would seem appropriate. I knew Jagger was taking me on some surveillance mission, but damn, I wanted to look good. The only things I had were black stretchy leggings and a black turtleneck. With my pale skin, I looked like a mime.

Then I realized what roommates were for.

When eleven rolled around, I stood on the front porch in the dark until Jagger pulled in. I hurried to his SUV, opened the door and got in.

"Hi."

He nodded.

I wished I could see better in the dark because I felt pretty darn sexy in Goldie's black leather jacket with the fitted waist. Although he was much bigger than myself, it still looked good, since I went with the leggings. I patted my pockets to make sure I had my beeper and glasses. Because I knew my blonde hair would stand out like a searchlight, Goldie had fixed me up with one of his turbans.

I always marveled at how good he looked in them. The black one I had on now had tiny black gems along the front. Under Goldie's insistence, I left several strands of my hair hanging out on the sides and as bangs.

It was true what they said about clothes making the man, because this outfit made me feel so damn good. And so damn sexy. I looked over to see Jagger since he hadn't pulled out of the parking space yet.

"Something wrong?"

It wasn't like Jagger to not speak his mind, so I figured he didn't have anything to say. He leaned over, touched my hair and said, "Tuck it all in."

Speechless, I could still feel his fingers on my hair, although I knew hair strands didn't have any feelings. I did as he said, but I knew in my heart that Jagger thought I looked good.

No, looked sexy.

He pulled into the Dunkin Donuts lot and drove up to the window.

"May I help you?" said a disembodied female voice.

"Two coffees. Black."

"Please pull up."

"Black? And not decaf. I'll be up all night, Jagger."

He looked at me. "That's right, Sherlock. That's the idea."

He handed me the coffee. I looked at him over my cup and took a little sip.

Black coffee is bitter. For the life of me, I couldn't see how anyone could enjoy it. Jagger had insisted I should enjoy the true flavor of the beans, but I insisted a half cup of cream and three sugars would taste a hell of a lot better. Like melted coffee ice cream.

As I busied my mind with the stupid coffee, I looked to see that we had pulled up past Mr. Wisnowski's house and stopped on the next corner.

Oh, boy.

My heart started pounding so loudly, I wanted to blame it on the caffeine, but knew better. Knew Jagger and how he worked. Knew the amount of caffeine in a little cup like this wasn't enough to cause an arrhythmia in my heart, and knew . . .

We were going to break in.

Sixteen

Jagger took my coffee cup away. As well he should, I thought, as I'd been watching the liquid splash about in my shaking grip.

"Look, Sherlock, we've never been here. You got that?"

I wanted to say we had, in fact, been there before, but he wouldn't let me in to look around once I'd sprawled out on Mr. Wisnowski's floor. "Okay. We've never been here. Now can we go?"

He shook his head.

"I got it. I can't tell anyone, not even Goldie or Miles that we've been here."

"Or Nick."

I nodded. "Look, I'm all for investigating medical insurance fraud, but as much as I want to solve my case, breaking and entering isn't in my job description."

He dangled a key in front of me.

Semantics.

Knowing it was Mr. W's, I opened my side door ever so gingerly and stepped out. Next door, the lights were on in Sophie's upstairs room. I figured that it had to be her bedroom since I'd already "toured" this house and remembered the floor plan. I sure didn't need Sophie looking out the window and seeing me.

Jagger looked around and walked up the sidewalk toward the back of the house. I followed close behind, biting my lips until I tasted blood. Okay, it was only saliva, but with my insides in a panic, I could have gnawed them down until they bled. It was either that or say something stupid to Jagger.

Thank goodness the moon was full tonight. No doubt Jagger had figured that into his plans. He moved around as if it didn't bother him in the least—and nothing frightened Jagger.

I felt a comforting warmth at the thought.

I really did feel safe with him, but hoped I didn't do something to ruin this night. I had been on surveillance with him before, but always on the outside looking in. As I walked into Mr. Wisnowski's kitchen and inhaled the dampness of a closed house in a New England winter, I now knew how it felt to be on the inside with Jagger.

For a second, I stood and watched him. He'd already put on his gloves outside, so I stuck my hands into my pockets and grabbed mine.

When I pulled them out, he looked at me.

"What?"

"Invest in some thin, black gloves." With that he turned and walked out of the kitchen.

I looked down at the chartreuse wool gloves my sister Mary had given me for Christmas four years ago and made a mental note to buy a new pair for work, although I could dispute the contention that chartreuse would leave prints. They were still damp from a snowball fight I'd had with Goldie and Miles the other day. Smelled like wet neon sheep.

Walking as silently as I could, I followed Jagger into the living room. "This is so creepy," I whispered.

He looked at me. In the dim light from the moon's reflection, I could see his smile. "What's the matter, Sherlock? Afraid of ghosts?"

I shuddered. Damn him. I hadn't even *thought* of ghosts until then. "No. That's ridiculous—"

Squeak.

I froze.

Jagger motioned for me to stay put. I didn't argue, but when he started to walk out of the room, my feet had other things on their minds. "Jaaaaaagger," I whispered and stepped forward. Little baby steps until I could see his shadow in the kitchen.

Any second now I knew the ghost of poor Mr. Wisnowski was going to come flying at us, accusing us of breaking into his house.

A light flew past the window.

A ghost!

"Jaaaaaagger!"

Suddenly he was in front of me. "Nice staying put, Sherlock. And keep it the hell quiet."

"Whaaat . . . was—"

He put his arm around my shoulder. "Relax. Mice have taken up residence in the place."

Another light flew by the window. I readied to yell "incoming!" but realized it was a car's headlights as it passed by. "Little mice make noise like that?"

"It wasn't exactly a screeching banshee, Sherlock. A few mice decided to try and get through the old cat door in the kitchen. Guess the door could use some WD-40." He chuckled, squeezed me tighter, and then let go.

I did *not* tell him that I thought I had seen the ghost of

Mr. W. Experience told me info like that should be kept to myself where Jagger was concerned.

Jagger opened drawers and looked behind every picture, knickknack and even under the braided red throw rugs. I joined in, not certain what I was looking for. I figured if it was medically related, I'd give a holler.

Actually we kept our voices to a soft whisper. His sounded sexy. Mine sounded hoarse, like a post-op tonsillectomy patient's. When we got to the bathroom, he opened the medicine cabinet and shined his flashlight at the contents.

It appeared as if nothing had been disturbed since Mr. Wisnowski's death. I wondered if he didn't have any family other than Sophie to come clean out the place. And she didn't seem all to eager to do any kind of physical labor. But when Jagger took several prescription bottles off the shelf, I was glad the place had been left "as is."

With my camera glasses in hand, I hoped I could get a huge leap in my case.

Fat chance.

"They all look legit for a man in his eighties. Heart meds, blood pressure meds. All with his name on them," I continued in my hoarse tone, wishing I could sound more like Lois the pharmacy tech.

Jagger put them back and closed the door. He stood there for a few seconds, and I assumed he was thinking. I said, "We need to think like an old man."

Even in the dim lighting I could see Jagger's eyebrows rise. "What?"

Damn. He thought I was crazy. "What I mean is, we need to think where an old man would hide something. My Uncle Walt has a secret drawer in his dresser where he keeps money."

"Thanks for sharing that info. Now if Walt gets robbed, I'll be the number-one suspect." He ran his gloved hand through his hair.

I sighed, and then turned it feebly into a cough.

"You all right?"

"Um." I couldn't talk because it had dawned on me that I was in this house, it was the middle of the night—and most important, I was alone with Jagger.

Nick likes me. Nick likes me. "Nick likes me."

Jagger turned. "So I figured, since he asked you out."

Oh . . . my . . . God.

The words had somehow snuck out of my lips in the hoarse tone, making me feel like a fool. It was such a dumb thing to say. Jagger now turned away, and I figured that was so I could melt into a puddle of embarrassment.

But, I pulled myself taller—well, as tall as I could with him towering several inches above me. "My mind wandered. I was . . . thinking of Nick." I coughed. "What next?" Good. That had come out convincingly nonchalant. I really was getting to be a better actress/liar.

Jagger motioned for me to follow. Once in the hallway he asked, "Okay, Sherlock. Where would you hide something if you were eighty years old?"

For a second, I had a flash of Peggy. Peggy would know where old Mr. W. would hide something even if only in her seventies. Then, fearful of becoming schizophrenic, I told myself that I really wasn't Peggy. Or, in fact, that I really was Peggy. To keep my sanity, I decided to think more like my Uncle Walt since I knew him so well. "Okay. Like I said, Uncle Walt has that secret drawer. Then there was the time he hid his hothouse tomatoes in his jacket pocket."

Jagger glared at me.

"What? They were wrapped in a napkin."

"So you think we should look in all the jacket pockets of Mr. Wisnowski's suits?"

I started to shake my head, then stopped. "Yes. Yes, I do."

Jagger paused, then moved aside, sweeping his hand in the air. "After you."

I led him up to the master bedroom and didn't tell him how I knew where it was so easily. Actually, I'd never made it up here, letting Goldie come while I snooped downstairs.

When I opened the door, Jagger aimed the light inside. It was truly eerie now. The bed had been made up as if no one had ever lived there, but beneath, I could see a pair of bedroom slippers. Old Mr. Wisnowski's bedroom slippers.

A tear trickled down my cheek. Maybe this job really wasn't for me.

I sniffled and tried to disguise it as another cough.

Jagger turned to me. Even in the dim light I could see concern in his eyes. "Did you know him?"

"Mr. Wisnowski?"

He nodded.

"I think I met him at a party with Uncle Walt and Uncle Stash. But no, I really didn't know him."

Suddenly I felt Jagger step closer. His arms were around me before I could sniffle again. "You can't let all this get to you, Sherlock. You'll never make it if you do."

He held me a few seconds.

It felt nice, comforting, and this time not in a sexual way. I knew he was right, but it was so damn hard. So damn hard not to let personal feelings, emotions get in the way. Seeing those "old man" bedroom slippers made me think of my uncles. Especially Uncle Walt, whom I'd always had a special place in my heart for, since I'd grown up with him living in our house.

"I know," I mumbled. Then I eased free. "Thanks. It just reminded me too much of my uncles. Do you think, Jagger, that my Uncle Walt's life could be in jeopardy?"

"Whoa. Where'd that come from?"

I told him about the conversation Uncle Walt and I had had about sex and the senior citizens. If I thought I was embarrassed talking to my uncle about that, right now I was mortified beyond belief.

Jagger, however, kept his oh-so-cool exterior and listened without comment. "Gut instinct tells me this whole thing is tied together somehow. If your uncle and Mr. Wisnowski were buying the Viagra from the same person— most likely Leo—then we need to keep an eye on your uncle too. And see who replaces Leo."

I couldn't speak. I stood there in the dark and felt my insides sink to knee level. Then, with Jagger looking at me and somehow building my confidence, I said, "Let's get going then."

We looked in all of Mr. Wisnowski's jacket pockets and pants too. Other than old receipts and more "love notes" from Helen, we came up blank. I started to fish around in the closet. Where else would an elderly person hide things?

As if old Mr. W's ghost had tapped me on the back, I swung around to see his very neat shelf of shoeboxes. Each box was labeled with things like WINTER BLACK, SUMMER BEIGE and SPRING TENNIS SHOES. I had to smile. My *Babci* had done the same thing. Then I noticed one box marked SHOES. Odd. In what season did Mr. Wisnowski wear them?

I reached up and took the box down.

"Find something?"

What I found was Jagger's breath on my neck. Shit. I could barely open the box, but managed, along with, "I'm not sure." I explained the labeling system and then opened the box.

Five prescription bottles sat there.

I lifted each one. Viagra. Viagra. All were prescriptions of Viagra. One in Mr. Wisnowski's name, the others all in different names, filled by Leo Pasinski.

"Goddamn," Jagger said. "No one needs that much of a boost."

I looked at him and was speechless, then shook my brain until I was coherent again. "These must be the ones he was using to either trade or sell to the other men."

Jagger was already taking pictures of them. His camera, this time, was a tiny ring on his left hand.

I followed suit with my camera/glasses, although this really wasn't my case. Still, if my Uncle Walt's life could be in jeopardy, I wasn't taking any chances. I moved the bottles to the side to show their labels. Beneath were several photographs.

Helen, smiling seductively as if she were trying to make Mr. Wisnowski horny. The other pictures were of Sophie and Leo. Family pictures. Odd that he kept them with his Viagra, but maybe this little box was filled with the "treasures" only an eighty-year-old could appreciate.

"Open the bottles to make sure that's what they are," Jagger said.

Why didn't I think of that? With my damp, woolly gloves, I managed to pour out a few into my palm. Blue pills. "Yep. They are the real things."

Bang. Bang.

We both froze. Jagger only for a second, me almost permanently. We finished taking pictures, shoved the pills back and returned the box to the shelf as if never touched.

The noise sounded way too loud for those little mice to be making. Jagger shut off his flashlight and took me by the hand. I fumbled in the dark, trying to remember what was in the room so I wouldn't bump into it. I'd be a mass of purple bruises tomorrow after knocking into so much furniture.

By the glow of the moon, we made it to the kitchen. Sophie's front porch light was on now. I motioned to Jagger, who looked as if he noticed too. With my hand in his, we made it out the backdoor, stopping only long enough for him to shut and lock it, and to stuff the key back under the mat.

I stood silently—partly because I knew I had to be quiet and partly because I couldn't believe how smoothly he had maneuvered around without making even the slightest sound. The mice were thunderous compared with Jagger.

We were outside when we heard footsteps along Mr. Wisnowski's driveway.

"Who's out there?"

I recognized Sophie's voice. She shined a flashlight toward the back porch. It would have caught us in its beams if we headed out the way we'd come in. Before I knew it, Jagger had yanked me toward the back of the yard. As far as I could remember, there was only the cemetery-type bench and Mr. Wisnowski's old shed.

The shed it was.

Thank goodness it was unlocked.

With the skill of a surgeon, Jagger opened the door silently and pushed me inside.

"Who is there?" Sophie shouted.

My hand flew to my face as Jagger pushed me further in. Sophie's light flashed toward us.

A gasp flew out of my mouth.

Just as fast as Jagger's did, up flew my other hand, which stifled any more gasps.

Suddenly I felt something fall off my wooly chartreuse glove and end up in my mouth.

I coughed and prayed it wasn't some bug.

I pushed Jagger's hand away. Whatever it was slid down my throat!

I looked down. Jagger seemed to realize something was wrong. He leaned near. "What the hell?"

In my softest voice I said, "Something was stuck to my glove and went into my mouth. Maybe a bug."

"There aren't any bugs in the winter time, Sherlock. Relax." He took my hand and held it out. Then he aimed his flashlight on it.

A blue pill was stuck there, nestled into the wool.

"What the hell?" he said.

As soon as he said it, Sophie's light shone under the door. "Stupid yard boy. Can't even lock up right after shoveling. I'll get him in the morning."

With that she clicked some kind of lock on the other side of the door. "You mice are doomed when I set my traps tomorrow."

Jagger looked up at me. "Jesus. You really swallowed a Viagra?"

And now I'm stuck in here with you.

Seventeen

I tried to vomit back up the Viagra in a very lady-like, very silent manner.

No such luck.

I made a mental note to carry syrup of ipecac from now on.

Not that the Viagra had been able to work in those few seconds, but I sure as hell felt my skin burning while Jagger looked at me—grinning.

Sophie had mumbled some more and apparently left.

Jagger shined his light around the room. No window. No other door.

I was locked in Mr. Wisnowski's shed with my fantasy man—and I'd just swallowed a drug used for sexual dysfunction.

I knew it also worked on women, enhancing their "feelings." And it worked in thirty minutes—and lasted up to four hours.

This could be a long night.

But a fun one.

"How soon can we get out of here?" I asked when my mind snapped back to reality.

Jagger looked at me. "We're probably locked in till daybreak when the kid comes back, Sherlock."

Locked in.

Oh, boy. All of a sudden my heart started to pound and beneath my gloves my palms sweated. Locked in. This was not good for my claustrophobia.

Jagger must have noticed. "Oh shit. You're not going to pass out like that time on the elevator."

"Pass out? Very funny." I became woozy. "I'm fine." The room spun. "No problem." My knees wobbled like a rubber band.

I ordered my brain to ignore the fact that we were locked in.

"Good." He grabbed a few burlap sacks from a pile and laid them out on the floor near the door. "Then make yourself comfortable." He sat down and patted the floor next to him.

I stood like a freaking mannequin.

"Oh," he said, grinning. "Maybe you want separate sleeping arrangements after you swallowed that . . . bug?"

I could try to sleep somewhere else, but the shed was only about six feet by eight feet, and filled with tools, shovels, a lawnmower and a snow thrower.

And, besides, if I tried to sleep somewhere else, Jagger would never let me live it down.

Or I'd have a full-blown anxiety attack if I couldn't be near the door.

"Move over." I flopped down, scrunched up a few burlap bags for a pillow. "Good night." I turned with my back toward him.

I knew he was still grinning.

For several minutes I laid there, telling myself that one silly Viagra wouldn't affect me.

Then Jagger shifted.

Only a little. A tiny little amount, but his leg brushed the back of my knee.

Viagra was like adding gasoline to my already detonated Jagger explosion.

Okay, time to pull out the Pauline Sokol, RN, ammo. I had to reach into my already confused brain to tell myself that the Viagra didn't do anything to increase desire in women. I'd read a study that said when Viagra was used on women, it increased the blood flow to involved parts and did help, but that one tiny "bug" pill I'd swallowed shouldn't do a damn thing to me—unless we "did it," and I doubted it—especially because Jagger was snoring softly against my back.

I'd never sleep a wink tonight, I said to myself.

My eyes burned from being so overtired. My back ached from not being able—no, not daring—to turn around. If I faced Jagger, I would see him, watch him, ogle him and drool over him—that'd be my undoing.

He shifted again.

"Damn it," I mumbled.

He turned over!

Now his arm had taken the liberty of resting on my shoulder. He moved closer.

I didn't know much about Jagger, but now I knew without a doubt that he was a "cuddler."

He started making some kind of moaning sounds. Not as if he were in any kind of pain, but more sexual in nature. More as if he were having a darn good time while he slept. At least that's how I heard them in my Viagra-induced state.

Yes, my Viagra had kicked in.

I felt heat tear through my body, landing in the most important area that Jagger could ever affect. It wasn't easy not to spin around, grab him, tear off his clothes, make mad love and keep kissing him until the damned medicine wore off.

But I was a professional and told myself that I could withstand this torture—for the case.

And, admittedly, for me to keep face in front of Jagger.

So, I stayed put, ignored my traitorous body, now enhanced by some chemical, and shut my eyes.

I felt as if I were being smothered after I realized we couldn't get out. Phobias were not life threatening, I reminded myself. So, a little sweat. A rapid heartbeat. No one ever died from being locked in an old shed.

I had to fall asleep to ignore my phobia—and Jagger.

After a gazillion novenas to Saint Theresa, I felt my eyes start to shut.

My nose was freezing. I opened my eyes to see Jagger's face, inches away from mine. The cold night had seeped into the tiny, unheated shed. Shivering took over my body, and I tried to turn back. Obviously in my sleep, I'd shifted toward Jagger.

This was not good.

His hold tightened.

I tried to ease free by sliding down toward our feet. It wasn't easy by the way he held me, but I kept moving inch by inch.

But for every inch I'd gain, his hold would shift, tighten or his legs would move closer, pinning me in. I took a deep breath, told myself the Viagra had to be out of my system now, when, in fact, I knew it must be at its peak.

I made it down past his waistline, ready to pull free and turn. Shutting my eyes, I paused.

"Viagra kicking in, Sherlock?"

My eyes flew open to come face to "fly" with Jagger's jeans—with him still in them.

Oh . . . my . . . God.

This didn't look good at all.

For a second, I couldn't move. Then, thinking as fast as I could, I started to mumble. I mumbled and shifted, praying my acting abilities would have Jagger thinking I was still asleep and wriggled up until opposite his neck.

Then my chin lifted toward his face.

His lips touched mine.

And my world would never be the same.

My eyelids fluttered open. I looked around and felt my forehead wrinkle. What a dream. This place was freezing, dirty and . . . Jagger stood near the door.

It wasn't a dream.

More a nightmare.

The last thing I remembered was Jagger's lips on mine. I looked under the burlap to see that I had all my clothes on—but no jacket. I know I went to sleep with my jacket on.

Did that really mean we had . . .

Knowing Jagger, he would have helped me back into my clothes after . . .

Then I remembered the Viagra and said a silent prayer that it hadn't gotten out of hand last night. I felt pretty tired, but that could be since this wasn't the Ritz, and I hadn't slept much.

If I'd made love to Jagger—surely I'd be floating on a cloud right now—not lying here on a dirty floor.

And Lord knows, if we really had sex, I'd want to have lived through every tiny second of *that* experience with him.

I decided I'd go with the theory we hadn't and never breach the subject with him.

He turned toward me. "Hey."

"Morning." My voice came out a raspy tone. Sounded a bit sexier than it had last night, but I knew my breath needed some help. First thing I always did in the morning, no matter who I was with, was brush my teeth and tongue.

Pauline Sokol, creature of habit.

With my hand over my mouth, I asked, "Did you get it unlocked?"

He gave me one of those looks.

"Okay. How are we going to get out if the yard boy doesn't come back?" I sat up and ran my hand through my hair. Medusa, look out. Trying to tame the strands, I said, "Should we call someone?"

"We've never been here."

"Oh, right." I got up, brushed myself off and touched my lips. They felt a bit swollen. Maybe we had shared more than one kiss? And why was my jacket off?

Damn, how I wished I could remember.

Not only to know whether I should be properly embarrassed, but there was that thing of if I'd had sex with Jagger, I'd want to relive it moment by moment, or maybe even have video—for my own use only.

I couldn't be that unlucky to have done "it" and not remember.

Goldie's jacket hung from a hook above my head. Not a good sign. I reached into the deepest recesses of my brain to see if I remembered hanging it there. *Nada*. Jagger could have hung it up for me.

I shook my head to get all these stupid thoughts out of it, stood, grabbed the jacket and put it on.

He watched me, silently.

Great.

"So, how do we get out of here?" I walked toward the door.

Jagger had pushed open the double doors only about three inches. The old padlock still did its job, holding them shut.

I pushed at one door. It creaked. "Can't you just push it until the lock pops?"

Jagger looked through the small opening. "Not until Sophie is gone."

I bent near to look. His breath heated my cheek, and the bastard didn't move away. As a matter of fact, I think he somehow managed to make his breath . . . hotter.

During the night, snow had fallen. Not much, thank goodness, but enough that the roads might be a bit slippery. I wondered if the neighbors had noticed Jagger's SUV parked down the street. At least he didn't stop it right in front of Mr. W's house.

The guy was on the ball.

"Oh. Good thinking about Sophie. Can you—" I pulled back. "She's coming!"

Jagger took a fast peek, then grabbed my arm. As he pulled me toward the back of the shed, he held a finger to my lips. I got it that I had to shut up, but didn't move his hand away.

Pauline Sokol, pathetic woman.

"Clean both driveways today, Todd. Someone is coming to look at the house," Sophie said.

"Yeah," a teen's voice answered. Obviously Todd. The yard boy.

Jagger and I looked at the shovel together. Todd had to come get it. The lock started to jiggle.

Jagger pushed me behind the lawnmower. I fell, but before I could conk my head, his arms were around me, easing me to the floor with him on top of me.

Todd, a lanky kid with acne and a black woolen cap, stuck his arm into the shed and grabbed the shovel. "Yeah, bitch-lady. I'll shovel real good. Wouldn't want your fat ass skidding down the drive and breaking the cement." He turned to look, probably to make sure Sophie was gone. Then he let out a howl of laughter.

I held my breath, which wasn't difficult since Jagger was squashing the daylights out of me.

A mouse walked across my leg!

Jagger's hand was over my mouth before I could scream, but a tiny muffled sound had come out.

Todd stopped laughing.

"Who's in there?" his voice shook like mine felt. "I'll bet just one of those damn mice. Yeah. You little shits, stop making so much noise. You're not going to scare me anyway, making me think old man Wisnowski came back from the dead."

Silence.

Bam!

Jagger eased up. With my face partially blocked by his jacket, I looked to see the door shut and prayed Todd had forgotten to lock it again.

We waited a few minutes.

Then Jagger got up, offered me a hand, which I had to take since I was folded like a pretzel and didn't think I could maneuver on my own. When I was able to stand, he turned and walked toward the door. Ever so gently, he eased it open.

Atta boy, Todd, forgetful teenager.

Squeak.

This time I knew it wasn't the mice. If Todd had decent

hearing, he might come see what was going on. Then again, a teen who thinks about ghosts more than likely would run the other way.

I looked at Jagger. "Think he'll come back?"

"More than likely he's got some earphones blaring. Come on."

He took my hand, stepped out, and looked down the driveway. Sure enough, there shoveled Todd with music playing so loudly I could hear it from where I stood. We worked our way around the back of the shed and ended up on the opposite street.

Jagger looked around. "Let's go."

We walked down the sidewalk, turned left and headed toward his SUV, which sat partially covered in white.

I think I finally took a breath.

"Hungry?" Jagger asked after he brushed off the snow just barely enough to see through the windshield.

"I hadn't even thought about food after a night like that."

He turned, grinned.

"I'm talking about almost getting caught breaking and entering." But truthfully his look wasn't far off. "Yeah. I guess I am hungry, but I can't eat like this."

He turned down Elm Street. "We'll go to a restaurant."

"No, I mean . . . my teeth. I have to brush them and then shower before I can eat."

At the stoplight Jagger turned to me. "Maybe next time you should bring an overnight bag with you on surveillance."

"Why I hadn't thought about—" I slapped his arm before he took off again. "Funny. I can't help having good hygiene. Anyway, I need to go home before I can eat."

"I'm starving."

"Okay. Compromise. I'll give you toast while I get ready."

He didn't reply but turned into the parking lot of my condo and shut off the engine. Once outside, I took a long, deep breath of fresh air. It really felt good to be outside again. I made a mental note to call my friend who was a therapist. Probably I could use some behavior modification for my phobia while doing this line of work.

Maybe even a little Prozac.

We walked up the steps, and I opened the door. When Jagger walked in, he stopped. I'd forgotten to warn him about the "jungle."

"Goldie lives here now too."

Without a word, he walked toward the kitchen. Spanky came running up to Jagger. He grabbed the dog, gave him a hug and held him. "Where's the coffee?"

I pointed to the pantry. "Don't make any messes. Miles can't take it. I'll be right back." I gave Spanky a pat, but the dog ignored me and nuzzled Jagger's arm.

Smart dog.

Once in the bathroom, I started to undress, then thought about Jagger being downstairs. Like a fool, okay a wishful fool, I rechecked the door lock. Yep, *unlocked*.

I got into the shower and turned the handle on full blast. The water felt wonderful after last night. Not that I got that dirty, since I had on my winter clothes, but on principle I felt cleaner afterward.

When I headed into my room to change, I remembered how long it had taken me the other night to pick out an outfit for my date. Then it dawned on me that I hadn't even thought about Nick all night.

That was not a good sign.

My "Nick likes me" mantra ran through my head until I was dressed in my jeans, long blue sweater and had my hair pulled up. There wasn't time to wash and dry it, so I went with the casual look. I reapplied my makeup and headed downstairs.

Something smelled good. Certainly wasn't plain old toast. Famished now, I opened the swinging door to the kitchen. Spanky sat on the floor watching.

Me, I leaned against the wall and joined the dog.

Jagger moved about as if he owned the place. Coffee perked. Bacon sizzled. On the griddle were two gigantic pancakes. He stood over them, slicing bananas onto them. Without looking up, he said, "Hope you like bananas."

For a second I thought he was talking to Spanky. "Oh . . . yes. But I've never had them in my pancakes." I managed to move away from the wall, take a mug from the table Jagger had set and filled it with coffee. After several yawns, I needed the caffeine.

I had to smile when I set the mug down on the table to put in my cream and sugar. He'd used Miles's everyday white pottery dishes. But instead of using napkins, Jagger had folded paper towels and set them next to them. The fork, knife and spoon all sat on the left side of the dish. I had the urge to correct it, but held back.

Did it really matter?

Obviously Jagger did things his own way—and that's what made him Jagger.

"This is so nice of you," I said, taking a sip of my coffee. "I thought we were going out to eat."

He looked at me. "Not before I showered."

I smiled, knowing he did it 'cause I was upset. "Touché. Who knew you could cook?" I sat at the table and took another sip of coffee.

"Jack of all trades."

I'll bet you are.

He turned around and set a plateful of bacon on the table, which he followed with the two pancakes too large to fit on a plate. Those he juggled on the spatula and pan while hurrying over to the table. My pancake he set down, folded in half.

"Thanks. This looks wonderful." I would *not* allow myself any "homey" or "sexy" thoughts of us sharing breakfast on a cold winter's day. So, I took the heated maple syrup and poured way too much over my pancake.

We ate in silence, which didn't surprise me. After taking the last bite, even though I was stuffed, I said, "I'm so full. You did a great job, Jagger." I had to get up and move around, or else I'd gain twenty pounds just sitting there.

He got up and started taking his dish to the sink.

"Oh no. House rules. Whoever cooks doesn't clean up." I stifled another yawn and got up.

He set the dish back on the table. "Good rule. So how long has Goldie been here?"

"Just moved in." After another yawn, I could feel him staring at me, probably wondering why the hell I was still there. "I'm planning on moving out."

He nodded. "Where to?"

I couldn't get the words "my parents' house" to come out of my lips, so I just shrugged. "Haven't looked around yet."

"Rent gets expensive . . . alone."

What? Was Jagger insinuating that we should move in together or had the Viagra rebounded?

"Tell me about it. You know of any cheap places? Oh, I don't mean cheap as in crummy. I mean nice, safe places that aren't too expensive."

"Do you think I'd set you up in an unsafe place?"

I let out a sigh. "I'm overtired and not responsible for what I say all day today."

Ring. Ring!

We both looked at the phone together. "Funny how sometimes even the ringer sounds impatient." I picked it up. "Hello."

"Pauline?"

"Yes, Mother. Who else would answer when you called my number?"

"Pauline, where have you been? I've been trying to get you all morning!"

I was about to tell a lie, but her voice sounded too concerned about something. "What's wrong, Ma. Daddy all right? Uncle Walt?" Oh, no! Had something happened to Uncle Walt like Mr. W? "Uncle Stash?"

"That one."

"Something is wrong with Uncle Stash?"

"Get over here right away, Pauline." She sniffled.

"Oh, my God, Mom! Call an ambulance!"

Her voice stiffened. "An ambulance couldn't fix this, Pauline." She hung up.

Jagger had already picked up the rest of the dishes and stuck them in the dishwasher while I had been on the phone.

"My mother—"

"I'll take you over there."

"I . . . I'll go alone. She sounded strange."

"You can't drive."

I grabbed my purse and keys from the table. "Yes I can." My vision blurred. Another yawn. He was right. I hadn't slept enough last night. "You're probably as tired as I am."

He walked to the front door, opened it. "I slept, Sherlock."

* * *

All the way to my mother's house, I kept thinking of Jagger sleeping and me a wreck all night. I vowed never to go on a "midnight mission" with him ever again.

Then again, I'd also vowed I'd never take a nursing job again, and here I was. If I learned anything, it should have been not to make any vows to myself where Jagger was concerned.

He turned down Pleasant Street, taking the back roads. He'd been to my parents' house last Christmas.

My mother liked Jagger.

No telling what was going on now, or what she'd say when I showed up with him at this time of the morning.

When we pulled into the driveway, I hurried out. Jagger was right behind. On the way over, I'd assured myself that Uncle Stash couldn't be sick or an ambulance would be needed.

Then again, if he were dead . . .

"Mom!" I shoved open the front door and ran inside.

"In here, *Pączki*," my father called out from the kitchen.

Running in, I said, "Daddy, what is going on?"

Mother stepped forward with a coffeepot in her hand. "Why didn't you tell me you were bringing company, Pauline? For heaven's sake, where are your manners?" She set the coffeepot on a hotplate shaped like a strawberry in the middle of the table. "How are you, Mr. Jagger?"

She always insisted on adding the "mister" and I couldn't explain that he only had one name—which I knew of anyway.

"He's fine, Ma. I didn't tell you because you had me so upset. What the hell is going on?"

Jagger touched my arm. "Relax, Sherlock."

"That's right, Pauline. Mind your manners and get Mr. Jagger a chair, and let him answer for himself."

"I've been fine, Mrs. Sokol."

Uncle Walt and my father sat at the table. I nodded to them and grabbed the chair near the wall phone. I looked at Jagger. "Here. Sit."

Mother shook her head. "Let me fix you some scrambled eggs."

"We already ate, Ma. What is going on?"

"What did you eat? Coffee? A donut?" She got up and went toward the refrigerator.

"Jagger made us pancakes!" I couldn't control myself now. Being summoned here for some emergency and then being fed again (because I didn't want her to know that we'd spent the night together no matter how—hopefully—platonic it was) was too much to take.

My entire family locked eyes with me. Mother's were the strongest, pulling the truth out of me.

"He came . . . we had work to do. After the work he made breakfast. Now why the hell am I here?"

Mother wiped her hands on her favorite winter apron. The one with red cardinals sitting on naked brown branches highlighted with snow. She looked me in the eye.

At first I thought she was going to go on about breakfast, pancakes and Jagger. But instead she cleared her throat. "Your uncle is getting married."

My eyes bugged out. I swung around to Uncle Walt. "Congratu—"

"Not him," Mother said. "Uncle Stash."

I felt my knees weaken. Jagger must have noticed, because his arms were on mine. I leaned into his chest for support. "Uncle Stash. Uncle Stash is getting married to someone he knows from back home in Florida?"

"No, *Pączki*," Daddy said. "Stash is marrying that woman. Helen Wanat."

I turned to see a tear run down Uncle Walt's cheek.

Eighteen

Through clenched teeth I managed, "Uncle Stash is marrying Helen? Helen?" That last word came out as a screech.

Jagger pulled me to the side. "Easy, Sherlock."

I know he meant to watch out for Uncle Walt's feelings, and I surely did care about them, but right now I was also worried about Uncle Stash.

Since I'd never liked Helen, I could only assume she was marrying my uncle for his money. Damn woman. Poor Uncle Walt never had as much as Uncle Stash, and Helen must have found that out.

I looked at Uncle Walt. He winked at me. He'd be fine, I knew then. But I eased away from Jagger, went to Uncle Walt and bent near his ear. "Her loss."

He took my hand and then looked at my mother. "Pauline and I have some business to attend to."

We do?

"I'll make up some sweet rolls," my mother said.

Daddy had gone back to reading the paper.

Uncle Walt motioned for Jagger to join us. We headed down the hallway toward his room.

"Sssh." He walked in and held his finger to his lips. Then he looked out the door as if my mother had followed us. Which, by the way, wasn't that far-fetched an idea.

But she hadn't. I told Jagger to sit in the stuffed chair by the window while I dropped down onto the bed. Uncle Walt stood near the door as if standing guard.

I looked at Jagger. We shared a smile. My uncle was so cute. I really hoped his feelings weren't that hurt.

"So, Uncle Walt. What do we need to talk about?"

"Helen," he whispered.

Jagger looked at Uncle Walt. "Sorry about that."

Uncle Walt waved a hand in the air as if dismissing Jagger's words. "Thanks for the condolences, son, but they are not needed."

"I'm confused," I said. "I thought you were . . . were 'involved' with Helen."

Uncle Walt moved closer to us. He sat on the edge of the bed next to me, but kept looking from Jagger to myself. "Oh, don't get me wrong. I had some 'fun' with the woman. I liked her. At first, that is. But, no way would I marry at this age."

I patted his hand. "You're never too old, Uncle Walt."

"Yes. Yes you are, Pauline. I wouldn't marry someone so much younger and have her stuck taking care of me. Why, Old Man Westerly married Hannah Carmichael when she was in her sixties. He was seventy-five. Now she spends her days visiting him in the nursing home. Done it for six years now. He doesn't even know who she is. No kind of life. No kind of life."

"So," Jagger asked, "you're not heartbroken that your brother is marrying Helen?"

"I'm upset all right, but not for the reasons you two

young ones think. No siree. Stash and I have never been close." He turned toward me. "You know that, Pauline."

"Hey, we all have our favorites." I patted his hand.

He smiled. "True. You are my favorite niece. Well, I have a special fondness for you since you never married and had children. The others are all so busy with their families. But not you."

Thank you for the reminder, Uncle Walt.

I decided to ignore that comment, since, in fact, it was all true and there was nothing to argue about. I also chose not to look at Jagger—but knew damn well he was grinning.

"So why bring us in here? What is so secret, Uncle Walt?"

"I think Helen can't be trusted." With that he leaned back a bit, and waited.

I looked at Jagger.

He shrugged.

"Okay, Uncle Walt. Helen obviously can't be trusted since she went behind your back and dated your brother. But what does that have to do with us?"

He leaned near, grabbed Jagger's and my arms and pulled us closer. "Don't you two youngsters understand? She can't be *trusted*." He looked at the door as if expecting someone to crash through it. "I'm surprised at you, Pauline. You too, Jagger. I thought you both were better at your jobs. A smart nurse, Pauline. Helen . . . is in on it."

Jagger and I looked at each other again. I wondered if I looked as confused as he did. "In on what?"

"Oh, my gosh. Okay. I'll spell it out. I started dating Helen more after Wisnowski died. Sure, I liked the company of such a vibrant woman, but then I got suspicious. Don't you see? I was dating her to help your case!"

"My case?"

"Yes, Pauline. I found a . . . Viagra tablet in Helen's living room!"

Jagger made a noise. To me it sounded like a failed laugh. He had turned toward the window, obviously not wanting to embarrass my uncle.

"How many did you find?" I asked.

"One, Pauline. But how many do I need to find? Maybe she sells them too!"

I touched his hand. Obviously his feelings for Helen were stronger than he wanted to admit to us. "Maybe she had it—" I couldn't say it. I couldn't say that maybe Helen had a Viagra for one of her "dates."

Because obviously she'd never offered it to Uncle Walt.

Jagger stood up. "Great job, Walt. I'd hire you myself if I could."

I wanted to ask whom he worked for then, but it wasn't an appropriate time. Uncle Walt was beaming because of his "investigating."

Jagger patted him on the back. "Yep. Great job. Look, can you do us a favor?"

Uncle Walt stood. "Anything. I'm at your disposal."

"Great. Don't say a word to anyone."

Uncle Walt "zipped" his lips.

I smiled.

Jagger continued, "Perfect. I knew we could trust you. So, no telling anyone, and stay clear of Helen."

"But," Uncle Walt protested, "maybe I should keep surveillance on her? Tell Stash about her?"

Jagger had begun to walk away, but turned back quickly.

I'd seen his smiling reflection in the dresser mirror and

wanted to thank him for being so kind, so considerate of my aged uncle.

"Leave the rest to us professionals, Walt. You did a great job reporting what you found. We'll take over from here." With that he held out his hand.

Uncle Walt took it in a shaky hold. "Well, then. My work is done."

I leaned over and kissed his cheek.

On the way out, Jagger said over his shoulder, "Maybe next week we can take my SUV out for a drive."

Tears welled in my eyes at the sight of the twinkle in Uncle Walt's.

"Thank you," I said to Jagger when we got into his SUV.

"No problem." He cranked the engine and drove off.

We'd snuck out the backdoor before my mother caught us and made us eat sweet rolls. They were always delicious, but I was still so full, and I wanted to talk to Jagger.

"You know, I never liked Helen."

He turned down Elm Street and stopped at the red light. "And?"

"And, well, do you think she is mixed up in this?"

He chuckled. "Pauline, *one* Viagra. You of all people should know the effects of that."

Since the vehicle was at a stop, I slapped at his arm.

He pulled away and my hand landed on the steering wheel. I learned then that my reflexes were no match for Jagger's.

"Very funny," I said.

"It is. But actually I'm not trying to be funny."

"Good. 'Cause you're not."

"What I meant was, no. I don't suspect Helen. Neither do the cops. What I suspect is that poor Uncle Walt is really miffed about getting dumped or that she never offered him a Viagra and, although he probably believes it, he's seeing something that isn't there."

I wasn't so sure.

"And if Walt starts something, our cases could blow up in our faces," he added.

I nodded.

When we pulled up to my condo, Jagger didn't turn off the engine. Good. What I needed now was a long nap. An all-day nap.

I tossed and turned and looked at the clock a gazillion times. Only twenty-five minutes had passed since I'd climbed into bed. Obviously I was overtired and the coffee Jagger made this morning must have been Miles's regular blend and not decaf.

I looked at the window. A light snowfall brightened the early afternoon. My first thought was to go for a jog. Maybe I'd feel better with some exercise. Then I told myself I'd probably slip on the sidewalk and break something. That was the kind of luck I usually had.

Leaning back, I propped my pillows into a pile and stared out the window. Was Uncle Walt even remotely right about Helen Wanat?

Or, more likely, were my negative feelings about her getting in my way.

I wasn't a good people watcher. Never could judge someone from the outside unless it had to do with their health. Jagger had said Helen was clean, and I knew damn well that he wouldn't say that if she weren't. Also, no way in hell was I going to argue with him where investigating was concerned.

He was a master.

And, a darn good "people watcher," it seemed.

He'd read Uncle Walt correctly and was even gentle with the old man's feelings. I liked that.

Ring. Ring.

First I looked at the phone. Miles and Goldie had gone shopping for the day in New York City. They'd left me a note on my door. I couldn't wait to see what outfits Goldie came back with. His black jacket hung from my closet door.

I thought about Jagger.

Ring. "Hello." I had grabbed at the phone so fast, I nearly fell out of bed.

"How's it going?" Nick's voice came across the line so clean, so fresh, and so deep.

My heart did a pitter-patter.

That was good. Nick's voice had the power to make me interested. After a bit of chitchat, with me filling him in on my case, he'd thought Helen wasn't suspect either. I could only hope that Uncle Walt wouldn't get hurt anymore, and planned to keep an eye on her. Nick also told me that I really had to get going on my case. Fabio had a short fuse.

I laughed. "No argument there."

"I miss you, Pauline."

I swallowed. Hard. "I . . . me too." Did that mean I missed him or myself? Flustered, I tried to correct myself, but felt at a loss.

His chuckling warmed my heart through the AT&T lines. "I'll see you tomorrow night. How about dinner?"

Exhausted, dinner was the last thing on my mind. But I truly wanted to see Nick. "I look forward to it."

With a promise to pick me up at seven, he hung up.

If I couldn't sleep before, I never would now. So, I got up, took a shower to perk up and got dressed. This time I wore the black leggings and turtleneck. Who cared if I looked like a mime? I wasn't going anywhere.

Once downstairs, I fixed myself a cup of tea, spread out my work photos on the table, and stared at them. No wonder Fabio was pissed. There really wasn't much to go on. I needed something soon.

I looked down at Spanky, who was snoring by the door, cuddled in his zebra doggie bed. A gift from Auntie Goldie. "What the hell am I going to do?"

"You have the keys to the pharmacy, jerk."

Jerk! My little darling had called me a jerk. Then I realized, yet again, that I'd spoken out loud with the wisdom of a five-pound canine.

I finished my tea, rinsed out the mug and set it in the dishwasher, and then gathered my glasses, beeper, keys and license. Not wanting to lug around a purse, I stuck twenty bucks in the pocket of my jeans. I then reached into the inside zipper of my bag and took out the keys to the clinic.

Pauline Sokol, insurance investigator rides again.

The clinic parking lot wasn't totally empty. Good, because now my car wouldn't stand out. That gave me pause. Then I told myself some cleaning crew probably worked on Saturdays and wouldn't take much notice when I unlocked the door with a key I had. Employees often came back over the weekend to finish up paperwork.

Me, I'd never been that much of a workaholic.

I reached into my jacket pocket and pulled out my new pair of thin black gloves. On the way there I'd stopped at a Wal-Mart. Jagger would be proud. I pulled off the tags, threw them in the trash bag beneath my dashboard and stepped outside.

This time I'd worn my Steelers parka instead of Goldie's sexy jacket. I figured if I got caught, sexy wouldn't help. Maybe my favorite football team would bring me luck. I checked the pocket of my jeans to make sure I had everything. The bulges said I did.

At the door, I paused, looked around and took out the key. The door opened without a hitch. As I walked inside, a man carrying a mop came from around the corner.

"Oh!" I stumbled back.

He looked at me, at the key. "I'm leaving. Lock up when you are done and stay off the floor on the west side of the pharmacy. It's still wet." He stuck the mop in the pail, which he shoved into the janitor's closet, grabbed a jacket and walked out the door, mumbling.

The only thing I got was "don't want no footprints on it." I nodded. I didn't want my footprints on the floor or anywhere else either. The fact that this man could identify me did little to worry me. He seemed in a hurry; he probably didn't even notice my Steelers jacket.

Lock up. Good. He'd made it sound as if I were the only one here. I turned toward the clinic and paused.

Suddenly an eerie feeling crept inside me. Not that I expected any ghosts, but the last time I'd broken into my workplace to snoop, I was nearly shot.

I told myself fate wouldn't be so cruel as to repeat that incident, and that I had a job to do. I was a big girl, with big bills. Adult bills that needed to be paid soon. Once inside the clinic, I stopped, listened. A clock, given by a drug company, ticked away in the waiting room. The only sound was the second hand passing by each organ—6 was a kidney, 9, a liver, and 12, a heart.

It was ten past the pancreas now and apparently adrenaline had boosted my second wind. I slowly walked through the empty clinic and headed toward the door to the pharmacy, praying it wasn't locked.

I twisted the handle and it clicked. Perfect. The door opened and I walked through, turning and shutting it. Then I stood for a few minutes, waiting. Nothing. Good. No one was around. Emergency lights glowed red above the doorways. There was also some white light coming from the floor area, most likely to discourage burglars.

I smiled.

Not that I was going to steal anything, but the light helped, since I'd forgotten a flashlight. A tidbit I was not going to share with Jagger. Across the waiting room was the yellow plastic "wet floor" sign left by the grumpy janitor. Good thing for grumpy janitors in a hurry to leave. I walked to the back of the pharmacy, where the medications were filled.

With my gloves on, I opened drawer after drawer. Feeling sure that all the narcotics were locked up, I'd never touch the safe, in case someone came in. That way I couldn't be accused of stealing drugs, and then lose my nursing license. A sobering thought, even for someone who never wanted to work in that profession again.

My heart sank. This was a waste of my time, I thought. I could have been doing more tossing and turning in my bed. I leaned against the counter and told myself I had to think like a pharmacist. A crooked pharmacist. A cheating pharmacist.

The area looked clean. Where would Leo hide things? Where would he put anything to do with Sophie? And had the cops already found what I might need?

I should have brought Spanky with me to tell me what to do. Now I needed a dog to help with my case. How pathetic was that?

Speaking of pathetic, I thought of the measly late Leo Pasinski. Then I noticed a file cabinet. I walked over, opened it and looked under B for Banko. Sophie's chart was not as thick as some of the others but it wasn't thin by any means. Much like the woman herself. I yanked it open and spread the papers out on the clean counter.

Damn. Leo hid things right out in the open. The old "reverse psychology," I guessed. Well, it did make things less conspicuous.

With my camera glasses on now, I clicked away. I tried to read each page as I clicked but thought I shouldn't take too much time there. I could study it all at home. One paper flew off the pile as I shifted the others.

I reached down to pick it up.

A prescription. Then I found prescription after prescription in Sophie's name—all written on a pad by the same doctor. Dr. Arnold Stabach. The only doctor by that name who I'd worked with at Saint Gregory's Hospital had died last year. I leaned closer. Sure enough, the office location was on Pleasant Street and at Saint Greg's where he'd worked.

Sophie or Leo must have stolen the prescription pad before he died. Then Sophie wrote them out and Leo filled them, or more than likely didn't. No wait. I had to think like a criminal. I paused. I chewed a strand of hair. I clicked my nail against my teeth. Yes. He must have filed the insurance claims on them and not filled the prescriptions. That way he could sell the pills—twice.

Very clever.

Bump. Bump.

My hands froze for a second. There couldn't be mice in the clinic making that kind of noise. I shoved the papers back into the folder, not caring what order they were in. Then I stuck the folder back in the file cabinet so it blended in and shut the drawer faster than the speed of a hummingbird's wings.

I silently tiptoed to the other side of the room. The noise seemed to come from behind me. So, I hiked myself up onto the counter, knocked the damned box of carob bars for another flying leap, and jumped off the other end. Tough luck, carob bars, I thought, as getting the hell out of there was more important.

Bump!

I looked from side to side and behind me. While still looking, I started to run. Suddenly the noise got louder. My feet flew out from under me. And I slid like Thumper on ice across the wet floor to land—at the feet of a *man*.

Nineteen

My head clunked against the floor as I spun around on my back. Ouch! I'd shut my eyes at first, then opened them to look up. Dark blurry vision. Ears ringing. Slight nausea. Concussion City.

Another janitor stood over me, mop in hand—glaring down and frowning.

What the hell kind of excuse could I use for being here?

And would he call 911, and would I be found out?

Suddenly he shook his head. Twice.

Even with my blurry vision, I had a déjà vu kind of feeling. "Janitor Jagger. Again," I mumbled, and then collapsed.

It was one thing to wake up in the arms of a gorgeous hunk of a guy, even disguised as a janitor, but another thing to wake up—and lose your pancake breakfast in his lap.

"Shit!" He grabbed a rag from his overalls.

I looked at him through blurry eyes. Okay, I'd only coughed up pancakes about the size of a half dollar, but it was, nevertheless, mortifying. "Thank goodness you chose that disguise today."

"You all right, Sherlock?"

I moaned. "How do I look?"

"We need to get you to the hospital."

"No. I'll be fine." I leaned back and shut my eyes.

Before I knew it, I was lifted up into his arms. I opened my eyes to see we were walking toward the door. I should have protested, but I felt like crap, and head injuries were nothing to sneeze at. So, I let Jagger whisk me off to the ER amid my humiliation.

He pulled up to the entrance of Saint Greg's, parked the car and hurried to my side door. There had to be a sarcastic comment for me to make, but the way I felt, I didn't have it in me to come up with one. Jagger took my hand and helped me out.

"Can you make it?"

Walking on legs of Jell-O, I said, "Of course. I only have a mild concussion. I'll live."

His eyes grew darker, which seemed an impossibility. Also as impossible was how much sexier it made him look. But beneath the sex was concern.

I was feeling better already.

Jagger walked me to the desk and insisted I be seen right away. A man bleeding from his nose sat on a chair in the waiting room. He looked more in need than I felt, but before I knew it, the nurse had me in Exam Room #2, after Jagger convinced the receptionist that he'd go over my insurance information with her so I could be taken care of.

How sweet.

The doctor came in and poked around, shone a light in my eyes, asked several questions and then left.

A few of the staff who remembered me from working there came in to say hi. One of the nurses was an old friend from my days working in OB.

"Hey, Sheila," I said. Did old Dr. Stabach die?"

She gave me an odd look. "What day is it, Pauline?"

I gave her an even odder look. "Saturday."

"Who is the president?"

I groaned and told her. I knew she was checking to see if my noggin was intact, but she hadn't answered my question. "Is he dead, Sheila?"

"Pauline, I sat a row behind you at his memorial service."

Damn. I knew that, but had forgotten. Had to be related to my head problem. "Did he have a son with the same name who's also a doctor?"

She took my arm and felt for my pulse. "He never married, Pauline."

So the prescription pad had to have come from his office. I couldn't wait to share this info with Jagger and—more important—with Fabio.

Even feeling as crappy as I did, I felt glad that my case was over. I could now get paid for nailing Sophie Banko, medical insurance fraud criminal.

Jagger came to the doorway. He looked like I felt.

"What? I'm *not* going to make it?" I chuckled, but he remained as stone faced as usual.

"You don't have any medical coverage, Pauline."

Oh . . . my . . . God. He'd used my real name. That meant business. "No insurance?" I screamed.

Sheila spun around. "This is a hospital, Pauline."

"Sorry." I leaned back and took a deep breath. Then I held my hand up and wiggled my pointer finger for Jagger to come closer. "What the hell are you talking about? Is that some kind of joke?"

He looked a bit hurt. I guess accusing him of trying to fool an injured woman was a bit insensitive. But no insurance! That had me riled up.

"The receptionist ran your number through several times. She even tried to call Fabio, but no one is there on a Saturday. I'm guessing he didn't make your payments for medical insurance yet because he considers you on probation. Weren't you aware of that, so you could make temporary provisions?"

I could only stare at Jagger. Not bad to look at to try to take your mind off an earth-shattering problem. Then I shut my eyes and started to laugh.

Sheila said she'd be back later, that I'd probably be going for a CAT scan and not to get loud again.

I peeked out of one eye and cursed her inside my head.

Jagger pulled up a chair next to my stretcher. "How do you feel?"

I opened my eyes and looked at him. "How do you think I feel after dropping that bomb on me? I don't even have enough on my credit card line to pay for this bill. Get me my shoes. I'm getting out of here." I pointed to the table where Sheila had set them.

Jagger remained seated.

"Put down this side rail so I can go home. I'll take some Tylenol and be fine."

"You above all people should know not to take any kind of pain medication which could mask serious symptoms of a head injury. What if you have a hematoma?"

"Just 'cause you disguise yourself as a doctor, doesn't mean you know what the hell you are talking about." Although he was on target with everything he'd said. Damn it. I couldn't just leave without finding out I was all right, and I couldn't afford to be here.

"You don't need your shoes yet," he said.

"I have to get out of here." I swallowed my pride and added, "I can't *afford* this, Jagger."

Sheila came in with a slip for Radiology. "You're going for a CAT scan."

"No. I'm going home."

Jagger stood and leaned near my ear. "The bill is taken care of. You can owe me." With that he was out of the room.

I lay there speechless. Owe Jagger. Owe Jagger? Owe Jagger!

Fate appeared to be out to get me again anyway.

Since I passed my CAT Scan with flying colors and started to feel nothing worse than a headache, I was released to go home. Again Jagger wouldn't take me to my car and let me drive, which, although I wouldn't admit it to him, was a sensible idea. Instead he took me to my condo and said he'd arrange to get my car if I gave him my keys. I had no problem trusting him with my Volvo.

It was *owing* him that caused me grief.

I'd learned my lesson co-signing that car loan for my ex-friend and never wanted to owe money to anyone. Least of all Jagger. Besides, if I had to pay him with what I earned from this case, I wouldn't have enough left to get my own place. Damn.

When we arrived at my condo, he got out and opened the car door again.

"A girl could get used to such chivalrous behavior." I stepped out and brushed his hand away.

He didn't answer. I looked at his stained outfit and felt horrible.

"If you want, I'll lend you something of Miles's and wash that for you."

We walked to the door. He took the key and let me in first. Spanky ran to Jagger.

"Traitor," I mumbled and flopped onto the couch.

"Miles doesn't look my size."

"Goldie is."

Jagger looked at me.

"What? He does have men's clothes, you know."

"Where's your Tylenol?"

"In the bathroom cabinet upstairs. Go into Goldie's room and get some jeans and a tee shirt. He really wouldn't mind." Besides, I wouldn't keep being reminded of how I had stained him.

Jagger headed upstairs, and I leaned back to rest. Spanky, maybe knowing I'd been hurt, jumped up and nuzzled next to my arm. "Oh. So you decided where your loyalty lies?"

It seemed Jagger was gone for a while. Maybe because I dozed off and on and held Spanky even tighter. I would probably have to ask my parents for money to pay Jagger back now.

I'd have been better off if the fall had killed me.

I heard footsteps and my eyes flew open. Jagger walked across the room—dressed in Goldie's clothes. His male clothes.

"Not one word."

I nodded. "Ouch." Someone with a concussion shouldn't nod. He'd found a pair of worn light blue denim jeans. The only "Goldie" thing about them was silver buttons on the pockets. Not just little tiny buttons, but rather large ones with a giant *G* monogrammed next to them. Jagger looked as if he wanted to yank them off. Hip-huggers with flared bottoms.

I nearly choked on a laugh.

On top he'd put on a plain white tee shirt. Goldie only wore them under his clothes, but I figured Jagger wouldn't be caught dead in one of Goldie's "gay pride" tees or one of the sparkly ones. In his hands Jagger held his rolled-up janitor suit.

He looked half James Dean sans pack of cigarettes stuck in his rolled-up sleeve and half—well, there was no hiding Jagger completely.

Yum.

"If you put your clothes in the hamper, I'll wash them and return them next time I see you."

"I'm not leaving in these things. Where's the machine?"

I smiled, but his look kept me from making a snide comment. But damn, how I wanted to.

After Jagger had his wash going, he came out of the kitchen with a mug of tea for me and a Budweiser for himself. "Hungry?"

I thought of how his pancake breakfast had ended up and shook my head. With the steamy mug in my hands, I sat up enough to take a few sips. "This hits the spot, although your Budweiser looks appealing."

"No alcohol for you."

"I didn't hear the doctor say that."

He looked at me. "I said that." Jagger settled himself across the room in the gigantic zebra futon. "You rest. Let me know if you need anything."

"Actually I don't want to sleep."

"You can trust me, Sherlock."

Flustered, I shifted, knocking Spanky onto the white carpet. "Oh! I'm sorry, sweetie." But the dog ran to Jagger, who picked him up and held him.

"Was your investigation successful before your fall?"

For a second, I didn't know what he was talking about. Damn. I wished I wasn't having short-term memory losses. Then it dawned on me why I'd been at the clinic. I filled Jagger in on my findings. "So, it seems Leo and Sophie were in cahoots. All her fake insurance claims have cost Fabio thousands. I'm so relieved to have this done with. On Monday I'm taking the pictures to be developed, then closing the case." I leaned back and sighed when I thought of my nice, fat paycheck.

Jagger held Spanky to his chest and rubbed behind his left ear. "You can't."

"Can't what?"

"You can't close the case yet, Sherlock."

I heard the words, but they wouldn't process. Damn my aching head. Then again, I couldn't blame this one on a head injury. "Like hell I can't."

"Look, Sherlock. You go getting Sophie busted now, and my case is blown to hell."

Talk about déjà vu.

"Now hold on. You did this with the Macaluso case. I am not staying at that clinic any longer. And I *need* my money now, Jagger."

"You don't need your money now and yes, you need to stay."

"No."

"Yes."

"No."

"If you leave and blow my case, Viagra fraud is going to continue. You want kids buying it and dying when they mix it with Ecstasy?"

I opened my mouth. Nothing came out. If Sophie was

mixed up in more than I'd found out about, I would ruin everything and maybe even hurt some of Uncle Walt's friends—or him.

"I hate you," I muttered and shut my eyes.

Twenty

With my eyes shut, I mentally let out all my anger, frustration and annoyance with Jagger for making me delay the completion of my case.

But the seething really didn't feel that good. It wasn't my style, damn it. I wish I could enjoy seething better.

"How much longer do you figure it will take?" I didn't even bother to open my eyes.

"You'll be the first to know when you can quit the clinic and nail Sophie."

"That doesn't answer my question."

"A few weeks."

"You'd say anything to get me off the subject and agree to stay on and help you."

"Then why'd you ask?"

Exactly. I couldn't bring myself to say, "Oh, yeah. Sure I'll stay there," so I kept my eyes shut and let my silence be his answer.

It was either that or let my mouth fly out with some terms that would make even bikers blush.

I actually did dose off. Maybe out of frustration and the need to escape my life right then. I woke to the aroma of food and the living room dark. The mantel clock said it was past seven.

It took a great effort to make myself get up, but I had to know if Jagger was still here or if my roomies were back. Spanky wasn't anywhere to be found so I assumed he was in the kitchen too. I stood, waited until I had my bearings and walked to the kitchen door. When I pushed, I thought I'd been transported to Italy. Not that I'd ever left the United States in my entire life, but I guessed this fabulous aroma would come from Roma.

Jagger sat at the table, writing on some kind of little notepad. The table was set with the white pottery dishes again. On the stove, pots steamed, sauce bubbled, and the oven light and wonderful scent said the garlic bread was nearly done.

"Smells wonderful."

He never looked up. "I thought you'd be hungry."

Most guys would apologize for taking the liberty of making themselves at home, but I figured Jagger never apologized for much.

When I sat opposite him, I marveled at his abilities, his looks and cooking skills too. What a catch. Then I wondered why no one ever caught him. Goldie had told me once about Jagger's divorce being painful, so maybe it had thrown him into a single life of work. Or maybe looks were deceiving—even though I'd seen some hints of humanity.

Without a word, he got up, served me a dish of spaghetti, salad he took from the fridge, and a slice of bread from the oven.

"Chef Jagger. Guess I'm dreaming now. Maybe my head injury was worse than I thought."

He poured me a glass of water. "No caffeine tonight."

I saluted him. "Yes, sir."

He smiled, fixed his own dish and sat down. We ate in silence for a good part of the meal. Not unlike Jagger. He wasn't one for small talk.

After my last bite, I wiped a napkin across my lips and said, "I'll have your money next week."

"The bills haven't even cleared the credit card company."

"Doesn't matter. I'll get the money from my parents and pay you what you've already charged."

He looked at me. "You want to owe your parents?"

I groaned.

"Thought so. Don't be so foolish, Pauline. Pay me when you can. I trust you."

And I knew he did, as I trusted him. What I was more concerned with was having a monetary commitment to *him*. One that would surely continue after our cases were solved.

Did I want that kind of debt?

And did I want it just to be able to hold on to seeing Jagger?

Jagger had cleaned the dishes, changed back into his janitor overalls and washed Goldie's clothes before he and Miles got home and began screeching like two mother hens about my injury. He left after giving them instructions about waking me throughout the night to make sure I hadn't passed away in my sleep. I kept reiterating that Miles was a nurse, which Jagger ignored each time.

Me, I kept thinking about that debt question.

When he'd finally left, I was exhausted and Goldie and Miles tucked me into bed like my two fairy godmothers.

Sleep wouldn't come since I'd taken that nap, but I lay in bed and rested, thinking. That was part of why I couldn't fall asleep.

I had to give Fabio something soon.

I needed to get paid.

And I needed to help Jagger—for all the right reasons.

I would stay on at the clinic and see what I could find out about the Viagra. That meant that I didn't have to dress up like Peggy anymore. I told myself how relieved I was.

Then it dawned on me that if Peggy "disappeared" without a trace, the seniors would call the cops. I had to do Peggy one more time.

Jagger called to check up on me and read me the riot act because I wasn't sleeping.

After a few fake static sounds I told him he was breaking up and put the receiver down.

Then I wished I hadn't.

That's when I shut my eyes and ordered myself to sleep.

"Suga. Suga? Wake up."

I opened one eye to see Goldie standing there in his royal blue peignoir. It looked great with his skin coloring but a bit eerie at night because he was sans wig and makeup. More like a bald Marilyn Monroe. "I just fell asleep."

"What day is it?"

I cursed him.

"Suga?"

"Going on Sunday. And don't ask me who the president is unless you want that royal blue thing in shreds."

After a typical Goldie shriek, he kissed my cheek and left.

He and Miles took turns annoying me all night until I screamed the ultimate threat: redecorating the condo in *my* taste.

The rest of the night, as far as I could remember, went by peacefully.

Ring. Ring.

I heard Goldie yell to Miles to get the phone so it didn't wake me. "Too late, Gold," I hollered.

Then I could hear Miles on the phone in their bedroom. "Yes, we kept waking her. No, she never was forgetful. Irritable, yes. Of course. Like her usual self."

I smiled to my pillows and figured it was the ER calling to see how I was. They often did that with patients who were sent home and might develop some kind of complications.

"No, we didn't give her any liquor. For chrissake. I am a nurse, Jagger."

Jagger!

I sprang up in my bed as if he'd walked into the room and seen me in my red flannel nightie. Whoa, boy. Moving fast was not a good idea. My head pounded. I flopped back. I knew I'd be fine if I moved at a more normal pace. Today I'd have to do Peggy and get that out of the way, since working at the clinic was so exhausting that I wasn't in a mood to go out at night.

Go out.

I remembered my date with Nick and my heart fluttered. I was thankful and impressed that my "friend" Jagger had called out of concern, but I repeated to myself, *Nick likes me!*

I heard Miles say a curt goodbye. I smiled again and got out of bed.

When I crossed the hallway to the bathroom, Goldie started admonishing Miles for waking me up by talking too loud.

"Gold, I'm fine. Actually the ringing woke me. If you're going to holler at someone, make it Jagger."

"Ah!" he yelled.

I laughed to myself at the vision of Goldie going up against Jagger. Too funny.

After I brushed my teeth, had a cup of tea that Miles fixed me and took my shower, I went through my "Peggy" wardrobe. "Hey, Gold. Got a minute?"

From downstairs he yelled, "What's wrong?" Then I heard the pounding of footsteps all the way up the stairs. They flew into my room as if I'd had some kind of attack.

"Take it easy, you two. I'm fine. Jagger has gotten you both too riled up. My head is fine. If it were Monday I'd be going to work." Ugh.

They sighed simultaneously. Miles settled in my stuffed mauve chair, and Goldie flopped on the bed like some diva.

"So, what is it, Suga?"

"Well, I never got the chance to tell you both that I've finished my case—"

They were up and dancing me around in seconds.

"Wait!" Miles yelled. "We'll make her sick. Are you sick, Pauline?"

"Oh, my God. Oh, my God." Goldie looked paler than me.

I laughed. "You two are way too gay sometimes. I'm fine. But even though I have enough to nail Sophie, I can't turn it in yet. I have to . . . shit, stay and help Jagger with his case."

Miles grinned.

Goldie frowned.

I stood speechless and . . . glad.

They prodded and prodded me for the details, and then I told them about having to be Peggy one more time.

Goldie got up and gave me a gentle hug. "I'm so proud of you. You thought of that all by yourself. Peggy must look fabulous today!"

With that the two set about making me age forty years.

After Goldie combed the last strand of my white wig, he turned me around.

"Damn." I looked at myself. He'd gone easy on the wrinkles this time, as if Peggy were happy about leaving. Miles made me wear Mrs. Honeysuckle's black shirtwaist dress with white piping. It came mid calf and my "Maciejko" legs looked damned good. He also pulled the hair of the wig up in a French chignon and today's makeup was more natural than overdone.

I turned to them. "Do you think I look younger?"

They laughed.

Miles leaned near. "Wait until Helen gets a load of you. The bitch will die of envy."

Goldie laughed. "Right. Then maybe she won't take Uncle Stash for a ride."

I groaned at the thought of Helen becoming my step-aunt. Thank goodness they'd live in Florida.

"Okay. I'm off. Good thing it's Sunday and there's a special luncheon at the senior citizens center."

Goldie said, "You take it easy, Suga," and Miles added, "Yeah."

They each kissed one cheek. I couldn't feel a thing with the makeup, but made a smooching sound back at them.

Spanky again barked at me, and I knew today was going to be a fabulous day.

*   *   *

When I passed down Pleasant Street toward the senior citizens center, I saw a spanking-new red Mustang pull out of Olive Street. The female driver, she looked . . . familiar.

My head swung around so fast, I had a moment of dizziness. After a deep breath, I leaned closer to the window.

The driver looked like Hildy!

Maybe my concussion was worse than I'd thought. Maybe I wasn't seeing clearly. Maybe Hildy did make "extra" money illegally and had killed Leo over some tiff.

My heart sank.

There was no way that she could afford that car on her measly salary, I thought.

There was a chance that it wasn't her, I told myself. I opened my window a bit for a breath of fresh air to revive me and heard a shout.

Apparently a black Toyota had pulled out in front of the Mustang. I was busy processing what the female in the Mustang had yelled.

Hang it!

How many other kids that looked like Hildy used that term? I could barely move. I sat staring at the green light until I heard some annoying honking. I started to move as the light turned red.

I was the last one who made it through.

I turned down Olive to follow her. She headed in the direction of her street. With each turn, I felt horrible. The least of my worries was that she'd see me and recognize me. Then again, if Spanky didn't know me, I don't think an unobservant teen would either.

But what about a murderess?

Where did the car come from?

All the way to her house I told myself that maybe she'd

borrowed it. But when she pulled into her driveway, I noticed the old car wasn't there. Hildy got out and bent to lock the door. I pulled up to the curb.

She looked as if she felt better, and why shouldn't she? A deep brown fur jacket, rabbit maybe, covered her. The knee-high boots she wore over her jeans looked brand new—and expensive. Italian leather, I guessed.

How could she afford all that?

I made a mental note to tell Jagger about all of this and added a prayer that there was some other explanation.

Hildy just couldn't be involved in the fraud—or the murders.

On the way back to the senior citizens center I decided I'd get something out of Hildy at work tomorrow. Surely she'd be there, since she didn't look sick anymore.

I, however, felt like crap after seeing her.

The parking lot at the center was quite full. I guessed I'd get to say goodbye to everyone in one fell swoop. Thank goodness. Jagger could have the disguise department. I hadn't even dressed up on Halloween as a kid. Hated it.

I pulled into a space, shut off my engine and put my hand on my car door. It pulled open on its own!

"Ah, Bellisima. How nice you look today." Joey the Wooer stood with his hand on my door. "Let me help-a you. It is a bit slippery. They really should-a cleaned this pavement better for us folks."

I wanted to say I survived a slide yesterday, but bit my tongue and smiled. "How nice you are, Mr. Joey." Peggy's tone had come back without a thought. I was really beginning to wonder if my masquerading was causing some kind of personality split for me. I liked Peggy.

Joey held my arm as we went inside. When we came up

to the table, he spoke rather loudly, "You look lovely to-day, Bellisima. Much younger."

I hoped my blush showed through my makeup since it seemed the appropriate thing to do after that comment.

Uncle Walt, Uncle Stash and Benny all nodded. Sophie merely stared. Helen kind of growled.

"You sure do," said Uncle Walt.

Green showed through Helen's makeup. She grabbed his arm rather possessively. And here I thought she had her sights on my other uncle. "Why so dolled up, Peggy?"

"Well—" I sat down after Joey held my chair and was once again sandwiched between him and Sophie. I ignored her lest I yell at her about being a criminal. "Unfortunately . . . it is my goodbye outfit."

Helen and Sophie perked up.

"Goodbye as you are going on a trip?" Helen asked.

"No, dearie. Goodbye as I am moving away. My mind isn't as clear as it used to be. My darling nephew is taking me to Arizona. I hear it's nice out there."

Helen beamed.

Sophie looked glad.

Benny said, "Well, we sure are going to miss you, Peggy."

My Uncle Walt stared at me a few seconds. "Darned if you don't look familiar today. Younger is right."

Uncle Stash clucked his tongue. "You've seen Peggy plenty, Walt. Of course she looks younger than you. Oh, by the way, everyone, Helen and I have some news to celebrate today."

I held onto the sides of my chair and watched Uncle Walt.

"We're getting married!"

Uncle Walt flinched.

Benny yelled, "Congratulations!"

Joey looked unreadable, as usual.

I tried to force a smile.

Sophie looked pissed. Jealous was maybe more like it. She probably wanted a man herself. Suddenly I felt sorry for her.

Then I could hear Jagger in my ear. "Don't get emotionally involved, Sherlock."

I shook my head and grabbed a roll. Joey passed me the butter, looking at me oddly.

"Everything all right, Bellisima?"

I slathered the roll and took too big a bite. "Fwine. Evewething is fwine."

Thank goodness my teeth were my own, and I didn't choke. Imagine someone doing CPR on me and finding all my padding as I died. My spirit would be too embarrassed to enter heaven.

After the meal, Joey insisted on dancing with me over and over. A few of the other men cut in, but Joey would always come back. I figured he was a bit overprotective, as any "old country" European would be after learning I was leaving. How cute. He held me tighter.

I was having way too much fun with him.

I was glad to be Peggy for the last time. My work was done as far as Sophie was concerned. I didn't think too much would be going on here with the Viagra fraud. We already knew the men bought it or traded their other medication for it.

Now we needed to find out who had replaced Leo.

I shut my eyes, letting Joey guide me around and prayed that it wasn't . . . Hildy.

Twenty-one

If I kept taking so many showers, I'd be permanently wrinkled in spite of the ones I was trying to
peel off. It was kind of sad washing away Peggy. I'd actually shed a few tears when I left the senior citizens center.
It was as if I was losing several old friends, and then there
were Helen and Sophie. Thank goodness Jagger had convinced me that Uncle Walt wasn't in any danger, or I'd
have to have kept up being Peggy. Now, I just let her fade
away. Goodbye, old friend.

Guess that was the life of a medical fraud insurance
investigator.

I consoled myself with the thought that at least I hadn't
become a full-blown schizophrenic.

But back to reality. Nick was due in a half hour. I really
needed to plan more primping time for the next date. I
scurried out of the shower and while still damp, dried my
hair and did my makeup. I went with the natural look that
Goldie had done on Peggy. Leaning closer to the mirror, I
was pleased. Muted browns and beiges worked with my
light complexion. Again I'd learned how to look better as
a woman from Goldie. What a hoot.

I threw on my robe and ran across the hallway.

Miles was coming up the stairs. "Stop running with a concussion!"

"I'm fine, you old mother hen." I laughed and opened my closet. "What should I wear for my date with Nick?"

Miles stood in my doorway, then leaned against the door frame. "This getting serious?"

I waved my hand at him in a "pshaw" kind of gesture. "I'm having fun, Miles."

Goldie came up from behind and set his arm around Miles's shoulder. "What are we discussing, and why isn't she dressed?"

"Her date, and we're here to help."

Goldie let out a whoop, and they hurried into my room. Tornado Goldie threw clothes from my closet until he found the "right" item. Miles sniffed all my colognes and spritzed me with the one he thought the sexiest. They were having as much fun as a kid let loose in the Magic Kingdom.

"Guess you should know what attracts men," I teased as Miles put me in a cream-colored slinky top. My breasts were not small by any means and the low-cut top showed off more cleavage than my morals allowed. He'd given it to me for my birthday last year. The tags still dangled from under the arm.

Goldie leaned back. "You go, girl!"

Miles shoved a pair of black heels at me. "You could kill yourself on the slippery sidewalks with these. Put them on."

"But you said I could fall."

"That's why you need to hold on real tightly to Mr. Nick Caruso!"

They high-fived each other.

"You two." I slipped on the shoes after struggling into a

pair of black pants that I had in my Goodwill pile. I insisted they were too tight. Goldie said they were sexy.

When I stood and straightened, I started to turn toward the mirror.

"Wait!" Goldie yelled. As he ran out of the room, he said, "Don't look yet."

I turned to Miles. "I can't imagine what he's going to lend me."

But after Goldie returned, had me stand still, and clasped something around my neck, he said I could then look.

I opened my eyes and gasped.

Miles whistled.

"Oh wow. Gold, this is perfect." He'd lent me a necklace. Not just any plain necklace, but a Goldie-size necklace of beige, black and deep burgundy beads of different sizes. It wasn't light by any means, but I'd suffer neck pain to look this good. Not that I wanted to exude sex, but damn if the necklace didn't call attention to my chest. What the hell. One time wouldn't hurt. I pulled them into a group hug. "You guys. You are too much. I love both of you."

Miles wiped at his eyes.

Goldie sniffled.

I smiled and grabbed my purse from the dresser. "Nick will be here—" The doorbell rang before I could finish. I kissed them each one more time and went out into the hallway.

"Think he's the one?" Miles asked Goldie.

I paused.

"No, but I hope he turns out to be."

I stood for a few seconds and then knew what I wanted to do.

I was going to sleep with Nick tonight—because I *wanted* to.

* * *

"Wow." Nick leaned over and kissed me as soon as I'd opened the front door. "You look fabulous, Pauline."

I really did!

"Thanks." I kissed him back, then momentarily felt as if I should put on a cardigan to hide my chest. "You don't look so bad yourself." And he didn't. I don't think Nick really could. He wore a jacket of a deep camel color and brown trousers that blended perfectly with an off-white turtleneck. His eyes even looked damn good.

I swallowed.

He took me by the shoulder and walked me out to his Porsche and opened my door. I refused to think of Jagger. No way was he entering into this night.

Tonight Nick and I really were an "us."

We headed to Madelyn's. The hostess sat us at the most secluded table, where Nick ordered Dom Perignon.

Me, I was more a Budweiser girl, but tonight I felt all giddy and sexy inside and decided the bubbly was a perfect choice, along with the crab-stuffed Maine lobsters Nick ordered.

The dinner was fabulous, and I filled Nick in on my case—even telling him I had agreed to work longer with Jagger. I could tell by Nick's look that he didn't like the idea, but he proved to be a professional when he said, "Make sure he pays you for your work."

I hadn't thought about that, but Jagger had paid me to help the last time. Although desperate for money, I never would have thought to ask for it. But looking at Nick across the table in the dim lighting and having my attraction bubble inside like the Dom Perignon, I decided that was the best way to keep my relationship with Jagger on the up and up.

No more foolish fantasies about Jagger.

I was hired by him and would get paid.

Nick leaned over and kissed my cheek. "Penny for your thoughts."

I smiled and decided although I didn't want to start out lying to my "boyfriend," I couldn't share those thoughts. "I think you are absolutely right about Jagger paying me to stay on."

I hadn't told Nick about Jagger's "loan."

After dinner we walked along the water's edge. Although near the end of winter, milder air had come up from the south. The full moon glowed so brightly that once we were past the restaurant's little white lights, we could still see each other.

I kept peeking at Nick and thinking, "He likes me."

Yahoo!

"Maybe you shouldn't be out in the cold too much," Nick said, wrapping a protective hold around my shoulders.

"I'm fine." I looked down at my shoes and held his arm tighter. "My head is fine. Besides Goldie and Miles wouldn't have let me out of the condo if they didn't think I was all right."

Nick laughed. "Have you thought about a place of your own, now that Goldie has moved in?"

"I think a lot about it, then they take such good care of me and insist I stay. I truly think they don't want me to leave. I'm the daughter they never had. It's not that I'm trying to convince myself of that, because the other option is . . . moving in with my parents." I groaned. "Maybe I do feel sick now."

Nick laughed, leaned over and kissed my cheek. "How about a nightcap?"

Hot milk was my usual "nightcap." "Sounds like a perfect way to end this wonderful night, but it's Sunday. I think even Madelyn's closes in a few minutes."

Nick looked at his watch. "You're right. I'm mixed up on my days. My trip to New York was a whirlwind."

"But well worth it, it seems." Over dinner he'd told me how he had gotten plenty of surveillance tape on his suspect and after tying up a few loose ends, his case would be over soon too.

What a weird, fun business, I thought.

"Guess we'll have to take a rain check."

My mouth dried. My heart started to pound, so I pulled a bit away before he felt it. My logical mind told me, "Don't say it."

But I knew what I wanted tonight, so I said, "Don't you have any nightcaps at your place?"

As soon as the very un-Pauline-like words came out, I felt my face burning.

Nick paused, leaned over and kissed my lips. "I like a woman of the twenty-first century."

All the way to his place I pictured the grin on his face and told myself this is what I wanted.

Then why were my hands shaking so much that I had to stuff them into my too-tight pants pockets?

For as little as I knew about Jagger, Nick was now an open book. He showed me around his penthouse apartment, which overlooked the Connecticut River. I found it hard to believe that he made such good money as an investigator, but then I realized I was looking at the job through *my* eyes.

Goldie did pretty damn good too.

Nick's place had a wall of windows in the living room, which was decorated in chrome and black and white leather. Very masculine, yet inviting. He poured us two glasses of Harvey's Bristol Cream, a smooth, delicious sherry I'd never had before.

After the Dom Perignon, and not being a big drinker, I was feeling very relaxed yet still in control of my faculties. Nick showed me pictures of his parents, who had passed away several years ago. He'd grown up in West Hartford, Connecticut, in what I knew was a rather wealthy section. As an only child, he attended Yale and followed in his father's footsteps, taking over the insurance company when he died.

"But after years of seeing the fraud people committed, I sold my shares of the company and now freelance to stop the criminals."

My first thought was that my mother would love that about Nick. Good looks and good morals. What a package. My second thought was, I want to kiss him.

So, being a woman of the twenty-first century, I set my sherry on the chrome-and-glass coffee table and said, "I'm going to kiss you."

His eyes widened, then without a word, he set his glass down and leaned closer.

I took his shoulders in my hands and pressed my lips to his. Wow! This wasn't as difficult as I'd thought it would be. Or maybe Dom and Harvey had given me a jolt of courage.

Nick took over and ran kisses along my neck.

I moaned.

Then he really took over, which entailed my top being lifted off over my head. Thank goodness I'd worn my clean underwear. Actually Goldie had made me wear my black, lacy push-up bra that he said made my shape look like a model's. For some reason I don't think Nick cared two hoots about my undies.

He kissed my lips and leaned back. "Soon there'll be no stopping."

"Who wants to?" my voice came out as sexy-sounding as Lois the pharmacy tech's. I was on a roll!

Nick stood and took my hand. "You sure, Pauline?"

"Nice of you to ask, but—" I stood on my tiptoes and kissed his lips. "Look, buddy, if you don't take your clothes off soon, I'm going to rip them off."

He chuckled. A deep masculine sound.

Nick had a huge bedroom with windows overlooking the city of Hartford, a huge television/stereo system with Surround Sound, which Frank Sinatra now crooned from and a bed on one wall the size of a small football field.

Our clothes lay strewn across the room as in some Meg Ryan romantic comedy. Not that any of this was funny. As he kissed along my neck again, I thought, oh, no, this isn't funny.

It's *delicious*.

Nick eased back, brushed my hair from my eyes. "One last chance—"

I touched my finger to his lips. I needed "it" tonight. Not that I was so horny, but with my last boyfriend now in jail, it had been a *long* time. "Don't you want to?" came out in that Lois tone again.

"Of course, but I don't want to rush you, Pauline. I like you too much."

Nick likes me!

Goddammit. Jagger's face started to appear before me.

I gasped, then refused to focus in on the vision.

A blurry Jagger disappeared.

Nick chuckled again, his chest vibrating against mine. "Don't sound so surprised."

"It's not that. It's—"

I couldn't say that I just might be using him for my own physical pleasure, which certainly was an acceptable twenty-first-century thing for a woman to do.

But it wasn't me.

I started to wind my finger in Goldie's' necklace, which was the only item I wore. How damn sexy was that? "I like you too, Nick. I really do. So, let's not stop."

He leaned to kiss me.

The necklace tightened on my finger. I tried to pull it out, but got sidetracked with Nick. Yum. It was wonderful, having him do all those things to me. I needed to hold him, so I yanked my finger free.

Beige, black and deep burgundy beads of different sizes flew into the air, snowing down on Nick and me—one slamming Nick in the eye.

Twenty-two

"Oh, my God!" I yelled amid the raining beads. "Are you all right?" I leaned close to see his eye. It wasn't even red. Thank goodness.

Nick looked at me. "Fine. I'm fine."

We looked around the black, beige and burgundy bead-covered bed. No way could we be comfortable on it.

"I'm so sorry. Sorry you got smacked in the eye and definitely sorry that our 'moment' was interrupted."

And it was. No going back.

Nick took my hand and kissed it.

Then, he looked at me and we started laughing.

It shouldn't have been so humorous, but it was either that, or I'd die of embarrassment in Nick's bed amid the damn beads.

How would that look in the newspapers?

Middle-aged, *single* insurance fraud investigator dies of embarrassment with the one man who had taken her to bed in months.

"I'm so . . . so sooooorry," I tried to say amid laughs.

He kissed me quickly and picked a black bead from my hair. "Guess it wasn't meant to be."

My heart sank.

He leaned near. "For tonight."

Ah. Sounded much less permanent.

After we dressed, Nick got a plastic baggie for the beads. He said he'd have them restrung. I argued politely enough that I should get that done, but he insisted. I sighed with relief since I didn't need any more bills. Goldie wouldn't have let me pay for it anyway, but on principle, it was nice having Nick offer.

It was nice having Nick, period.

He took me home and kissed me at the door.

"I'll call you tomorrow."

And, again, I knew he would. There was nothing worse than a guy who said he'd call and never did. Women could usually tell when that line was fake. With Nick it wasn't.

I turned to watch him go and noticed my car parked in the rear of the lot. Not my space, but at least Jagger had kept his promise to have it returned. Too tired to move it, I decided I'd rather risk getting a nasty note from the neighbor in 10B, whose space it was in.

Goldie and Miles were asleep on the couch when I opened the door. I smiled and shook my head. Would my mother be waiting up for me if I moved back home?

"Oh, shit," I mumbled.

Miles opened an eye. He tugged at Goldie. "She's home."

"Who . . . Suga!" He sat up, rubbing at his eyes. "So, tell us."

I looked at Miles in his black silk pj's and Goldie in the blue peignoir, looking striking this time. He hadn't removed his makeup or wig for the night yet. I hoped I looked that good to Nick, pre bead explosion.

Goldie leaned closer. "My necklace."

I hurried over to him and gave both of them a hug. "Oh, Gold. I'm so sorry. It's got to be fixed."

He looked surprised and a bit upset, but said, "No problem. My friend Jerry is a jeweler."

"It popped and the beads fell all over. Nick is having it restrung."

"Oh. Oh?" Goldie winked at Miles. "That's great, Suga. No problem with the necklace. I'm surprised it broke, though. It was quite expensive and imported from Johannesburg."

I looked at my finger. A red ring from where the necklace had been wrapped glared at me. "It didn't break easily."

"Enough with beads," Miles said. "How was your date?"

"I like Nick. It was fine."

They yelled, "Fine?"

Goldie leaned near. "I'm hoping the broken beads at least had something to do with . . . you know."

Miles slapped his arm.

I laughed. "Okay. It was wonderful. A wonderful date. Nick is wonderful. I *really* like him."

They high-fived each other and laughed.

"Look, you guys don't have to wait up for me like this. I feel as if I'm imposing on your lives."

They screeched in horror.

Miles took me by the arm. "You belong here. We want you here."

Goldie joined in with, "You're like a sister to us, Suga."

"A sister?" I asked.

They laughed. "Okay, we mother hens need someone to watch over, and we want it to be you," Miles said.

"I feel as if I was just born. A bouncing six-pound baby girl."

Knowing my true birth weight, Miles eyed me.

"Hey, it's *my* fantasy."

We all howled, hugged and kissed.

Goldie said, "Now get some sleep, Suga. You have work tomorrow and need to be fully recovered."

I shook my head. "Yes, Mom."

On my way to my room, I heard them giggling and knew none of us was ready for me to move out yet.

Last night I had slept the best I had in months. I credited it to Nick and smiled as I drove into the parking lot of the clinic. Okay, the fact that I didn't have to move back to 171 David Drive could have added to my slumber.

Then my heart sank, knowing I had to keep working in nursing. I had vowed twice now not to get back into this profession, but Jagger had other plans for me.

This was the last time for sure.

When I opened my door and got out, I looked around for Hildy's new Mustang. Only a white one sat on the far side of the lot, and I knew that belonged to a guy in the clinic. Hildy had to be back at work today, I told myself.

I really needed to know how she got that car.

I hurried inside and stuck my belongings in my locker in the nurse's lounge. One of the other nurses came in. "Hi."

"Hello, Pauline. Light morning today," she said, sticking her purse in her locker.

Good. I had to get in contact with Jagger then, and see what I could find out about Hildy. When the nurse left, I took out my cell phone and punched in #1.

"Leave a message."

"Oh, hi, Jagger," I started to say, then realized it was his voice mail. Hmm. Why wouldn't he answer his phone? What if I needed help?

Knowing him, he'd be there.

I shrugged, said I needed to talk to him and went out to work. My first patient, Freddy Wentwhistle, a young guy with red hair, glasses and a mustache, had come in for a pain in his knee.

Gotcha, Jagger!

When I showed him into the examining room, I shut the door. "Look. We need to talk. Why didn't you answer your phone?"

"Talk?" Freddy looked a bit scared. "You called me, ma'am?"

"Stop pretending. No one can hear us. Hildy has a new car."

Freddy stood and hobbled toward the door. "Oh. That's nice for . . . Hildy." His voice trembled.

"Oh, my." I stepped back so he wouldn't bolt on me with his bum knee. "Aren't you Freddy Wentwhistle from Manchester?" I'd quickly looked at his chart to see he was from Hartford.

"No . . . no."

"I'm so sorry. I was mistaken. Please sit back down, Freddy, so I can take your blood pressure." Which must be sky high after thinking I was nuts.

The rest of the morning I was more cautious of accusing other patients of being Jagger, although a Mr. Smith and Mr. Jones looked very suspicious.

Jagger never did show up.

That I knew of.

At lunchtime, I hurried over to the pharmacy.

Kathy was sitting at Hildy's desk writing on file cards.

"Oh, hey, Kath."

She didn't look up. "Hi, Pauline."

Lois was at the counter with a patient and gave me a suspicious look. She seemed not to like me, although we really hadn't met. Then again, everyone here was on edge after Leo's death, the police investigation and being overworked.

I ignored her and said, "Can Hildy go to lunch now?"

Kathy looked up. "Why the hell do you think I'm sitting here?"

"Hildy still out sick?"

"The bitch quit."

I know Kathy continued complaining because her lips were moving, but my mind was reeling on its own. She quit! How could Hildy leave a job she claimed to need so much? Oh, shit. This really looked bad for her.

Hildy had something to do with the fraud—and Leo's death.

I knew it.

And where the hell was Jagger?

After I'd left the pharmacy with a giant knot in my stomach, I realized I better try to eat something since I had a half day to go. I needed some fresh air, so I decided to walk across the street to the diner Goldie and I had gone to before.

I opened the door to the fragrance of grease and the humming of a crowded room. Smoke wafted through the air, since only half of the diner was smoke-free. I stood next to the "Please wait to be seated" sign, looking around the room. None of the other staff was here today so I'd have to eat alone.

The hostess came up to me. "One?"

I nodded.

She took a menu and guided me to a booth at the end of the room. "This is all I have, unless you want to sit at the counter."

"This is fine." I sat down and took the menu from her. Still upset about Hildy, I looked for something that'd be digestible with a knotted stomach.

A shadow crossed over my menu.

I looked up.

Jagger, dressed as plain, regular, gorgeous Jagger, stood there. "Hildy left town."

As he sat, my mouth dried and my heart jolted. I'd have to stick with soup for lunch now. "What do you mean?" I asked stupidly. Jagger spoke perfect English, and I'd "gotten" that Hildy had run away.

He waved to the waitress. "Coffee." He looked at me.

"Arsenic." With the news of Hildy, I needed arsenic.

Jagger shook his head. Only once, thank goodness. "And a cola for her."

"What do you . . . how do you know about Hildy?"

Jagger had bent his head to look at the menu and only shifted his eyes upward to speak volumes to me.

"Okay," I said as the waitress set down my cola. I looked at her. "New England clam chowder."

"That it?"

I nodded.

She rolled her eyes as if soup wouldn't garnish her a very big tip. Keep rolling your eyes, lady, and there'll be *no* tip.

She gave Jagger his coffee.

"Tuna on whole wheat. No tomatoes," Jagger said.

She gave him a colossal smile and bent to get his menu while sticking her boobs in his face.

I curled my lip.

When the waitress left, Jagger looked at me. "Anyway. She's gone. Moved out. Her landlord said she left everything except her clothes—and an envelop of cash to pay the rent and utilities to date."

"Oh, shit. She also drove away in a brand-new Mustang. A hot red one."

"Mustang?"

"I saw her Saturday and followed her."

"Jesus, Sherlock. Did she see you?"

"Of course not. I was Pe—" Yikes! I almost blew my cover! Even if it was Jagger, him knowing about Peggy was on my no-no list. Even though Peggy wouldn't surface again, I wanted to keep at least one thing from Jagger. I know he'd seen me as half-Peggy when he popped up in my backseat, but he hadn't questioned me then, which meant I had to live with him thinking I wore polyester and comfortable shoes.

Felt good to know he didn't know *everything* about me.

A picture of Nick and the beads flashed before my eyes. Surely Jagger didn't know about . . . naw. I was thinking stupid thoughts because I was so upset about Hildy. "This doesn't look good for her. Huh?"

Jagger took a sip of coffee. Good enough answer for me.

"Damn it. I really liked her. She was so poor and in need of a friend. I thought I could help her."

Again he looked over the mug.

"Okay. Okay. Don't get involved. Don't get emotional. But in my heart I still think she's innocent."

Jagger set down his mug. "Is your heart always right?"

I thought of my ex. The now incarcerated criminal boyfriend. "It has its moments."

"Look, Sherlock. You have to give up your nursing help-everyone mentality to do this job. You're not trying to help. You're trying to convict, uncover fraud."

The waitress came over and set Jagger's tuna sandwich down. "Anything else, big boy?"

I groaned.

"Not for now, doll." He winked.

I cleared my throat after looking at her empty hands. "My soup?"

"Soup?"

"New England clam chowder. You wrote it down." I stupidly pointed to her apron where she kept her order book.

She never looked down, but stared at Jagger.

"Oh, yeah. Chowda. Be out soon." After a wink back at "big boy," she left and after a prolonged amount of time brought me a now cool soup.

I didn't have time to send it back, so I ate it, telling myself it was piping hot. I wished I could tell myself not to care so much about Hildy, like I'd convinced myself that the soup didn't taste all that bad. I finished it and looked at my watch. "I have to get back to work."

"Meet me at the backdoor when the clinic closes."

I didn't have time to argue, but I'd been thinking all day about Nick calling me. I had been really looking forward to seeing him and also not having to go to Bingo tonight. But the case had to get settled soon.

And I had to find out about Hildy.

I saluted Jagger with two fingers like in my old Girl Scout days and left.

All the way through the crowd, until I got to the door, I felt him staring at me—but didn't dare turn around.

* * *

At five, the receptionist turned the phone lines over to the answering service, and I said good night to everyone and walked out the front door. I got into my car and drove around toward the back.

Dr. Handy was getting into his car as I drove by. He gave me an odd look, and I figured he was wondering why I wasn't driving out of the lot. Shit. At least I didn't have to talk to him.

Jagger's SUV sat amid the few cars in the back lot. I guessed the cleaning crew had already come in and was at work now. I hoped I didn't run into Grumpy Janitor.

I got out next to Jagger's SUV. He waved me in. When I sat down, he drove off, leaving my car there once again. Oh well, guess it would miraculously show up in my condo lot tomorrow morning when I needed it.

"Can't I go home and at least change?"

At the stoplight, he reached into the backseat and pulled out my navy overnight bag.

"What? How'd you get that?" I took it and looked inside to see my black gloves, a black top and black jeans along with my boots. "Did you break into my condo?"

Did I really need to ask?

"How do you know your roommates didn't give me the stuff?" I noticed him grin as he looked straight ahead at the other cars.

"I'm going to ask them, you know."

"I have no doubt."

I really wouldn't. Some sleepless night I might need a fantasy about him rummaging through my clothes, and if my roomies had given him the stuff, I'd have nothing to dream about.

We pulled into Dunkin Donuts. He looked at me as if I should be able to read his mind.

"Okay. I'll go change." When I opened the door, I turned. "Damn. I'm getting pretty good at reading your mind now, Jagger. Look out."

"Then you must have read that you should call Nick and cancel tonight."

My hand froze on the door. How'd he know? After a few seconds of embarrassment, I started to slam the door. After the *bang*, I leaned close to the window. "Goldie's beads."

He gave me one of those looks again along with the shaking head thingie.

Phew. This time I could "read" that he didn't know about the fateful "bead" incident.

In the ladies' room, I kept mumbling to myself about "feeling as if Big Brother was watching me all the time." Sure it was good when I was being shot at, but now that I had a love life, I sure as hell didn't want "Big Boy/Big Brother" knowing any details. "You're being paranoid, Pauline," I told myself and also agreed.

Once dressed, I went outside to the SUV. Jagger had gotten us coffee and my French cruller. My usual French cruller. I was that predictable to Jagger. And I hated that.

Suddenly I really had a craving for a glazed.

Twenty-three

"Where are we going?" I asked Jagger as we drove down Olive Street.

"You tell me."

I looked at him. What the hell was he talking about? After a long pause, I realized Jagger was giving me a lesson in Fraud 101. Obviously he didn't think I was ready for 201. "Well, Hildy moved out. Mr. W's house is done. Sophie is probably home, since there's no Bingo now." I looked at the cars passing by and tried to think. Where else did we need to go?

Jagger glanced at me.

"I'm thinking."

He looked straight at the road. I figured we weren't going to the clinic or pharmacy. "We've already searched the pharmacy several times, so that can't be where we are going." I paused when we passed Pleasant Street.

At the red light, he turned toward me. "Cheater."

"No . . . I . . . okay. So you already passed the turn."

He took another look at me and when the light turned green, he started to go. I could get more hints when I saw which way he drove.

He pulled into the parking lot of McDonald's and parked. "You need to think harder, Sherlock."

I mumbled a few times and then kept asking myself what we had missed. I ran a litany of suspects through my head, but most had already been mentioned. Hildy was gone to who knew where. Aha! I looked at Jagger. "You found Hildy!"

"No."

"Shit." It seemed as if hours flew by although it was probably more like twenty minutes. I thought again and again about both of our cases. Then it dawned on me.

There was only one place that we hadn't broken in to yet. One place that could hold the answer to all our questions.

"Leo's."

He cranked the engine. We were off.

I felt real damn proud of myself.

Jagger, however, never said a word—but I took that as a sign of praise, coming from him. Hey, I'd gotten to realize that *not* having him shake his head at me was tantamount to getting a gold star on my homework.

We pulled around the corner and into a subdivision. A rather nice-looking subdivision of huge houses lit up like New York City after dark.

Leo, I soon learned, had lived near the river. His house was a rather large one and not too shabby. Very modern, made mostly of cement with large columns and round sections as if someone had put it together like a Tinker Toy house.

Not a house an ordinary pharmacist could afford.

Jagger pulled down the street into the parking lot of Mario's Bar and Grill. Although the name sounded as if bikers frequented the place, nothing but BMWs, Mercedes, and SUVs sat in the lot. Inconspicuous. That was Jagger and me.

He shut off the engine, collected his flashlight and gloves and looked at me. I reached into the suitcase he'd brought me and took out my gloves. "I'm still going to find out if you broke into my condo to get these."

He grinned.

I stuck on my gloves and hat that Jagger held out toward me. A basic black wool cap was next. I figured he'd want me to tuck all my hair into it this time. I did that and even shoved the collar of my coat up higher so my pale complexion didn't reflect any light.

We walked in the opposite direction of Leo's house and then turned and walked several blocks until we were behind it.

Damn, this guy was good.

My fear of getting caught breaking and entering was nullified as I kept telling myself that Jagger might be FBI or a cop or whatever. He did have Lieutenant Shatley on his side. He'd never arrest us. As Jagger jimmied a lock on the backdoor and managed to open it without a sound, I told myself that Lieutenant Shatley had probably said, "Sure. Go take a peek at Leo Pasinski's house. No problem, my friend Jagger."

Jagger didn't turn on his flashlight but took my arm and guided me into the darkened hallway, where he fiddled with the burglar alarm on the wall as it made a little *beep-beep* sound. I hoped he was shutting it off. I surmised he didn't know the code, but also figured Jagger *knew* how to get around something like that.

The night was about to begin.

I soon stood in the kitchen still marveling that Jagger

was so smooth. So knowledgeable. So adept. Adept at breaking and entering without a trace. That shouldn't be a good thing, but in our business it sure as hell helped.

He leaned close to me. "Don't try this on your own."

I should have been insulted, but he was right. I could just imagine the cop's lights and them calling on a bullhorn for me to come out with my hands up, and Goldie and Miles crying in the parking lot while my mother yelled at the police all the while serving sandwiches made of leftovers. My heart started to beat a bit faster. Then I looked at Jagger's silhouette. He still hadn't put the flashlight on.

My heart slowed.

"What makes you think I couldn't do this on my own?"

In the dim lighting, his eyes sparkled as he grinned.

"Bite me," I muttered.

I turned to look around the kitchen. It was even eerier than Mr. Wisnowski's house, since dishes still sat in the sink. The timer must have been set on the Mr. Coffee machine, because it had made a pot and turned itself off. How sad. Leo left for work one day and never came back—but the coffee got made.

A sad life indeed.

Jagger took my arm and led me down the hallway and up a circular staircase. "Investigators are not above the law, Sherlock."

I knew that was a warning. And a damn sensible one at that. But I also knew that doing something like this with Jagger, although illegal, could only be a good thing. He really was trying to teach me the business, but his needing my help meant we did things his way—not the way I'd be doing them by myself.

I didn't even own a gun.

Jagger, however, did. Probably more than one.

We walked into a giant room with glass walls overlooking the water. In the center of the room was a circular bed, covered in a black silken bedspread with white pillow shams and a mirror above.

I felt my face grow hot and hoped Jagger hadn't noticed the mirror.

Jagger not notice something, and I did. What a joke.

"Swinger Leo," he mumbled.

I forced a laugh. It was truly embarrassing, talking sex to Jagger even if in the line of duty. He opened drawer after drawer. Having no clue as to what to look for, I turned around. And gasped.

In the corner of the room was a huge porcelain tiger standing on its hind legs. Bigger than Jagger's six plus feet.

Jagger's hand grabbed mine. "It won't eat you, Sherlock. Try to keep the hysterics down."

"Hysterics!" I yelled hysterically. Then I decided to take a few deep breaths.

I didn't need to look back to know he was shaking his head. "Stop doing that." I walked toward the tiger. "This one's face looks like the one Goldie has on his sparkly shirt. Did I ever tell you that the tiger's eye on Goldie's shirt is a mini video camera?"

I felt Jagger close behind me. His flashlight clicked on, aiming at the tiger. "You don't say."

"I do say. It was funny. One day he took a video of me with his shirt. Well not the shirt per say. The eye of the tiger was a big gem that popped out. Well, the eye was a camera, not a real gem. It's amazing what technology can do nowadays."

"That a girl, Sherlock."

I turned around, but Jagger eased past me, still shining the light on the tiger. Its eyes, actually. He reached up and touched the left one. Nothing.

"Oh, my! You don't think . . . Do you think the eye . . . ? Naw. That'd be way too coincidental. . . . Do you really, Jagger, think—"

Before I could finish my nervous rambling, Jagger touched the right eye. The silence in the room was deafening. Then there was a *pop*. I looked down to see the "eye" in Jagger's hand.

And behind us a wall safe's door flew open.

Jagger leaned over and whispered in my ear, "We've never been here."

Again with the warning as if I was going to call the Associated Press to tell them we broke in to a dead man's house.

"What do you think is in the safe?"

He looked at me.

"Okay. So we should go look to find out." I was beginning to think Jagger just liked looking at me. At least I told myself that foolishness in order to save face.

I followed him to the safe. He kept the flashlight on now.

"Jesus. Look at this."

I leaned closer. Momentarily, I couldn't comprehend what I was looking at.

"What . . . what is it?" I managed to ask as if I'd never spoken the English language before.

The flashlight remained aimed inside the safe. "Leo had quite the business here. There is a downside to being a nerdy perfectionist though."

"Like what?"

"The fool has notes here, spelling out his entire scheme. Even graphs of revenue and sales. What a shit."

Hildy.

That made me think of Hildy.

"Is anyone's name . . . on anything?" Please, not *Hildy's*.

Jagger went about taking pictures of everything. This time he had a tiny camera that looked like a tiny camera. "Hildy's name is not on anything, Pauline." He took the papers, spread them on the bed and clicked away.

I stood in a huff for a few seconds. "I was thinking about Sophie. Sophie Jones."

Without looking up, Jagger muttered, "Banko. Sophie *Banko*."

And *Hildy* Jones.

I couldn't get the kid out of my head and said a silent prayer that we were wrong about her.

But as much as I believed in miracles, this time I didn't think even my Saint Theresa could right Hildy in this one.

While I stood there stewing about my concern and admitting I really shouldn't get so involved or care so much about someone like Hildy, a possible murderess, Jagger cleaned up the bed and put the papers back.

He took out a stack of bills, still in their wrapper. Next to it was an empty one. Obviously some of the money had been taken. By Leo?

Or Hildy?

"Pasinski was two-timing the insurance companies," Jagger said. "He'd send in the fake prescriptions Sophie gave him, then 'fill' other prescriptions with the medication and sell it to someone else."

"We knew all that already." I felt my chest poof out, pointing that out to Jagger.

"But what we didn't know was that the reason he 'filled' the empty prescriptions was to let someone working in the pharmacy know which ones they were."

Damn. I stood there a few minutes, hoping that the epiphany Jagger just had would sink in. But for the life of me, I didn't know what the hell he was talking about. And, I hated to say "I don't follow," so I bit my lower lip.

He shut the safe, returned the tiger's eye and led me to the bathroom. "There's a mole in the pharmacy."

My mind flashed to those tiny furry creatures without eyes. At least I didn't think they had eyes, and I surely didn't need them to burrow through people's yards, ruining their grass. Then I shifted back into investigator mode.

It wasn't easy being in this house alone with Jagger—with no one knowing where we were.

And that big bed with the mirrored ceiling.

Jagger could take advantage of me, and I'd be helpless.

Make that hopeless. I was hopeless.

Switching gears, I said, "A mole. There is . . . you think it's Hildy. You think she was the one he was giving the clues to, and she'd know what to do to commit the fraud. And you think she either messed up or got greedy. You think she killed him to keep all the profits." I stepped further into the luxurious bathroom—

And fell *splash* into a sunken tub.

"Shit!"

Jagger started laughing.

I was hollering for him to get me out. My boots, soaked through and through now, weighed a ton. Cement shoes were like Air Nikes compared with these.

"Give me a damn hand and a damn towel!"

He switched on a small night-light near the sink, opened a cabinet below and then threw two fluffy black towels at me.

I caught them in midair.

"Use them, fold them up and put them back were we found them."

Clever. Who would check Leo's cabinets? "I'll turn to ice when I go outside," I mumbled as he helped me out of the tub. My first thought was that I was glad to have on all black and a heavy-duty winter coat. I looked down at my clothes just to make sure nothing was transparent.

"Not going to win any wet tee shirt contests tonight, Sherlock."

"I'm not . . . ha, ha."

Did he mean I could win one if I had on summer clothes? *Pauline!* I screamed inside my head until it hurt and brought me back to sanity. I did as Jagger had said with the towels and stood for a few minutes feeling sticky and wet. Material clung to every part of my body.

"We'll get out of here so you can slip into something more comfortable."

There were two ways I could take that suggestion. Remaining professional, I went with changing to dry clothes.

"Why do you think Leo filled the tub and left it like that before he went to work . . . and never returned?"

Jagger leaned against the counter. I could see pride in his eyes. He nodded this time. "Good question."

I beamed.

"Maybe he was going to take a bath and was running late."

"Shit. How un-mysterious. How unromantic. How logical." I curled my lip and bent to wipe up the floor.

Jagger chuckled. "Ready?"

"Well, we didn't look in his medicine cabinet yet." I actually had thought of something before Jagger had! I leaned past him and opened the medicine cabinet above the sink, certain we were going to find a gigantic bottle of Viagra.

A box of Tampax fell out.

Jagger lifted it up and shoved it back on the shelf. "Did you really think someone as smart and crafty as Leo Pasinski would keep anything in this cabinet that could get him found out?"

I would have. "No, but shit, Jagger. Whose are these?" I pointed to the blue box. "And these?" A round container of birth control pills were next to a Lady Schick razor.

"Leo lived with someone."

I swung around. "Who?"

"If I knew that, we wouldn't be here unless she died with him and no one's found her body yet."

"Ah. You don't know who he lived with then."

"Or that he lived with anyone."

Slam.

Jagger looked at me.

"Do you think . . . Leo's house has mice?"

He pulled me so fast, we forgot the night-light when we went hurrying down the hallway. "Jagger," I whispered. "The night-light."

"Christ." He pushed me into an alcove in the hallway. "Stay put."

"I'm not sleeping in any shed, you know."

I leaned out and turned my head so I could hear if someone was really downstairs.

Click. Click.

His girlfriend.

Jagger came up behind me and before I could scream from fright, he had the foresight to cover my mouth.

I pushed his hand away and whispered. "It's a she. She's an *it*. She's down there."

"Slow down, Sherlock."

"She's down there, Jagger. A lady. Leo's lady."

"You saw her?"

"No. I stayed put. I heard her clicking across the tile floor."

"Clicking."

"Heels, Jagger. Someone wearing spike heels is down there. Unless Goldie has a clone, I'm guessing it's a woman. Leo's woman."

Jagger shoved a finger over my mouth and pulled me toward the stairs. He never gave me the time to question him.

What could I say? I trusted the guy.

Despite my legs feeling as if they had no bones in them, he pushed us up close against the wall across from the banister.

Before I knew it, we were through the living room and near the front door. I noticed a light blinking on the alarm system next to the door.

"Fuck," Jagger mumbled.

He'd noticed it too.

He motioned for me to move to the side, and without even a thought, I found myself inside the foyer closet, amongst moth-scented wool coats and two full-length minks—and Jagger's shoulder crushing my left breast.

Pain and pleasure really were a hairline away from each other.

Click. Click.

In the darkness of the closet I could hear my heart

beating and figured it'd race itself into some life-ending arrhythmia.

The footsteps passed us.

She must have walked into the carpeted living room and, hopefully, up the stairs.

Jagger eased to the side and opened the door a crack.

We looked through it together.

Yikes.

On the landing of the stairway, reading some mail, stood Lois Meyers.

Twenty-four

"Lois the pharmacy tech? What the hell is she doing here?" I whispered to Jagger.

In the darkness of the closet he said, "That's what we need to find out. Maybe she's his accomplice at the pharmacy."

"That would make Hildy not guilty."

"Where'd she get the money for her car, to pay her rent and to leave?"

I felt his shoulder press into mine. Forget it, I told myself. I had to keep my wits about me for the case. To get it done and over with. To get paid. To help the police catch a murderer.

I whispered, "You need to pay me for helping you."

"Did you think I wouldn't?"

Shit. "Of course not."

Jagger eased me to the back of the closet. "When I give you a signal, follow me without a word, and fast."

I nodded, then realized that more than likely he couldn't see me in the darkness. So, I whispered, "Okay."

Suddenly footsteps came down the stairs again. This

time they weren't heels, but it still had to be Lois. At least I hoped no one else was here. Jagger took me by the shoulders and held me tightly as if he expected me to run out of the closet and get caught.

Shit. Sometimes he didn't give me any credit for brains.

The front door opened. The burglar alarm beeped until she must have put the code in. Then the door shut.

Silence.

Jagger eased open the closet door only enough to see out and listen. He stood for several minutes that way. In the distance a car door shut, an engine cranked and a car pulled away.

Jagger opened the door all the way, grabbing me at the same time. Not taking any chances, he pulled me across the living room, into the kitchen and to the back hallway, a kind of mudroom.

The way we came in.

We were just about to open the back door as a car pulled into the driveway with its lights beaming right at us!

He shoved me back, and there I was, in the laundry room, right off the mudroom. At least it was lighter than the closet and much bigger. Piles of clothes covered the floor. There was a bit of light shining through the curtainless window from an outside floodlight.

Jagger held his finger to his mouth.

I curled my lips, yet again, at him. Any dummy would know not to talk.

The backdoor opened, footsteps followed, the door shut. Thank goodness the door to the laundry room was closed. Nevertheless, my breath held in my chest until I thought I was going to pop like the tiger's eye.

Woof. Woof.

A dog! Lois had brought a dog back with her, and it sounded *big*. I could only hope it had a cold and stuffy nose so that its sniffing abilities were impaired.

Footsteps came closer to our room. Jagger pushed me to the floor and covered us in the laundry.

Yuck! Dead Leo's dirty clothes on us! I gagged but kept my mouth shut, which didn't seem humanly possible. I was learning a lot in this business. And one thing was that the dirty clothes helped cover our scent.

A loud sniffing sound came close to the door.

Maybe not.

"Get the hell over here, Bruno. You're not getting in the laundry to play no matter how good it smells to you. Come."

I said a fast, abbreviated prayer.

The footsteps then grew distant. She must have gone upstairs with the dog.

But was it for the night?

Would the pooch come back? Did it have free reign of the house so it could?

"Do you think she's gone upstairs for the night?" I whispered, praying she had since I was about to scream, wearing these wet clothes.

Jagger shrugged. "Stay here."

He opened the door, stuck his head out and walked toward the backdoor.

Good. He'd fiddle with the alarm system again, then we'd be home free.

"Fuck," Jagger muttered. He came back in, shut the door and looked at the pile of laundry. He checked the window and cursed something about the alarm system. "Make yourself comfortable," he said.

I looked down. "What? What the hell are you talking about? I have to get home and change."

"Look, Sherlock. I'd like nothing more than to be home in my own bed right now too. But Lois did something to the freaking alarm. I can't bypass it without the entire system sounding full force and notifying the cops, not to mention the neighbors, her and the mutt. We'd never make it out the door before she or her dog came at us."

I readied to ask where his bedroom was since I thought maybe he lived in his SUV, but there is a time and place for everything so I asked, "Do you think the dog will come back down?"

"Doesn't Spanky sleep with you?"

My eyebrows rose at the very thought. Yes, he did, but having Jagger know that felt like an invasion of my privacy. How *did* he know that? "Have you *seen* him in my room?"

"Relax, Sherlock. I'm not a Peeping Tom. Everyone I know who owns a dog lets them sleep in their bed. We can only hope Lois is like all dog owners—and tomorrow morning is not laundry day."

Good assumption, but my mouth went dry anyway.

Tomorrow! I'd be here again with him and then have to go to work at the clinic or call in sick. Very tempting. I started to make little moaning sounds as I fixed a pile of laundry to lie down on.

"Not too comfortable in wet stuff?"

I looked at him in the dim light. "You are one observant guy, Jagger. I'll give you that."

He took off his jacket and started to unbutton his shirt. Unbutton his shirt!

Oh my God!

I'd never sleep tonight or any night with that vision. He had on a crewneck white tee under the black shirt. His arms looked muscular but not overdone in the short sleeves.

I blew out a breath.

"Here." He held out his jacket and shirt. "That's the best I can do unless you want to change into Leo's dirty stuff."

"I'm fine." I sneezed.

"Change," he just about ordered.

When Jagger talked to you in that tone, you could only do what he said. Damn. He was more and more like my mother.

"Turn around."

He did a three sixty.

"Funny. Turn around and stay around so I can get these wet things off." As soon as he did, I tugged at my wet gloves amid frequent groans. Even though the tub water had been cold, it felt as if the material had been melted onto my skin. "Shit."

Jagger looked over his shoulder.

"Turn around!" I yelled in a whisper.

"I've seen your naked *fingers* before, Sherlock."

He came closer and took my hand. After several tugs, he had my gloves off. "Do not touch anything in this room now."

Damn. I hadn't thought about that. Maybe I should have kept on the wet gloves. Now that they were off I could get the jacket and shirt off, no problem.

Wrong.

The jacket didn't let me down though. My Steelers never would. After several tugs, I gently set the wet, and now smelly, down parka on the floor. Then it was time for the turtleneck. I pulled and made it halfway up my midriff. That was it. The thing stuck there as if glued on like Peggy's wrinkles.

I moaned. I tugged. Moaned again and tugged more. A panic attack threatened. Silly, sure. But when I lost control over anything to do with my body, my heart started to race, my palms sweated and my mouth became the Sahara. "Oh. Oooooooh. Oh! Ack!"

Jagger had lain down on his pile of laundry. "Keep it down."

"I'd love to if I could get this wet crap off of me. *Ah choo*!" Before I could cover my mouth the sneeze sprayed out. Damn!

Jagger flipped over. "Christ, Sherlock. Can't you get undressed any quieter?"

"Never mind. I'm going to just go to . . . to . . . to sleeeeeep." Another sneeze.

He sat up, ran a hand through his hair and got up. "Come here."

My feet froze to late Leo's tile floor. "I . . . no. I'll be fine." Two more sneezes.

"You'll have pneumonia before daylight."

"You have to come into contact with someone who has the cold virus to get sick. Just 'cause I'm wet and cold doesn't mean I'm getting—"

Jagger's hand muffled my sneeze, but I was afraid I'd slobbered on him. How the hell did I get myself into these situations?

"I'm going to help you peel that wet shit off and then you are going to put on my dry shirt and jacket. You can't borrow a pair of Lois's pants 'cause we could be found out. We don't take things from suspects. Then you are going to stop making noises as if you're having an orgasm."

I couldn't even think of how embarrassed I was now.

Very.

"You suspect Lois then and not Hildy?" My voice came out with way too much optimism, but at least it took the conversation off the "O" word.

Jagger ignored my question and grabbed onto my shirt. If I liked my men rough, this would have sent my insides into a tornado. But he was only trying to help me get comfortable and not die of pneumonia or get caught.

What a guy.

His hot, yes hot, fingers brushed my navel.

I bit my tongue.

Slowly he turned me around so my back faced him.

What a gentleman.

The material clung so tightly, he had to lean into the back of my legs.

The turtleneck budged.

His breath burned into my neck.

I was ready to suggest he just breathe on me a few seconds and the clothing would be dry. But, I stood there shamelessly knowing he could see the back of my bra (as if that would be a sensual turn-on for Jagger) and didn't say a word. I merely wiggled as he tugged.

"Goddammit."

The material lifted off my head. I felt him pressing his shirt into my hand.

He never turned me around until I was properly dressed in his shirt—inhaling male.

Another sleepless night loomed.

"Put this on too." He shoved his jacket at me.

I took it and put it on over the shirt as I began to shiver.

He looked at my legs. "That shirt is so long on you it comes down to your knees." With that he turned and laid down.

"Well, I guess that means I can take off my pants."

"You're on your own for that, Sherlock."

I stood silent, with no comeback. Then I reminded myself where we were and why. I bent to fix my makeshift bed.

With his back to me, Jagger said, "Don't touch anything."

My hands froze. I stood and kicked with my feet until the pile was puffier. Then, and it took a good hundred hours, I shimmied out of my pants. I refused to take off my undies.

Finally, while listening to his soft snoring, I settled down into my pile of laundry.

And my head hit a hard object.

I turned to start digging in the laundry to remove it, then remembered my gloves were off. I looked at Jagger.

Talk about how innocent someone looks while asleep.

Innocent—and delicious.

I told myself to lie down and keep my mouth shut and try to rest even if I never fell asleep. If I did doze off, I figured Jagger would wake us both in plenty of time to get the hell out of there. How though? I had no idea, but believed daylight could fix just about anything.

I lay back down. "Ouch." The object poked into my head where I must have had a lovely shade of purple under my hair from the concussion.

I tried to move to the side. My head fell off the pile I'd fixed as a pillow. "Damn," I whispered. Then I lifted my head back and tried to move it so that the object didn't poke me again. My neck started to hurt.

I tossed, turned, moaned and groaned.

"What the hell is wrong with you?" Jagger said in a sexy throaty whisper. "Are you trying to get us caught, or merely annoy the hell out of me?"

"Annoy the hell out of you. I have nothing better to do."

He sucked in some air and blew it out in a long, slow, obviously irritated breath. "What is wrong?"

"Something in the laundry is sticking into my head."

"Is it sharp?"

"No. I . . . don't think so."

"You're going to have to learn to sleep in all kinds of odd situations while on surveillance. Ignore it."

"Don't you think I tried to, along with moving from side to side? It's not easy not being able to touch anything either, you know."

He sat up and leaned toward me. "Where?"

I pointed to the spot that had been like a gargantuan pea and me the princess. "Right there. Please move it."

He blew out air again.

"Further to the left."

"Yes, Sherlock."

"You don't have to be so grumpy. I'm really not doing this to piss you off."

I watched him pull apart the pile of laundry. A white lab coat was on the bottom of the pile.

Leo's lab coat.

Eeyeuuw.

"What is in there that hurt me?"

Jagger, I noticed, moved very gingerly while reaching into Leo's lab coat pocket. I thought that a good idea so that he wouldn't disturb or break anything. I made a mental note to work like that when on my cases alone.

He pulled out a pen. "This the culprit?"

"It felt . . . bigger."

"Bigger. You have some extraordinary feeling in your skull?"

"Funny. I do, however, have a gigantic bruise and know that it felt bigger."

He reached in again and pulled out a prescription bottle. "Imagine. A pharmacist with a lethal weapon like a prescription bottle." He set it down and moved back to his pile. "Nightie night, Sherlock."

I looked at the bottle and wanted to move it, but had to stick my hands into my pockets. This was not going to be a good night. Not at all. When Jagger shifted, the floodlight beams highlighted the bottle.

"Jagger!" I whispered a yell. Our voices would probably be changed forever after having to talk like this all night.

He sighed. "Another lump in your pillow?"

"No. The bottle. The prescription bottle."

"Christ!" He grabbed the bottle and shoved it into the lab coat, which he stuck under his own head.

"I shouldn't even say anything."

"Good."

"I should let you sleep on that lump and hope it pokes a sinkhole in your stubborn head."

"Good idea. 'Night." He turned his back to me.

"Jagger. That bottle is for Lanoxin."

He didn't turn around. "Lan what?"

"Lanoxin. It's digoxin. A cardiovascular drug used to treat congestive heart failure. To regulate the heart rhythm."

"Like the stuff Hildy had?"

Shit. I hadn't thought of that.

"Well, yeah." Not much to go on, but again, I didn't want her involved. "Mr. Wisnowski's name is on this bottle."

Jagger turned over. "Go on."

My chest puffed out like a peacock's feathers. Guess my nursing was finally good for something. "Okay. Mr. W's name is on it. So, this was probably a prescription Leo had filled for him. But, maybe he never got to give it to him. Or, wait. Let me see it."

Jagger obliged.

I smiled.

He held it in his gloved hand and turned the bottle so I could read it in the light of the window. "Anything?"

"The dose is appropriate for someone Mr. Wisnowski's size. But you have to be careful with digoxin. The risk of toxicity is increased if someone also takes diuretics and loses calcium and potassium. The heart can go into tachycardia."

"Tachycardia?"

"Too fast. It beats too fast. Or the overdose of digitalis can cause arterial fibrillation or atrioventicular block."

"In laymen's terms, Sherlock."

"Mr. W's heart would go haywire if he overdosed on this medication. Without getting too technical, it would either beat erratically or too weakly, quivering like a bowl of Jell-O, all of which could cause . . . death."

"But if he didn't overdose?"

"It's tougher in the elderly to monitor the doses. Mr. W was a slight man and could have reached toxic levels over time."

"How common is that?"

"I've never worked geriatrics, but I'm guessing it is possible. Although if the doctor monitors the patients correctly, they'd pick up on early symptoms and probably be doing blood work to check 'dig' levels all along."

Jagger held the bottle closer. "Anything else look suspicious?"

I studied it a bit longer and shook my head. I felt a bit disappointed that I hadn't "discovered" some fabulous clue.

Jagger leaned closer.

I moved back a few inches. Maybe he just wanted to keep me warm?

He opened the bottle and poured out a few onto the palm of his glove. "Right dose?"

I glared at the pills.

He took his flashlight out and beamed it toward them. "Tiny, round and a light greenish color."

"Zero point five."

"And?"

"The label says zero point one two five."

"Christ. Four times the prescribed dose."

I looked at Jagger. "I'm guessing Mr. Wisnowski would never know what dose was what color. The prescription was just filled a month ago, too, and I'll bet before the doctor had a chance to check the 'dig' level. Leo could have gotten away with murder doing that over time."

"He *did* get away with it."

Needless to say, I didn't fall asleep until early morning. I kept thinking how diabolical Leo was to kill Mr. Wisnowski so slowly over time.

When the sun peeked through the window, Jagger shook me gently until I woke. He kept his finger on my lips in case I'd forgotten where I was.

We gathered all my clothes and shoes and put the prescription bottle back in place. I figured Jagger had taken a bunch of pictures of it while I dozed. With the room back in order, he told me to follow him.

"Lois's taken the dog out the backdoor."

I only hoped they had walked down the street so we could get away.

My hopes were seriously dashed after Jagger and I snuck out the door only to hear Lois mumbling something about hurrying up, along with a litany of curse words.

Faster than the speed of light, Jagger had pushed me into the back of the spruce trees. Thank goodness they provided some cover.

Pokey spruce needles dug into my cheeks as we stood there. Lois came so close I could see her eyes were barely open. She grumbled and yanked at the dog, who looked *me* right in the eyes! A low growl started from deep in his throat.

"Leave the squirrels alone, Bruno, and get the hell over here," she yelled to him and pulled him into the house.

I let out my breath.

Then Jagger pulled me away from the bushes, holding onto my arm all the way to the car.

My legs were freezing with the shirt and jacket only coming to my knees.

But he was a gentleman when we got into his SUV, wrapping me in a blanket and turning the heat on full blast once the engine warmed.

"Here," he said as we pulled into the Dunkin Donuts parking lot and parked on the side. "Let me get your face."

Before I could ask what he meant, he had pulled a first aid kit out of the glove compartment and started to wipe an alcohol pad on my right cheek.

"Ouch!"

"Sorry."

I half expected him to tell me to "suck it up," but he didn't.

I ignored the pain of the spruce's scratch, concentrating on my "doctor."

He pulled back.

I touched my cheek. "Thanks."

Before he could see my now ruddy-hued complexion, I swung around to look out the window. A red Mustang drove by.

"Hildy!"

Jagger looked at me. "You're not starting that again."

I waved my hands around, pointing—and poked Jagger in the nose.

"Aye!"

"Oh. Sorry! But she's getting away. Hildy is leaving!"

Jagger looked as the red Mustang drove down the street, then started his engine. Before I could remind myself how uncomfortable I was in this outfit, we were tailing her down Olive Street.

What if it *wasn't* Hildy?

Twenty-five

"Hey! Watch it!" I yelled to Jagger as he wove through Elm Street, nearly hitting a parked car.

The red Mustang seemed to be evading us.

God, now I actually hoped it *wasn't* Hildy.

Driving like that, maybe she was thinking we were following her. That would mean she had something to hide.

Like killing Leo.

We pulled through a parking lot, heading the Mustang off at Oak Street. The tires screeched as it pulled to the side, hitting the curb with a thud. Jagger was out and running to the Mustang before I could wrap the blanket around my legs and waddle out.

He opened her door. "You all right?"

Hildy stepped out.

I dropped my grip on the blanket, letting it fall to the frozen ground.

Hildy looked more confused than afraid. I bent and grabbed at the blanket, then shoved it around me again.

"Pauline?" She leaned closer.

"Hi, Hildy." I sounded so matter-of-fact, I was actually embarrassed.

Hildy looked at me as if I was nuts. "What the hell is going on?"

"You tell us," Jagger said.

I poked his arm. "Let her talk."

"Talk?" She looked at him, the SUV and then at me. Up and down at me. "Looks like you two have more to talk about than I do. Why were you chasing me?"

"Why were you running?" Jagger asked.

"Nice job," I muttered to him.

Hildy looked a bit teary-eyed. "I thought someone was following me. Maybe my mother's boyfriend. He's done it before, and now more than ever he's after me. But, hey, you two were chasing me? Why?"

Did you kill Leo? was on the tip of my tongue. Thank goodness I bit it back. I knew Jagger wouldn't want me to ask that question. I had no idea if that was something only the police could ask. There was that Miranda warning thingie. I didn't want to blow this.

I looked at the car. Her furry coat. The Italian leather boots.

"Where did you get all of this?"

Jagger cursed.

Oops. I shouldn't have said that, but it came out without a thought.

Hildy gave us a look of teenage "attitude." Shit. She was going to clam up on us. Jagger was going to kill me now.

I had to think fast to remedy this situation. "I . . . I missed you at work, Hildy. I've been worried about you."

That did it.

Hildy's look softened.

In a childish whisper, she said, "No one's ever worried

about me. Well, no one in a long time. Since my grandpa died."

"I'm sorry to hear that, but—"

She looked at Jagger. "Oh shit. You think I have something to do with Leo's croaking."

It wasn't a question.

Jagger looked at her with the look that made you tell the truth. Look out, Hildy!

"Did you?" he asked, bending toward her. Looking deeper.

"Jesus H. Christ. I can't even kill a mosquito in the summer."

"You can't!" I said happily.

Jagger leaned next to me. "Easy does it, Sherlock. Don't get involved."

I pushed at his arm. "She can't kill a bug, Jagger. How could she kill Leo?"

He rolled his eyes. "Do you know how many convicts on death row 'could never kill a fly'?"

I almost asked how many.

Instead, I turned to Hildy. "You didn't have anything to do with it?"

She shook her head.

In my gut I knew she was telling the truth. Then I caught the hot Mustang behind her. "How . . . how could you afford—"

She looked over her shoulder. "Oh. That."

Jagger said, "Yeah, that."

I poked him again.

"My grandfather . . . Popi, I used to call him. I loved him. He was always there when I needed him as a kid. Then, he got sick a while ago. My mom stuck Popi in a nursing home and wouldn't tell me where he was. That's another reason I was leaving. I was so pissed at her for that. She was always jealous of our relationship. Popi had come to stay with me a few times last November."

"Did he take digoxin?"

She looked at me as if some snake had crawled out of my mouth like in an alien movie. "What the hell?"

Jagger said, "We noticed a prescription bottle in your apartment."

"Oh, in the drawer. Yeah, that was his. You opened the drawer?"

"Pauline needed a tissue."

She looked from him to me. "Oh."

"What about the car? Your job?"

I had to call in sick today. No question.

Hildy looked pissed. "You know, I don't have to tell you two anything."

"Rather tell it to the police?"

"Jagger!" This time I nearly knocked him down with my shoulder punch. "Stop it. She's only a kid."

He raised his hands. "Take it easy, Sherlock."

"Hildy, how could you afford all of this?" I looked at the car and her outfit.

"I'm only telling *you*, Pauline, because I like you." She turned away from Jagger and said, "My Popi died. The will was read a short time ago. My mom and her three sisters thought they'd get it all. Popi wasn't rich until he won the lotto two years ago and saved most of it."

"And he left some to you." I looked back at Jagger as if to say, "Nyah-nyah."

He shrugged.

"No. He left me all of it. When I found that out, I high-tailed it out of that damn job even though Leo was gone. I hated it. This morning I checked out of my hotel room. Oh, I called in the day the money came. You know the day I was sick and you two came over."

I nodded. "So you're moving away."

"I'm going back to see my mom. Maybe give her some of the money. Shit. She is my mother, even if she sent her goon after me."

I touched her arm. "That's nice. The seeing your mother part. Not the goon part."

Jagger groaned. "A freaking fairy-tale ending," he said, coming closer. "Why was the name ripped off the prescription bottle?"

She looked at me. "I was so pissed that my mom wouldn't tell me where he was, then he died. I was so sad and angry. I did it in anger. Ripped the name off but saved the bottle for a memory. I even put aside all the clothes I'd had on when I found out he was dead and never wore them again. And his slippers. Popi had left a pair of slippers at my place. I still . . . wear them."

I patted her arm.

Jagger came closer. "Don't leave town until Lieutenant Shatley has talked to you—"

"Jagger!"

He looked at me. "Relax, Sherlock. I'll give him a call. He'll see her today and check out an alibi and her story."

Hildy moved closer, gave me a hug. "Thank you for everything."

Through my vision blurred with tears, I smiled and said, "Have a great life, kid. You deserve it." I looked over her shoulder to see Jagger's face.

If she didn't murder Leo, it said.

As I watched Hildy drive off from Jagger's SUV, I turned to him. "That isn't a story. It's the truth."

He shook his head.

Twice.

After Jagger dropped me off, and I explained my "outfit" to Goldie and Miles without going into details of where Jagger and I had been, I took a shower worthy of the Guinness Book of World Records.

I finally turned it off when I thought I heard one of the neighbors banging on the pipes because I'd used up all the hot water in the complex. While still wrapped in my towel, I faked a scratchy throat and called the manager of the clinic.

Then I snuggled into my red flannel nightie with the black ribbons on the sleeves and crawled into bed. Thank goodness Goldie and Miles had taken care of Spanky and gone off to work. I'd shoved Jagger's clothes into a plastic bag to remind me to wash and return them, after the urge to save them as a momento threatened. I shut my eyes.

Peace, quiet and *sleep*.

Ring. Ring.

Thank the good Lord for answering machines. I rolled over.

Beep. "Pauline? Pauline, is this you? No, it doesn't sound like you. Maybe it's your gay roommate. Miles? Is that you, Miles? Or Goldie. Is that you, Goldie? The voice is too high maybe for a man. I can't tell who is talking. Is this that machine?"

Beep.

I smiled and kept my eyes closed, wrapping the covers tighter. How wonderful to be in my own bed. Dorothy had it down pat. There was no place like home.

Ring. Ring.

"No!" I shouted to my pillow.

Beep. "Pauline? Pauline is this you?"

I rolled my eyes. My mother really was an intelligent woman, but sometimes she didn't come across that way when it came to electronics. They still didn't have cable, cell phones, cordless phones, or a VCR.

"Okay. Whoever this is, tell her she needs to go to that Helen woman's for dinner tonight. Daddy and I can't go. We have to go to Mary's daughter's ballet recital. Uncle Walt says he has to go to Bingo. That Helen woman invited us to celebrate her . . . oh, my Lord . . . engagement to Stash. The fool. When will those men learn to think with their brains and not their—"

My eyes flew open.

Beep.

"Mom!" I yelled out, then laughed until that was the last thing I remembered.

From a distance I could hear the ringing of the phone yet again. *Leave me alone, Mom*, I thought. Then I realized the room was dark now. I opened my left eye to see the digital numbers: 5, 1, 0. I had slept all day!

Well, my mother would say that my body needed it. If she only knew. Then I sat up in bed with a jolt, remembering mother's phone message.

I had to go to Helen's house for dinner.

Maybe I'd slept through it. Since the phone kept ringing, I grabbed the phone before the machine got it. "Hello."

Uncle Stash's voice was filled with so such excitement that I couldn't say no to dinner at seven.

I did say that I needed more time, and we settled on seven thirty. Great, I thought, after hanging up. I needed more time to fully wake up and make myself look presentable.

I decided that for Helen I'd settle for partially awake and looking human.

Once ready, I took care of Spanky, then left a note for my roomies telling them I'd be back in a few hours. They both had my cell phone number if need be. I thought about Jagger and wondered what he'd done today. Maybe gave all his info to the police along with clearing Hildy. I really hoped that last part was true.

When I stepped outside, the cold air slapped my face, waking me up. Okay, as much as I didn't want to go, I'd do it for my uncle. Stash was not my favorite, but he was family, and we'd always had a close-knit family. I'd do my part and be very polite about it.

Uncle Stash had given me directions to where Helen stayed. I'd corrected him on the phone, saying that he must have meant where she *lived*. No, he'd said, where she *stayed* since giving up her apartment to move to Florida with him.

Helen sure didn't let any grass grow under her feet.

I pulled into the parking lot of the Family Suites. It was a small complex on the Hartford side of town where people rented efficiency apartments for a month at a time. The parking lot wrapped around the back of the building. Helen's place was on the first floor at the far end of the unit. Past a snow-covered wrought-iron patio set, I could see my Uncle Stash sitting on the living room couch through the French doors. The curtains hadn't been pulled, but the parking lot bordered the woods, so I guessed not many folks came back here.

I shut off my car and walked to the front door of #43. I could hear jazz music coming from Helen's. Okay. Maybe she wasn't all that bad. But her marrying my uncle still got under my skin. The wind sent my hair flying, reminding me how cold I'd been last night, so I stepped closer to the door and poked at the doorbell.

The chimes had only rung once when the door flew open. Helen stood there, purple hair sprayed like a rubber wig, a rather tight red dress revealing a little pooch of an abdomen, thick black glasses with rhinestone sides, and heels that Peggy never could have maneuvered in.

Guess Helen was young at heart.

"Come in, dear," she said, moving to the side.

The place was well lit, decorated in monotone beige and had a small kitchenette to the left of the living room. Helen took my black wool coat. I missed my Steelers jacket, but down took a long time to dry.

"Hello, Pauline," Uncle Stash said, standing up. "What can I get you to drink?" He looked toward a brass liquor table filled with various bottles. Their age group had cocktails at every function.

"Beer would be fine."

I followed Helen and sat on the couch, feeling strange. I looked around the room. Even though it was a temporary place for Helen, it looked so impersonal. I would have stuck out a family picture or two. When I looked at the kitchenette, I noticed the stove was empty. No pots or pans on it. Geez. Maybe the invitation was only for cocktails, and I'd starve to death in a few minutes, after sleeping through breakfast, lunch and my afternoon tea and cookie break.

"Dinner will be ready in a few minutes," she said.

I didn't argue, but wondered how the hell that was going to happen. Uncle Stash handed me a Budweiser still in the can. Helen looked at him, but she never admonished him for not giving me a glass. My first thought was that she didn't have the class someone who looked like her should have had. I wasn't being nice. Maybe I was still mixed up from being tired and groggy.

I took a sip of my beer and set it next to last May's issue of *A Buyers Gallery of Fine Automobiles*. Helen, a car buff? Then I noticed the address label. Uncle Walt's. She must have gotten it somehow when they had been "dating."

I shuddered.

I loved my Uncle Stash even though I wasn't that close to him. I didn't want to see him get hurt. Uncle Stash had retired from IBM years ago and it was rumored in my family that the guy had some bucks. I know he'd talked about buying stock way back when.

Hmm. Did Helen know the value of "way back when" stock?

The door chimes rang.

More company? I thought no one else in my family could make it. Suddenly my heart stopped. I hoped these two mismatched lovers hadn't planned to fix me up!

"Dinner's ready," Helen chirped as she got up to answer the door.

The scent of fried rice and egg rolls filled the air. Dinner is ready is right. I smiled to myself as the Chinese food deliveryman gave Helen a dirty look before he left. Must have stiffed him on the tip.

Throughout the entire meal they talked about Florida. I pictured myself hanging from the curtain pull.

Helen went on and on about how sensitive her skin was to the sun and did Uncle Stash have a cover over his lanai.

I pictured borrowing Jagger's gun and shooting myself in the foot.

Then Uncle Stash talked incessantly about Helen. Her

hair. Her lovely nose. Her perfect teeth. The way she walked. The way she . . . yadda, yadda, yadda.

I pictured myself drinking every bottle of liquor on her brass table and drifting off into quiet oblivion.

Ring. Ring.

I jumped.

Helen got up to answer the phone while Uncle Stash followed. Geez. Were these two already joined at the hip?

Still, I guessed I was glad that my uncle was happy.

"Oh, dear. Oh, my. Damn it."

I looked up. She didn't look as concerned as her words sounded.

Uncle Stash asked, "What is it, sugar pie?"

I gagged on a bite of my Moo Goo Gai Pan.

"Okay. We'll come right now." She hung up the phone. "We have to go take Sophie to the hospital."

"Is she all right?" I asked.

Helen looked at me oddly, then nodded. "Sophie is our friend from Bingo. She got her toe stuck in the faucet of her bathtub."

I wasn't supposed to know who Sophie was! But the vision of the large woman attached to plumbing nearly had me busting my sides, trying to keep in a laugh. "Oh. So she is all right?"

"Yes, but we have to go drive her. Her neighbor helped get the faucet off the wall, but it's still on her toe."

"Jiminy Cricket," Uncle Stash said.

"Well, you two go ahead. I'll clean up and put the rest of the food away so it doesn't spoil. I'll lock the door on my way out."

Helen nearly jumped on me. "No!"

Uncle Stash took her into his arms. Senior lovers. Cute.

My Moo Goo Gai Pan worked its way up my throat.

"Don't worry so much about everyone. Sophie will be fine. Pauline is a dear to offer to clean up. You know you don't like to anyway. Let's go. She'll be fine. Besides, she hasn't finished dinner. You don't want to make a bad impression on your soon-to-be family."

I held up a forkful of Gai Pan for her to see.

She rolled her eyes at me. Hmm. Not exactly a good impression on the Sokol family.

They argued for a few minutes, until I reminded them that Sophie's toe might be turning black from lack of blood so they scurried out.

I shook my head and thought about calling Goldie and Miles for a good laugh, but started to yawn instead. I couldn't wait to get home and back to bed. I figured I'd get the go-ahead to end my case from Jagger soon. After all, Lois Meyers had to be the accomplice. Even Jagger couldn't argue with me on that one. She had lived in luxury with Leo.

'Nough said.

I cleaned the table, sink and counter. Then I went to stick the liter Coke bottle back in the refrigerator. I opened the door.

Other than the Coke, it was empty.

Twenty-six

I looked at Helen's empty refrigerator.

No one could be on that kind of diet. How odd. She had to have been living here at least a few days to be so settled. Why hadn't she shopped?

Oh, well. I had more on my mind than Helen's diet, even if it was odd that she had no food in the fridge. She probably just ate takeout. The investigator in me opened a cabinet door.

Empty.

The next held the dishes and glasses that obviously came stocked with the studio apartment. No food was to be found anywhere.

My gut said there was something wrong here. I sat on the couch and stuck my feet on the magazine on the coffee table. I should just go, but I needed a moment to think. Maybe Helen really was living with someone else and only kept this place to fool my uncle!

I mean, I was no Emeril when it came to cooking, but I at least kept dry food like cereal and bread around. If she really lived here, I'd assume she'd have *something* in the cabinet.

Damn.

She was lying to him and marrying him for his money. I'd have to find out for sure and warn him so the bride would be left at the altar. My foot slipped on the slick surface of the table, sending the magazine to the floor.

A letter fell out.

I went to pick it up and stick it back. After all, it was none of my business—until I read the handwritten name "Stash" in the first paragraph. On closer inspection it was more a note than a letter.

And, it was about my uncle. I tried to put it back in the magazine, but knew Jagger would tell me to read it.

Okay, I used that as an excuse to read it.

"Damn. I was right."

Helen had written to Sophie about marrying my uncle for his money. "Why Sophie?" Hmm. They must have been closer friends than I thought. Or maybe Helen was going to split the money with her. Maybe Helen was in on the Viagra dealings too. Who wasn't?

I looked at the letter one more time to see if I'd missed anything.

"Didn't your mother ever tell you to not be so nosy?"

I swung around to see Helen. "Oh . . . this." I looked at the letter as if I had every right to be holding it. "It fell when I put my feet on it. I mean, I put my feet on the . . . shit. You are not going to marry my uncle!"

She stared at me.

If I thought Jagger and my mother had a way with their eyes, Helen was a master at instilling fear into one's heart with hers. "You shouldn't have ruined everything, Pauline."

I sized her up. Seventy. Maybe seventy-one. Slight frame with her little Buddha-belly. I could take her.

Then, she reached into her purse and before I knew it, I was looking at the barrel of a shiny metal gun. Caliber unknown, since I had no clue about weapons.

I couldn't take her.

"Helen," I said and then laughed. "I'm not going to say a word." I zipped my lips like Uncle Walt had done. "No siree." I started to walk toward the door. "No one has to know. You too lovers will have a great time in Florida. Don't forget sunblock of at least SPF thirty." I laughed again. Sounded fake.

"Take another step and you'll have a hole through that pretty face."

"You think I'm pretty? My skin's not too pale?" Shit! What the hell was I saying? My nerves had gotten the best of me. Remain cool. You are a professional. You beat death once before. You can do it again. Hey, at least I wasn't in an elevator this time.

Helen's gun made a clicking sound.

I jumped. She must have done something to take off the safety or something like that. Who the hell knew? All I knew was that I had to remain relatively calm and . . . lunge at her.

The gun flew into the air. Helen landed on the couch.

And her hair-sprayed purple hair ended up—in my hands!

I looked down at her.

Beneath the wig was plastered down black hair. And up close, her skin was pretty damn smooth. And that voice. Deep and sultry. Shit.

She looked at me and started to swing her arms wildly. *Lois Meyers?*

She smacked my right cheek. "Ouch!" Before I had

time to comprehend that Helen, or Lois, had just tried to kill me, she had slugged me in the jaw. "Damn!"

For what seemed like hours, we hit, pinched. Helen/Lois even bit me once, and I screamed so that maybe a neighbor would hear. But no one came. Then again, it was an end unit and pretty damn secluded. Good choice, Helen/Lois.

"My uncle is going to come and . . . and he'll fix you!"

"Ha! Forget him."

I grabbed her by the black hair half expecting it to come off in my hand. "Did you . . . did you hurt him?"

"I didn't kill him, bitch. Not my sugar daddy." She lunged at me and kicked me in the abdomen.

My breath whooshed out. Earlier I had hesitated to hit an old lady, but now that Helen/Lois had maybe only ten years on me, I let her have it. Before she could slug me back, I got her on the floor and pinned her down with my knee.

She flipped me like a pancake.

Shit. Helen/Lois had probably never cooked a pancake in her life. Now she had me in the "missionary" position but her intentions were lethal. I noticed her eying the gun, which had landed under one wheel of the brass liquor cart. She pressed her fingers into my throat.

I started to gag.

With one hand, she bent as low as she could get and reached the gun.

I had to think fast. The last time I was faced with artillery, I used reverse psychology on the guy to get a confession. Of course it'd be no good if I died. Still, not ready to give up, I looked at Helen with pleading eyes.

She eased her grip and now held the gun in my face. "Get up."

While choking and rubbing my throat, I stood and

flopped down on the sofa. "I'm guessing a cola is out of the question?"

"Don't give me any shit, Pauline. You ruined everything. Now I have to clean up your mess."

I chuckled. "Hey, I cleaned up your apartment."

She shot daggers at me from her eyes. "Shut up and let me think how to get rid of you."

I wasn't about to give her any help on that issue. "Helen, I mean Lois, you don't want to get into more trouble. I mean, marrying my uncle for his money is one thing, you smart cookie you, but murder? You don't want to commit murder. Ever."

"Ever again, you mean."

Gulp. I think I read somewhere that the first kill was the hardest—then it was like riding a bike and got easier and easier.

Or was that falling off a horse?

Either way, I looked at Helen, thinking criminals like to brag when they are about to kill the person to whom they brag to. If I could get her to confess everything, she'd be nailed when I reported it all to Jagger.

Of course, dead Pauline Sokols tell no tales. Couldn't let that happen. My insides were in such knots, though, having a panic attack seemed like a walk in the park compared to this. I tried to nonchalantly click on my beeper camera. Even if I didn't get good shots, I'd at least get her confession on tape.

She looked disgusted.

"I'm sorry I ruined it for you." Maybe that would loosen her up.

"Goddamn men."

"I hear you on that one."

She waved the gun at me. "Shut up. I need to concentrate. Couldn't listen to me. He just couldn't listen. We'd be in Rio right now living off millions. But no. He wouldn't listen."

"So you killed him." I had no idea what she was talking about, but threw that out for conversation enhancement.

"Wouldn't *you*?"

Oh, boy. Helen/Lois may be snapping. "Well, depends on what he did." I caught her attention as if taking her into my confidence, all the while praying she wouldn't shoot the freckles off my nose.

"First he kills his freaking uncle who found out too much and wouldn't agree to be a player. Then, he nearly shits in his pants when he hears the police might be investigating—"

"Mr. Wisnowski's death," I muttered.

She shrugged. "Leo deserved it too. He could have made us a mint on the Viagra. Stupid shit."

I shut my eyes for a nanosecond. It couldn't be good to shut your eyes when someone held a gun to your freckles, but in that nanosecond I realized Hildy was innocent.

Thank God for small wonders.

I couldn't wait to tell Jagger.

Jagger. Suddenly the situation slapped me in the face. Would I ever see him again? My parents? My siblings? Goldie? Miles? Spanky? My uncles? Nieces? Nephews? My future kids? God willing.

I paused.

If my life flashed back to my birth and fast-forwarded to today, I was a dead woman.

Oh well, that possibility meant I had nothing to lose. "You killed your partner Leo?"

"No, stupid."

I was ready to argue with her when she said, "My dick of a *husband*, Leo."

Yikes! That made Lois Sophie's daughter-in-law. Small world.

"My God. You killed your husband with the medication, committed insurance fraud and sold Viagra illegally to kids and the seniors."

"Look, Miss High-and-Mighty, I'm going to kill you too. When I left my Daddy and Mama at age sixteen, I said I'd never be poor again. Never. Never eat from trash bins. Never wear holes in my clothes."

If it wasn't for the gun, I might have started to feel sorry for her.

"All planned. Already rented out Leo's and my house. So, you see, I've worked too hard and put up with too much shit to let years of planning go down the toilet because of some fucking niece of my fiancé's."

"Medical fraud insurance investigator." Oh . . . my . . . God.

How and *why* did I say that?

Helen leaned back. The gun waved in the air. "You little snitch. Damn you!"

Pop!

"Ouch!" I yelled, and then screamed until my lungs hurt worse than my arm.

Crash!

My mind started to whirl. Helen had fired, but I was still alive. At least I thought I was. The room grew darker and almost foggy. However, there was a nasty sting in my arm, which seemed a good sign since I didn't think there was pain in the afterlife. I heard another crash. When I looked toward the French doors, I hallucinated that Joey the Wooer had just thrown a wrought iron patio chair through it.

And, as if that wasn't enough, Joey was armed.

And just shot the gun out of Helen/Lois's hand.

"You're gonna make it," a deep voice said.

I opened one eye to see Joey the Wooer gazing down on me. He held me in his strong arms. If I wasn't in pain and groggy from obviously blacking out, I'd admonish myself for noticing.

"Is this heaven?" I mumbled.

Joey laughed.

Sounded familiar.

I shut my eyes.

They say hearing is the last sense to leave a person.

I could barely open my eyes, but heard some kind of commotion.

"You could have gotten yourself killed. Don't ever take a chance like that again, Sherlock."

Sherlock. Sherlock? Sherlock!

No one called me that except . . . I looked up with blurry vision and blinked and blinked again. Helen/Lois stood near the kitchenette, getting cuffed by two cops at her sides.

I blinked one more time to make sure I was seeing what I thought I saw.

Joey had taken off his hair. Not really taken it off leaving him bald, but uncovered more hair. He actually had dark, black hair now. Maybe another wig. Who changed wig colors mid-shooting? I had to blink again. His mustache was gone. I looked to see his "old man's" suit on, but this sure as hell wasn't any old man holding me.

He wiped a cloth across my bullet-riddled arm. Okay, it

was only grazed, but shot in the line of duty had to be worth something.

His gentle touch took me by surprise.

"You. You're Joey?"

"Who else could make sure all the old geezers didn't hit on Peggy?"

Yikes. That's why "Joey" acted so weird, almost possessive of me around Nick. Even in my fog of being shot, I wanted to ask him if we had . . . you know . . . that night in the shed, but oh, well. There was that time-and-place thing again. Waiting for an ambulance didn't seem the time to talk about sex. What could one more mystery about Jagger hurt?

He lifted my head and stuck his jacket under it.

Nice touch.

"She was a real looker that Peg." Fabulous Jagger-grin.

"Oh, God. Take me now," I mumbled. If only embarrassment were a means to suicide I'd be growing wings right now.

Jagger shook his head, oh-so very Jaggerlike. Warmed me inside. Then, he wiped my arm again and whispered, "You did good, Sherlock. *Real* good. You just might make it after all."

And don't miss Lori Avocato's next thrilling
Pauline Sokol Mystery,

ONE DEAD UNDER THE
CUCKOO'S NEST,

coming in October 2005.

Please turn this page

for a preview.

After my goodbyes to Adele and Goldie, I hurried outside. When I saw the black Suburban pull into the lot, my heart did a stupid happy dance.

Too much caffeine in my decaf coffee. Had to be it.

Jagger pulled up next to the curb and looked at me.

"What?" I shifted from foot to foot. "I wore the damned scrubs like you said."

"No purse. I said don't bring a purse for this job."

Shit. I'd forgotten. I really had to pay more attention to the details. Especially Jagger details. "I'll go give it to Goldie—"

"Get in."

He looked anxious to leave so I hurried around the other side of the car and got in. Nick always opened the door for me. Jagger, well, was Jagger.

"Take out your essentials and leave the purse under the seat," he said as we spun out of the parking lot.

I gave him a dirty look, figuring his eyes were on the road, but he stopped at the light and looked at me. "Essentials. No crap like makeup, perfume, or money. You won't need money."

"Fine." I'd learned a long time ago not to argue with Jagger. Okay, what I really learned was *when* I argued with him, I lost. I opened my bag, took out a comb, lipstick, new key chain from Nick and tried to nonchalantly take out a Tampax—just in case.

When he jammed on the brake, the Tampax flew out of my hand, harpooning itself on the lambskin collar of Jagger's aviator jacket.

He pulled to a stop sign, turned and shook his head.

I reached over and grabbed the Tampax without a word. Somehow that made me feel empowered. If I'd broken down into hysterical sobs, as I wanted to do, or died of embarrassment, which was my second choice, Jagger wouldn't respect me. One more shake of his head and we were off.

Another thing I'd learned about Jagger was when he shook his head at me once, he was perturbed. Two shakes, well, no one would want Jagger shaking his head at them twice. *Exasperated* was the word I'd associate with two shakes.

We turned onto Interstate 91 headed north.

"You said this was only going to take a few hours. Where are we going?"

"Airport."

"Airport!" flew out of my mouth so fast a hiccup followed. I ignored it like the harpooned Tampax. "I'm not flying anywhere." Not being a frequent flyer, I needed a few doses of Prozac before stepping down the long jetway to confinement, and I didn't bring any.

"No, you are not." He turned off the airport exit and before I knew it, we'd pulled up to the curb beneath the "Arrivals" sign.

"You can't park here," I said after reading all the warning signs. "You know how tight security has gotten since 9/11."

This time he merely looked at me. No head shaking.

Made my day.

"That state cop is coming over. You better drive around the airport a few times."

The cop came near, leaned over, and looked at me. "No stopping—"

Jagger bent forward.

The cop looked at him, tipped his hat to me and said, "Have a nice day, ma'am."

Often when I was with Jagger, the same physical things happened. Heart arrhythmias. My high IQ tanked. And jaw problems. The "problem" was that my jaw would drop down to my chest when he'd say or do something oh so very Jagger-like.

"What the hell? Why didn't you have to—" No need to finish. It was foolish to ask Jagger anything. He was as closed-mouthed as a clam dug out of the Rhode Island beaches. I should have known and not wasted my words.

"There." Jagger motioned his head toward the far door. "There she is. Mary Louise Huntington. Go get her."

I looked up to see a young woman with blonde hair about my length coming out of the door. I stepped out of the car and squinted. "Holy shit. She looks like me!"

"Ata girl, Sherlock."

Pleased that I'd figured something out, but having no clue as to what, I started walking towards the woman who was now followed by a nun. Another state cop came out of the far door near the baggage claim amid a crowd of people. A flight must have recently landed.

When I got closer to the woman, I said, "I'm here to escort you." To a mental institution, but I didn't say that out loud. "I'm with him." I turned around and pointed.

That jaw thing happened again.

No black Suburban.

No Jagger.

No idea what the hell I was doing.

I only hoped the woman, who looked even more like me close up, wouldn't freak out and give me a hard time.

"I need to pee," she said and turned around. The nun was nowhere in sight now.

"Oh, wait," I shouted as I followed her inside. She hurried toward the ladies' room near the baggage claim carousels. "I'm supposed to stay with you."

I bumped into an elderly woman, coming out of the ladies' room.

"Watch it, bitch!" she shouted.

Appalled that a granny would speak that way, I offered an "Excuse me" and went inside. Mary Louise must have gone into a stall. I leaned against the sink and waited. "Er . . . you all right?"

Silence.

Jagger surely would be back from driving around the airport by now. He would do more than shake his head if I messed this case up.

"Look, Mary Louise, is it? I need to know that you are all—"

The door opened.

My jaw dropped to my nipples this time.

Mary Louise Huntington stood in front of me as if I were looking in a mirror.

"I . . . did you notice how much we—"

She took off her jacket. Beneath she wore drab blue scrubs.

Just like mine.

What the hell?

Before I could say a word, she hurried out the door again. I followed close behind. "Oh, no, lady. You are not getting me into trouble with Jagger."

The nun approached, dropped her black carry on bag and bumped into me. "Oh, sorry, Sister. I'm not usually . . . ouch!"

I looked down at my arm. A syringe was pulled out. A syringe that the nun was now tucking into the sleeve of her robe. It gave me a chill.

A haze started to cloud the room. Or maybe it was . . . my . . . mind. My mind was . . . fuzzy. Fuzzy Wuzzy was a bear. Stop that, *Pączki*. I laughed. The fuzzy nun pushed me into the bathroom. "Ouch." I bumped my head on the wall. "Daddy calls me *Pączki*. I giggled, stumbled. "It's a Polish prune-filled donut." Jagger.

Where the hell was Jagger?

I rubbed at my arm. Make that three arms. I saw three arms attached to me on one side, four on the other. "You pinched me. That hurt. Nuns shouldn't . . . pinch . . . what did you give me? I hope to hell that syringe was sterile!"

Without a word, she pulled off her veil.

He?

He pulled off his veil, and he wasn't at all like Goldie. It didn't seem as if he usually dressed like a nun. I pushed at his chest and made it to the doorway of the rest room. Thank goodness there was no door that I had to open. My three arms felt as if they were made of rubber. Whatever was in that shot had kicked in, and I felt like crap.

My mouth dried.

My skin prickled.

My heart raced until the room spun, turned dark and started to wink out.

In the distance, on the other side of the glass door, watching—stood *Jagger*.

AGATHA AWARD-WINNING AUTHOR
JILL CHURCHILL

The Jane Jeffry Mysteries

BELL, BOOK, AND SCANDAL
0-06-009900-3/$6.99 US/$9.99 Can

When a famous ego-squashing editor is undone
by an anonymous poisoner at a mystery convention,
suburban homemaker Jane Jeffry and her best friend
Shelley Nowack jump right in, ready to snoop,
eavesdrop and gossip their way to a solution.

THE HOUSE OF SEVEN MABELS
0-380-80492-1/$6.99 US/$9.99 Can

While helping to restore and redecorate a
decrepit old mansion, one of their fellow
workwomen ends up dead, leaving Jane
and Shelley to try and nail the assassin.

MULCH ADO ABOUT NOTHING
0-380-80491-3/$6.99 US/$9.99 Can

Jane and Shelley's scheme to improve themselves
dies on the vine when the celebrated botanist
slated to teach a class at the Community Center
is mysteriously beaten into a coma.

A GROOM WITH A VIEW
0-380-79450-0/$6.99 US/$9.99 Can

While Jane plans a wedding for the daughter
of a prominent, wealthy businessman, someone
suspiciously slips down the stairs to her death.

PERENNIAL DARK ALLEY

Be Cool: Elmore Leonard takes Chili Palmer into the world of rock stars, pop divas, and hip-hop gangsters—all the stuff that makes big box office.
0-06-077706-0

Eye of the Needle: For the first time in trade paperback, comes one of legendary suspense author **Ken Follett's** most compelling classics.
0-06-074815-X

More Than They Could Chew: **Rob Roberge** tells the story of Nick Ray, a man whose addictions (alcohol, kinky sex, questionable friends) might only be cured by weaning him from oxygen.
0-06-074280-1

Men from Boys: A short story collection featuring some of the true masters of crime fiction, including Dennis Lehane, Lawrence Block, and Michael Connelly. These stories examine what it means to be a man amid cardsharks, revolvers, and shallow graves.
0-06-076285-3

Fender Benders: From **Bill Fitzhugh** comes the story of three people planning on making a "killing" on Nashville's music row.
0-06-081523-X

Cross Dressing: It'll take nothing short of a miracle to get Dan Steele, counterfeit cleric, out of a sinfully funny jam in this wickedly good tale from **Bill Fitzhugh.**
0-06-081524-8

The Fix: Debut crime novelist **Anthony Lee** tells the story of a young gangster who finds himself caught between honor and necessity.
0-06-059534-5

 PERENNIAL **DARK ALLEY**

An Imprint of HarperCollins*Publishers*
www.harpercollins.com

DKA 0405

Murder and mystery with a Southern twist— delightfully deadly mysteries by

KATHY HOGAN TROCHECK

FEATURING CALLAHAN GARRITY

EVERY CROOKED NANNY
0-06-109170-7/$6.99 US/$9.99 Can

Callahan Garrity is trading in her police badge for a broom and a staff of house cleaners. But soon she finds herself right back in the middle of a mystery when a client's pretty, pious nineteen-year-old nanny disappears.

TO LIVE AND DIE IN DIXIE
0-06-109171-5/$6.99 US/$9.99 Can

Callahan and her crew discover the bloodied body of a young woman —and are soon on the trail of a priceless Civil War diary stolen by the killer.

HOMEMADE SIN
0-06-109256-8/$6.99 US/$9.99 Can

When her cousin Patti is found dead, Callahan just knows that her surburbanite cousin's death is too strange to be accidental.

HAPPILY NEVER AFTER
0-06-109360-2/$6.99 US/$9.99 Can

When a singer is found passed out next to the dead body of her former producer, it's up to Callahan to find the real killer.

HEART TROUBLE
0-06-109585-0/$6.99 US/$9.99 Can

When a roadside murder turns up the heat on simmering racial tensions, Callahan must trap a mean, mad killer.

IRISH EYES
0-06-109869-8/$6.99 US/$9.99 Can

A St. Patrick's Day celebration ends badly when Callahan's ex-partner is shot dead during a robbery.